PENGUIN BOOKS

The
TAILOR'S
GIRL

Fiona McIntosh is an internationally bestselling author of novels for adults and children. She co-founded an award-winning travel magazine with her husband, which they ran for fifteen years while raising their twin sons before she became a full-time author. Fiona roams the world researching and drawing inspiration for her novels, and runs a series of highly respected fiction masterclasses. She calls South Australia home.

T0363016

FIONA McINTOSH

The TAILOR'S GIRL

PENGUIN BOOKS

PENGUIN BOOKS

UK I USA I Canada I Ireland I Australia
India I New Zealand I South Africa I China

Penguin Books is part of the Penguin Random House group of companies
whose addresses can be found at global.penguinrandomhouse.com.

First published by Penguin Group (Australia), 2013
This edition published by Penguin Books, 2021

Cover photography by Lee Avison/Trevillion Images
Cover design by Louisa Maggio © Penguin Random House Australia Pty Ltd
Typeset in Sabon by Samantha Jayaweera © Penguin Random House Australia Pty Ltd

Printed and bound in Australia by Griffin Press, part of Ovato, an accredited
ISO AS/NZS 14001 Environmental Management Systems printer

 A catalogue record for this
book is available from the
National Library of Australia

ISBN 978 1 76104 239 3

penguin.com.au

For Jack McIntosh

… who dreams of having his suits tailored at Savile Row.

I

NOVEMBER 1919

The man startled awake and stared at familiar bubbled paintwork on the ceiling, but the more he tried to grab for the dreamlike memories, the more they drifted away like gossamer spider-silk floating on a breeze. The night terrors left behind a telltale marker, though: an acridity that he could taste in his throat. It carried the metallic tang of blood, the sickening stench of rotting flesh and human waste, the pervasive charcoal aroma of gunpowder, or of old tobacco, sweat . . . but mostly the chilling, acidic taste of fear. He was assured by those caring for him that he was reliving life in the trenches – *It's common enough; Don't worry, it will pass* and other kindly placations – but none helped to stop the recurring nightmare.

He shivered beneath the hospital sheet, printed in blue at one corner with the name of his present home, Edmonton Military Hospital. The blanket was rough and insufficient but his small iron bed was near the radiator. He felt comforted by its ancient, wheezing presence and wondered how many other men had lain in this very bed and why. To the casual observer he looked well enough. The injuries had healed sufficiently and now a limp was the only visible indication that he'd sustained an injury on the front line. It was the invisible scar that he carried inside that was far more sinister.

He couldn't remember how he'd been injured and, because he'd been delivered as a 'missing soldier', the medical team couldn't tell him either. They'd agreed that given the timing of his injuries, and the particular crisscross style of his bandaging, he must have spent a period in a field hospital, perhaps in Flanders, before a stint at a base hospital, most probably at Rouens in France. And so he had come to accept that he'd likely fought at Ypres.

Repatriated several months earlier, he had been brought here to London. Through most of that time he had been unconscious from serious concussion, as well as intermittently rattling with fever from infection. He could recall nothing prior to June 1918, other than the vivid images in his sleep that fled as soon as he surfaced. His first clear memory was waking up on a ship as it crossed the Channel to England. It was summer – July, he recalled. Men were singing, smoking, talking quietly in corners, while others groaned from their wounds. Everyone was as hot as he felt and preferred being out on the decks but no one complained. They'd all experienced hell and survived it. He remembered staring blank-faced at the scene around him, confusion his only emotion – he simply couldn't remember what they were all trying to forget.

'Morning, Jonesey.' A bright voice cut into his exasperation, bringing him back to the present. 'Brrr . . . it's a cold one.'

'Good morning to you, Nancy,' he said, finding a smile for the nurse who never seemed to lose her humour.

'How are we?' She began checking his pulse.

'*We* are just fine,' he said, mightily impressed by the blinding whiteness of her starched pinafore apron that contrasted with the navy-black uniform beneath. Both provided a monochrome backdrop for her hair, painted from a fiery palette. Nancy wore her nurse's hat as far back as she dared and ringlets of golden-flame curls escaped. She wouldn't turn heads, but he defied anyone not to find her attractive. Her perkiness was seductive; it shone through even while she counted, looking at her fob watch with its upside-down face.

'You certainly look fine,' she finally said. 'And, may I say, very handsome too in spite of that beard.' She winked.

He rubbed his jaw, still refusing to remove the unruly growth that had emerged dark and un-greyed.

'Perhaps someone might recognise you if you shaved,' Nancy said archly, plumping his pillows. 'Are you going to get dressed?'

'Is there any point?' he said, mimicking her cheery tone.

She gave him a play slap. 'Yes, Mr Jones. For a start I'd love to know your real name. You certainly don't sound like you belong here.'

'Where do I belong?' he asked, standing for her so she could arrange his bedclothes. He strolled to the window, trying to disguise the way the slipper on his left foot dragged on the lino like a soft sigh.

'Oh, some posh place down south, I suspect,' she answered.

He pondered this. 'Maybe I'm a great actor.'

'I'd have recognised you.' She shook her head, frowning. 'I think you were a solicitor, or a banker,' she said. 'I'd definitely go on a date with you then.'

'Did I ask you out?' he said, swinging around, embarrassed. He fiddled with retying his dressing gown.

'No, but I am waiting for an invitation now that you can walk and we're finally in peacetime.' She gave him another knowing glance.

Peacetime. It was meaningless to him. 'What's the date, Nan?'

'November nineteenth, although you won't be the first to ask that today, I'm sure. I think the whole country is still in a state of hangover.' She laughed, shaking her head. 'I keep pinching myself it's over. Four years . . .' She sighed, snapped her fingers. 'And over just like that. What was it all about?'

He was the wrong person to ask. He turned to gaze back into the well-kept grounds of the hospital – he'd been told that glorious shows of flowers had once adorned the front entrance but the garden beds had served as vegetable plots for the past few years. Next spring bright petals would erase that patch of history as they burst into bloom once again. He was in a wing they dubbed the sanatorium, a remote part of the hospital that had been enjoyable when there were four of them but his three companions had been claimed, returned to their families, and now the sanatorium's distant location only heightened his isolation.

Another small garden outside was still ringed by barren, thorny rose bushes. The lawn looked crispy with frost and he saw a robin perched on a near-naked bush, where it had found space amongst the burnished orange of rosehips and was warbling his melodious tune. He presumed the songster was male from the U-shape of the olive-brown forehead. *How do I know that?* he thought. The robin looked as lonely as he felt and its tune, reaching him through the glass, sounded as plaintive as his mood. He understood, knowing this bird liked the quiet as much as he did.

'Right, Jonesy. I'll be back shortly. Will you have showered by then?'

'Definitely. I'd hate to disappoint you.'

She squeezed his arm. 'If only all patients were as easy as you. You're welcome to stay forever.'

Her words chilled him. He knew she meant them kindly, but he revolted at the jest.

'You're one of the lucky ones,' she added. 'You see that pretty woman there?' She nodded beyond the window and he saw a dark-haired woman in a navy suit and tan gloves walking down the pathway that cut past his wing. 'I heard today that she lost her brother a little while back. He'd be about your age; she said he was thirty-three. She sounded so broken over it . . . as though it happened yesterday.'

'Lost?'

'Died in action but no information about it – his body left behind, buried as another nameless soldier in 1915. Ypres, I think she said.'

He blinked. 'Where I was?'

'We're assuming you were from there,' she said, waving a cautionary finger.

The woman had disappeared behind the hedge. 'Who is she visiting?'

'No one, as such. You know, where you sit out there, all grumpy most days, is also the delivery entrance.' As he nodded Nancy shrugged. 'She was dropping something off to the hospital director. She must have waited for him in the tearoom. I overheard her talking about her brother.' Nancy became matter-of-fact again. 'Right, into the shower and then you can join the communal breakfast —'

'Oh, Nancy, I'd prefer —'

'Yes, Mr Jones, I know what you'd prefer but . . . hospital orders.'

'What about the Spanish flu?'

She blinked, looking momentarily distraught. 'We lost another two through the night. And two more nurses – that's four of our girls now.'

'Nan, I'm so sorry,' he said, feeling ashamed for ruining her mood.

'It's a dreadful thing, not choosy at all. Beth Churcher was a great nurse – we all loved her. She died in two days. That's all it took. One moment healthy, the next that awful lavender-coloured skin pigment that would have told her she had a death sentence.' He shook his head with regret. He didn't know Beth, but he could see Nan was heartbroken. 'And young Joey Nesbitt. He was going home in a week or so. I didn't know the other gentleman or nurse but we were briefed at the meeting this morning. And they won't be the last,' she said, her expression mournful now.

'All the more reason, surely, for me to remain here,' he tried.

Miraculously, Nan agreed. 'This end of the hospital is quite deserted. You probably are protected, and I haven't worked the same wards as Betty – one in which Tommy and the other fellow died.' She dug up her smile again. 'All right. You stay here. I'll bring some food in shortly. But don't forget, tomorrow's the Peace Party. I've had your spare shirt laundered. Everyone's putting on their best clothes. I'll leave a razor.' She winked again as she left him.

He couldn't imagine how a party could be deemed wise given the flu epidemic that was sweeping the nation. Only last week while sitting in the garden he'd heard through the privet hedge a family passing by. One of the children was singing a rhyme and he suspected she hardly understood the macabre words:

I had a little bird
Its name was Enza
I opened the window
And in-flu-Enza.

Spanish flu, as it had been nicknamed, was on a grand killing spree, and had no sympathy that Europe had already lost a generation of young men. It was now going to kill their parents, their grandparents, their sisters and brothers, their aunts and uncles and cousins . . . their friends.

Some were saying this disease was worse than the Black Death and slaughtering faster than any war could. He'd read that it had begun in the trenches. Soldiers who didn't succumb on the battlefield took the illness home – some believed it erupted in Scotland and headed on a murderous path south, killing in the thousands. He'd read a figure that by October more than one quarter of a million Britons, most of them formerly healthy, were dead from Spanish Flu.

And now they'd begun dying here in the hospital.

He returned his attention to the path that had carried away the bereaved young woman. The sound of her heels on the bricks echoed dully in his mind, and he felt envious of her freedom to walk away from this place.

The dreams were now worse, filled with a yellowy-green killing mist and men stumbling around blinded, dying of suffocation, bowels emptying in a final pitiful humiliation as bodies sank in slimy mud that was knee-deep. No one had names, uniforms gave him no clue, and his companions had no faces – some had been blown away, others unrecognisable.

Today he woke resentful, hating that he was no one. He belonged to someone, surely!

He showered briskly, secretly still thrilled at the novelty of being left alone to his ablutions. He wet the cake of soap that Nan had left with the razor, which was already screwed together and enclosed a new blade his experienced thumb told him, though where he had gained such experience was anyone's guess. The soap was dry and cracked from lack of use. Nevertheless, its flaws smoothed out the moment water came into contact and as he lathered up his beard, the sharp, medicinal odour of coal tar filled the small bathroom. For just a fleeting second the pungent fragrance whisked him somewhere and he was sure he was a child, sitting in a bathtub with the impression that a uniformed older woman was smiling approvingly as she wrapped him in a big white towel. And then the vision was gone; his awareness hadn't lingered on her face but the large hands, with sausage-like fingers and no rings, were achingly familiar, the distant voice beloved. Then, he couldn't find that memory again, couldn't hear her soft mutterings any more – no matter how much he inhaled the strong, oily smell.

Jones snatched a flannel to wipe the steam from the mirror. The old glass had tarnished, its silvering breaking down in the bevelled edges and particularly where the holes for screws had been made. Small metallic pinpricks peppered one side of his reflection, which he stared at moodily. By almost smothering half of his face in an odd shadow, it seemed to mock him. He was only half a man; the other half – the side that knew itself and who he was, where he came from – was a ghost wandering the battlefields of Ypres . . . if that was even where he'd been.

Why couldn't he recognise who was looking back at him with the flop of shiny, near-black hair and those haunted eyes? *They match your school blazer*, he heard in his mind, but who had spoken those words? Which school had he attended whose pupils wore indigo? The bathroom pipes suddenly juddered loudly, and he flung down the razor into the sink where the metal clattered against the enamel and the pieces fell apart, echoing how he felt inside. Broken. Dismantled.

Instead of shaving he rinsed his face, drying it roughly in a low rage of frustration, the petrol-like soap smell still clinging to his beard. Nancy would not be pleased. He dressed obediently in the freshly laundered and ironed shirt that had been returned. His only suit – a hand-me-down from who knew where – was old, worn at the knees and faded at the elbows, frayed on two of the button-holes. It offended him on some level but in truth it served its purpose and fitted him well enough. He had no genuine grounds for complaint, especially as most returned wounded soldiers were given an instantly recognisable saxe blue suit, with oddly white lapels and a bright-red tie to wear. Nan, who'd taken such an inter-est in him, had brought this suit from home. Her cousin's friend didn't need it any more. He had not asked the obvious question but had wrinkled his nose at the faint whiff of coal.

'Wear it more and air it out,' Nancy had suggested with a soft punch. He knew she liked touching him playfully. 'Then that moth-ball smell will disappear.'

Perhaps naphthalene would chase off the Spanish flu bug, he thought humourlessly now as he straightened the jacket.

He immediately headed into the small garden outside his ward. Fresh air, he was sure, would lift his spirits and blow away the smell of the coal tar. It was milder weather today, possibly even planning to rain. Moody clouds were assembling like a gloomy council, but he stepped outside anyway, after ignoring his greatcoat on the hook near the door. He loathed that coat. It had been cleaned but still it stank of death. Instead he'd put on a woollen jumper beneath his jacket that one of the volunteers had knitted for him. He liked its mossy colour and hoped she'd see him wearing it at last.

He waved to one of the nurses passing in the near distance – she was older but he responded to her no-nonsense ways.

'How are you feeling today, Mr Jones?'

'Oh fine, fine,' he said, giving the stock answer. 'Looks like rain,' he added, moving to the next stock item of conversation.

She looked up. 'You'd better not linger out here.'

'I shan't. Everyone seems busy,' he added, pleased he'd found something fresh to remark on.

'It's the Peace Party – we've finally got around to it. We can look forward to the happiest of Christmases.'

'Plenty to celebrate this year,' he agreed, and then regretted it because so many would be mourning precious family members.

'Yes, too true,' Sister Bolton replied, lifting a cheery hand in farewell. 'See you at the party. There's a new parcel of Tuxedo arrived from our American friends. By the way, a shave would be nice.'

He nodded as he waved; he could use a fresh supply of tobacco. Memories may desert you, he thought, but oddly, addictions don't. He obviously needed to taste a cigarette right now because just talk of Tuxedo made him want some. He lit one of the last cigarettes he'd rolled, inhaled deeply and felt the nicotine hit the back of his throat, its earthy taste reminding him – just for a heartbeat – of being buried. But there was no point in chasing that strand; he'd learned it was pointless teasing at a notion and he forced himself to trust the doctors' advice that his mind would yield its memories when it had healed.

'It's just like your leg wound, Jones. It needs time.' One wit – Nancy, he realised it must have been – had suggested that another bump to his head might bring his memory back. He sighed at how easy that sounded, and considered asking Nan to bring in a hockey stick and see if her theory worked.

Being outside had begun to weave its magic. At least he was no longer upsetting himself. The doctors had assured him that memory loss was being seen in injured soldiers suffering from something they termed 'shellshock'. He'd talked with a psychiatrist as part of his recuperation and Dr Vaughan had suggested that his devastating fracture of memory, though uncommon, was on the rise and not surprising given reports of what Allied soldiers had faced on the front lines.

So why had he been left feeling like some sort of malingerer? If he could remember, he would, damn it! He wasn't looking for sympathy; he was sure he wouldn't have used memory loss as a way out of the seeming hellhole they'd dragged him from. Well, he wasn't going to spend another day in this place being mentally prodded and looked upon with pity, waiting to be recognised – to be found and claimed like lost luggage. It was time to make a decision.

As the notion slotted into place, a robin – perhaps the same one – began a melodious song, and in that instant, breaking cover from behind the bushes and surprising him, was the pretty woman of yesterday. He habitually reached for a fob watch which was no longer there, but he decided it had to be about the same time. Today she was dressed in grey but the traditionally sombre colour looked anything but gloomy on her; the suit was fashioned precisely, fitting her body perfectly. She wasn't wearing the billowy war crinoline that most of the women he'd seen outside of uniform wore. Instead, clean lines prevailed on a skirt still long enough to be considered demure, with neat pleats to allow an open stride, but the fine styling made it possible for him to imagine the curve of her legs, which were neither especially long nor short. He wasn't sure why he noticed her outfit so keenly or why he had concentrated sufficiently to remember yesterday's navy ensemble. Perhaps he'd been involved with clothing or cloth before the war? Before the abyss, as he'd begun to think of it – the place into which all of his memories had been tipped and buried with the rest of the dead.

Without permitting so much as a heartbeat to censor himself, he called out, 'Er . . . excuse me, Miss?' She paused, turned his way. Now he'd done it. 'Pardon me for interrupting you.'

'Yes?' she asked. He liked her voice. It was slightly husky.

'Er, do you have a light?' he said, glad that his cigarette had gone out.

She shook her head. 'I'm sorry, I don't.' No, it wasn't husky, he thought. It's smoky. He liked it even more now that he could see her mouth front on. It was generous, with clearly defined lips as precise as the cut of her suit.

He shrugged. 'Do you have a minute to give me instead, then?' The mouth he'd been admiring widened slightly into a small smile. 'I don't bite, I promise,' he added.

'How can I help you?'

'Will you sit with me for a few moments?'

She held her head to one side, as if weighing up his request, then looked around, checking to see if anyone else was nearby. She was probably wondering whether he was sweet or just plain strange. Sweet obviously won out, because she approached. Either that or a wave of pity had swept through her.

'I can stand with you for a few moments,' she offered. 'You have a lovely spot here amongst the rose bushes.'

'It was a perfumed nook just a few months ago,' he admitted. 'But then I see myself as a man of winter, so perhaps the bare rose bushes suit me.' He held out a hand. 'I'm Jones,' he said, feeling suddenly and for a rare moment grateful to be alive in the presence of luminous beauty.

Dark eyes, lamp-black in the glum light, nevertheless sparkled with internal amusement. She shook his hand gently. 'Just Jones?'

Her clear complexion was neither pale nor olive – somewhere in between – and the cold had pinched her cheeks so they blushed attractively. Hair the colour of a moonless Flanders night was pinned behind her head, and she wore a hat tipped jauntily with a striped feather pointing backwards from the hatband.

'I'm afraid so,' he said, desperate not to let go of her, but he did. 'I say, I do like that rakish feather.'

She grinned. Its effect felt like he'd walked in from the cold to a warm hearth. 'You've lost your name?' she remarked with slight incredulity.

'And my memory with it,' he added and wished he hadn't. He had wanted it to come out as a cheerful, plucky remark. Instead it sounded helpless.

'Oh.' Now she looked mortified. 'I'm sorry, I didn't mean to —'

'Please don't apologise.' He cringed. 'I'm tired of people feeling sorry for me. I have everything to be thankful for,' he said, lying to himself. But he decided in that single tick of his life that he shouldn't lie to her. 'Actually, that's not quite true. I don't feel all that grateful but I do feel glad in this instant that I survived.'

She nodded, as though immediately understanding his dilemma, and joined him at a modest distance on the bench they now shared, which pleased him. 'My brother didn't survive unfortunately.'

'So I hear.'

'Pardon me?'

He flicked the ash from his cigarette and in what appeared to be another habitual motion he put the barely smoked cigarette back into his pocket, carefully saving it for later. 'One of the nurses heard you talking about your brother in the tearoom.'

She blinked. 'His name was Daniel.'

'I'm sorry.'

'I am too. I miss him terribly and my father misses his son desperately. I'm not sure I'm enough.'

'Oh, I can't believe that. You would be for me.'

She gave him a startled glance.

'I'm sorry again. I don't know why I said that. I've clearly been a long time out of the company of beautiful young women, or my injuries have scrambled my filters . . .'

His admission made her smile again and he saw it warm up her gaze. Her eyes were the darkest chocolate, he noted, not nearly black as he'd originally assumed. 'So, what is to be done with you?' she asked.

He shrugged. 'Who knows? I have only a nickname, and no clues to where I hail from, which company I fought with, or even where I was fighting. I gather my uniform jacket was missing when I was discovered or they'd have some clue. I just keep hoping that some family is going to walk up and gasp with joy that they've found me.'

'And you have nothing at all to go on?'

He shook his head. 'I don't know what I used to be. I don't even know how old I am. I do remember a dog, though – a fox terrier, I think.'

'Well, there's a start,' she said, her tone brightening.

'I'm told I could be recalling the cigarette dog that roamed the trenches or even the ratters we were apparently all grateful for, so it's not really a clue to my background.'

'Oh dear,' she said, and for some reason – probably awkwardness, he thought – his explanation made them both chuckle. 'Any other options?'

'Obviously I don't wait for anyone to come looking,' he said with a sardonic grin. She waited. 'May I ask a favour of you?' he added, again without giving himself time to lose his courage.

'It depends what it is.'

'Would you help me escape?'

Alarm was back in her expression now, her gaze shrouding with worry. 'Surely you should —'

'They have no idea what to do with me. I've been here nearly five months and no one has been able to find even a remote connection for me.'

'It's early days. The war is only just —'

He shook his head. 'I think I really will go mad if I have to stay another night here. I've made a decision to leave. I'm going today, come what may. But I have no idea of where I'm going. I don't even think I know how to catch a bus or a train. I certainly have no money to do so.'

'But what can I do?'

'Just point me in the right direction. If you can get me even a few miles from here, I shall be fine. I simply need to get out of the hospital's reach so it can forget about me – another casualty of the war.'

'I'm sorry, Mr Jones, I really don't think —'

'Please.' It was embarrassing to beg. 'I doubt I'll ever have a better chance than today.'

He saw her resolve give behind those kind eyes. Maybe she was thinking of Daniel.

'I'm a fully grown adult, in case you hadn't noticed,' he added, and it broke the tension. She looked at her gloved hands, but he caught the grin as she lowered her head. 'I'm sure I was perfectly capable of looking after myself before the war, so I shall just learn to do so again. I know I'm not helpless. But in here I certainly feel that way.'

She regarded him again and it wasn't pity he saw. Instead he sensed her own ambition and strength, and perhaps she felt it was right that he was allowed to be independent.

'All right. I can't see how it is a crime to help a war veteran.'

'Really?'

She nodded. 'How do we do this?'

'It's the Peace Party today.'

She nodded, waiting for instructions.

'You see, everyone will be distracted once the festivities begin. Just take my arm and walk me out of the compound. I will not trouble you beyond the end of this path. If you could tell me in which direction to head, I should also be grateful.' His attention was caught by a glint of gold amongst the bushes. A wind was gusting up and had blown some leaves away. 'Hang on a moment,' he said, rising and limping across the lawn, realising it was a coin that had rolled against a naked, thorny rose bush.

'Aha!' he said, triumph in his voice. 'A half sovereign. Now I have means. It was meant to be.' He returned. 'I know someone is missing this, but they say what goes around comes around.'

She gave him a wry glance.

'And in the same spirit, one day I will pay you back for your kindness. If you make my dream come true, I'll do the same for you one day . . . I promise.'

She shook her head, amused by his whimsy, but held out her hand. 'It's a deal. I'm Eden. Eden Valentine.'

Even her name was lovely. 'Thank you, Miss Valentine,' he murmured and kissed the soft suede of her glove.

2

Edie Valentine was moving in amused bewilderment that a stranger – with no memory, no name – had recently taken her by the arm and accompanied her down the path towards a side gate of the hospital.

'We should be in conversation, I suspect,' he murmured. 'It distracts people, reassures them we are meant to be walking together in this direction.'

'What shall we talk about?' she managed to say through her bemusement.

'Well,' he said, sounding cheerful, 'how about you tell me why you're visiting the hospital? That should get us to the hedge and then soon you can be rid of me.' He smiled his encouragement, even patted her hand as though they were extremely good friends.

'All right,' Edie said. 'Yesterday I was here to collect some money and today I made a delivery to the director of the hospital.'

'And what were you delivering?' He gestured politely for her to go first as the path narrowed.

Edie relaxed slightly, charmed by his manners. 'It was a suit. The director is . . . well, my father's a tailor and Mr Donegal likes how my father styles for him.' She cleared her throat and pointed. 'Mr Donegal has been too busy to . . . um . . . it's not far now.'

Music struck up suddenly as a gramophone wheezed into life and this was clearly the cue for the merrymaking to start in earnest, because voices began to drift into their hearing, carried on the breeze. A woman's laughter erupted.

'She sounds like a hen that's busy laying an egg,' he remarked.

Edie chuckled as more clucking laughter followed and she enjoyed a mental image of the hospital henhouse. 'It's lovely to hear happy voices,' she admitted, not meaning to sound quite as wistful as she did.

'You're doing awfully well, Miss Valentine,' he assured her in such a gentle tone she cut him an equally tender smile.

'I'm not used to intrigue. You seem comfy enough with it.'

'Well, maybe I was a spy during the war,' he said, giving her a wink.

'Oh. Do you think so?'

He shook his head. 'No, I don't. What is your father's name?'

'Abraham. Abe.'

'Does he have a shop?'

'Yes. It's called Valentine & Son. Oh, look!' Edie gushed, delighted that London's grey sky was now polka-dotted by brightly coloured orbs, rising above the hospital rooftop as one. Gradually, individual balloons broke from the pack to ride a pocket of wind to unknown destinies. She was aware that her companion had followed her line of sight but that he had swiftly dropped his head as someone appeared from around the nearby hedge leading a bicycle.

She felt instantly guilty and her stomach clenched that a delivery boy – a grocer – might suddenly take an interest in her new career as an escape accomplice. Edie reminded herself that Mr Jones was not a criminal. She met the young man's appreciative gaze with a bright salutation. 'Look at the balloons,' she said, diverting his eyes upwards from her, hoping he would not remember the man by her side. 'It's for the party. There's cake,' she grinned.

They passed the youngster, who touched his cap politely.

'And son?' Mr Jones continued conversationally.

She blinked, tracking back in her mind to what they'd been talking about. Edie nodded with a shrug.

'Forgive me, I don't mean to —'

'No, that's all right. Daniel had been groomed since childhood for the trade. My father always wanted him to continue the business.'

'Of course. And have you learned the family trade as well?'

She sighed gently. 'I am a seamstress, yes.'

'Can you cut and sew a suit for a man?'

'Of course,' she replied, wishing she didn't sound quite so defiant.

He paused, allowing her to go first through the opening in the barrier between the world outside and the grounds of the hospital. Light traffic sounds instantly impacted but still it was mainly the cheer from the party that clung around them.

'Then the business is safe, surely?' he frowned, following her.

Edie shrugged. It was a moot point. 'We are here, Mr Jones,' she said as they emerged from beneath a small arched gate, nearly hidden by the tall privet hedge, and onto the pavement.

She watched his face relax in wonder; it must seem like a whole new world after his time at the hospital.

'It does,' he agreed, and Edie was momentarily embarrassed to realise she'd offered this thought aloud.

The jolly dance music felt distant now that the hedge provided a solid barrier but she experienced a fleeting thought of wishing Mr Jones had asked her to dance. She'd heard of whole neighbourhoods taking to the streets to celebrate the sheer joy of having peace again and no more young braves giving up their lives so hopelessly. She shook the notion away, allowing her attention to be captured by the colourful patriotic bunting that hung between lampposts on the street at the side of the hospital.

'How do you feel?' she asked, as it suddenly occurred to her that she might have just helped a sick man escape.

'Free,' he admitted. 'Just like one of your colourful balloons.' He looked up briefly and then returned her gaze, amused, and she couldn't help but wish she could see that same slightly boyish grin without the beard that she was sure he hid beneath. 'Thank you, Miss Valentine. I haven't forgotten my promise. I am in your debt.'

She smiled, cleared her throat of the small dam of confusing emotion that had invisibly clogged it. He was a stranger; she shouldn't feel such a connection to him. 'So, in which direction will you go?'

He shrugged. 'As far from here as possible; where do you suggest?'

'If you don't mind me saying, you sound as though you're from the south. But while I wouldn't suggest you head for London, maybe you could start a journey with a village close to London in mind.'

'Perfect,' he said. 'I'd better get on with it, then, as I suspect it's going to rain.'

'Here,' she said, digging into a cloth bag she carried. 'Take my umbrella.'

'It will rain on you as much as me, Miss Valentine.'

'But I don't have so far to travel.'

'Where are you headed?'

'Golders Green.' She could see it meant nothing to him.

'May I walk you to the bus stop?'

Edie looked up as she felt the first raindrop splash on her shoulder with a dull plop. She pushed up her umbrella. 'Why not, and then we can share this.' She ignored the guilty pleasure at staying in his company for a few more minutes. 'Pity about the party revellers.'

He unselfconsciously took her arm again, pulling their bodies closer to get beneath the umbrella as the raindrops began to fall heavily and insistently. They laughed and ran together, arriving slightly breathlessly into the shelter.

'Didn't do us much good,' Edie grinned, brushing water from her jacket.

'But here comes a bus,' he said, nodding at the slow vehicle lumbering towards them in the distance. The motorbus had an open top and the hardy couple upstairs were drenched, as was the driver down below who was equally open to the elements. Unlike his passengers, however, he was covered head to toe in waxed coveralls. 'So your timing is impeccable,' Jones replied. 'I presume this is yours?'

'It is,' she said, frowning. 'Will you be all right?'

'I have my lucky half sovereign.'

'Oh, wait, please,' she said, digging again into her bag and finding her purse. 'I meant to say that you should not use that half sovereign.'

'Why?'

'It's too much. Here,' she said, pushing a silver threepence into his hand. 'Save your lucky coin. You're going to need it.'

'I couldn't possibly accept your money —'

'Please, take it. I cannot in all good conscience leave you without it. Anyway, you were the one who said what goes around comes around. I'm sure someone will do me a good turn. Besides, if Daniel had . . .' She stopped, shook her head. She didn't want to keep mentioning Daniel. It had been four years now. Time to let the dead rest.

He folded the coin back into her gloved hand, shaking his head with a sad smile. 'I shall be —' The bus suddenly backfired loudly and accelerated towards the pavement. In that split second, Jones crouched and covered his arms over his head.

Edie leaned down. 'Mr Jones?' He said nothing but she heard him groan; her pity went out to him. She grasped what the explosion had provoked. 'I think you'd better come with me.' At his look of mystification, she added, 'Please. I can't leave you here.'

Jones allowed her to take his hand and lead him onto the bus. Even though she didn't relish being open to the inclement weather, Edie presumed he wouldn't want to be crowded by other passengers.

'Upstairs all right?'

He nodded, looking suddenly grey. Edie guided him up the stairs into the rain and to the back where they were alone.

'Take some deep breaths,' she urged when she noted his forehead looked damp from anxiety rather than rain.

'I'm so sorry,' he murmured, staring at the seat in front. 'I thought I was ready. I don't even know what I'm scared of. My memory won't tell me. I just reacted. Habit, I suppose.'

The rain eased off to a drizzle and then stopped almost as fast as it had arrived.

'It's perfectly understandable,' she assured as she shook out her umbrella and closed it. 'And although I don't know much about it, we've all heard how ugly it was in the trenches and on the front line. I imagine you were ducking for cover constantly. You have to give yourself time to heal, but also for your mind and body to accept we're in peacetime now. Perhaps for a while every backfire, every loud crack or voice, will disturb you.' She squeezed his arm, which was pushed against her. 'You're going to be fine,' Edie soothed above the rumbling noise of the bus as it jerked forward.

'I feel I have burdened you, Miss Valentine.'

'Not at all,' she said, helplessly pinioned by his sad gaze, looking out from the darkest of blue eyes. She wondered what on earth she was going to do with him, but she knew now that she couldn't just walk away from Mr Jones. She had to acknowledge that neither did she want to walk away from this handsome, somewhat helpless, fellow. 'Does it help to talk?'

'I don't know. Talking is all I seem to do, but it's all meaningless.'

'Well, if it's any consolation, I'd give anything to talk to Daniel again. And there are people out there who must feel the same way about you. Please don't lose heart.'

He finally turned to look at her. 'Thank you, Miss Valentine. I shan't.'

'Call me Edie.'

'Then you must call me Jones.'

They shared an amused glance.

A notion occurred to Edie. 'Don't think about this too hard, but why don't you just say the first man's name that comes into your head?'

He hesitated only for a heartbeat as he listened. 'Thomas,' he said, and then frowned.

'Thomas?' she repeated, as though testing it against him. 'I wonder why.'

He shrugged.

'You don't look like a Thomas, but I think Tom might suit you.'

'Tom,' he repeated. 'Why, yes, it sounds rather cheerful and I like it.'

'Does it sound familiar?'

He shook his head. 'Sound? No.' Edie let out a silent breath of disappointment. 'But curiously, there's something about it that *feels* vaguely familiar.'

'Really?' She brightened, beaming at him.

'Yes. Although don't ask me to explain it.'

'Then Tom you shall be, unless formal introductions are called for, and maybe if we keep that name close, it may come back to you why it was your first choice. It's a beginning, don't you see?'

'You are very good for me, Edie. Why didn't the hospital suggest that?'

'I'm no doctor.' She leaned close to whisper. 'But I do think women are more practical.'

He smiled. 'Where will you drop me off?'

'I'm not going to drop you anywhere. I'm taking you home with me to meet my father.' It had slipped out before she'd given herself time to consider it. Tom was like a lost, needy animal. If she didn't help him, who would? And she had agreed to get him out of the hospital, after all.

And why else? The question was posed in her mind in her father's voice. She ignored it.

Tom stared at her as though she'd suddenly broken out into a strange language. 'But why?'

She shrugged. 'I feel responsible.'

'You shouldn't. I coerced you. You've done enough.'

'No, I wouldn't be happy to let you continue until you've acclimatised a little more to the – um – the outside world. Abba . . . my father, is a wise man. He'll know what to do. Perhaps you need to be with friends at least for a night. He won't mind.'

'Friends. That sounds so nice and normal.'

'You are normal, Tom. You're just wounded. Your mind has been hurt in the same way that another soldier's arm or leg has been.'

The conductor arrived. 'Afternoon.' Then he frowned. 'Is it afternoon? Who can tell with these grey skies?'

'Two, please,' Edie said, handing over her threepence.

'Thanks, luv.' The conductor's gaze lingered on Edie as he handed her two tickets before he wandered off.

'Should I punch him on the nose, do you think?'

She smiled self-consciously. 'Even a year ago that conductor would have been a woman. I'm sure women miss their roles, now that men have returned.'

'Yes, I imagine they must have felt great freedom and now must return to their lives at home.'

She nodded – he spoke the truth – but in her mind she heard the word 'prison' rather than 'lives'.

'He has the wasted and haunted look of a returned soldier,' Tom continued.

'How can you tell . . . I mean, without memory to clue you?'

'A logical question. Perhaps it's simply because his conductor's uniform swamps him and I'm drawing a conclusion, right or wrong.' He narrowed his gaze. 'But didn't you see that look in his eyes?'

She shook her head.

'Desperate for companionship, but distant . . . somehow unsettled?'

Edie shrugged. 'I didn't, I must admit.'

'I believe I've seen that look a thousand times over, or so my gut tells me. I probably possess it too.'

'You're very handsome and not at all distant,' she assured, and then felt her cheeks warm uncomfortably. He gave her a sideways glance but said nothing, turning instead to look at passing traffic, which was thickening as they skirted London central and then bypassed it.

'Evening News, Schweppes Water, Oakey's Knife Polish, Claymore Whisky, Iron Jelloids . . .' he recited softly.

'Pardon me?'

He shook his head. 'Just reading the advertisements on the other buses. It's hard to believe a war has just finished. It all looks so colourful and bright.'

Edie didn't believe much looked bright in the depths of November at all but perhaps everything would after the trenches. 'Anything ring a bell?'

'The whisky, maybe.' He grinned disarmingly and Edie knew that even in the short time she'd spent with this man, his charm was infectious. There was something about his straight bearing, his careful, courteous manner and his quiet way of speaking that she found attractive.

'Well, Golders Green is the end of the line, so just take in the sights. You never know.'

'Do you mind if I smoke?'

She smiled and shook her head as he reached into his pocket. 'But my father might.'

He struck a match and lit the cigarette he'd tapped out of a small packet. There was only one remaining. 'I shall make this my last, then,' he said, with no tone of regret.

'Why?'

'New beginnings. Everything about today feels new and I want to feel as though I've started a new life.' He took a final long drag before casually flicking it away.

They travelled in near silence for the rest of the journey, although Edie became all too aware of the warmth that connected them, through his common carded wool flannel suit to her more expensively woven yarn suit. There was a burn like a Catherine wheel firework hissing between them, except this one was spinning and spitting invisible sparks inside her. It felt dangerously exciting.

———

A petite woman, striking in her deep crimson coat, alighted from a taxi outside Edmonton Hospital's main gate and asked the driver to wait. As she approached the entrance, observers would have noticed that the visitor was as daring in her design as in colour, for the coat was actually a cape fastened with an oversized button on one side. A narrow, midnight-blue skirt emerged from beneath it to land above her ankles, and her gloved hand reached instinctively to her navy broad-brimmed hat as a gust of wind threatened to unseat it from Apollo-golden hair, which was neatly parted and pinned around both ears.

At the hospital reception she was told that the Peace Party was underway for the patients. When she said she was seeking one in particular – a gentleman, one of the returned soldiers – she was asked to wait.

Sister Bolton was just tipping a beaker of warmed elder cordial to her lips when she was called to the nurses' station. She tried not to roll her eyes.

'Who wants me?'

'I was asked by Miss Fairview to find you.'

'Why?'

The girl looked ready to shrug but caught herself in time. 'I'm not sure, Sister. I think she might have mentioned an important visitor.'

'Very well. Run along, Smith.'

Bolton strode towards reception, her lips helplessly pursed at being pulled away from the celebrations she hoped would breathe some happiness into the depressed lives of her returned soldiers as they healed, convalesced and tried to forget what they had experienced on the battlefields of Europe. So many were still recovering from serious injuries, and most were facing the worse battle of trying to recover from much deeper scars, which even her determined team and its care might never heal.

She arrived in the main lobby to be introduced to a young woman who smelled of exquisite spiced floral perfume and was dressed so expensively she was almost convinced a curtsey might be due.

'Oh, hello, Sister Bolton,' the woman said and her effortless greeting persuaded Sister that the visitor cared not about social status. 'I was told you were the person I should talk to.' The beam of the visitor's smile warmed up the frost that had settled about Emilia Bolton. 'I'm Penelope Aubrey-Finch.'

'Miss Aubrey-Finch.' Sister Bolton nodded, and shook the navy-gloved hand, feeling the caress of softest kid against her skin. 'How can I help?' Her gaze flicked to a young man who'd lost the best part of both legs, amputated at a field hospital during the Battle of the Somme. She watched her patient being pushed in a wheelchair to join the party before returning her attention to Miss Aubrey-Finch, mindful of not letting it rudely wander again.

'. . . and I've been searching all the military hospitals and establishments where returning injured soldiers have been brought,' she said.

Sister Bolton understood. 'Of course. Your father? Brother?' she said.

'Neither, actually. An extremely distant cousin,' she said, then added, 'So distant as to be more like a friend than blood . . . um, a very special friend.'

The elder woman found an encouraging smile for her, understanding immediately the toll that these sorts of searches took on the families. So much hope, yet potential despair waiting at every turn.

'And clearly an important one if you have taken so much care in hunting him down.' She watched the young woman falter. Penelope Aubrey-Finch struck her as exquisitely beautiful – like a fragile butterfly – and it occurred to Sister Bolton to wonder why such a young woman was here alone on this mission. 'Did anyone accompany you?'

Miss Aubrey-Finch smiled and shook her head. 'No. I've taken it upon myself to find cousin Lex. I have a car waiting.'

'Lex?' She frowned. 'You can leave your umbrella here to dry off. Come with me.' She called by the reception to request a mask, which she handed to her wealthy visitor. 'It's a precaution only, but may I suggest you wear this? Influenza is rife and we do suggest it for all our visitors.'

The woman nodded. 'Thank you. I'm getting quite used to covering my face,' she said, impressively unperturbed by the caution.

'You'd make a fine nurse,' Sister Bolton remarked as she gestured for her guest to follow.

Penelope Aubrey-Finch fell in step and as they walked the corridors they discussed her journey from Belgravia, where her parents were spending the festive season. 'My family home is in York but I schooled in London and Switzerland, and I guess I feel more comfortable in the south.'

'Of course,' Sister Bolton replied, imagining the privileged life of this young woman who could barely be past twenty, but Miss Aubrey-Finch and her heady fragrance, immaculate clothes, fine manners and especially her bright, engaging way was extremely hard to dislike.

'. . . given up, except me. I believe with all of my heart that he's still alive, perhaps injured.'

'I understand.'

She led her visitor into the 'dining room' – as the nurses called it – which had become the main undercover venue for the Peace Party, although it was thinning out now that the rain had stopped and people had headed into the gardens to spot the freedom balloons that had been released.

'Here, my dear. All but the sickest of our soldiers are gathered. Do you recognise your cousin? I have to warn you, though, we have no one here called Lex.'

Miss Aubrey-Finch paused carefully before each of the men, and shared a kind word or two before she moved on to the next. Sister Bolton was impressed by the young woman's composure but especially how magnanimous she seemed in making sure her friendliness fell upon each soldier, some with legs in bandages or arms in slings, others with their heads still wrapped in linens or eyes covered with patches. She noticed their visitor didn't flinch as she met each and all the patients. The men were left grinning as their visitor returned to the nurse with a shrug. Yes, indeed, a fine nurse this one would make.

'I'm so sorry,' Sister Bolton said when it was obvious the distant cousin was not amongst the men.

'Don't be. You've been so kind to allow me to interrupt a special day,' Miss Aubrey-Finch replied, her eyes misty but her voice steady. She pulled away her mask.

'Believe me, dear, we don't mind interruptions such as yours. If I could send any one of these men home today with you, it would be my best Christmas present ever.'

Her companion smiled. 'Thank you. I wish I could take them all home and see them laughing again.'

'We can visit the ward next. There are two . . . er, no, three other men, too unwell to attend the party.'

Miss Aubrey-Finch brightened. 'Thank you.' She slipped her mask back on as she followed Sister Bolton.

More disappointment followed as the three patients predictably were not the cousin she sought. 'Sincere thanks, all the same,' she said and shook Sister Bolton's hand again, this time without gloves, and the older woman noticed her companion's hand was soft and unmarked, her nails perfectly kept and buffed until they shone.

'I do wish I could have brought joy to your family's Christmas, Miss Aubrey-Finch.'

Penelope gave a sad smile. 'The perfect Christmas gift.'

'Don't get disheartened. I applaud your determination. If he's alive, you will find him.' She had to ask. 'Is he your fiancé?'

Penelope Aubrey-Finch shook her head. 'No, Sister, but I'd be lying if I said I don't hope for that to be the case.' The older woman noticed a shadow ghost across the young woman's open face. 'There's never been anyone else for me.'

'Well, perhaps leave a description and a photograph or a —'

'Oh, heavens! I brought one. I quite forgot.' She rummaged in a satin side pocket within the small, navy leather bag where she'd slung her gloves. 'Here,' she said with a sigh. 'That's him.' She smiled. 'It's a few years old now, and Lex always loathed having a photo taken —'

Sister Bolton took the photo and stared at the figure her companion pointed to. She blinked and frowned, then shook her head. 'I'm so sorry, but . . .' She hesitated.

'What is it? Do you know him?' her companion pleaded.

The older woman's expression became thoughtful before she shook her head in slight frustration. 'I don't recognise this man, I have to be honest . . . but there's just something familiar about him. I don't know what it is – the shape of his head or just the way he's got it slightly cocked to one side like that. I . . .' She gave a soft sigh. 'I really can't say.'

Her visitor gave a small groan. 'It's not a great photo, I'll admit, especially being a more distant group shot and everyone in tennis whites.' She shrugged. 'Happier times.'

'You've tried all the military hospitals?'

'Near enough. I have written to them all, though, and given a most detailed description of Lex.'

'Well, you're certainly doing everything you can. Um . . . have you tried any of the mental institutions?'

Miss Aubrey-Finch gave a small gasp. 'No. Should I?'

Sister Bolton lifted one shoulder. 'So many of our soldiers came home wounded physically but also mentally. Take our Mr Jones, for example. That's not his real name. It's just what we call him.'

Miss Aubrey-Finch regarded her in puzzlement. 'Why?'

'He is suffering from shellshock and remembers nothing, not even his name. Those with amnesia at Edmonton are arbitrarily given common surnames – we've had four. Mr Smith, Mr Green, Mr Brown and Mr Jones. It affects the soldiers in numerous ways. Some become moody, others completely withdraw. There are terrible night terrors and I've heard of some men, normally peaceful, gentle folk, turning violent without warning.' She shook her head sadly.

'Has no one claimed them?'

'Oh, indeed. Smith, Green and Brown have already been returned to loving families.'

'And Mr Jones?'

'Completely lost. He has no memory of who he is.' She blinked into the distance. 'Funnily enough, he's the one that I was thinking bore a curious echo to your dashing-looking friend.' She smiled at the young woman who seemed pleased by the compliment. 'Can I see that photo again, please?'

Miss Aubrey-Finch handed her the photograph once more and Sister Bolton studied it before biting her lip. 'You know, it could be him. Similar height, build . . .'

Sister Bolton heard her visitor give a soft gasp of hope.

She continued. 'He has no memory since he regained consciousness. We believe he was hurt in late 1917 at Ypres, transferred to various places and institutions, finally coming to us a few months ago.'

'He last wrote to me from Flanders! Lex is here?' the young woman exclaimed, tears arriving helplessly. She clamped a hand to her masked mouth. 'Really?' she added in a tremulous voice.

Sister Bolton straightened. 'No, I am not sure about that at all, Miss Aubrey-Finch. Please do not get your hopes too high. But there's something about this fellow in your photo. Mr Jones refuses to shave his beard for some reason. I spoke to him barely an hour ago. Let me find Nan, who knows him best. Wait here, dear. I don't understand why he isn't at the party.' She turned back to the dining room and spied Nancy sipping a ginger beer and giggling with two of the patients.

Sister Bolton strode over to the trio. 'Excuse me. Nan, where is Mr Jones?'

Nan's expression clouded with bewilderment. Sister Bolton waited.

'Er, I left him in the garden.' Nan frowned. 'He was dressed in good clothes,' she continued, thinking back over her morning.

'Yes, I spoke to him. He said he'd see me at the party.'

Nancy's expression lost its amusement. 'Is he in his ward?'

'Go check, quickly. I have a visitor with a photograph of someone who bears a resemblance. Let's not miss an opportunity to find his family.'

———

While Sister Bolton returned to calm Penelope Aubrey-Finch's rising hopes, Nan hurried back to the ward where Jonesy lived alone these days, and as her sinking heart suggested, she found it empty. He'd been in a slightly strange mood this morning – more of the bad dreams had disturbed his sleep and he had seemed curiously quiet, almost wistful, when she'd done her early rounds.

He'd promised he'd shake a leg with her on the makeshift dance floor in the dining room if she played something bright on the gramophone. Had he deliberately misled her? She didn't think he would lie to her face – didn't think he'd lie at all. But why would he disappear today? What was so special about today that might prompt him to walk out of the hospital? She checked in all the bathrooms, spare rooms; even ducked out into the gardens in case he was moping in a drenched nook somewhere, but she came up wanting. Nancy returned to the waiting women with a haunted expression and hated the way the beautiful visitor's expression brightened eagerly.

'Well?' Sister Bolton demanded.

'I can't find him anywhere, Sister. I think Jones may have left the hospital.'

She watched Sister Bolton close her eyes momentarily with frustration. 'The side gate. We kept it unlocked for small deliveries. It was so rarely used.'

Nan nodded. 'I think that's exactly what's happened, Sister.

His ward windows look out that way. He's been watching people come and go for months.'

'What are you saying?' their guest said, her gaze darting wildly between them. 'He's escaped?'

'Escaped?' Sister Bolton repeated and couldn't fully mask the incredulity in her voice. 'No, my dear. Our patients are not prisoners. I presume he has exercised his right to discharge himself and has chosen to make our lives more difficult by ignoring the paperwork.'

'Where would he go?'

Nan shook her head. 'To my knowledge he'd never even looked beyond the privet hedge. He was traumatised, Miss, he had no memory, and was terribly haunted by nightmares. I would never have thought Jonesy . . . er, Mr Jones, would leave the hospital grounds without aid or encouragement.' Or without saying goodbye, she thought forlornly, trying not to consider the small candle she carried for him.

'You said he was shellshocked. Is that the word you used, Sister Bolton?' their visitor asked.

She nodded. 'Yes. He may not show visible wounds, but he's injured nonetheless.'

'He has a slight limp too,' Nan added. 'Shrapnel wound that's healed but left its scar.'

'But he could be anywhere!' Miss Aubrey-Finch exclaimed, and they could see how hard she fought to retain her composure.

'Come with me, dear. What we need is a cup of tea for your shock and then we'll see what can be done.' Sister Bolton led the finely dressed woman away and Nan was left feeling hollow. She didn't even know if the weeping beauty was Jones's wife but she had been right about one thing – the patient she'd fallen for had been no regular Tommy.

3

They alighted the bus at the terminus and set off in the direction of the town of Golders Green.

'That's a nice smell,' Tom remarked, sniffing the air.

'Bagels,' Edie replied.

'What is a bagel?'

She laughed. 'I suspect you'll find out later. I'll let it be a surprise.' She pointed. 'Down this way.'

'Where's your mother, Edie?'

'She died.'

'I'm sorry to hear that.'

Edie shrugged. 'It's all right. I never knew her so in a way I'm lucky that I don't have to miss her as we do Daniel.'

'You and your father sound very close.'

'We are. And now we . . .' She stopped whatever she was going to say. 'We have to head across the High Street and then we're home,' she said.

'Home?' He looked surprised to be staring at a main street ahead, with mansion apartments above the stores.

'It's quite a large apartment above the shop.'

Edie had begun walking but Tom lagged, still staring into the distance at the row of mansion apartments, when a lorry drove by through a large puddle. It kicked up a torrent and splashed the back of him. He yelped and Edie found it impossible not to explode into laughter.

Tom grinned. 'Not very heroic for a returned soldier, am I?'

'We must hurry and get you out of those wet things. You really will freeze.'

They scuttled along, holding on to each other once more as the clouds chose that moment to burst again. There was no point in opening an umbrella. With slitted eyes to the deluge, they ran, finally making it into the High Street that was bustling with people despite the inclement weather. She pushed into a dark shop and a bell rang distantly.

'Abba?'

A smallish, round man emerged from a doorway behind a counter. Silver-haired and with a luxuriant beard to match, he smiled at the arrival of his drenched daughter but his expression clouded as he caught sight of her companion. 'We have a visitor?'

Breathless, Edie hurried to kiss her father. 'Abba, this is Mr Thomas Jones. He's . . . er, he's a returned serviceman from the front.'

His manners overcame his reserve and he crossed the floor to shake hands. 'Mr Jones. I am Abraham Valentine.'

'Mr Valentine,' Tom replied, bowing slightly as he shook his elder's hand. He sensed the awkwardness immediately and needed to save Edie any tension with her father. 'Forgive me, Sir. Your kind daughter took pity on a stray in the rain, I'm afraid. I promise I will not interrupt you longer than a few minutes to dry off slightly.'

'Abba, I'll explain. Let me get Mr Jones out of his wet clothes and —'

Valentine's bemused expression intensified. 'Why don't I help our visitor out of his wet things, Edie, my dear, and you can perhaps make us a pot of tea?'

'Of course,' Edie said, cutting Tom a look of soft apology.

'Come with me,' the older man offered. Tom allowed himself to be led into the back of the shop, where patterns hung from pegs with names of people scrawled on them, and bolts of cloths and barrels of buttons were piled high. Threads and yarns and an assortment of odd-looking tools hung from hooks as did a range of huge scissors. He smelled wool and found it deeply comforting but didn't know why. 'Now, let me see. What can we find you?' Valentine pointed. 'Why don't you shrug off those wet things over there, while I hunt down some garments? You're a 34-inch waist normally, I suspect, but you look like you've got some pounds to put on yet to reach that. I'll see if I have something in 32. And a jacket? Mmm, leave it with me.' He disappeared around a corner and a door closed softly. Above, he heard floorboards creak as Edie presumably moved around in the family's apartment.

Then he could make out muted voices: Edie's sounding beseeching while her father's sounded grave. It seemed he hadn't been able to save Edie the interrogation.

Upstairs, Abraham Valentine regarded his daughter with amazement. 'He's a perfect stranger and you're an engaged woman!'

'He needed help, Abba,' Edie appealed.

'But he was in hospital. Worse, he's a mental patient, I now learn!'

'No, that's not what I —'

'Why would your help be best?'

'He needed to escape.' Edie knew that came out wrong. But it was too late. Her father's gaze had already widened.

'Escape?'

'He was trapped in his loss of memory, I meant. He says he needs to find out about himself, perhaps start tracing where he came from, find his family.'

'Which, presumably, a military hospital was already doing on his behalf!'

'He'd been there five months with no news,' she bleated, returning to making the tea, so her father might miss how upset she was. She wondered if Tom could hear what they were saying.

'Daughter, what makes you think you can help where the whole military bureaucracy of Britain cannot . . . hmm?'

She rounded on him but kept her expression even. Abba never responded well to exasperation. Calm was her only ally. Edie spoke softly. 'I didn't set out with the intention to help him trace his roots. I followed your creed that if someone asks for my help, I should give it. He asked. I simply allowed him to accompany me out of the hospital grounds.'

She watched her father's expression soften and hurried on.

'It was raining. The bus backfired loudly,' she said, remembering how traumatised Tom had looked; how his gaze had momentarily been so far away. 'And I noticed how it upset him. You've heard of shellshock?'

He nodded.

'That's what Tom is suffering from, I gather.'

She saw her father's eyebrow arch at the familiar use of their guest's name.

'And the bus backfiring disturbed him enough that I simply could not leave him where he cringed, drenched and forlorn. I suggested he come home because I thought you'd know what to do. I said you would help.'

He nodded. 'And so I will, as you knew I would. Set the tea tray in the sitting room. I shall bring him up.'

She moved to hug her father. 'Thank you. He's terribly grateful and polite, Abba.'

'They all are, my beloved,' he murmured and kissed her head. She frowned as she watched him move down the hallway towards Daniel's old room but didn't linger, realising Tom had been left too long already.

Downstairs, feeling faintly ridiculous, Tom stood in his shirt, which the damp hadn't reached, and socks and underwear provided by the hospital. Both were itchy. Finally Valentine arrived holding two suits.

'They will both fit. Which do you prefer?' he asked.

Tom appeared taken aback by having the choice. 'Er, the darker one, I think.'

'You have good taste, Mr Jones. This is made from the finest merino wool that money can buy.'

He assumed Valentine wanted him to appreciate this fact so he touched the sleeve and felt the soft, fine yarn. 'It's excellent. One hundred crimps per inch?'

Valentine stared at him with astonishment and Tom shrugged. 'I have absolutely no idea why I should ask such a question. Did I say something wrong?'

'Not at all. In fact, it's rather enlightening. Here, please try it on.' He offered the suit.

The trousers were a perfect fit, the length only a shade too short.

'I'll drop that hem in a few minutes for you, son. I'm told you're recovering from war wounds,' he remarked, twisting Tom gently to regard the seat of the trousers.

'I am, yes.'

'Well, these will fit your waist for now but they won't as your health improves. Your chest size attests to that.'

'I wouldn't know,' Tom admitted, dipping an arm into the jacket sleeve that Valentine expertly slipped onto his shoulders, habitually drawing both hands across as if to straighten the cloth and remove any stray lint.

'Yes, snug, as I presumed,' Valentine remarked. 'This was made for someone who had a 32-inch waist and a 37-inch chest. You are 34 and 40 for future reference.'

'I am more than grateful to use it until my suit dries.'

'I wish you to have it. Let us say it is a gift from a grateful family to a brave soldier who may even have fought alongside its favourite son.'

Tom blinked.

'It can set you on your way forward so you look spruce and ready for the challenges ahead. Now, come, my daughter is laying out some tea for us.'

Tom, surprised by the generosity but not game to argue, duly followed Valentine upstairs and emerged into a dim but not inelegant sitting room, where Edie looked up from laying out items from a tray. Her expression changed from a welcome smile to surprise and he realised it was because of his new clothes.

'Abba . . . are you sure?' she said, cutting an anxious glance at her father, who was already seating himself.

'Daniel has no further need for it,' he replied. 'Now, I'm guessing Jones is not your real name,' he said, inviting him with a wave to make himself comfortable.

'No.'

'Edie has told me what she can about your situation, but why don't you explain?' he said, eyes genial but not fully able to disguise his suspicion. He gestured to Edie and as she began to pour the tea, Tom had no choice but to tell Valentine his life story, which consisted of only five months of dull routine, all of its dreary nights spent in a hospital bed anguishing over lost memories.

4

Valentine had sat silent, listening to the man who was interrupting an otherwise uneventful life that Abe had deliberately carved, minute by terrible minute, since that dark day four years ago when news had reached them of Daniel's death. His beautiful, bright, intelligent son, who hurt no one and yet felt it was his duty to take up arms and defend the country that had given his family a home two generations earlier.

Sir. It is my painful duty to inform you that a report has been received from the War Office notifying the death of . . . He hadn't read on. He had left the pale-eyed lad who had delivered the telegram with Edie. His daughter and the telegram boy stood on either side of the door watching him turn his back on them.

He recalled now how he'd been so unable – no doubt unwilling – to absorb the enormity of what he'd read in that opening sentence that he'd shocked Edie by wordlessly going straight into the backroom to begin cutting a pattern. If he could lose himself in the comforting sound of the shears slicing through good cloth, kicking up the chalk as he followed the soothing white lines of his work, maybe he could lose the truth of that telegram. Those markings never let him down – they always guided him; they were dependable. And then a small voice had spoken to him. *They can be rubbed away,* it said. *Like Daniel.*

Daniel had been as reliable and solid as Abe's white chalk and yet he'd been equally vulnerable, when a German bullet from a strafing machine gun had caught him in the neck, they later learned. On the days when Abe felt bright he rationalised that Daniel was lucky to suffer instant death: no pain, no limbs cut away, no shock of blood loss or mates comforting him with hollow words as he slipped away. One moment his boy had been vital, full of life; the next his son was gone, his body an empty vessel like the spent cartridges that littered the death fields.

'Hmm?' he said, looking up from his saucer, roused from his memories.

'Abba. Are you listening?' Edie repeated, frowning with concern.

'Yes . . . yes, of course,' he replied. He sipped the dregs of his tea and as he placed his cup and saucer back down on the small side table next to his armchair he plucked a tea leaf from his tongue. Right away, he wished he hadn't. His long-dead wife, Nina, had maintained such a thing was an omen. Apparently her eldest aunt had possessed the 'sight' and one of her notions was that to remove a tea leaf from one's mouth should prompt a forewarning. He remembered Nina's whimsical remark that followed: 'Esther would say that whoever has come into your life or whatever you are doing at that moment has important resonance. Don't ignore it.'

Why had he plucked that tea leaf off his tongue? Now he felt obliged to pay more notice to the mysterious Tom or defy Nina. And one never defied Nina. *But why now, my love?* he pleaded silently. Why with this gentile stranger whom his soon-to-be-married daughter clearly found as irresistible as a homeless puppy?

'Why were you not in the Friern Barnet Mental Asylum?' Abe suddenly piped up.

He knew his daughter bristled at the query but watched their guest smile without, apparently, taking offence and begin explaining in the softly spoken way he had. Abe stared at the man seated opposite. He was taller than Daniel, who was an inch shy of six feet. Although Jones claimed to have no memory, he was not without self-possession. He sat straight-backed but to some degree relaxed, as if not intimidated by this audience. He was respectful but Abe decided that this respect was being accorded simply to his elder rather than to someone he considered his superior.

His daughter's intrigue was his uppermost concern; at twenty-three she was not prone to the histrionics he'd heard or witnessed in his friends' teenaged daughters, but she was nonetheless vulnerable. The loss of her brother had affected her profoundly. His love for Edie, the only member of his small family left, was inestimable, and he'd be damned if he was going to let some good-looking sapper returned from the front line with a shrapnel wound and a sob story steal her heart, which was not only promised but about to be wed. Abe Valentine had planned this for his daughter. Levi's son, Benjamin, was a perfect match.

'Pardon me, but did you say you *were* in the mental asylum?' Abe queried.

'I did, Sir, yes. But I was moved because that institution was for the insane . . . and in terms of the returning soldiers, it was mainly used for the men who were troubled.'

'You were neither, I take it?' Abe offered, masking the dryness of his comment.

Tom put his cup and saucer down, smiling thanks at Edie. 'Memory loss might have made me disgruntled, even irritable, but it does not make me hostile, or a hazard to anyone or anything around me, Sir. To put it frankly, I believe I've done the War Office a good deed by ridding it of a problem.'

'And what do you propose to do now?'

He watched Jones blow out his cheeks and already knew the answer. 'I'm not exactly sure. This morning I simply wanted to put distance between the hospital and myself. I was tired of being paraded before hopeful families only to watch them shake their collective heads with deep disappointment.'

'That must have been humiliating,' Edie murmured.

'It was. And ultimately heartbreaking. I couldn't watch another family's despair because I wasn't who they needed me to be, and with each shake of the head my own heart hurt a little more. Besides, I want to make my own decisions – I'm sure I must have in civilian life before the war. I see no reason why I shouldn't now. I'm not sick. I simply have no recall.'

'Surely the authorities can reunite families in a more sensitive way?' Abe said, dabbing his beard out of habit with his large white handkerchief.

'Maybe, but given the circumstances I suspect they're doing their best. There are so many soldiers still lost, I gather, still trying to find their way back. I don't mean to criticise or sound ungrateful. As soon as I knew the Spanish flu had reached the hospital I wanted to get out.'

At Abe's startled expression, Tom raised his hands to show there was nothing to fear from him. 'I was in a completely protected wing, but I wasn't going to wait for it to find me, Sir. I assure you I am in good health.'

Abe blinked. 'My problem is that you've encouraged my daughter to break the law.'

'No law was broken, Mr Valentine. I have been released from the army. I am a free man with a free will. I just didn't choose to exercise it until today. Edie is in no danger from me or my actions.'

'That's good to know, Mr Jones, because Edie is about to be married.' It was as good a chance as any to press the point, he'd decided.

Edie cut him a glare. 'Well,' she said, standing. 'Abba, you have an appointment in less than twenty minutes. Mr Fletcher will be here and you still have to check over his suit.'

Abe quieted his daughter with a weary nod of submission as he pushed himself up from his chair. Tom stood too. 'Well . . . it's been a pleasure to meet you. Forgive me, but you heard my daughter's instructions. Edie will show you out . . . er . . .' He could hear the rain pounding on the roof again and felt guilty at his urging that it was time for their visitor to leave.

'Thank you, Sir. I'm really most grateful for your indulgence and especially, of course, to Edie for helping me as she did this morning.' He offered his hand and Abe clasped it. 'I learned about Daniel. I'm deeply sorry for the loss of your son. I was at Ypres. I believe I still dream about it.'

Abe blinked. 'You fought at Ypres?' His random thought that their guest may have fought alongside his son wasn't so far-fetched after all.

'So I'm told,' Tom said with a sad smile. 'I remember nothing, but the limp is a reminder because whatever explosion wounded me took my memory as well. Apparently I was transferred from Flanders.' He shrugged.

'My son died in the second battle.'

'Maybe I'm the fortunate one, Sir, because I have no memory of it, but I did see a lot of men at the hospital who were ghosts. They survived the battle but it seemed only their bodies came back. Their spirits had fled.'

Abe frowned, sickened by what he was hearing. He knew Tom was gallantly trying to convey the message that perhaps Daniel had even been fortunate to die over there rather than return as one of those ghosts. As he shook his visitor's hand, it occurred to him that he'd never been closer to Daniel in four years than through this stranger right now. No body had been returned; there was no grave to visit, only memories and grief. He felt the bleak sense of despair rise again.

'And where did you say you will go now?' he said, clearing his throat, aware he was repeating himself.

Tom shrugged. 'Whichever direction beckons,' he said, sounding surprisingly cheerful. 'I shall probably rent a room for the night and make a plan for myself. Er, by the way, this suit, Sir, I . . .'

'You are to keep it, as I said.'

Tom nodded. 'Then I'll wear it proudly.'

Valentine glanced at his daughter, seeing the pain in her expression, although she would not meet his gaze. He knew what she wanted of him.

'Listen . . . son . . . I don't wish to cast you out into —'

He saw genuine concern erupt across their visitor's face. 'Please, Mr Valentine. You're not. I haven't felt this optimistic since I returned from Europe. Really, each passing minute away from the hospital and its gloom improves my humour. Your family has been so kind. Perhaps one day I can visit and repay that kindness. I have a debt to your daughter anyway to keep.'

'Oh?'

Edie shook her head, looking embarrassed. 'It's nothing, Abba. A few words in jest.'

He returned his attention to Tom, whose gaze held him steadily. The man was no trickster. Abe sighed. What could it hurt? 'I was going to suggest that you are welcome to stay . . .' Tom blinked in surprise and Abe found himself shrugging self-consciously. 'At least until you get on your feet and set yourself a direction, a purpose.'

'Oh, Abba!' Edie said and flung herself to hug him. 'Really? I knew you'd help. You see, Tom – I told you he would know what to do.'

Jones looked startled as well as dumbfounded. 'I . . . I don't know what to say, Sir. I feel I should leave. You've already been more than —'

'Tosh!' Abe said, waving a hand as he made the decision. 'I now have work to do. And I'm not suggesting you sit around and twiddle your thumbs, young man. You can earn your keep until you move on to the next stage of your journey.'

'I know nothing about tailoring.'

'Who said anything about tailoring?' Abe chuckled. 'There's always coal that needs shifting, errands to be run. I have bolts of fabric that I haven't had the strength to get to . . . Edie?'

'I'll show him. You get on with Mr Fletcher's suit.'

'I shall see you for dinner, then, Tom,' Abe said and nodded, muttering to himself about hating to be late for clients.

Edie threw Tom a look of triumph. 'Say yes,' she urged.

'How can I refuse either of you?'

She clapped her hands. 'I'm pleased. Now when you next set off, I hope you'll feel less chaotic. Come on, then. I'll show you where everything is, although maybe it's best you change back out of that suit. It's Italian cloth,' she added, as though he should be mightily impressed.

———————

By dinnertime Tom had restacked the two coal scuttles and after cleaning up had given over what remained of the day to shifting some of the bolts of cloth from a towering stack to manageable, easier to navigate pillars in the storeroom. But there was plenty more to be done.

He was relieved they hadn't suggested he sleep in Daniel's room and was glad the family had the space in the apartment to give him a spare room, which Edie had made up for him. It was sparse but more than adequate. After washing his face and hands, and dressing in the trousers of his loan suit and his shirt and jumper from the hospital, he appeared at the doorway of the small kitchen.

'Good evening,' he said and Edie glanced his way, standing back from her stove to look at him with appreciation.

'Good evening to you, Tom. Well, you've got colour back in your cheeks.'

'Nothing like a bit of physical work,' he said, pretending to pump his muscles. 'I've been far too long in that hospital mooching around.'

'I'm pleased for you,' she encouraged and they shared an affectionate smile before Abe arrived, having changed for dinner and now wearing a round, flat cap only large enough to cover his crown.

'You can lay the table if you want, Tom,' Edie said. 'Everything you need is in the sideboard. And you may want to light the candles too.'

'At the double,' he said, saluting Edie and disappearing around the corner into the adjoining room. There were two sideboards. Inside the closest one he saw that it was full of all the right accoutrements.

It didn't take him long. Perhaps it was the habit of being in the army and doing things quickly but he found a damask cloth that he shook out of its perfectly ironed creases to lay across the table. Matching napkins and rings soon followed. In a mahogany box he discovered the cutlery and laid out three places. Behind one of the cupboard doors were glasses. He moved to the wall to admire his work. Perfect. He put the candelabra he'd spied on top of the sideboard onto the table and added four new candles, which he lit. It felt so homely and he realised how much and how long he'd been yearning for this sort of normality.

Tom returned to the kitchen where father and daughter were arguing gently over the seasoning of whatever was about to be ladled into a large tureen.

'The table awaits!' he called, not wanting to cram into the kitchen as well.

As his companions arrived, their chatter stopped abruptly. He looked at them, surprised, and then followed their bemused gazes to the table. He didn't know what had caught their attention. The table was set precisely. The silver and crystal glittered beneath the candlelight.

'Is something wrong?' he had to say.

They both rushed to reassure him, voices stumbling over each other.

'It's just . . . a simple meal,' Edie added, taking in the sumptuous scene before her.

Tom looked back at his handiwork. He still didn't grasp the dilemma.

'Tom, my boy, since when did you eat with silver cutlery and drink water from crystal glasses on a Tuesday?' Abe asked, and Tom heard the glee in the old man's voice. 'Look, Edie, our guest is expecting several courses, it seems,' he said, pointing to the two sets of forks and knives and dessert fork and spoon laid neatly at each place. 'I hope you've made pudding too, daughter.' He chuckled with obvious delight.

Edie set the tureen down and now that Tom looked at the dish, it was a simple lidded pottery bowl. The silver tureen he could see was glinting at him from the cabinet. But Edie's eyes sparkled with similar amusement to her father's.

'Abba, how long has it been since we've used the good crockery and cutlery?'

'Too long, child,' he admitted.

'It's wonderful, Tom,' she said, turning to him. 'Thank you.'

'Is there an alternative?' he frowned.

She pointed to the other, more modest-looking sideboard. 'In there. Our daily cutlery and crockery. This is our best ware,' she said, glancing back at the fine table that was laid out. 'But what a treat. Maybe it's a clue to your past, Tom.'

He was aware of his hosts sharing puzzled glances despite their encouraging smiles. Abe handed him a small dark velvet *kippah* to cover his crown. 'Won't hurt to wear it around the table,' Abe said, slight apology in his tone.

'I'll be glad to. Tomorrow, I'll keep working in the storeroom.'

Abe nodded. 'You've already done more than I anticipated.'

Tom smiled at Edie, who shifted the tureen and lifted the lid to reveal a stew. His eyes widened and they both noted his expression and waited. 'I don't know why I was expecting chicken soup with dumplings,' he said in explanation.

Abe waved a finger. 'My grandparents were born in London but I believe we originally came from Russia or eastern Europe.'

'Cooler climes, hence the hearty stew that's part of our culture,' Edie finished, seating herself.

'Let us pray,' Abe said.

Tom bent his head, hands in his lap, hoping this was the right way to pray at this Jewish table. His inclination was to clasp his hands, or better still to reach towards Edie's hand and hold it in a hush of pleasure. But even though he wouldn't dare, he took silent joy in reminding himself that she had held his hand twice today on the journey here and even now that memory of touching Edie's gloved hand was setting off an unexpected series of physical reactions that made him clear his throat as Abe Valentine quietly thanked God for the food on his table, for his family's health and for the improving health of their guest seated at it. Tom felt, too, the unfamiliar warmth spread through him, which spoke of a thin sense of belonging for the first time in his new, short lifetime and felt empowering.

And as Edie stood to take his plate and serve, he deliberately positioned his fingers so that he might 'accidentally' touch hers. Letting go of the plate and the fingertips he skimmed seemed far harder than it should have and she glanced at him, amused, when she pulled away and felt the tension still in Tom's clasp. Her dark eyes looked soulful in the lamplight she'd added to help illuminate the room, and despite his best intentions not to think further about Edie's life and her plans, Tom gave in to irrational thoughts about her fiancé . . . particularly how much he envied him.

'Forgive the oil lamps,' Edie said. 'We do have gaslight but Abba suffers from short breath if we use it for prolonged periods. We'll turn it up later in the sitting room.'

Tom grinned. 'Candles and lamps are far more romantic anyway.'

'Expensive to have both,' Abe cautioned softly as he busied himself unfurling his napkin to place on his lap.

Edie reached for the ladle to begin dishing out the stew, serving her father first, before Tom, then herself. She handed around warmed bread rolls with a hole in the middle and as Tom helped himself to one of the intriguing breads, his hand brushed Edie's, this time genuinely by accident. The bread dish wobbled, she looked startled and now he was sure it wasn't just him feeling the frisson that had begun to invisibly spark and crackle between them.

'Forgive me,' he said.

Her expression evened although she did not fully meet his gaze and immediately began talking to her father about the suit she had delivered today at the hospital. It gave Tom a chance to break the roll that was studded with chips of salt. Inside the lightly crisp shell was soft, spongy dough that became delightfully chewy in his mouth.

'This is amazing!' he said.

His hosts stopped speaking and regarded him, surprised by the outburst.

'That's a bagel, Tom,' Abe said. 'You'll eat plenty of those while you live with us.'

While you live with us. He liked the sound of that.

'It has a wonderful flavour,' he admitted. 'I taste onion.'

Edie smiled. 'And a hint of wild garlic.'

Tom tucked into the stew, which was as hearty as Edie had promised, and she'd managed to cover the small amount of meat that rationing imposed with a variety of vegetables.

'Have more,' Abe encouraged. 'You need fattening,' he added, although Tom became aware that neither of his hosts had put much on their plates. It occurred to him only now, as he felt obliged to take a second helping, that they were probably holding back to ensure their guest had plenty.

'It's delicious, Edie, thank you.'

'You're most welcome.' This time she watched him and it was Tom who looked away, unsettled by the intensity in her eyes that made his throat catch; he hadn't felt this attuned to anything or anyone – or so alive – for as far back as he could recall.

They ate quietly for a time.

Tom broke the silence. 'Um, Mr Valentine . . .'

'In my house, at my table, I am Abe.'

'Abe,' Tom repeated. 'Those bolts of fabric in your storeroom.'

'Yes?'

'There seemed an awful lot to be holding in stock.'

Edie cut her father a rueful glance.

'Have you been talking with my daughter, Tom?' Abe said, humour still in his tone.

'No, Sir,' he answered honestly, frowning. 'I stopped counting at sixty-two bolts. There seemed to be twice as many and more still to count.'

'It's a contentious topic,' Edie quipped.

'What's your point?' Abe asked, shaking his head as Edie offered another helping from the paltry remains of vegetables in the tureen. 'Thank you, dear. It was as good as your mother's.'

She stood to take his plate and Tom saw how she laid an affectionate hand on her father and wondered what it might feel like to have Edie squeeze his shoulder like that. His mind was wandering and Abe was waiting.

'Curiosity, I suppose. Do you really need that much fabric? I mean, is it wise to hold that much stock? Especially in these times. How many suits do you make in a month?'

'Oh, perhaps eight,' Abe replied far too quickly.

'Don't fib, Abba. You're lucky if it's four . . . on average,' Edie said, reaching to take Tom's plate. 'You make *up* to four new suits – it's probably more like three – and we work on another six maybe.' She glanced at Tom. 'My father offers repairs, adjustments and so on. And as these are not prosperous times for anyone, the majority of people are making do with older clothes being given a new lease of life.'

Her father nodded sombrely in agreement. 'They say the Jewish tailors got fat and rich on making uniforms for our soldiers. I don't know anyone who fits that description.' He shrugged. 'Maybe tailors elsewhere in London.'

'Or up north,' Edie suggested. 'Abba tends to serve people of nearby neighbourhoods. He's never really looked beyond.' She gave her father an affectionate look that spoke of reproach. 'And yet, Abba, you're so talented. Everyone says so. It's why the director of the hospital refuses to go to anyone else, and Mr Linden, the wealthy industrialist, refuses to have his suits tailored by anyone else.' She smiled sadly. 'Mr Hughes, Mr Frayne, Mr Beeton, Mr —'

'Enough, Edie . . . enough,' her father said, sounding weary. It was obviously an old debate, Tom decided, so he changed the focus.

'The dust on some of that fabric suggests it hasn't been looked at in a long time. And yet the quality is superb.'

Abe nodded. 'I've stockpiled over the years and bought a lot before the war, but these are not times . . .' Again he shrugged, not finishing his thought.

Tom frowned as he reached towards something, unsure of what it was but going with it anyway, because his thoughts could run independently like this at times. The door to his past was locked but the invisible part of him – his soul, his spirit . . . whatever it was that made him who he was – could slip across that barrier and access his experiences pre- and post-war.

'For the poor this is a time of austerity. Not for the wealthy, though.' As Tom spoke, the elder man set his glass down and studied him. He ignored the scrutiny and continued, becoming more animated. 'Rich people will now want life to return to normality as much as possible. They'll want to be hunting, going to balls, theatre in the city, opera, engagements, weddings . . .' He cut a look at Edie at the mention of nuptials. 'Parties for any manner of reasons, cocktail evenings and grand gatherings . . . all of which require new, expensive suits. As we turn the corner on 1919, most will want to rebuild their lives, although none of us who were on the battlefields probably can —'

'Unless they've lost their memory,' Edie chimed in, still busily clearing away the quarter plates and the salt and pepper cellars.

'Exactly,' Tom said, waving a finger, 'but the majority of people will be pushing themselves to look forward, reinvent their lives as best they can. The affluent, however, will do that through business, through festivity, through new ventures. And they will use their houses, their new cars, their holidays, their women and wine to prove it.' He held Abe's stare.

'You speak with such authority, Tom,' the old man observed.

Tom shrugged. 'But doesn't that make sense to you? Isn't it obvious?'

Abe nodded, relenting. 'I suppose so.'

'Well, fine clothes are part of that resurgence, surely. What shows off wealth faster than mink and tuxedos?'

'So?' Abe said.

'Shift the cloth.' Tom finally reached his point. Privately he hadn't realised that was where he'd been headed with this conversation but suddenly it made sense. 'Why store it if you can't use it? Sell it on. I presume you bought it at brilliant pre-war prices?'

'I did. But no one here is going to buy it in Golders Green. There is one other tailor. We both do all right, but —'

'Forget Golders Green, Abe,' Tom said, waving a hand and eyeing Edie, who had paused in the doorway. 'Where do the truly wealthy go to have their suits made?'

'Savile Row,' Abe and Edie said at the same time.

'What is that, a shop?'

They both laughed. 'Savile Row, my boy,' Abe said with an avuncular nod, 'is a place. It is the high altar of British tailoring.'

'Why?'

Abe shrugged as Edie ducked back to the kitchen. 'Because these are the tailors to royalty, to the nobility, to the gentry and to the fabulously wealthy. The tailoring community that looks after these rich people base themselves there.'

'So why aren't *you* there?' Tom asked.

'Why indeed!' Edie said, returning with some cheese.

'Abe?' Tom pressed.

The old man sighed. 'My daughter's right. This is a contentious subject. She's been nagging for years, and Daniel before her. He had dreams that Valentine & Son would open on Savile Row.'

'And you won't consider it?'

'Tom, I'm about to turn seventy. What can I say? I had my family late. And now, I've raised my family . . . and lost half of it. What is the point in striving? We're comfortable. We aren't starving, we aren't struggling to meet bills, although one can always do with a little more. But tell me why I would keep the dream alive for Savile Row when Valentine & Son can never be?'

Tom didn't need to look at Edie to know she was staring at the tablecloth as her father had spoken so earnestly. His honesty hurt Tom so he could only imagine how Edie was feeling.

'How about Valentine & Daughter?'

The tailor looked dumbstruck momentarily, turned to regard Edie, who had turned away to place something on the sideboard, and so he looked back at Tom. 'What do you mean?'

'What do I mean? Perhaps I don't know anything about your trade, Abe, but I gather that Edie sews as well as any man.' He didn't mean for it to come out as an accusation but that's how it sounded. Suddenly he wished he'd never opened this box of hurt, knowing Edie's eyes were watering but he couldn't look at her. Nevertheless he was too far down the track with his argument now. 'Doesn't she?'

'Yes,' Abe answered, as though bullied into it.

Tom shook his head, shrugging. 'Surely you want to secure a future for Edie?'

'And you think Savile Row is it?'

'Right now I don't know Savile Row from the street your house is on but you do. Only you can tell me the idea is ludicrous.'

Abe nodded, glanced at his daughter. 'Are we having coffee, Edie dear?'

At the threshold between kitchen and dining room she flinched as if stung. 'Yes, of course.'

'We'll take it in the sitting room,' Abe said and motioned at Tom. He didn't look happy.

Tom gave Edie an apologetic glance, firstly for stirring a pot he now realised he should have left untouched, and also for the cheese she'd laid out that remained untouched.

In the sitting room a small coal fire bounced with blue flames and gave off a vaguely sulphurous smell. Abe turned down the gaslight and darkened the room further so the heavy furnishings fell into deep shadows.

'Sit, Tom,' he said, as he lowered himself into a comfortable-looking armchair near the hearth. He waited until Tom was seated opposite. 'Why are you putting ideas into my daughter's head? It can come to no good.'

'Forgive me. I didn't mean to intrude. But this was Edie's notion, not mine.'

Her father nodded, which covered the flash of surprise that Tom detected in his expression. 'Eden Valentine can sew beautifully . . . better than her brother.' He murmured a brief and private beseechment for forgiveness that he should say such a thing about his dead son before he continued. 'But she is a woman . . . I want to say "in case you hadn't noticed" but I am still sharp enough to realise that you have indeed noticed her.'

Tom cleared his throat. 'Edie is beautiful. I —'

'Eden is also promised, Tom,' Abe cut across him softly, then fixed him with a mournful gaze.

'Yes, I've gathered as much. Of course, it is nearly 1920 and today's woman has the well-deserved luxury of —'

'She will marry Benjamin Levi next month,' Abe said, ruthlessly dashing Tom's embryonic hope that there might be a chance for him.

'So soon?' was all he could force out beneath the weight of Abe's heartless revelation.

The old man continued, oblivious to Tom's pain but not to his intent; the younger man heard the warning in his tone. 'He's a good boy. They've known each other since nursery days. Our two families decided on this course before my darling Edie was born. He has prospects . . .' Abe let that hang.

'I dare say,' Tom said, clearing his throat. 'But Edie has dreams for her tailoring.'

'She is a seamstress . . . a dressmaker.'

'And yet you have her sewing suiting.'

Abe's expression, despite the low light and the dancing flames, appeared as wintry as the November night outside.

'What exactly has Edie been saying to you . . . a stranger?'

Tom shook his head. 'It's perhaps what she didn't say. She mentioned the dream of having her own shop.'

'Ah, yes, the dream of a little girl, which a lone parent, lonely himself and very much in love and proud of his daughter, perhaps indulges. But this is not the aspiration of a woman. Soon she will have responsibilities of being a wife, a mother . . .'

'Forgive me, this is none of my business, I realise, but Abe, the roles of women are surely changing. You're talking about the women of a previous century, not the modern woman who has been running the country in the absence of the men who were busy getting killed on the battlefields of Europe and beyond.'

He regretted the outburst immediately. It was insensitive, critical and patronising.

'You're right, Tom, this is not your business. Edie will marry and she will live under the rules of her husband's household. I think we should talk about something else.'

5

Edie leaned back into the corner and wiped away silent tears. Dear Tom. He'd gone into battle for her without even being asked. Had she led him into that fight? Maybe she had. She couldn't pretend to herself that she'd not encouraged him, remembering her daring opening conversation with the stranger, her even more daring entertainment of helping him escape the hospital, the intimate smiles, their closeness on the bus, their laughter in the rain . . . Who was she kidding that she didn't feel a current passing between them? She nearly dropped the bread plate when he accidentally touched her, and how she didn't tremble over her father's blessing she would never know. She was also sure she was not imagining that Tom had begun to believe they might become more than new friends. If the way he'd resisted letting go of her hand after the prayer was a glimpse behind the polite mask he'd put on for her father, then she needed to dissuade him quickly.

Her father had been dreaming of linking the Levi and Valentine families since her mother's passing more than two decades previous. She'd heard the shock in Tom's voice at her father's remark about how soon the wedding was, and yet she'd also heard how unflinchingly he'd taken on Abe Valentine and argued for her. Few people would. Her father was one of the elders of Golders Green; his words were heard, his advice heeded. His words echoed, each like a small punch: 'she will live under the rules of her husband's household'.

More rules. Men's rules. Her dreams and desires? Irrelevant. And here was a stranger called Tom, fighting for her right to make her own decisions. While she, cringing in the shadows, had never yet found the courage to say to Abe Valentine what her brave, battle-scarred soldier had just said, blundering into the no-man's-land that was Jewish custom. Her father had not lied. She had known Ben Levi since both of them had been old enough to walk and talk. Their two mothers had been close friends and when Ben had been born his mother had looked at pregnant Nina Valentine and wished that she were carrying a daughter. They'd agreed that if the child were a girl, then she would be promised to Ben. Their families would join. Her father was simply following the plan . . . but no one had asked Edie whether this pledge suited her. She had always known of the betrothal to Ben. She'd just not taken it seriously enough and now it was too late; marriage was almost upon her.

Edie stared at the rose-gold ring she'd taken off this morning and forgotten to put on before she'd headed to the hospital. It was back in place now, proclaiming that she was 'spoken for', with its tiny embedded diamond catching the light, and she had to quickly swallow a sob. Age had caught up with her and so had Ben and their mothers' promises. In twenty-seven days she would meekly agree with the rabbi that she was now to be known as Eden Levi. Meanwhile a man she knew so little about was willing her to cling to being Valentine, and to fight for her dream. Most of all she sensed that Tom was silently tapping into her own fears that regret was just twenty-six nights away. Everything that had happened since meeting Tom confirmed that she did not want this marriage as much as everyone else around her did. She was a helpless mario-nette dancing beneath strings being pulled by others.

But Tom had no strings. Tom was free. She was helplessly drawn to him, wanting to learn more about him, to spend time with him, even though Abba's glares forbade it and Ben would loathe him; but then Ben loathed any other man who might potentially show interest in her. She'd learned that the hard way when she was seventeen and had attended a local gathering with one of her peers from her father's synagogue. Ben had made a terrible scene when he'd caught sight of them laughing in a café together. It was only then that the full realisation of what her mother's promise to Ben's family meant hit her – exclusivity, control, power. But how does a daughter remain dutiful if she defies her parents' wishes? And once Daniel – her only conspirator – had died, she felt it was now her duty more than ever to remain obedient. It was a demonstration of her love and commitment to the Valentine family.

Wedding arrangements had gone ahead, with Ben's mother masterminding them in the absence of Nina. Edie had become resigned, but then there had never been an alternative; no one had challenged Ben's presence or sense of ownership of Edie until tonight . . . until she'd heard that catch in Tom's voice when Abba had reinforced Edie's engagement.

She couldn't help enjoying the way he watched her, that lingering gaze of his that made her blush and feel deliciously uncomfortable. The private smile they'd shared in the kitchen felt like a thousand words were carried within it . . . all of them dangerously romantic. Tom's very presence was exciting. She wanted to march into the sitting room and yell at her father that the best she had with Ben was fun memories and secrets from childhood – a past, but no hope of a future.

She heard the men shifting in their seats in the room next door, and she tiptoed hurriedly to the kitchen to pick up the tray. Wiping her eyes with a handkerchief and pinching her cheeks, she whisked the tea tray into the hall, nearly bumping into Tom.

'I thought you may need some help,' he said.

'I'm fine. Thank you,' she said and then smiled. 'Oh, well, you can take this. I've forgotten the milk.'

She pushed the tray towards him and felt his fingers touch hers as he took it. It was surely deliberate. Edie was convinced that if she looked down at her hands now she would see scorch marks where Tom's fingertips had caressed hers. Instead she swallowed, rubbing her empty hands against her apron as he turned back to where her father waited. Tom looked so suddenly imposing in the low light. Her father was clearly unwilling to let her have any more moments alone, perhaps fearing she could become susceptible to Tom's obvious charm. Well, it was too late for that . . . she was ready to surrender to it.

She returned to the sitting room. 'Are you warm enough, Abba?'

He nodded silently, taking the cup of coffee she offered. Edie could still feel the men's previous conversation hanging uncomfortably in the air. She plunged in as though she was none the wiser to what had been discussed.

'Did you resolve the questions of the fabric?'

'We didn't,' Abe admitted. 'Tom was going to tell me his plan.'

Tom gave a rueful shrug. 'No plan, just a notion for how to make that fabric pay you back.'

'Do you suggest I just travel to Savile Row in the city and hawk it on a wheelbarrow?' Abe asked.

'No. I'd suggest you make up a set of samples – a sort of catalogue – so you can show your fabrics to the buyers. How many tailoring salons are there?'

Abe sighed. 'It's growing. Perhaps six at the moment, but I know of two more that may open up soon enough.'

'That's eight to sell to.'

Abe shook his head warily.

'It's a good plan, Abba,' Edie pressed. 'At least Tom has a relevant suggestion about that fabric – all I did was nag.'

'I don't want to go cap in hand to Savile Row,' Abe admitted finally. 'I don't want to be the desperate Jew. I am doing just fine.'

'But you agree, the cloth is just wasted money if we don't use it or sell it.'

'Of course! I have scores of pounds tied up in my storeroom.'

Tom sighed. 'All right. How's this, then, Abe? You get the buyers to come here and I'll triple what you paid for it. Use me as an intermediary and keep yourself at a distance.'

The old man laughed. 'Triple. Now that's a business I'd like a part of.'

'I'm not lying. I'm confident.'

'I can see. I have to wonder from where this confidence springs when you have no memory and my daughter tells me a mere bus backfiring can turn you into a gibbering heap.'

Edie gasped. 'Abba, that's not fair.'

The old man shrugged.

'I'm sorry, Tom,' Edie said for him.

'Don't be,' Tom said. 'Your father speaks the truth.'

'And what do you get out of this, Tom?' Abe demanded quietly.

'Nothing, Sir. I only want to see it happen. I'm grateful for the generosity shown to me. It's a way of returning your kindness.'

'You want no cut, Tom? Is that what you're telling me?'

Tom looked at his elder, frowning. Abe was clearly unsettled by his approach. 'Cut? No, not at all. I simply see an opportunity for your family. Abe, you've taken me in. You've fed me. You've been kind to me and, more so, understanding of my condition.'

'I'll stop you there, son,' Abe said, holding up a hand. 'It is Edie here who has shown you those courtesies. She is her mother's girl through and through.'

Tom shook his head. 'From what I see she's the tailor's girl through and through . . . because Abe, while Edie looked upon me as an injured animal, you saw the man and you're the one who has taken me into your home. In just a few hours I've invaded your privacy, you've said prayers with me, broken bread with me, even given me your precious son's suit, for heaven's sake. You've given me work that made me feel useful and productive again. And this work has given rise to an idea that prompts me to believe I have a fully engaged mind again, even if my memory has failed me. You've made me feel as though I have something to contribute again to the world.'

'All that from some old clothes and a stew, Tom?' Abe said, chuckling.

But Tom would not let him make light of it. 'Abe, because of today I know I can build a new life for myself. I'm going to stop reaching for the past, picking at my mind as one picks at a scab. It's done. It's behind me. And the war is over. I realise I'm lucky I don't remember all of it. Today is the first day of my new life. I'm going to make a good life, Abe, and I hope you and Edie will always be friends in it.'

Edie was staring at the flames but she couldn't hide the water in her eyes at Tom's provocative words. He had to look away from her.

'I'm pleased for you, son,' Abe admitted. 'I'll help you. Let's get you started in this new life of yours. I'll bring some of the buyers to the shop. I'll give you four weeks. You get me my money back on the cloth and whatever you make on top is yours.'

Edie shifted to look at her father, open-mouthed. Tom said nothing, waiting for Edie's lead. 'Do you mean that, Abba?' she whispered.

He gave her a quizzical look. 'Why shouldn't I?'

Edie's gaze moved to Tom. 'Do you hear that, Tom?'

'I don't know what to say, Abe.'

'Don't say anything. Let's see your mettle first, son. These buyers are tougher than you imagine,' the older man said, tapping his nose. 'Mostly Jews, and we are not known for giving away our money freely.' He chuckled at his own remark and Tom sensibly held his tongue. 'They'll beat you down.'

'Let's see, shall we?' Tom said.

'Indeed. I'll set the idea in motion tomorrow.' Abe stood. 'I have coffee with one of the tailors at Gieves & Hawkes. He won't be able to resist taking the news back when I tell him about the beautiful cloth I have.'

Edie grinned. 'This is exciting.'

'Too much excitement for me, I'm afraid,' Abe said and kissed his daughter. 'Good night, my darling girl.' He reached a hand out to their guest. 'Sleep soundly, Tom. You have a big adventure ahead.'

Tom grinned. 'Good night, Abe. Thank you again for your hospitality.'

Abe made shooshing noises but Tom saw warning in the hooded expression he cast and knew what it meant.

When Abe had shuffled out, Edie turned. 'Thank you, Tom.'

'What for? Good gracious, the Valentines have —'

'You know what for,' she said softly. 'I'm afraid my father is extremely old-fashioned. He struggled to let me out to fulfil my war duties. It's only because I said he should think of Daniel that he relented.'

'What did you do?' Tom asked, putting his cup and saucer back on the tray. It meant he could sit closer to the fire . . . and to Edie.

'I helped to produce supplies for the soldiers. I sewed shirts, bandages, absolutely anything that a needle and thread could do, I did. I often felt I should work in one of the munitions factories. Those girls – they called them canaries – took on such dangerous work with poisons.'

Tom shook his head. 'Edie, everyone was doing their bit in the very best way they could. Why were they nicknamed canaries?'

She smiled sadly. 'Their skin took on a yellow tinge because of the sulphur they worked with. I couldn't help but envy them that courage. They really felt part of the war effort.'

'And you didn't?'

She shrugged. 'Perhaps I should have joined the Land Army and helped the farmers grow the food for our soldiers or something.'

'Your skills may have saved lives, you know. Only a talented seamstress could have turned out the goods you made with such speed or dexterity.'

'You're sweet, Tom, thank you.'

'I'm going to make Abe change his mind, you know.'

'About what?'

'I think you know the answer to that.'

'He will not agree to my own salon.'

'No, Edie,' he said, laying a tentative hand across hers. 'About Benjamin Levi.'

She pulled her hand away. 'Don't, Tom. You . . . you don't understand.' She picked up the tray, standing in a hurry.

He, too, stood, taking the tray from her. 'Do you love him?' he whispered, staring hard at her.

'It doesn't matter what —'

'Do you love him, Edie?' Tom pressed, his voice low and urgent.

She shook her head, staring at the tray. 'I'm not even attracted to him. He's my oldest friend – that's how I think of him.'

'That's all I need to know,' he said. 'Good night, Edie. Thank you for a wonderful evening. I'll leave this in the kitchen, shall I?'

She nodded, looking slightly ashamed but in equal measure excited. 'Sleep well,' she said to his back, knowing full well that she wouldn't.

The next day passed uneventfully as Tom worked quietly and diligently in the storeroom, coordinating the cloths – now that he had made an inventory – into colours and fabric styles. Abe returned from taking coffee with the tailor from Savile Row, reporting back that evening over dinner that the seed had been sown.

'Now we let him water it,' he said, stirring the chicken soup in his bowl to cool it.

'But what about the other tailoring houses?' Tom asked.

'News travels fast, son,' Abe assured, sipping neatly from his spoon then waving it at Tom. 'Eat. You've worked hard today.'

Tom looked around. 'Are we not waiting for Edie?'

Abe continued eating. 'She's not joining us this evening.'

'Oh?'

The older man looked up and as he dabbed his beard with a napkin he regarded Tom with a meaningful stare. 'Tonight she shares her meal with close family friends. She's just readying herself to leave.'

Disappointment ached through him and his appetite was instantly lost; Tom had toiled all day knowing that the reward would be Edie at sundown: her smile, that smoky voice, those sideways looks he desperately wanted to interpret as interest in him beyond the polite. He had planned to find some time alone if he could; wanted to hear her laugh unguarded as he had when they'd met at the hospital. Around her father she was so careful and dutiful it put Tom on edge. But now she was leaving him for the evening with only Abe for company. Suddenly the gentle, meaty fragrance no longer tantalised as it had just moments ago. He looked at the shallow bowl, steam rising; the rice that Edie had thrown in for some extra staple had settled at the bottom. A flash of colour to the side caught his eye and he looked to the doorway where Edie stood, dressed immaculately and stunningly in scarlet. She was pulling on gloves and appeared determined to refuse him eye contact.

'There's plenty more,' she said to the room. Tom sensed that her bright voice sounded forced. He wanted her to meet his gaze.

'You look lovely tonight, Edie,' Tom remarked evenly but it was her father who responded.

'Enjoy yourself, my dear,' Abe said. 'Don't forget that checklist either. I need to know for Benjamin's suit.'

Tom eyed Edie, although she was nodding at her father while tying on a silk scarf. The bright red dress seemed to hang effortlessly from her shoulders. The belt was part of the dress itself but didn't cinch at the waist. She had a tiny white collar and matching cuffs with studs of black that echoed the overcoat she reached for.

'She assures me this is the new look that's coming,' Abe said. 'What do you think?'

'Did you make that?' Tom said to her.

She nodded with a shy smile, still avoiding his gaze. 'Yes. This dropped waist is quite daring, but —' She shrugged. 'It's what every woman will want to be wearing soon.'

'Don't even ask how she knows these things, Tom,' Abe said, forcing Tom to break his gaze away from Edie. 'It's a mystery. It's magic. It's . . . osmosis. She just absorbs it from everything she reads, hears, sees.'

'Well, it's incredibly eye-catching. Lead the charge, I say,' Tom remarked, punching the air, which made Abe grin over the bread he was breaking.

'I don't know about that, Tom,' Edie admitted, touching her hair self-consciously, turning away from him.

Abe waved a finger. 'All you need to care about, my love, is that Benjamin Levi likes how you look in it.' His gaze slid back to Tom, slow enough to register, fast enough that Tom was left staring at someone who was tucking into his food as though no conversation had passed.

Tom pasted on a smile he wasn't feeling. 'So that's why you're not joining us,' he said, picking up his glass for something to direct his annoyance at. He swirled the water expertly.

'It's not wine, Tom,' Abe remarked.

'Have a lovely evening, Edie,' Tom offered.

'Thank you,' she said, finally forced to meet his eyes, and in that glance he registered soft pain.

Whether Abe registered it too, he didn't reveal. 'Give the Levi family my respects,' he said brightly. 'Tell Moshe it's time he came in and got his suit spruced too. We've a wedding in a few weeks.'

'I'll do that, Abba,' she said, avoiding Tom's eyes again.

He would not be ignored. 'How are you getting to your friends' house?' Tom suddenly asked.

She smiled but it was brittle. 'I walk. It's not very far.'

'Nevertheless, it's cold and icy. Let me walk you there. See you indoors safely.' He glanced at Abe. 'I'll leave Edie at the corner if she prefers but I think I was raised, I'm certain, to see a lady door to door.'

'What fine manners our Tom possesses, dearest,' Abe said with only a hint of dryness. Tom knew he'd trapped the old man. For him to refuse his daughter a safe escort would be churlish. 'Go ahead, young man. But it's barely five minutes away.'

'All the same,' Tom said, leaping up.

'Your dinner will go cold,' Edie complained but with no heat in her tone, Tom noted.

'I feel sure I ate a lot worse in the trenches. Cold soup will not daunt me. I can warm it again.'

She nodded, and Tom was confident she was trying to mask her pleasure at the turn of events. He hoped the angels were smiling on him tonight.

'All right. To the corner, then,' Edie said. 'Thank you, Tom. Night, Abba. Don't wait up.'

Outside the front door, Tom offered his arm. 'Your father didn't try to stop me.'

'He's made his point, I'm sure. He knows I won't defy him. And he knows you wouldn't risk betraying him.'

'He's very confident, clearly.'

Edie sighed. 'Let's walk,' she said and he noticed she declined to take his arm.

'How does tonight work?'

'What do you mean?'

'You sit and talk with his parents present, or do you just say hello to them and then go out alone?'

'Tonight I shall have dinner with the family at their house.'

'Is this what Benjamin wants too?'

She wasn't offended by how quickly he'd advanced the conversation to what obviously mattered most to him. She shrugged and it was a sad gesture. 'Benjamin asked me to marry him when he was nine and I barely seven. He didn't know then – and neither did I – that this is precisely what our four parents intended. He's not changed that desire.'

'But now you're triple that age with a mind of your own and aspirations that —'

'That I am not permitted to entertain, Tom. You must forget about what I shared with you.'

'I can't.' He pointed to where some ice had formed on a puddle and she neatly sidestepped it.

'Well, put it out of your mind then, because it has no future. I rely on my father's income and soon I will rely on Benjamin's. He's a lawyer.'

'I'm happy for him,' Tom remarked dryly.

'Cross here,' she said, pointing, and this time she did take his arm. Instantly a current of need as much as desire sizzled through him.

'What about if you had the means?'

'Means?'

'The financial means to set up.'

She laughed. 'You're such a dreamer, Tom,' she said, but it wasn't spoken unkindly. 'I do love that about you.'

'So you do love something about me?' he remarked as the smell of baking bread elevated the pleasure that her spirit-lifting words had achieved. 'Do they bake through the night?' he asked, as they passed the bakery, deliberately distracting her.

'Tom, don't —'

'Don't what?' He couldn't be polite any longer. 'Don't tell you that I think I fell in love with you the moment I saw you?' Even in the thin pool of gaslight from the street lamp he could see her blanch with surprise. His mental injuries had surely affected his natural inhibitors to be quite so raw with his emotions. Had he always been this candid? He pressed on, heedless that he was being too direct, too fast. 'I can remember exactly what you were wearing, how you'd styled your hair, that your footsteps resonated in my mind hours later. Or maybe you'd rather not hear that I fell deeper in love when you joined me on the garden bench at the hospital, and that once I saw you smile just for me I knew I couldn't ever love another woman.'

She'd stopped walking and he could see her breath was short, slightly ragged, as it steamed around her in the freezing evening. 'Tom, this is your vulnerability talking. You've felt lost, lonely, anxious . . . Perhaps I was the first person to show you the sort of friendship you sought, but —'

'No, Edie, don't do that.'

She swallowed. 'Don't do what?'

'You mustn't patronise me. I've lost my memory but I haven't lost my ability to rationalise, to know what I want, to know how I feel at this moment. And I know how I feel about you. It's sudden, perhaps even shocking – for both of us – but I feel it all the same. And I hope it doesn't sound preposterous to you.'

'Tom, I . . .' She looked lost but he sensed she was not horrified or offended by his admission. 'Listen . . . you might have a family somewhere. A wife, a child! Your name could be John, or Edward.'

'Is it that I'm not Jewish?'

'Yes! No,' she said, then sounding forlorn, her shoulders slumped. 'No, definitely not that.' She gave a wry smile. 'You actually look quite Jewish with this beard of yours.'

He grinned in spite of the tension. 'Do you know something, Edie? You are the only woman I've met since I woke who hasn't asked me to shave.'

She lifted a shoulder. 'I'm used to men with beards. I'd like to see you clean-shaven, of course,' she added.

'Aha!'

'Why haven't you? Shaved, I mean?'

It was Tom's turn to sigh. 'I think I've been working hard to convince myself that once the beard goes, the real me is waiting and I'll recognise the man in the mirror immediately. But while my heart likes to believe this, my head is assuring me that I will stare back at him, just as confused and angry that I don't know him.'

'So?'

'So then all hope is gone.'

'Rubbish!' she said, sounding both dismayed and angered by his belief. 'You are *you*, Tom. You're alive, you're getting stronger, you have all your faculties. Your memory is damaged, that's all. It will return when that wound heals and, if it doesn't, you *did* return. So many didn't!'

He stared at her, holding the awkward silence between them as she searched his face, willing him to agree. Finally, Tom nodded. 'Thank you.'

'Don't mention it,' she said and laughed gently, a sound that he knew could push away night terrors and fill his dreams with brightness. 'Shave your beard only when you feel ready to accept the man beneath it precisely how he is and not despise him.'

'You dodged my question, Edie.'

'I can't even remember it,' she said in a droll voice, but unable to look at him. She walked on. 'Come on, I can't be late. And I think my eyebrows are frozen.'

He would not be deterred. 'You remember very well that I told you I've fallen in love with you and I think you're fearful,' Tom said, falling into step alongside her.

'Fearful?'

'Of disappointing Benjamin, disappointing the families, especially disappointing your father and then, of course, those prospects Abe spoke of. I apparently have none.'

'All of it,' she said, 'though perhaps the last is of little importance to me.'

'Edie, give me a chance,' he said, running around her as she doggedly cornered into a new street . . . a darker way of houses, a lone dog barking in the distance and each home backlit behind curtains like heavily lidded eyes watching them.

'I —'

'No, don't say any more. When you're sitting with Benjamin and his family tonight, think about . . . well, just think about this conversation and what perhaps you're not saying.'

'I hardly know you, Tom,' Edie said in a small voice.

'You know me, Edie,' he said, his voice confident. 'And you know I'm what you want. I think big. So do you. We'd make a good team, you and I. As for who is in my past, I am absolutely certain if I were married or even just engaged, I would feel that connection somewhere. Or rather, I wouldn't be able to feel about you as I do. All of me is yours if you want me. Marry *me*, Edie. Don't think too hard – just follow that instinct of yours that served you well when you helped me leave the hospital, and bring me home. It led us here . . . to now. There was a reason we met.'

Without warning, Tom pulled Edie down a small alley they'd paused by, which offered a cut through to the next main street. He glanced both ways before pulling her back into shadows against the cold brick; he waited a couple of heartbeats for the protest from her that didn't come. Hidden from sight of those ever-curious window gazers and with moonlight weakly illuminating one half of Edie's beautiful face, he saw a fire glittering in her eye and he knew she was his.

And as Edie opened her mouth to respond to his challenge, he prevented her words by bending close to touch his lips to hers; something he had wanted to do from the moment she'd sat on the bench and smiled for only him, reigniting a fire that had known no warmth for much too long. She didn't resist him, and although it had been a long time, Tom's panic instantly dissipated as he realised his fear was unfounded. It seemed one never forgot how to kiss.

And he lost himself in it. Nearly eighteen months of anguish in hospitals and three years, he was sure, of terror and despair in the trenches, all obliterated in seconds by the touch of Eden Valentine, who, tentatively at first, soon showed that her feelings for him were more than cursory or plain charity.

She matched his passion and he helplessly closed his eyes on the world as he felt her thin arms reach up and hold him closer, clasping around his neck, pulling him into her private space. In her kiss he tasted everything he already knew about Edie: her generosity, her joy in life, her intensity, her dreams and, most of all, her hope. It passed from her to him as he caressed her warm neck, her sweet straight jawline, her expressive, welcoming mouth with his lips, wishing desperately he could kiss her with abandon and not feel worried that they might be seen.

He pulled back finally and her breath came short and hard, the cold turning it to instant steam that drifted and curled around his breath, keeping the connection strong. Her lips were swollen slightly and all the more desirable for their soft bruising. He could see her eyes glistening moistly and as she wordlessly stepped around him, she caressed his cheek gently, allowing her gloved fingers to trace his bearded jaw before she hurried towards the gaslit street. Once again he heard Eden Valentine's footsteps retreating from him.

Edie could barely breathe as she hurried away from the alley. She knew it was a freezing night and yet she worried that her cheeks were burning: with embarrassment, with guilt, with shame, but mostly with passion . . . such a new, exciting sensation. Only last night she'd been wondering what it would be like to be held close by Tom. Over dinner, with her father's eyes closed as he spoke his blessing, she had sneaked a glance at their guest, his dark head bent in prayer, respectfully wearing the *kippah* of her family's faith, and she had imagined what it would feel like to be kissed by him.

She'd been wrong. Her imagination had lied.

Her only experience of kissing was watching screen stars at the cinema with puckered lips or cheeks quickly pressed together after a perfunctory peck. And Benjamin's kisses, of course – dry, brief, boyish. But Tom's kiss! She felt both freshly excited and embarrassed just recalling it. Tom's kiss had been deep and thrilling, like an exciting secret shared. His tongue had been soft but searching, demanding she respond . . . and she had. Such shame and yet . . . no shame at all, for kissing Tom was a thing of beauty – an experience she could neither regret nor give up. Now she'd tasted his lips, she wanted them again and again . . . and she wanted his mouth all over her. She blushed once more at her cavalier attitude even though as she dwelled on

Tom's kiss – the hardness of his body, the need she felt as he pulled her so close – she could see Ben's house in the near distance.

She didn't want to arrive. Edie didn't want anything connected with the Levi family to intrude on her surrender in an alleyway with Tom. She half gulped, half laughed at her outrageous behaviour. What would her father think of her? Truly, did she care now that she remembered how Tom's passion had prompted flashing circles of light behind her closed lids? Being out of control was not Edie's way but with Tom it suddenly hadn't mattered. She *was* his prisoner. If she had to have a keeper, let it be Tom! If everyone around her insisted that a man was required to give a woman's life meaning, then let it be Tom who helped to shape her future, her life. *Please, please*, she begged in silence, let it be this stranger, this intriguing man she was helplessly attracted to who spoke to her ambition and dreams, who made her feel talented and special, important to him, and every inch of her desirable. *Please forgive me*, she cast out, while trying to ignore the more dangerous notion that her worst action was yet to come.

She put a hand to her fiery cheek – she was appalled! She was also thrilled. Kissing deeply in a dark alley, desperately wanting to feel him press himself harder against her, an aching and hot desire to disrobe and lay flesh against flesh . . .

Stop it, Eden!

How had she permitted it? And yet there was nothing remotely dirty or desperate about it. If anything, as she forced her breathing to calm and her mind to feel less chaotic, Edie knew what had occurred was beautiful. She had never felt so desired and had never wanted anything so badly before. Ben was filled with fervour for her, but Tom left Benjamin behind in his single kiss. If passion could become a person, it was Tom, she thought, trying not to smile at her notion and trying not to think of the remnants of the warmth he had prompted low in her body.

Benjamin! Oh, what a traitor she was. But as she stood outside the Levi house, lurking in the shadows once again and grateful for the moon now hidden behind night clouds, she told herself this feeling was perhaps inevitable.

Tom's arrival into her life was meant to be. It confirmed all her reservations about her engagement to Ben. Nothing about her relationship with him could be considered as anything but sisterly. From that first mad decision to help Tom, she knew she had done so because she found herself irresistibly drawn to him, and then yielded control.

Intuition. Instinct. Chemistry. All those primitive elements had taken over and Edie now felt slave to their mastery, although until this moment she'd tried to ignore it, dismiss it as a fanciful crush.

She understood now, though, that she'd been deluding herself. Whenever Tom stood nearby she held her breath – had he noticed? As he slept in the room next to Daniel's, she lay awake in hers – restless, anxious, her dreams when they finally came filled with yearning. Tom's voice, Tom's laugh, Tom's touch . . . She wanted all of it.

Ben's kiss? She gave a choked sound of guilt as she pushed herself to approach the stairs of his home but could not climb them as she remembered Ben's lack of ardour – cold, swift, self-conscious. He was so devoted to her and perhaps he believed devotion could become romantic. He did love her – of this she was sure – but he'd had no other girlfriends, wanted no other woman.

Maybe he hopes I'll learn to love him in the way he loves me? Edie thought sadly as she stared at the Levi's front door, like a prisoner being shown the door to her cell.

'It's not going to happen,' she whispered to the pigeons cooing softly on the rooftop of the Levi house.

Edie touched her lips softly and the memory of Tom's stolen kiss returned. He was such an exceptional man, a leader, with impeccable manners. *Except when he's dragging unsuspecting young women into alleyways*, she thought, amused. Abba had suggested privately that Tom might have served in a hotel dining room but Edie was thinking more along the lines that he had likely belonged to a fine household.

'No, Abba,' she'd disagreed. 'He notices too much. He is aware of expensive things. And his talk about money? He's seen what wealth can create. A butler, perhaps?'

They were no closer to solving the riddle of Tom.

Edie realised she still had her fingers to her mouth and her body was still buzzing with a tingling excitement of Tom's hands cupping her chin, before dropping to pull her body closer and harder against his —

'Edie? Is that you?'

She nearly squealed in embarrassment at the familiar sight of Ben's narrow shoulders and lean body. He was wearing the jumper his mother had knitted last year. It was tight, making him look even more skinny. 'Yes . . . yes, sorry, Ben.'

'What are you doing out here in the dark?' he asked, as he skipped down the three steps onto the pavement to meet her.

'Is it Eden?' came his mother's familiar voice.

'Are you all right?' Ben was suddenly at her side and the moon peeped out from behind the cloud. In its spotlight she'd arrived fully onto the stage of shame. An accusatory finger of light . . . or perhaps a reassuring caress of heavenly light that understood, that gave permission, that told her to follow her heart and be happy . . .

Ben repeated his question, the moonlight painting the top of his short, wiry hair with silver, and she shook her head, forcing a smile. 'Of course. I suddenly remembered something I'd forgotten. I'm sorry, I was just thinking it through.'

His brow knitted but she saw relief ghost across his expression. 'That's not like you.'

'Edie, dear, whatever are you doing standing out there in the shadows . . . in the freezing cold?' his mother admonished.

'Pardon?' she said to Benjamin, buying time. Could they tell she'd been kissing another man? Then her mind snapped into cold fear. Had Tom kissed her neck? Yes, he had, briefly. It had felt amazingly seductive. She was sure it wouldn't take much on her sensitive skin to draw the kind of bruise she'd seen on others. Edie touched her neck self-consciously, and as Ben helped her with her overcoat she loosened her scarf, terrified, trying to glimpse her neck in the mirror. Not a trace to be seen. Of course there wasn't. There was nothing vulgar about Tom.

She threw a look over her shoulder and out the open front door as Mrs Levi bustled back into the sitting room from the hallway, while Ben was hanging up her coat. He turned to close the door but in that moment Edie glimpsed a familiar shape across the road, standing on the common, and she knew Tom was watching her.

She closed her eyes fleetingly and took a breath to steady herself. *Oh, Tom, whatever do we do now?*

6

Tom turned as the door of the Levi house closed and shut Edie off from him; he had seen that shy glance over her shoulder, though, and he sensed she knew he was out here, wishing he could steal her away from the family that was drawing her ever closer to its bosom. Was she thinking of their kiss and wanting more? His injured mind scrambled with fresh distress while his nerves still trilled the message of pent desire. *Edie!* If he never got his memory back and all he had was Edie, she would be enough. Ben could not have her!

A lone nightingale sang above him and somewhere, for a few dazed moments, he was lost in a fraction of a memory of identical birdsong. The whizzing, horrific bang of bombs that took lives and shattered families suddenly echoed loudly in his thoughts and his head hurt. In his mind's eye he saw the brave fall, smashed backwards, picked off like metal targets at a funfair, but these were men with families, with loves and dreams; these were men showing the ultimate courage, prepared to make the greatest sacrifice – and they were dead before they felt the cold hard ground of foreign soil. The nightingale sang harder as though it alone had the power to conjure his memories and he saw other soldiers staggering, bleeding, some having lost a limb, stupefied, and the images became far worse until he thought his head might explode. Then the vision dissolved and he was back in a quiet park of Golders Green and the nightingale was still singing, but only to impress a female, not to punish him.

Nightingales . . . that's right! One of the nurses had told him other soldiers had remembered the call of these birds, seemingly unfazed by the shocking sounds of war, and how in the rare, over-whelming silences they would stun the soldiers by suddenly breaking into beautiful and haunting song. If he could remember that small detail, why not the rest?

'I know it's in there,' he murmured as he threw a final glance at the cosy light glowing out of the windows of the Levi house and forced himself to turn away. Before long he found himself sitting at a pub bar and counting his sorrows over a shot of whisky he afforded from the little coin that Edie had lent him. The smoky caramel vapour hit his taste sensors before the liquor burned on its way past his gullet, and reminded him of the fire that kissing Edie had stoked. While the spicy aftermath hummed in his mouth, he could still taste Edie, still smell her perfume on him, still feel her touch. He wanted to close his eyes and live through the kiss again but people in the bar would likely think him strange as well as lonely.

No, Benjamin could not have her. Benjamin would smother her, crush her dreams and control her . . .

'Fight him for her, matey,' an older bloke with silver side-burns urged. He was sitting nearby and Tom realised he had been speaking aloud.

He gave a small shrug. 'Maybe I will.'

'Twenty-fourth battalion,' his companion said, holding out a hand. Tom aged him at around forty.

He shook hands firmly. 'No idea which battalion.' Tom grinned. 'The Boche stole my memory.'

'Yeah, well, maybe you're the lucky one.'

'It's what I tell myself when I can't remember my childhood, or my friends in the trenches.'

'I saw you limp.'

He nodded. 'Ypres, I think. Third battle, or so I've been told. I came home in mid-1918 with no notion of who I was or where I'd been.'

'Ah, Passchendaele.'

Tom sank the contents of his glass and it burned again like a fiery meteorite as it descended. He winced. 'You?' he groaned out.

'A hellhole called Beaumont-Hamel. The Somme.'

'You look well for it.'

'I'm a good actor,' the man said, drawing circles on the counter in the beer that had frothed over and down the side of his tankard. He dragged hard on a cigarette and blew the smoke into the dense cloud of nicotine fog that hung above their heads.

Tom understood. 'Aren't we all?'

The older man sighed. 'I'm Alfred . . . Alf. I used to be a bookmaker.'

'Used to be?'

He shrugged. 'I still keep an eye on the gee-gees,' he said with a wink. 'I just don't make a business out of it. I bet just for myself . . . beer money and chips, you could say.'

'Have you family?'

Alf nodded. 'I did. Lost my wife and daughter to the influenza.'

Tom's expression clouded in sorrow. 'I'm sorry for you.'

'How ruddy stupid is that? You come home from the Western Front, having survived bombs, machine guns, mustard gas . . . and watch your wife struggling to breathe, your little girl wasting away in a matter of days. Both dead within a fortnight. Me, the great hero, able to stay alive, but can't save the ones I love.'

Tom didn't know what to say. There were no words of comfort that could possibly be meaningful. Instead he caught the barman's eye and gestured for another shot. It was poured and Tom slid the glass along the bar. 'Toss that in your beer.'

'I usually stay away from the hard stuff. Long story. But thank you. Drink it yourself instead with me.'

Tom hadn't planned on another, but he took the glass back and raised it to clink against Alf's tankard. 'Cheers then, Alf. I'm Tom . . . I think.'

This caught Alf's sense of humour and he spluttered a laugh into his beer. 'Silly sod. Now look what you've done.' He licked the froth from his lips. 'What about you?'

Tom explained his situation and told Alf a lot more than he meant to, except he sensibly withheld names and occupations as he figured these neighbourhoods were small enough that Alf could know the Valentine family. He realised he must have spoken for a while because when he looked again at his glass his whisky was finished and Alf's tankard was dry. He felt horribly sober . . . and could still feel Edie's arms around his neck.

'Oh . . . I see,' Alf was saying. 'So you think if you can provide the means, then this beautiful young woman might agree to be your girl?'

Tom raised and dropped his shoulders theatrically. 'I want her to be more than my girl, Alf. I want to marry her.'

'Cor, blimey, you're moving fast, lad.'

'Am I?'

'Just like Pretty Penny,' Alf said and winked again, clearly a habit.

Tom stared at him, flummoxed. 'Pretty Penny?'

'Cheltenham on Saturday. She's primed and ready to win big, though no one is rating her.' Alf tapped his nose this time in a new conspiratorial gesture. 'Long odds, money to be won, lad.'

Tom's gaze narrowed. 'How much?'

Alf laughed, pushed his glass forward towards the barman. 'How long is a piece of string?'

'How much if I give you half a sovereign?'

His companion's expression changed, eyes widening to reveal faded blue eyes that had been hooded until now. 'That's a lot of money to wager, lad.'

'I want to win a lot of money.'

Alf dithered, looking uncomfortable.

'Come on, Alf. You said yourself she's primed. You're betting on Pretty Penny. I trust you.'

Tom watched Alf stub out his cigarette in the nearby ashtray and blow the last fetid lungful of smoke into the room. The older man rubbed his chin and Tom noticed his fingers drumming on the counter. 'The odds are fifteen to one presently.' He smiled. 'Odds against.'

Tom shook his head in puzzlement.

'That means the bookie will pay you your earnings plus your stake back. Fifteen to one is a huge return, odds against.'

Tom caught on fast and was aware that anything connected with commercial gain made easy sense to him. Was this a clue to his past? 'I'll take thirteen to one. You take anything you can earn off the top.'

'What? You're mad, matey. You're giving me a pile if we win.'

'*If* we win. If we don't, I'm losing a half sovereign. Besides, if she wins, I won't be criticising the fellow who gave me the tip.'

'Why don't you go bet it yourself, take all the winnings?'

Tom shrugged. 'I don't know how. I don't think I want to learn, either. I can't risk being seen in a betting shop by certain folk.' He thought about Abe as he made the remark.

Alf thought about this. 'All right, son. Let's do this. I'm giving you thirteen to one. Unlucky for some.' He held out his hand again.

'I've been lucky so far,' Tom quipped as he dragged the coin from his inside pocket. 'Numbers don't frighten me.' He dropped the half sovereign into Alf's palm where it shone dully, depicting a man on a horse, a dragon cringing beneath his triumph. It felt prophetic. Tom knew every bump and dent in that coin. On the reverse face was the head of George V. 'Don't ask me again if I'm sure,' he said, pre-empting whatever Alf was opening his mouth to say. 'Win me a small fortune, Alf.'

Alf whistled, spat playfully on his palm and shook Tom's hand. 'Deal, my boy. Back here Friday afternoon.'

Tom nodded. 'If you're not here, I'll know we lost.'

'No hard feelings?'

'None.'

'You're very trusting. What if I go and spend your money on beer?'

'You won't. I think I'm an excellent judge of character.'

'Well . . . let's see what Pretty Penny can do for your heartsickness, lad.' Alf lifted a hand in farewell and left the pub.

Tom waited another five minutes to be sure he was steady on his feet and then opened the swinging pub door into the frosty air. It made him cough it was so fresh and cold as it hit his lungs. The whisky was keeping him warm inside and he tried to ignore the tug of another memory connected to the liquor. He found himself reaching down by his side as though looking for something – a flask, maybe – because he could hear the call of hounds and the trumpeting of a hunting horn, and then the thought instantly dissipated in his mind like the smoke dispersing from Alf's cigarette.

When Edie got home, it wasn't much past nine-thirty and Abe was sipping a brandy near the fire.

'Ooh, you've brought in Jack Frost with you, my girl. Get that overcoat off and come and sit by the fire with your old man,' he grumbled.

She arrived to kiss him and he winced theatrically at her cold cheek.

'Don't go on,' she admonished. 'It's actually a beautiful, moonlit night.'

'Did Ben walk you home?'

'Of course.'

'Didn't come in?'

Her gaze narrowed. 'As you can see, he didn't,' she replied, holding her palms out to the flames.

'Why not?'

'Because I didn't ask him in, Abba! He has a busy day tomorrow, and so do I,' she said, trying to keep her tone light. 'Can I get you anything?'

He shook his head.

As she walked away, she worked hard to keep her enquiry as casual as possible. 'Where's Tom?' She disappeared into the kitchen and then held her breath, waiting.

'He went to bed early. A headache or something.'

She didn't reply and kept the disappointment contained in the kitchen. Once she felt ready, she reappeared in the sitting room. 'The Levis send their love, as always. We had a lovely evening.' She sat down. 'Gefilte fish.'

'Good . . . good.'

'So, Tom's headache . . . Did you offer any of those aspirin you swear by?'

Her father glanced up from his book over the rim of his glasses and fixed Edie with a stare. It was the look she feared, the one that seemed to be able to see behind the words to what she *wasn't* saying. It took a measure of her actions before she even knew she would take them. 'I did,' he said.

She waited.

'We both agreed it was probably the whisky and sleeping it off was the best course of action.'

'Tom was drunk?' she asked, startled.

'I didn't say that,' Abe continued in the same, quiet manner.

'But why would you give him Scotch when you know he's recovering from —'

'Firstly, Edie, I'm sure you of all people have realised that Tom is his own man. He may appeal to you in your young, generous mind as a boyish soul who is lost, injured. But Tom is undeniably strong and someone used to having his way. Trust me, child, when I say there is nothing inherently helpless about our guest.'

Edie didn't want to listen but she dared not roll her eyes or even look away when her father impaled her with his 'look of truth'.

'I am not Tom's keeper. If Tom chooses to drink Scotch and pay the price for it, that's his decision. What's more, I did not ply Tom with any liquor. He told me he'd wandered into a pub and got chatting with some folk.' Her father glanced down and Edie knew it was all he planned to say. Within his words was the reprimand and the caution he knew she would hear.

And, as if he knew about the kiss, he added, without looking up this time, 'What details on the wedding?'

She knew before she said it that she shouldn't, but the kiss had made her brave. 'I didn't really want to discuss it tonight with them.'

Abe Valentine deliberately placed his book on the small table next to where he sat. In a practised action he removed his glasses, folded them slowly and rubbed his eyes. 'Sit down, child,' he said.

Edie took a deep breath and did as asked. Here it will come: her father's fury. And Edie knew it would be delivered in the identical calm, sane manner in which he might advise her about cutting a pattern or chalking up on fabric. Abba knew all about self-control. But then so did she.

'Is there something you wish to tell me, Edie?'

That shocked her. She thought she had been settling down for a lecture. She had not come to grips with her feelings, let alone formulated the right words to explain them.

Her silence was no doubt telling. Abe leaned forward, giving a small shake of his head. 'Well?'

The words spilled without warning. 'It's moving so fast, Abba. I'm not yet sure I wish to marry Benjamin Levi.' Edie's surprise in her unplanned words stared back at her in her father's expression, but his hurt forced him to look down and then away towards the safety of the fire, whose warmth suddenly couldn't touch the falling temperature between him and his daughter.

'Why?' he demanded in monotone.

Yes. *Why?* Edie thought. *Tell the truth.* 'Because I don't know whether I love him.'

Her father nodded ponderously.

She pressed on, suddenly in a hurry. 'Actually, that's not true – I do love Benjamin very much. It's just that I love him like a brother and that will always be a problem for us.'

Her father finally regarded her. 'What do you mean?'

'We're friends. I worry that I would struggle to take it beyond that. And I think it would make us both unhappy.'

'Benjamin Levi worships you!'

'I know,' Edie replied sadly, leaping up to cross the heartbeat of distance between them. She crouched by her father's knees and took his hand. 'I know it. But that only makes it worse. I feel . . . smothered by how he regards me. I think Ben believes his love should be more than enough to satisfy me in my life.'

'Well,' her father said, shaking his head. 'I have never heard a girl complain about being loved too much.'

'Abba, hear what I'm saying,' she pleaded. 'Ben and I have been the closest of friends since childhood – you know that. He has never been with another to know any different.'

'Surely neither have you.'

She felt the blood flush upwards and despite her resolve she looked away.

'Edie?'

She shook her head, feeling the sting of tears. She couldn't lie but she dare not tell her father the truth. Torn between duty and desire, she remained silent.

'It is acceptable . . . perfectly normal to have doubts at this stage. I think your mother wept herself to sleep in the week before our wedding. She was so fearful of leaving her family . . . starting a new life. This is all to be expected.'

'I just don't love him. Not the way you loved my mother . . . and still do.' Her father lifted her chin to look into her moist eyes as she spoke. 'I want to be in love like that.'

She could see that she'd sounded a chord in him and that he felt sad for her. 'I think Tom has much to answer for,' Abe said softly. 'He has distracted you from Benjamin; made you question your commitment.'

Edie felt as though she'd been punched. She faltered, as the tears came. 'No, Abba . . .'

'The man has entered your life like a meteorite, caught you in his blaze.'

She shook her head but felt the hopelessness of her denial; she hated hurting him like this.

'He's putting ideas into your head.'

'No. The ideas were always there, Abba.'

He nodded sadly, watching her intently. 'How can I help you, Edie? You know all that I want is your happiness.'

It was her chance. She would never have such an opening again, she was sure. 'Daniel always urged me to follow my dreams, Abba.'

He said nothing to this, as though refusing Daniel's name to be mentioned in connection with this conversation about not loving Ben. 'And Tom?'

'I want you – no, need you – to give him a chance.'

'To steal my daughter? Absolutely not.' Abe Valentine stood, wincing, and she knew it was the stab of arthritis from bending over a cutting and pattern bench for most of his life. She stood too and allowed him to tenderly gather her hands in his own and lean forward to kiss them. 'I love you, child, but you are naive – and I say that with utmost respect. That's part of what makes you irresistible and beautiful. You see the best in everyone. You are generous and affectionate.' He sighed. 'I imagine sooner or later Tom will discover the truth about himself.'

'So?'

He shrugged. 'Only pain waits for you then.' As she opened her mouth to speak, he raised a finger. She knew not to defy it. 'Go to bed, Edie. Think carefully on what I say. Your mother wanted this. I want this for you too. Benjamin is a fine young man from a good Jewish family.'

'I'm tougher than you give me credit for, Abba. Remember, while you lost your wife and son, I lost my mother and brother too. We both have our grief and we have both survived. Now I have my dreams. Let me try.'

'Are you sure Tom feels the same way about you?'

Edie was quietly stunned that her father had sliced deep to the crux of where this conversation truly lay.

'I . . . I haven't asked him,' she said, convincing herself she spoke the legal truth, ignoring the fact he'd declared himself to her only hours earlier. She had to protect her father's feelings.

'Benjamin offers robust health, stability, good family, income and a reliable future. I can honestly say to you that Tom offers none of this —'

'At this stage, Abba,' she interjected and he nodded.

'Well, tell me how Tom with nothing but a borrowed suit and no memory is going to give you a house, support a family, provide you with that dream of the shop you want, Edie?'

'I can't tell you how. All I can say is that Ben would never give me the shop, even if we did have the money. Ben wants me pregnant, rocking babies to sleep and cooking his meals.'

'Is that so unreasonable?'

'Abba, I want to be the designer of beautiful women's clothes and bridal wear. I want to be the owner, the founder. I want the atelier,' she said, shrugging as though in apology for having such aspirations.

He gave a slow sigh. 'And you think Tom can give you this?'

She bristled. 'I don't need Tom to give it to me. But I don't want to marry for convenience or a safe future. I don't want to be pushed together with someone for the rest of my life who I don't love as I should. I want to choose for myself . . . in everything, from the career I have to the man I love and ultimately choose to marry.'

Abe tutted quietly. 'I would be lying if I didn't say you are wounding me with this conversation. I too must think on it and reach a decision. I am your father and will not be denied my responsibilities to you.' He nodded with another soft sigh. 'Off to bed with you, Edie. Busy day ahead.'

She rose and gave her father a lingering kiss on his cheek. 'Consider how much you adore my mother to this day and ask yourself whether you want anything less for me in my marriage than that sort of love. Please.'

7

The following morning, setting aside any awkward feelings about the conversation of the previous evening, Edie presented her father with a bowl of porridge, ladled with most of the cream from the top of the milk bottle and a generous dollop of honey. She had made a large pot of oats and hurried back to the kitchen to stir the slowly bubbling, gloopy mass that would keep Abe's and Tom's bellies full and warm for hours.

'Tom!' she called down the hall. 'Breakfast!' She came back into the dining room. 'Where's Tom?'

'Do you know, child, you ask that question a lot,' Abe observed. 'He's left to do the Goldberg delivery and to run some errands.'

'Goldberg?' she said, looking astonished. 'But I haven't given him directions.'

'He'll be fine. I wrote them out for him in the end.'

'Abba, you haven't delivered to that customer in years. He always collects.'

'Tom is a grown man, Edie. Let him be. He's trying to find his own way.'

'What if he gets lost? What if he has one of those attacks?' She felt suddenly distraught. 'What if he doesn't come home?'

'So this is home, now?'

'Abba, don't.'

'Stay calm, child. Let's see how resourceful he is. I want a demonstration of his spine.'

'His spine? He's returned from the front! I don't think any of our soldiers need to demonstrate their courage. We can't begin to imagine what he's seen or experienced!'

'You miss my point, Edie. If your Tom ends up cowering in a bus stop again, I feel my concern that this man is no good for you is well founded and that he should be in a hospital where he belongs, letting the authorities find his real home, his real family.'

'Why are you being so heartless?'

'I don't believe I am being heartless.' She watched her father ponder this and then shake his head. 'No, I don't believe I could ever be accused of that, whereas your behaviour towards Benjamin might be construed that way.'

Edie stared at her father as though he'd slapped her. 'The problem with this conversation will always be the same, Abba,' she finally said, surprised at how calm she sounded. 'Benjamin is who *you* want for a son-in-law. But this is my heart we're talking about, so I can be as heartless as I choose about who it beats for. You love Benjamin more and more, I'm sure, because he behaves like Daniel,' she said, only fully grasping the truth of this as she spoke. It felt like a revelation and she blinked with the shock of it. 'He is a good Jewish son from good stock. He even looks a bit like Daniel – so lean and with that slightly curly hair. And Daniel was as serious as Ben has become.' She saw her father wrestle to keep his emotion in check and she loathed herself. 'But no matter how hard you wish it, Abba, you cannot replace your son. He is gone. He died, bravely, pointlessly, stupidly, even – because I never agreed with him volunteering – but he found the courage to give his life for his country, to make the world safer for those of us left behind. How ridiculous then that I would squander the chance he's given me by spending it with someone I can't love the way you want me to. I want to marry who I choose and because I love him with all of my heart, not because of a promise made between two old friends who loved each other and believed they could force their children to do the same!'

She watched her father's mouth purse at the reference to her mother.

'You would marry out of our faith, child?' His voice had a low ring of shock to it.

'I didn't say I was marrying anyone out of our faith, Abba,' she replied, her expression exasperated but it couldn't hide the flare of hope that glittered in her eyes. Edie heard the lack of sincerity in her words and suspected her father knew she was lying even to herself, so she spoke the truth, harsh though it would be for him to hear. 'But I wouldn't hesitate to if I loved him. This is 1919, not the Middle Ages!'

Abe began to shake his head, his face grave. Had they both heard the name 'Tom' in the word 'him'? 'I could be glad your mother isn't alive to hear this, my daughter. She would turn in her grave.'

Edie was beyond sparing her father's feelings, and although this was the first genuine disagreement they'd had since Daniel's departure, she refused to back down. 'My mother loved her husband. Why would you want anything but that for me? I don't love Ben and never will.' She needed to get off the subject of marriage because Edie knew it was a nest of vipers that would need untangling with an unlikely happy outcome. 'And how could you send Tom out without breakfast?' she added, deliberately knowing it would draw his ire, but at least it would distract her father from this marriage question.

He snorted, looking genuinely irritated with her. 'The man survived the trenches. I'm sure he can survive a morning without porridge.'

'But I notice you can't, Abba,' she replied, turning on her heel, feeling her cheeks burn with angry disappointment but coupled with guilt for snapping at her father and for revealing all that she had.

He suddenly appeared behind her with his empty dish. 'Daughter, the man wants to prove he is capable. Let him prove he is independent.' He shrugged. 'Stop fussing. He is not a child.'

There was a ring on the bell. She frowned in confusion but couldn't yet lose the anger and hurt that Tom had been clearly coerced into leaving this morning without seeing her. She had so much to say to him and her sixth sense was screaming at her that something was desperately wrong.

'Now, who can that be at this early hour!' she said.

'I know who it is,' her father muttered and disappeared before she could object.

Edie busied herself clearing away the dishes, making more noise than she knew was polite, but she had to rid herself of her fury somehow.

Edie heard whispers and swung around in surprise to see a group of familiar women; at their helm stood Benjamin's mother, Dena.

'W–what's this?' she stammered.

'Morning, Eden, darling,' Dena said, overly brightly. 'In the absence of our beloved Nina,' she nodded at Abe politely, as though practising rehearsed lines, 'I have agreed to be your guardian in the week prior to the marriage ceremony.'

'What?' Edie replied dully. 'The wedding . . . i–it . . .' She glanced at her father, stammering. 'I don't understand.'

The women advanced. There were only three but they were like a trio of fat, black mother hens who gave an impression of the armoured vanguard of an operation that had been set in motion.

'Edie, last night we sensed some reticence on your part regarding this marriage that has been planned for most of your life. Dear, we know it feels like a big step, but it is the most natural journey in the world for a woman of your age, of your faith, and especially with an ideal man who worships you. Benjamin doesn't want to wait.' She beamed her pleasure to everyone, taking in Edie with her scan of the dining room where they now all stood. 'Ben and your father both agree we should bring the wedding forward.' Edie had to repeat the word *forward* in her mind silently. She wanted this to be a joke but no one was smiling . . . no one but Dena, and Edie knew Aunt Dena well enough to sense when she was faking it. 'Why wait?' Dena was saying with an obvious shrug. 'You two precious souls have been joined and promised since birth.' She tittered, glancing at her sentinels. Edie was sure they were going to pounce on her and truss her up, ready to present to Ben. 'Samuel and Ben are speaking with the rabbi now about the *ketubah* – we must get the marriage contract officiated.'

'Abba?' Edie moaned, her sense of betrayal escalating. 'What's happening?' He must have used the shop's telephone, which her father was so proud of, to call the Levis last night; she felt ill at the thought.

'It's for the best, daughter,' he said but his voice was not steady, his mouth trembled as he spoke.

'Come, Edie, we must prepare you for your wedding.'

'Prepare? When exactly are you thinking this marriage might take place, Aunt Dena?' Her mind was filled with dread and even though she'd demanded her question, Edie shook her head as though she didn't want to hear the answer.

Dena giggled but behind the amusement, aimed to disarm, pressed a fierce determination to have her way. 'We thought tonight. The Levi family is ready; it has been for years.' She glanced at Abe. 'Your father is also ready, child, to hand you over to your husband . . . a very special man.' Edie was so shocked by Dena's admission that she had heard nothing more since Dena had uttered the word 'tonight'. *Tonight?* It was ridiculous. It was cruel. It was not going to happen. *Tom! Where are you?* her head and heart screamed.

If Dena saw it, she ignored Edie's dismay. 'There is the ritual bathing, and —' She shook a fat finger. 'No meeting of your betrothed. Not until tonight, anyway, when the *ketubah* will be read and the Torah, and we shall witness the joining of our families.'

'Stop this!' Edie interrupted.

The three older women gasped and the porridge bubbled angrily behind her. She could feel its heat on the stove and it echoed how she was feeling in this moment – churned up, ready to boil over.

Edie rounded on her father. 'Abba, what have you done? How could you discuss such a turn of events behind my back? This is between —'

Edie felt the light sting of a slap. Dena had clearly lost patience. It wasn't hard; it wasn't even a full-handed, open-palmed swing. It was the sort of tap that a parent might give a wayward child speaking back to them. It didn't hurt, it barely made a sound, and still Eden gave a choked gasp, inhaling with horror as she understood what had just occurred.

'Listen to me, Eden Valentine,' Dena was saying, but Edie wasn't listening. She didn't want to hear another word from Mrs Levi, who had just taken a step too far. She glanced at her father with his head hung, and eyed the two silent friends who suddenly looked as uncomfortable as Abe.

Edie wished she could slap Dena Levi right back but her small remaining reserve of patience and respect forced her to clap her hands loudly instead, surprising herself but mostly surprising Dena, whose words died instantly.

'Dena, be quiet!' She frightened herself by her outburst and her courage to snap at an elder. 'Tonight is Shabbat. I would like you and your family to join us for dinner and I am going to have a private conversation with Benjamin and then we are all going to say prayers together, take bread together and sort out this situation. But I can assure you I will not be getting married tonight, certainly not on Shabbat, nor in the immediate future either. You can take your bathing implements back to your house and you can tell Ben and Samuel that no marriage contract will be discussed with any rabbi without my father present and without my sanction. I have rights, Dena, the main one of which is to agree to my wedding . . . which I do not agree to tonight.'

Dena's mouth was open but her voice silent. Edie's gaze slid to her father, who nodded once.

He sighed. 'Dena, my daughter is right. Shame on us. This is an ambush. Although our ancestors might have done such a thing, I cannot. Please come tonight as Edie suggests. We are family. We will sort this out.'

Dena glared at them both. She raised the same forefinger now in threat; bangles jingled at her wrist and she took a step forward so that Edie could count the spidery wrinkles forming at the woman's lips, making her lipstick bleed slightly into the grooves. 'Do not,' she began, in an icy voice, 'hurt my son.'

Edie swallowed, and could feel a blockage of tension in her throat. 'I do not wish to hurt Ben.' She turned away deliberately, leaning against the sink to steady herself, and waited for her father to show their visitors out.

When he returned she was waiting for him, but despite her scrambled thoughts, past experience of intense grief had taught her how to find calm through the greatest storms.

'Abba,' she said softly as he arrived, his expression sheepish.

'I know you're angry, Edie, I —'

'No,' she said, taking a slow breath as she lied, 'I am not angry. I am disturbed.'

He raised his gaze to meet hers but said nothing.

'I feel frightened that you would put me into such a position as you did just now.'

Abe sat down heavily in one of the dining-room chairs and held his head. 'What a mess.'

Her heart hurt for him. She knew he wanted only happiness for them both; in his mind Ben represented that for her – she understood this. Edie quickly moved to reassure him, crouching by him and taking his hands. 'It needn't be a mess,' she said, tears springing, but she refused to let them spill. 'We just have to be honest.'

'I only want what's best for you!'

'I know, Abba, I know. But Ben is not the one.'

'Are you sure?' he pleaded, searching her face. She knew he referred to Tom but couldn't bring himself to say it.

And she faltered . . . how could anyone be certain about something as capricious as matters of the heart, which she knew so little about anyway? 'No. But is there any surety in life? All I know is that marrying Ben now is a mistake.'

Abe gave a long sigh of regret. 'I suggest, child, that you make Benjamin aware of your feelings before you explore those you have for Tom. The Levis do not know about a change of heart . . . towards another. All they know is that I was anxious about your modern thinking and whether your commitment to the marriage this year was still there.'

Edie wanted to wince but surprised herself by seizing her chance. 'I certainly will,' she said and watched her father's expression change to wary.

'He's going to break your heart, Edie.'

'Why?' she asked with soft exasperation.

Abe shook his head. 'Intuition.'

'You've been wrong before. He may surprise you.'

'I cannot change your mind so I must now fall back on my duty as your father. I insist that Tom show me his worth to you.

I presume you are not denying me my paternal right to make sure my daughter is well cared for.'

'I would be upset if you didn't. But be fair. Give him a chance – that's all I'm asking.'

He blinked and she saw he was angry with her. 'Benjamin will return with me from synagogue. Samuel will bring his mother over later. I cannot throw Tom out, but when he returns I will ask him to spend the evening elsewhere.'

At least her father anticipated his return. 'What do you expect him to do?'

'I don't care. He can go amuse himself in a pub again or at the cinema but this is family business and does not include him . . . even if he is a marriage wrecker.'

Edie refused to react to the sting of her father's words. 'I shall need money to buy food for our guests tonight.'

'Buy for five, not six,' he warned and walked away from her. 'Take the money from my drawer.'

———

Edie escaped into the High Street, her mind scattering with worry for Tom. She didn't believe her father would send him off with the deliberate intent of becoming disoriented and lost. But she could sense the depth of her father's disappointment and despair. The thought of losing Edie to a stranger might prompt him to act irrationally. Nothing in his life had gone to plan, and now here she was denying him the one brightness that might bring him happiness in his remaining years.

Edie felt the familiar prick of duty but it was instantly challenged by the memory of last night's kiss. Tom's recklessness and physical display of his emotion was seductive beyond all her previous fantasies. She'd caught herself smiling this morning as she'd brushed her hair. *Marry me, Edie!* he'd implored.

And he'd meant it. Of this she was certain. The curiosity, though, was that she had woken with no doubt in her mind, either – she wanted to say yes. It was laying her open to pain, beginning with her new role as an outcast amongst her community if she did marry a non-Jew. Denying her father of watching his only child marry properly in the faith beneath the gaze of the rabbi would bring shame to their house, plus it would tear apart the two families who had been friends for all of her life. Was she ready to cause such despair?

Yes. She loved Tom. And no amount of soul-searching could change that fact.

Love at first sight. Tom had changed everything and Edie now refused to settle for anything less than this incredible new feeling. Suddenly she didn't even want to lose sight of Tom, not for a moment. But there was also the notion that if her father's warnings came to pass and Tom offered her no financial security in her future, she didn't care because it was enough that Tom was *in* her future. Just the thought of being able to embrace him each day, kiss him, hear his gentle voice, catch that lovely smile . . . Edie sighed silently as she walked past familiar stores: the cobbler, the tobacconist, the greengrocer. Even though she'd known him only for a few days she'd caught herself studying the minutiae of Tom; liking the angle created by his lowest knuckle on his thumb when he held a mug of tea, listening for that soft way he cleared his throat, observing the neat manner in which he manipulated his spoon while eating his breakfast porridge, or how he worked his knife to butter his toast. And when he was contemplative she noticed that he silently drummed a tune on the table, a wall or his thigh with the middle finger of his right hand. She'd wondered repeatedly at which tune might be in his mind. She wanted to know everything about him but she wanted to know nothing about his past, for there, of course, lurked others . . . perhaps a romantic connection.

A man of his looks and charm would hardly be unnoticed by women. No, Edie didn't want to know a single moment of what had gone before in Tom's life since he'd taken her hand and she'd led him onto the bus.

And since the kiss she'd been thinking about his hands in an entirely different way, imagining them on her, reaching for her, squeezing her close, holding her tight, touching her —

If her father asked her that question of this morning again – about whether she was sure – she'd say she was . . . one hundred per cent sure. Edie wanted Tom.

And she made a decision then and there, queuing to get into the butcher, with the familiar raw smell leaking out of the carcasses of animals that hung behind the shop counter. If Tom asked her again to marry him, she would say yes, but she had to be certain he hadn't been carried away in the passion of the moment last night. She would wait for the question to come and it would need to be sincerely asked.

'Don't let me down, Tom,' she murmured and then cast out silently, *Come home safely*.

She finally stepped into the butcher's shop, scuffing through the sawdust, and was standing at the marble counter within a couple of minutes.

'Cold enough for you, Edie?' Eli was an old friend of the family.

She grinned her answer. 'Hello, Eli. Is that joint of beef tender?' She pointed behind him.

'Yes, my girl,' he said, reaching over the counter and pinching her cheek, as he had done since she was a child. 'Just like you. I've just butchered that leg. It's beautiful meat.'

'I'll take it, please.'

He nodded, picked up the joint, slapping it into his palm and smoothing the layer of fat on top. 'Should feed six. Don't cook it too long, Edie.'

He began wrapping it in large white sheets of paper, then pulled a pencil from behind his ear and totted up something on a small notepad. He twisted it around so she could see the amount and then put a finger to his lips and winked.

Eli was too good to her. She dipped into her purse for the few shillings he was charging her. 'Are you sure?' she murmured as she handed over the coins and ration coupons.

He nodded. 'Of course I'm sure. Your father has done my family many good turns. And meat is at a ridiculous price at the moment.'

She shrugged back and grinned. 'Thanks, Eli.'

'My best to Abe.'

She put the beef into her basket and decided she could afford some eggs. She'd noted Tom liked to drink milk, so she considered an extra pint, and perhaps an extra loaf of bread. Then she remembered tea-leaves. That would all tally up to another sixpence. She darted into the bakery and the grocery shop, making conversation with the women alongside her about the weather, what she was cooking tonight, her father's health . . . the usual topics, while adroitly steering their attention away from her personal life. Out of respect for Shabbat, which demanded no toil be done from sundown, Edie calculated when she must get her beef into the oven before the hour arrived when her father would no longer want her working in the kitchen. Edie mentally ticked off the meal – it would go far if she added some additional vegetables. The potato casserole could cook alongside the beef.

By the time Edie arrived home, put her food away and prepared the meat, it was nearing one p.m., and still there was no sign of Tom. She duly made her father a simple lunch and a pot of tea, which she carried down on a tray into the shop.

'Ah, you're back, my love.'

She nodded and pecked him hello. 'I thought you'd take it down here as you're busy.'

'Thank you, child. Are you feeling brighter?'

She nodded, giving him a sad smile. 'I'm not looking forward to this evening.'

He reached for her hand and kissed it. 'We shall stick together, us Valentines.'

'Promise?' she replied, slightly archly.

He nodded. 'I couldn't bear for you to be unhappy when I knew only happiness with your mother.' Her spirits rose. 'Two new suit orders today,' he continued.

'You see? We're going to be fine.' She looked genuinely happy at the news.

'If I was a younger man I might entertain that idea of Savile Row.'

'Abba, you have no intention of opening your shop on Savile Row. I think you're just too comfortable here.'

Abe sighed. 'We do all right, don't we, Edie?'

'Of course we do. There are so many people in a worse situation than us.'

'You sound so like your mother.'

She grinned. It was one of his favourite sayings. 'Do you want me to hem Mr Goldstein's trousers this afternoon?'

'Yes, thank you, dear. Will you watch the shop while I drink my tea?'

She shooed him to the back and sat at the counter watching the world go by from the shadows of the shop, looking out of its large front window, getting on with her hemming, but really with an eye on the passers-by, hoping to glimpse Tom. She disappeared to check on her food and to iron a tablecloth, taking pleasure in using the damask in his honour – even if he wasn't welcome to share the meal with them – before returning to her spot near the window to gaze out and hope to see him arriving home.

There was no sign of Tom by nearly quarter to four and Edie had kept a lid on her panic by ensuring every long minute of the day was as occupied as the previous one. She'd even cleared out a drawer of old cotton reels . . . anything to remain distracted.

She heard the bell on the door jangle but knew it was simply her father seeing Mr Tomlin on his way. Abe reappeared where she was working, brushing lint off two new suits in readiness to show customers on Monday.

'Well, my child, it is time for Shabbat. I have closed the shop.'

'You go on up, Abba. I'll be a minute or so more.'

'The sun is nearly set, Edie.'

'I know.' Normally she might have left it at that but today had heralded a new beginning in Edie's life, in her attitude. They both knew it. 'I want to unlock the side door before I come,' she said. She put the brush away and busied herself as though it was a perfectly feasible notion.

Her father did not turn and leave but regarded her. 'Edie, maybe this is for the best . . .' he began.

She would not permit him to say it. 'I'm sure he will be home shortly. He knows we observe Shabbat,' she said, matter-of-factly. 'And I'll leave it to you to tell him he is unwelcome at tonight's dinner table.'

His gaze softened but she knew he was hiding his true feelings. This time it was relief, even some satisfaction, as though his warnings had been borne out. 'Tom has been gone all day, child. Perhaps he has taken this opportunity to move on painlessly.'

She kept her voice even, though her belly felt as if it was filled with snakes twisting and sliding over each other at the notion that Tom had left her without farewell. 'No. Tom's not a coward, Abba. He would wish to say goodbye and thank us if he was leaving.'

Edie knew her father wanted to say that Tom could be lost, but she saw him resist it.

'Besides,' she said, 'if we leave it unlocked, then Ben can let himself in.' She smiled innocently. 'Go, Abba, change for Shabbat. I'll be up in a minute.'

He left and Edie took a few moments to quell the fluttering fear that wanted to take full flight. As she moved to the door to turn the Closed sign around, she stared out into the twilight as people hurried home before the sun set fully and she asked any of the angels that had kept Tom alive through the war to now bring him back to her.

'I promise I'll say yes. I cannot ask him to convert his faith but you know he's a good man. Instead I promise to be a loving wife who never breaks faith with my husband. Just bring Tom back to me,' she said softly, realising she was praying, not just casting out a hope.

There was a knock at the door and she was startled. Hope flared. She smiled sadly as she opened the door. 'Evening, Ben.' She kissed his cold cheek, feeling hideously awkward. Her feelings of dread and guilt, coupled with fear for Tom and fear for what was going to happen later this evening, only intensified when Ben showed no expression but his usual good-natured grin.

'I was worried I'd be late,' he said, giving her a hug.

'Right on time as usual,' she assured. 'Ben?'

'I know,' he said, cutting her off. 'We'll talk after synagogue.'

She nodded. 'Go on up. Abba is waiting.' She turned away, aware that they were both avoiding the inevitable. 'I'm just locking up,' she fibbed. 'I'll be up in a moment.'

Ben disappeared. It seemed ludicrous that he was still pretending as though everything was as it had been a few days ago. His mother had admitted that only this morning he was discussing the wedding contract with the rabbi.

Edie felt a skewer of regret for him while giving another wistful glance into the gloomy November night. It felt cold enough to snow. Tom was not prepared for the harsher elements, although she admitted to herself once again that he had emerged from war where others had succumbed to its traumas. Tom was a survivor, a small voice assured her in her mind.

She sighed and joined the men upstairs for a brief prayer and a sip of wine, and then her father and Ben kissed her farewell as they headed to the synagogue for Friday prayers with the rest of the men of Golders Green. In the interim, she listened for the telltale sound of Tom's return that never came while she laid the table with their best crockery and crystal, which somehow kept him with her.

8

Edie and Ben sat opposite one another in the sitting room while Abe remained in the dining room, awaiting the arrival of Dena and Samuel.

She had no idea how to begin the most difficult conversation of her life. The clock ticked ominously, reminding her of the awkward silence stretching between them. Gas lamps added no cheeriness to this scene and when the flame of the fire suddenly guttered, she felt obliged to start the horrible conversation, as clearly Ben wasn't going to. She'd expected him to be in a foul mood. Instead he appeared in control of his emotions and it dawned on her then that perhaps at the synagogue her father had suggested he take a conciliatory approach, as Abba no doubt believed there was now every likelihood Tom was not going to return. It made sense suddenly because she knew Ben had a temper, although it was also true that his childish propensity for anger had matured into an adult's ability to disguise it, channel it differently. She began politely. 'How was synagogue?'

'It was a good service,' he replied, giving her a small smile, and she realised Ben was not going to make it any easier for her.

Edie felt her patience give and shifted to a more direct approach. 'I can't marry you, Ben,' she said, her tone flat.

He shrugged. 'I gather you're nervous.'

His condescension made it easier. 'That's not it.'

'Your voice is trembling.'

'I feel uncomfortable having to confront you with this awkward situation.'

'Well, I want to marry you, Edie. You know that.'

'I do. But that doesn't change how I feel.'

'And how do you feel?'

She wasn't ready for such a question or his composure. Anger would have been far easier to confront. Edie hesitated as she reached for an appropriate response. 'Well, I feel . . . unhappy.'

'Unhappy?' His tone was measured.

He was using his lawyer's negotiating skills.

'Unhappy that I risk hurting you with this decision, but very determined. I cannot marry you, no matter how much Aunt Dena threatens.'

'I see. But you can't give me a reason why?'

'I don't love you . . . not the way a wife should.'

'How do you know how a wife should love, my darling? How do you know that how you love me isn't perfect?'

'Please don't, Ben. Don't twist my words. Save that for your courtroom. I do not feel a romantic love for you.'

He shook his head, his gaze slightly mocking. 'Compared to what?'

'To the love my parents felt.'

'Your mother died at your birth, Edie. You have no concept of their relationship.'

Edie swallowed her resentment at his patronising manner and decided she could no longer shield him from the truth. It was fair that he knew, no matter what the repercussions were. 'All right, then. If you must hear this, I don't love you in the way that I love someone else. Is that what you wanted to hear?'

He laughed. 'Well, that's certainly intriguing,' he said in a cryptic tone and gave her another condescending glance. Obviously

Abba had warned him privately about Tom's impact on her. She could hear familiar voices outside.

'Your parents are here.' She sighed.

'Shall we join them?'

'Ben?' He turned back. She hadn't wanted to hurt him, but Edie knew she now had to be clear even if it did wound. 'Nothing they say, or you say, can convince me to change my mind. I do not love you as I should.'

'Well, I shall and always will love you. Shall we?' He gestured to the door and Edie felt powerless against his devotion . . . no, his obsession.

———

As they all held hands for the blessing that her father was preparing to give over the small feast she'd laid out, Edie heard distant footsteps and her heart leapt. A small sound – a sob – escaped, which she disguised as a cough. She craned to hear, eyes closed for the telltale sound of their side door that creaked when it opened.

'So be it,' they said together in Hebrew, although Edie was one beat behind because she paused on hearing a familiar groan of floorboards from downstairs.

'That will be Tom,' she murmured, relief making her want to weep. Her heart was pounding so hard that she had to stand for fear of her guests noticing.

'Our houseguest,' Abe said, not looking at Edie. 'He won't be staying for dinner.'

She turned from the table and suddenly he was there – tall and broad, cheeks shining and pinched from the cold, teeth gleaming within a broad smile. In fact, his powerful presence felt overwhelming in the door frame in that instant and she sensed her whole body react to it with a rush of warmth, a choke in her throat, her pulse quickening further still. She wasn't sure her voice would be steady – her hands certainly were not and she was glad one was laid firmly on the back of the chair.

'Hello, Edie,' he gushed, and the chill came in with him and seemed to settle around her guests.

'Tom, welcome back,' Abe said politely. 'Come meet the Levi family.'

'Thank you, Abe. It took some effort but I found my way. The suit was delivered on time this morning, Sir.'

Abe cleared his throat. 'We have some family matters to discuss, Tom, so I thought you might drop by the pub for a counter meal. These are our oldest family friends. This is Benjamin Levi, Edie's —' He looked desperately uncomfortable.

'I'm Edie's fiancé, or at least, I think I am,' Ben said, trying to make it sound sardonic but it came out forced. Edie felt sickened. 'My parents . . . Samuel and Dena.'

Tom grinned disarmingly, offering to shake hands, and Edie turned away, embarrassed. 'Hello, Ben. I've heard plenty about you,' Tom said.

'All good, I hope?' Ben replied predictably, Edie thought, and then winced as he laughed at his own jest; Ben sounded suddenly nervous. Tom was having an effect on him too, it seemed. 'And I've been hearing plenty about you too, Tom. Edie couldn't stop talking about you at our house last night.'

Edie felt suddenly hot with shame.

'Well, that's encouraging,' Tom said.

Edie prayed her voice remained casual and steady. 'Tom, do you want to freshen up?' She hated that her father had already publicly dismissed him.

'Not yet, Edie,' he said and she turned back frowning, her breath suddenly trapped in her lungs.

Abe fixed him with one of his disapproving stares. 'You should, son. You smell like a brewery.'

'Yes, forgive me for that. However, I haven't drunk anything stronger than a pot of tea at a small railway café, Abe, but I have been to the pub, it's true, and today walking around these neighbourhoods has given me time to think.'

Everyone waited expectantly and watched as Tom dug into his inside breast pocket and shocked them by pulling out a roll of money. 'I know this is not the appropriate moment, Abe, but I'd like to save us all a lot of time and trouble and buy the bolts of cloth from you.'

They all stared in dull shock at the money Tom had placed on the sideboard. It looked grimy and well used. The Levis shared a confused look with each other and then back at their host, while Edie noted Ben's gaze had not moved from Tom.

Ben spoke first. 'Good heavens! That looks to be several pounds,' he said, in a forced levity.

'Several indeed,' Tom replied, glancing once at Edie. 'Seven, to be precise.'

She blanched, thunderstruck. 'How did you come by this money?' It was clear to her that Tom was not deterred by having an audience; in fact, he looked glad to be having this conversation publicly.

He dug into another pocket and pulled out a half sovereign. 'Remember this, Edie?' She nodded, pale with shock. Tom shrugged. 'I wagered it. I won it back, plus thirteen times its value.'

'Wagered?' Abe said, the most stunned of Tom's audience. 'On what?'

'On Pretty Penny.'

Their guests gasped again in surprise.

'Have you been to the races today?' Abe asked, sounding so shocked that Edie stepped closer to him and laid a calming hand on his arm.

'No, Sir. I gave my only coin to someone I met a couple of days ago. He wasn't keen to take it, but I insisted because I was determined to repay your hospitality. Now I can do that and can offer you a premium for your cloth if you'll accept it.'

'You're buying Abe Valentine's cloth?' Ben queried, bemused. 'What, all that fabric stored out the back, gathering dust?'

Tom nodded.

'What's the catch?'

'No catch, Ben,' Tom replied, his tone cool, almost with a hint of warning.

Abe opened his palms in dismay. 'But, Tom, you don't know the first thing about that cloth, or about tailoring.'

'This has nothing to do with tailoring, Abe. This is about commercial enterprise. We agreed, didn't we, that you needed to shift that cloth?' He glanced at Edie. 'Didn't we?'

She bit her lip, wondering where Tom was leading her with this conversation and whether it was wise to have it now, in this company. She breathed out, trusting him. 'Yes,' she said. 'The three of us agreed that the cloth was useless sitting in a storeroom.'

'Thank you,' he said. 'Abe, let me buy it and sell it on at no risk or embarrassment to you.'

'But, Tom, my father has spoken to the buyer from Savile Row. Why would you —'

She watched Tom lock stares with Abe before a small, wry grin appeared in his expression. 'Your father hasn't taken coffee with the fellow from Savile Row yet.'

Edie turned to her father. 'You did, though, didn't you, Abba? Gieves & Hawkes. You said —'

'I haven't yet, child,' her father replied smoothly.

Edie felt her heart sink. Abba had been toying with Tom.

'What's going on here, Abe?' Dena asked but won a glare from her husband.

Tom proceeded as if he and Abe were the only ones in the room. 'So let's not even ask you to do that, Abe,' he continued. 'You're a proud man. You're a great tailor and you don't need to give the impression that you need Savile Row to take the cloth off your hands.'

Edie turned to her father. 'Is that troubling you?'

'I would appear like a peddler,' he admitted. 'Desperate.'

'I can save you that heartache, Abe. Here's the cash,' Tom gestured again at the grubby pile. 'More than you had anticipated and I will take only what we agree is fair, which is perhaps one third of what you have stockpiled. Right now it's earning nothing.'

'Well, I'm sure Abe has plans for that cloth,' Ben began. 'I mean, if money is required, I'd be happy to ask my —'

'Don't, Ben,' Edie warned, desperate for this scene not to become any more intense. She saw the flame ignite in Tom's expression, and it burned brightly in his eyes as he shifted his attention to the man she was promised to.

'Firstly, Ben, you're missing the point. But it's best you don't involve yourself, for I don't have to ask my family for money.' Ben opened his mouth in expected indignation but Tom continued. 'I have my own money right here.'

Ben stood, his chair scraping back. 'Now, listen here, Tom, or whatever your name is. I have every right to be involved in my fiancée's future. As a lawyer, it's my duty to advise Abe on anything he might want to involve himself in commercially.'

'Really? And what about Edie?'

'Tom,' Edie said, but it was too late. Her suitors had locked horns and nothing could prevent the inevitable tussle.

'What *about* Edie?' Ben challenged.

'Her future, for starters.'

'Edie's future is with me, as my wife. She may deny that right now, but I'm sure my parents and I can convince her —'

'Is that it?' Tom said.

'It?'

'Is that all Edie has to look forward to? Being your wife, I mean?'

Ben looked back at him, aghast. 'What are you saying?'

'Too subtle for you?' Tom mocked and Edie felt the pain of the parry of words as the man she loved drew first blood from the man her father loved. 'You're entitled to follow your heart, your dreams. How about Edie?'

Dena clearly couldn't keep her silence a moment longer. 'Abe, who is this stranger who —'

'What dreams?' Ben interjected, as he looked at Edie, then at Abe, who was suspiciously silent. 'I know she is a splendid dressmaker.'

'Have you asked Edie what she looks forward to doing with her life, other than being your wife, mother to your children, keeper of your house? You don't excite her now, how do you plan to keep her interest for years to come?'

Ben blinked and Edie felt a wave of sorrow. She cut Tom a look, pleading for him to stop. She saw his expression soften.

'Will someone stop this man?' Dena demanded.

'Be quiet, mother,' Ben murmured.

'Enough!' Abe struggled to stand but shook off Edie's helping hand. 'Tom, I think you have breathed a new and fiery wind into our home that might bring about change that will burn everyone it touches.'

Edie watched Tom take a slow breath. 'I'm gathering you wish me to take my fire elsewhere, Abe,' he offered.

Abe nodded. 'Let it burn in your own belly, son. It will cause pain here.'

'Pain for whom, Abe? For Ben, who wants to marry your daughter? For his family that feels entitled to her because it was agreed before she was even born? For you, who wants Ben as a son-in-law because that's what your wife wanted? Or for Edie, who isn't getting a say in any aspect of her life?'

The old man raised a finger of caution.

Ben's composure deserted him and he began to splutter his objections. 'Who are you to come into this house and speak so directly as if you don't owe a great debt to the Valentine family?'

Tom looked away from Ben as though he barely mattered and fixed his attention on Abe. 'I owe a debt and am well aware of it, Mr Levi. Which is why I plan to pay it back tenfold. Abe, please, as a business venture, allow me to buy your cloth and then I will leave your household.'

Edie gasped inwardly. No, surely he wouldn't leave her?

Abe finally sighed. 'All right, Tom. Maybe it will set you up, get you started in life again.'

'It will,' he replied. 'I will not hand the money across your Shabbat table. But you know it is here. Can we shake on the deal?'

'I do not deal on Shabbat. But you have my word that we have agreed on our exchange,' Abe said. 'You can collect the cloth whenever you are in a position to. In the meantime, I wish you to take one of those pounds and go find yourself a hotel in London, pay for some time to organise your thoughts, feed yourself and make a plan.'

'Abba . . .' Edie let go of the breath she had been holding tightly since Tom had begun talking about her dreams. Even Ben had fallen silent. So her suspicions were correct; her father had betrayed her at the synagogue after their talk of the Valentines sticking together.

'No, it's all right, Edie,' Tom said gently. 'Your father is correct to ask me to leave. And I will go, but not before I have an opportunity to ask a question.'

'Go ahead,' Abe said. 'Ask me anything,' he challenged, his jaw suddenly sticking out as if he was determined to wrestle back control in his household.

'It is not a question for you, Abe,' Tom admitted. 'My question is for Edie.' He turned now and regarded her. She could feel his will urging her to look up and meet his gaze. She did so, convinced the rapid drumbeat of her heart could be heard by all and momentarily dizzied by its insistence.

'Edie, will you marry me?'

It should not have been a shock for her and yet as he posed his question so earnestly – those dark blue eyes of his as stormy and exciting as she could recall – she realised she couldn't speak for the emotion that choked in her throat. But over the top of Ben's shocked words claiming, 'What did you say?', his mother's sudden shriek of rage and her father's protestations, she nodded and smiled over the helpless tears of joy that watered.

Finally, her voice came, strong and steady. 'Yes, Tom,' she replied. 'I will marry you.'

———

It had been a risk. But given his success gambling on Pretty Penny, Tom had decided his luck was running and there would never be an easy time to ask for Edie's hand in marriage. In fact, he'd convinced himself as he climbed those stairs to the Valentine household that it might even be best coming out in a rush and seeing what happened.

He'd already accepted that Abe could have sent him off on an errand that might get him lost, so he'd taken a disc of tailor's chalk with him that he'd seen in the workroom. As he walked he'd left surreptitious markings on walls, pavements – even on a lamp-post – that would guide him back to the woman he loved. Abe could never know just how much Tom loved Edie and that if it took his last breath, he would have given it to find her, to come back for her. And today, when Alf had gleefully presented him with his winnings, he knew this would be the opportunity to prove he could take care of Edie. Plus he still had his lucky half sovereign.

When he'd arrived back at the apartment he saw Benjamin Levi sitting in the place he had occupied only the night before. Glimpsing the relief in Edie's eyes that he'd made it home safely, Levi's innocently smug attitude and Abe's pointed remark about him frequenting a pub only strengthened his resolve. He knew asking Edie to marry him brought a raft of problems to her life, not the least of which was betraying her faith . . . certainly in the eyes of the people who surrounded her. He was prepared to convert to Judaism if that would help, but he didn't bother offering for somehow Tom didn't think even that would be enough for Abe Valentine.

So while he could feel Abe's despair and hear Levi's jabbering confusion, his mother's horror above them both, all he could concentrate on was Edie's murmured agreement to his question and the joy that lit her expression. He took Edie's hand now and without asking anyone's permission, he kissed it softly and in that second, as his lips caressed her skin, he knew he would never be alone again.

Someone had finally claimed him.

9

EPPING, JULY 1920

Edie stared at her husband's slackened expression of sleep from the vantage of her pillow. His dreams had become so much more peaceful since their wedding. She could remember hearing him cry out in his sleep from his room in Golders Green, and when she'd asked him about it, he'd shrug and say he didn't remember. Or she'd wake to the sound of her father and Tom talking in hushed tones in the early hours. Edie knew that Abe sympathised, and gave Tom company at those lonely times. Edie sighed with quiet gratitude, for since that painfully awkward confrontation with Ben, her father had resigned himself to the reality that she would marry the newcomer in their life. Abba had found a way to swallow his pride, and for her sake had made it easy on Tom. She knew her father was not yet fully convinced that Tom wouldn't let her down, and yet he'd watched her bloom in every way since that night.

And now she was about to give him a grandchild. More than anything in the world, Abe wanted more Valentines, and the fact that a new generation was beginning pleased his aching heart, reassured his private anxiety and restored his faith in life. She was sure when she'd shocked the household that evening by brazenly accepting Tom's offer of marriage in front of Benjamin, and adding to her oldest friend's humiliation by throwing herself into Tom's arms, that her father had finally believed life's turns were determined to torment, or perhaps even kill, him.

'You'd make yourself an outcast for a gentile?' Ben had stated, clearly rattled as he had been so confident of seeing Tom off, with her father's support.

Edie remembered how she'd smiled sadly at them while she felt Tom's large hand embracing hers. 'No. You are the ones who make me an outcast.'

'Must be one of those shotgun weddings,' Dena had hissed as they'd gathered up their belongings to leave.

Abe had gasped at the insinuation, glanced horrified at Edie, who had shaken her head to reassure him. She replied simply, 'I am doing my best friend a favour. You will see, Benjamin,' she'd said, ignoring his mother now. 'When you truly fall in love you will know how different this feels.'

And from that moment her father had seemed to grasp fully how Edie felt about Tom. Any underlying hostility, no matter how passive it had been, Abe banished and the wedding had been a joyous event that was deliberately kept small for Tom's sake.

Abba had, surprisingly, been a picture of happiness and she wished with all of her heart she had a photograph of the three of them together but a fire that had burned down the studio and the sweet shop next door had taken her wedding plates with it. She hoped this would be rectified soon with baby photos. But the truth was she needed no photo of Tom, for every angle and line of his face she had sculpted into her memory. She noticed he had begun using scissors to trim his beard a little closer and keep it neat, which she appreciated but didn't mention. She didn't ever want to be one of those nagging wives.

She studied his face again, noticing the dark lashes that lay against his cheeks and the thick crescents of his eyebrows that she liked to kiss. 'Like furry caterpillars,' she'd once whispered as they soaked together in the bath. Edie recalled how she'd lain back against his broad chest, safe in his arms, floating on top of his thighs, both cocooned in a womb of deliciously warm water while a frosty, spring Sunday morning was heralded by the village's church bells.

'The bells make this feel a bit naughty,' he'd whispered.

'Only for a gentile,' she'd replied and sighed as he'd nudged aside her damp hair to kiss her neck while his hands cupped her breasts, his fingers teasing at her nipples. Edie remembered how she'd groaned softly then, needing him inside her but not wanting to rush the pleasurable anticipation. But it seemed Tom did, for his hands were seeking out new amusement, his kisses becoming harder, more urgent.

Edie remembered now how she'd swivelled around in the water to face him, desperately wanting to hold him, to look at the love in his eyes. She had promised herself repeatedly that she would never take his love for granted. She would cherish it, make it precious, always return it.

'We must go on a proper honeymoon when we can afford to,' Edie said.

'Where? Name the place.'

'Paris,' she sighed, before adding, 'then Venice.'

'On the train?'

'Slowest way there so I can enjoy you right across Europe,' she teased.

'New York can wait, eh?' he said, knowing that she often talked about visiting that city.

'Everything can wait. Take me back to bed.'

Barely towelling themselves dry, they'd tumbled back into their bed, which had retained their body warmth, and they stilled their inevitable shivering with skin on skin beneath the heavy blankets until the trembling stopped and the lovemaking began. It was that Sunday morning that Edie was sure they'd created their child.

She smiled now in memory, staring at Tom's even, symmetrical and perfectly shaped lips. She wanted that mouth on her now, and in moments like these she caught herself in wonder at her desire for this man. For a woman who had kept such tight control over her passions, Tom had been like a key fitting into her lock and opening the lid on the real Eden Valentine. How lucky she was to have been presented with Tom. How easy it would have been to dismiss his cheeky offer in the hospital grounds that day.

'Life's strange, isn't it?' Tom murmured sleepily without opening his eyes.

She smiled, realising he knew she'd been watching him. 'Is it?' she whispered.

'Just imagine if I hadn't been sitting on that bench outside the hospital as you happened to walk by.'

'Oh, Tom. I was just having the same thought.'

'That's because we're one,' he said in a gritty, morning voice. He pulled her close and she did kiss him now. Softly and lightly, not wanting him to wake fully. Then she turned so Tom could cup his body around hers and she could feel his full, sleepy warmth down the length of her body. She snuggled tighter, pulled his arm around her, and naturally it caressed her ripe belly, tight as a drum. She felt a twitch of movement behind her and grinned.

'Tom,' she warned. 'This is a big day.'

'You're telling me,' he groaned. 'I've never felt this big.'

Edie convulsed with laughter. 'No!'

'Oh, come on. Send me off with a lovely —'

'Tom! No. I'm going to make you a huge breakfast for your first trip alone into London and you can save those um . . . big plans, for tonight.'

'My reward?' he drawled.

She risked a peck but pulled away quickly. 'Our celebration that you did it . . . conquered the demons!' She leapt as nimbly out of bed as her new bulk would permit before he could grab her. 'Shower. Breakfast will be ready in fifteen minutes.'

He sighed and rolled over. 'Right. But we have a date tonight in this bed.'

'Or even the bath . . .' she said, cutting him a coquettish grin.

Tom looked up from his newspaper as she poured his tea. 'How are you feeling today?' he asked.

'A bit tired. But I was told to expect that. He's been kicking for hours. He's a restless soul.'

'He?'

She smiled. 'I guess we'll know in a few weeks.'

'You should tell me if you're not sleeping,' Tom said, closing the paper and giving her his full attention.

'And what can you do?' she teased.

'I could rub your back for you. I could sing to our child.'

'Oh no,' she said, feigning horror. 'You have a terrible voice – you'd make the poor mite squirm even more.'

He clutched his heart. Edie laughed again and tried to wriggle away from his grasping hands. 'Oh no, you don't. Where's my morning kiss?'

She loved these moments and knew the time was fast approaching when their selfish, wonderful existence would be profoundly changed. She appreciated how children shifted the focus in a marriage and suddenly that euphoric, youthful effervescence of being unable to stop touching the man you loved turned to a desire to wrap your hands around the precious child he'd given you and not let go.

'Again,' he urged, always hungry for her affection.

Edie kissed him longer this time, reluctant to pull away.

'Now, really mean it,' he said when she did.

This time they kissed slowly, deeply; Tom pulled her onto his lap, making a low sound of pleasure, and stroked her belly, her breasts, until she gave a soft sigh.

'Tom . . .' she groaned.

'I know. Tonight.'

They both shared an affectionate smile.

'No, I was going to say I can't imagine that I could ever love a child more than I love you.'

'I can't imagine it either,' he said and she hugged him as close as her belly allowed, burying her face into his neck. She inhaled Tom – he smelled of soap froth and Brilliantine, which he used sparingly to slick back the thick dark hair that had grown since they'd met. He no longer looked like a returned soldier with that close-cut short back and sides. Now he looked like a film star, she thought fancifully . . . if not for the beard.

Mercifully his terror of loud sounds had eased and while Tom still did not enjoy crowded places, he was growing more reliable and emotionally steady with each passing day. Edie had accepted that the still slightly haunted look in his eyes was an aspect of her husband that might never leave him.

'I'm going to speak to your father about when you're giving up work.'

'Don't,' she said. 'I'll do it.'

'I've told you that he can live with us. Epping is hardly a long way away and I wouldn't mind.'

'I know, but he's not going to leave Golders Green. Besides, he's an old man now. Set in his ways and used to being head of his own house.' She nodded at the cup nearby. 'Drink your tea. It's nearly time.'

'Well, he can't be too set in his ways – he's about to have a grandchild arrive in his life.'

She gave a happy sigh.

Tom drained his cooled tea. He stood and hugged her from behind. 'Let's call him Daniel if we have a boy; Nina if it's a girl.'

Edie swung around in his embrace. 'Do you mean that?' she asked.

'Why not? They're both lovely names . . . family names. I like the idea of a family name.'

'Are you still glad you took mine?' She searched his face.

'Edie, I swear you're still looking for the chink in my armour that is going to shatter me into a million pieces.'

She looked down and smiled self-consciously. 'I do. I always think of you as a gift from the angels.'

'And what they give, they can easily take away . . .' He trailed off. 'I know the saying. Your father repeats it enough.'

She grinned. 'Really? Daniel or Nina?'

He kissed her. 'Shall I write it in blood?'

Edie swiped at him, then her face contorted. 'Oooh,' she grimaced. 'Little rascal. Feel him,' she said, reaching to place Tom's hands on the small, neat bulge protruding between them.

He waited and then beamed her a proud smile. 'He might play for England!'

'Our new FA Cup Champion. Aston Villa?'

'No! Manchester United, of course.'

'Why, when you live just outside London?'

He grinned and shrugged. 'Don't know. A throwback, perhaps.'

'You don't come from the north. We agreed on that.'

Tom gave an expression showing he didn't care. 'The mystery of my past no longer intrigues me. I'm not interested to know who I was. I'm only concerned with who I am now.' He pointed at Edie. 'Your husband.' He lowered his finger to point at her swollen belly. 'His or her father.' Then he turned the finger on himself. 'Soon to be self-made and disgustingly wealthy, outrageously dashing —'

'And sometime modest bookkeeper,' she cut in.

'What time is your father arriving?'

'The train gets in by five, I think. Certainly before sundown. You know the rules.'

'Well, I shall try not to be late tonight but as I'm not Jewish and make no pretence to be, please explain to him that I'm not being disrespectful about Shabbat. It's just that I have a surprise for you.'

'And what's that?' Edie said, reaching her arms around him.

'Well, I think I'm finally going to take the plunge and shake up Savile Row.'

She sucked in a thrilled breath, eyes shining with astonished pleasure. 'Truly?'

He nodded. 'It's high time. I'm weary of the buyers coming to your father's shop and purchasing our cloth in dribs and drabs. I've been slack and otherwise distracted,' he said, pecking her head. 'But we've got a lot still to shift and what we need right now is a solid injection of cash. I want to make the trip count rather than just be a test of my ability to travel alone.'

'What do you mean?'

'Well, I plan to load the cloth onto the wagonette and it will all be sold to Savile Row in a single swoop.'

'All of it?' she asked.

'Yes. Solly Goldman has organised it with me, and with full sanction from your father,' Tom added.

'It's your cloth, Tom. You bought it fair and square. You don't need Abba's permission.'

He shrugged. 'To be fair, we've been living off the proceeds since the wedding so I'm not complaining, but I want to cash in.'

'Is now a good time, then?'

'Yes, although most wouldn't think so. Perhaps not even Abe, but I feel it instinctively.'

'Perhaps, Tom, you were once involved in business.'

'A runner on the stocks floor, maybe? Numbers and money do make sense to me.'

'And fine clothes,' she reminded archly. They shared a smile before Edie grew more serious. 'Abba says a depression is coming.' She tried not to make it sound like a challenge to his instinct.

'I suspect it is if you consider what is happening politically and industrially . . . and the problems in Ireland don't help. But the sort of people having their suits tailored at Savile Row aren't short of a bob. They will be robust in a time of crisis because they are financially savvy and have the "fat" to protect them. They won't stop the privileges they allow themselves but they may cut down or choose a less expensive option.' He shrugged. 'The rich don't like to lose face, Edie, particularly those who move and shake in London.'

'I don't know how you know these things, Tom.'

He blew his cheeks out. 'Intuition, I suppose. We all have our gifts.'

'So you're thinking that if you can sell the remaining cloth at once you'll make a small fortune in one swoop because the price will be irresistible?'

He grinned and kissed her. 'You make a fine businesswoman, Edie.'

'I'm proud of you. It would have made me happy just to know you're finally going to see Savile Row.'

'I'm sure it would have.'

She heard the subtlety of his words. 'Would?' she frowned.

His expression turned sheepish as she waited. 'I'm going to London, but I'm not going to Savile Row. Solly's handling that bit.'

'But why?' she asked, bewildered. 'If you make it up to London without feeling anxious those are the hardest yards covered, and you might as well go all the way to Savile Row. This is your sale, your chance to derive all the benefit. I want the buyers to meet you – Tom Valentine, entrepreneur.'

'I don't have an ego that requires having to personally close a sale. I've set it up. Solly knows what I want and he's an honest man. He gets his cut. I don't have to do anything except help load it onto the cart. Suits me.' He winked. 'No pun intended.'

'So you don't feel confident about going up to London alone?'

'That's not it. I want to go to London – have to in order to prove to myself that I no longer have to fear travelling alone. But confronting my fears may take too much out of me and I don't want to risk facing Savile Row with a blurred mind or weakened in any way when negotiations have to be done. Solly's my emissary. Next time I won't need one but the cloth we've got stockpiled needs to be shifted now and can't wait for me to be feeling confident about travelling into the heart of the city. We have to strike now, Edie, before the economy sinks further.'

She looked downcast, not ready to let the debate go. 'If you're feeling as strong as you appear and sound, then I really do think you should go. There may be all sorts of opportunities. You can't keep doing accounts for shopkeepers, Tom. You're so much better than that. You think big always. Ignore the fear, risk going into central London and close that deal yourself. Lead the sale.'

'Travelling alone that far will challenge me.'

'But you won't be alone,' she countered, knowing he had meant just the trip from Epping to Golders Green, but she chose to ignore it for the sake of her determined argument that he close the deal. 'And Savile Row will seduce you,' Edie said, excited again and with a plea in her voice.

'What is it, Edie?'

'Pride, I suppose,' she admitted, shrugging. 'I want them to know they are buying Valentine cloth from a Valentine. And envy. I would give anything to be able to spend time at Savile Row. It's a man's world, though. My father is quite a revolutionary in the way he has always encouraged me in his trade and allowed me to meet his clients.'

'I'd tell you to come with me but I don't like the idea of you travelling this close to our child's arrival.'

Edie waved a hand as though she didn't need to come today. Instead she prodded his chest. 'Someone important might see the potential in you that I know is there. You might be offered a wonderful new job on the Row.'

Tom grunted. 'I doubt it very much. This is where I want to be. Right here with you and our new baby in our sweet little home, with our vegetable garden and my roses. And besides, I like being self-employed. You can never make it big if you're employed by someone else.'

'Make it big?'

'I want to give you so much. And our child . . . children!' He smiled and held her. 'I don't want to go to work every day of my life for someone else. I want to be that someone else.'

She stopped their debate with a kiss. 'I love you, Tom Valentine.'

'I love you more, Eden Valentine.'

She shook her head. 'I doubt that.'

'I can prove it.'

'Go on, then.' She grinned.

'All right. When I am paid for the remainder of the cloth, the money is yours.'

She looked at him perplexed. 'For what? You're the financial brain in this family.'

He smiled, his eyes twinkling with mischief. 'Come with me.' He took her by the hand and led her out to his garden shed where he had an old leather satchel hanging up that Abe had given him. It was one of the many items Abe had gifted to his 'children', as he called them now. Everything from furniture to cooking pots and pans had found their way into their tiny but happy home.

As Tom took down the satchel Edie shook her head in wonder.

'Hold your apron out,' he said.

She did as he asked and Tom upended the satchel – out of it fell money. Lots of it.

Edie stared at the notes and coins in stunned silence. 'What is this, Tom?' she finally whispered, all amusement fled. 'Have you robbed a bank?'

'Honestly earned, invested and reinvested until I turned a profit during difficult times on the share market.'

'What do you know about stocks and shares?'

He shrugged, nodding. 'It's a good question. Nothing, but I learned very quickly.'

'I had no idea.'

'I couldn't have you worrying. It's why I never used any of the money that I earned doing the shopkeepers' books. You remember the seven pounds?' She nodded. 'I won more than that but kept a few pounds back for us. I thought we may need it if your father turned his back on us. All of this is earned through that original fund.'

'Pretty Penny, you mean?' she asked. He grinned. 'What made you do it?'

'You did, Edie.'

She frowned. 'I don't understand.'

Tom undid a front flap of the satchel and withdrew some paperwork. 'You will when you read this.'

'I prefer you to tell me. You're scaring me.'

He smiled and his eyes were round and filled with warmth. 'Nothing to fear. It's exciting. I have taken on a lease.'

Her gaze narrowed. 'A lease . . . for what?'

'For the atelier you dream of. I considered Petticoat Lane. I even thought long and hard about Lavender Hill, but you need to go after the real money, Edie – and the real money is spent in places like Sloane Square. Your new salon is on the King's Road. With the sale of the cloth today, you can afford to set up that shop with everything you need to start the dressmaking and bridal business.'

Edie felt as though a million words were crowding into her mind at once, backing up in her throat, but she couldn't get a single one out. She looked down at the money piled into her apron and back up to Tom's face, speechless.

Tom continued, filled with laughing enthusiasm. 'It's time to climb out of the shadow of Abe Valentine and especially that of your brother's. This is only about Eden Valentine, and her atelier.'

Edie continued to stare at him.

'All the paperwork is done for the shop itself. I have spoken to a lawyer who is handling everything. All the details are in here. We can go through it together . . .' He paused and laughed again. 'Once you get over the shock. But in all honesty, you don't need me.'

She took a deep breath. 'I don't know what to say.'

'Nothing to say. Just follow your dream, Edie.'

'But our baby?'

'We'll work it out. There are so many people looking for work, and we can set up a nursery at the back of the salon.'

She felt as though a rabble of butterflies had suddenly been startled in her chest.

'Edie? This is what you want, isn't it?'

She nodded through helpless tears, which she tried to sniff back while she responded to her husband's searching look. 'It's more, Tom. You've given me my dream – my salon, a child . . . and you. Is it fair for one person to have so much happiness at once? I feel dizzy with guilt.'

'Don't you dare,' he warned. 'You've spent your whole life being dutiful. Now it's your turn to chase the stars, and I'll be there, watching you proudly. So make me proud, Edie. Take this opportunity and don't worry about anything you can't control. Life is always going to get in the way of the best laid plans. But I'm here . . . I'll always be here for you.'

'Promise me.'

Tom kissed her long and tenderly, pulling away only when they both needed to take a breath, and even then leaving only the space of a single finger between their lips, which he now touched to her mouth. 'Hush, Edie,' he murmured. 'You have nothing to fear.'

IO

When Tom and Edie had been firm about leaving her family home above the shop and moving out of London, Abe had been inconsolable to begin with.

It had felt harsh at first to leave the old man behind, but no amount of Edie's pleading or Tom's urgings could encourage him to join them in the cottage that they'd stumbled upon one summery afternoon while picnicking in the Epping Forest.

Sitting humbly away from the Jacobean hunting lodges and various country manors were quaint workers' cottages and small lanes meandering through unspoiled countryside. Edie had fallen in love with the region and one particular abandoned cottage, its scrambling hedge of honeysuckle gone wild, while an arbour over the broken gate dripped with wisteria and nasturtiums. Ancient rose bushes, whose main shafts were nearly as thick as Edie's arm, bloomed sweet and bountiful in dazzling colours and scents. Flowerpots on the window ledges had long ago dried and cracked, their flowers withered, but somehow they managed to still look cheerful, perhaps aided by sentries of sunflowers that kept a vigil in beds lining the front of the house.

It was ramshackle, inside and out, but Edie could see strong bones, assured Tom they could afford somewhere like this, and it would work for them.

'You make me nervous, Edie,' he'd admitted, frowning at the restoration challenge ahead.

'I'll make this a home so fast you'll hardly catch a breath, and the railway station means the seventeen miles to London is easily covered. It's perfect. My father can still visit and I can get into and out of town to pick up work and deliver it back to Abba.'

Tom had nodded, deep in thought. 'I like that it's a market town.'

'Every Monday apparently,' she'd said.

Within weeks the newlyweds had moved in and begun turning the cottage into their home. As Tom kissed his wife now, both standing either side of their repaired and freshly painted front gate, she sighed.

'What's wrong?' he frowned.

'Nothing,' she replied.

'Tell me.'

'I can't bear us to be apart.'

He tutted. 'You go up and down to London all the time.'

'I do, yes. But you are always safe here and waiting for me. This time you're leaving.'

'You have nothing to fear. Just be relieved that I feel independent enough to do this.'

'I'm so proud my heart feels full enough to burst.'

He looked at her quizzically as he inhaled the scent of honeysuckle. 'And?'

'I'm frightened it might burst.'

'There you go again,' he teased. 'I am going to London to make us a cold fortune with our magnificent European cloth and then we're going to celebrate. You're going to have our baby very soon, then you're going to open the salon . . . and we'll really be on our way.'

'No straying into pubs today.'

He shook his head. 'I'm not a child.'

'I know. It's why I haven't sewn our address into your jacket,' she said sadly. 'But I wanted to.'

'Please stop worrying, Edie. I am recovered and now it's time I started proving that.'

She couldn't argue with this logic. 'I did sew something for you, though.'

He shook his head in query.

'Look in your breast pocket.' She mustered a grin. 'The invisible one.'

He pulled out a red handkerchief, ironed and folded neatly. He frowned. 'I have a handkerchief,' he said, tapping his outside breast pocket.

'Not like this one,' Edie said. 'Open it.'

He shook it out and noticed that the middle had been neatly cut away in a specific shape. Tom gave a sad smile. 'I do believe, Eden Valentine, that you have my heart.'

Edie opened her hand to reveal the heart-shaped scrap of red cotton upon which she had embroidered their intertwining initials. 'Forever,' she answered. 'And I'm going to keep it safe right next to my own.' She grinned, pushing the small piece of fabric into the front of her blouse, tucking it into her bra.

He raised an eyebrow. 'I'll be back to claim it. In the meantime, you should know that I don't ever want it to be anywhere else but there.' He kissed her softly. 'Back before you know it.'

She nodded. 'I'll miss you the whole time.' Edie hugged him hard and then he was gone, striding down the small lane, wearing the new navy suit her father had made for him recently. She noticed him pause to exchange a few words with Mrs Bailey, who was cutting some roses in her garden, and then he lifted his hat again for Mrs Charmers, who was pushing her new baby in its pram. She craned to watch him before he turned the corner and headed up towards the main road for the bus into town to meet Sol.

Oh, how Edie wished she possessed Tom's easy way with others. He seemed even more at home in their new country setting than she did. A soft summer breeze blew her hair off her shoulders.

'Being in love hurts, doesn't it?'

Edie swung around. It was the barmaid from The King's Head, where she and Tom had dropped in a couple of times and couldn't help but notice the laughing, loud woman behind the bar. If the give-away wrinkles were an indication, then this was a woman past her prime but Edie had noticed that Delia took care with her appearance. She surprisingly looked even more youthful with her hair in a ponytail and no lipstick or rouge.

'Delia, isn't it?'

'Good memory. Where's your handsome fellow going?'

'Hello. I'm Eden Valentine. Is it obvious how much I love him?'

'Then and now.'

'Tom's my husband.' She absently stroked their unborn child. 'I was watching him go for the day.' She looked away self-consciously.

'Why so worried?'

Edie found herself explaining to the relative stranger at her gate about her husband's lost memory, how they'd met, fallen in love and that they'd moved away from the city to help him heal fully. She even told her companion about her plans to open a bridal salon.

'Not just bridal, of course . . . I'd like to do the whole trous-seau and the honeymoon garments. Ultimately I'd like to offer a range of clothes off the hanger for the busy woman – at work, at play, at home.' She lost the misty look in her eyes and refocused on Delia. 'Today, though, it's all about Tom and knowing he's safe.'

Delia shrugged. 'You have to let him go sometime. Next time will be easier. And soon you'll be waving him off, glad to have some time to yourself for a while,' she said, slapping Edie playfully. 'I can't wait to push Bert out of our flat.'

'Do you live above the pub?'

Delia nodded and her expression clouded. 'We never could have children,' she said, glancing at Edie's bump, but she brightened almost immediately. 'But it does mean we can work our long pub hours and Bert said we should take a holiday next winter. Maybe go somewhere warm.'

'Lucky you,' Edie said.

'You'll have your hands full by then, I suspect.' Delia winked. 'Have you got family nearby?'

Edie shook her head.

'What about friends? Have you made many?'

She shrugged. 'Not yet.'

'Well, you two have probably been too busy,' Delia remarked dryly, glancing again at Edie's swollen belly. 'Come on, I've promised my Bert a nice fruit pie tonight.'

'Come on where?' Edie frowned.

'You do know the best blackberries in Britain grow at the bottom of your lane, don't you?' Delia asked.

Edie looked back at her vacantly.

'Oh, my heavens. Go fetch a bowl and tonight you are going to have a warm blackberry and apple pie waiting triumphantly for your man's return.'

Edie giggled. 'I've got an apple tree laden with fruit in our garden.'

'Excellent.'

Edie hurried back into the cottage, returning with a big glass bowl.

Delia casually linked an arm. 'Come on then, Eden.'

'Edie,' she corrected.

'Good, because I have to discuss your hair.'

'My hair?' she said.

'We're cutting it. You're young, Edie! Wear it in the new bob style.'

Edie looked back apprehensively at her new friend with a mischievous expression.

'What?' Delia said.

'Tom likes it long.'

'So does every man, but this is the 1920s! How old are you?'

'Twenty-four,' she answered.

'Well, then!' Delia replied as if that was the answer to all ills. 'There isn't a woman under thirty who isn't rushing out to have her tresses cut off. And you've got thick, dark, shiny hair that other women would kill you for. You can lead the charge in London, Edie.'

'Why don't you lead the charge?'

'Because I'm hitting forty-four! If you open this salon, aren't women going to be looking to you for fashion advice?'

'I suppose so.'

'Cut your hair, girl. I heard on the radio that barber shops in New York are being flooded by thousands of women every week, all wanting to be shorn. London will be next. You've surely seen the fashion magazines?'

Edie nodded.

'Must be quite intimidating for the men.' Delia laughed. 'But we have Madeleine.'

'Madeleine?'

'Great hairdresser turned amazing model and now retired from Paris, who lives near the pub and can cut your hair in the latest style. We can probably do it this afternoon and you can surprise your fella not only with a hot blackberry pie, but with a sexy new haircut.'

'Delia, I'm not sure . . .' She began to shake her head.

'Oh, he'll love it.' She patted Edie's arm as though a deal had just been done. 'Now, tell me more about your handsome husband. I have to warn you, if I was twenty years younger . . .'

Edie's laughter could be heard echoing down the pretty country lane with high hedgerows and tangles of blackberry canes.

————————

Tom was perspiring lightly from their efforts and was now trying to cool himself by sipping a ginger beer in Abe's kitchen with Sol. Abe was stirring a pot on the stove.

'Hot today, Abe. Is soup a good idea?' Sol remarked.

'Every day's a good day for chicken soup, Sol.'

Sol winked at Tom. 'We're all loaded, Abe.'

'Good. I'm glad we're rid of it.'

'Not rid of it yet,' Tom cautioned. 'I won't trust a sale until I have the man's money.'

'Listen, Tom, come with me today.'

'Sol, you must have suggested that ten times already,' Tom sighed.

'Let's make it a round dozen, then. Come with me. Abe would prefer it. I know I would. You should close this deal.'

'Now you sound like a Valentine. I'm happy to work behind the scenes.'

'You did well, Tom,' Abe assured. 'Feeling all right?'

'I'm feeling great,' he admitted. 'There was something powerful about catching the bus alone, walking alone, being entirely in charge of myself. But Edie frets, as you know.' He didn't add that it was near empty on the bus, that the conductor kept him distracted with chatter for most of the way, or that the traffic was light. Tom knew it would be busy from Golders Green into London proper and all those sounds of people and cars, animals and hectic city life could threaten his present calm.

Abe nodded. 'I have to admit to being a bit sad that you won't see Savile Row. It's just a hop and a skip into central London. The Row is special place . . . even for Edie. As a child, before she was old enough to attend school, she used to hold my hand and come with me to all my appointments. They'd give me my week's work and I'd bring it back here, do the jobs, then deliver the suits back to the various shops.'

Tom frowned. 'I didn't know that.'

Abe shrugged. 'Yes. I took their overflow, but when my wife died, I think I turned a bit crazy for a while. I didn't trust myself to find new business or measure up a suit properly. But Edie loved Savile Row even then. She used to play with the buttons and satin edging, and she was fascinated by the huge shears. It's not a place for women, though.'

Tom sighed, imagining what it would feel like to tell Edie he'd been to the Row. 'I'll tell you what, Sol. I'm feeling pretty good right now and I wouldn't mind a lift a bit closer into the city. Drop me off somewhere because I'd like to buy Edie a gift and we are finished here earlier than we planned.'

'Is that wise?' Abe turned to fix Tom with a gaze. 'You're better off sticking with Sol and going all the way.'

That made his mind up. 'I don't need to be babysat constantly. I won't go all the way to Savile Row but I do want to test my boundaries. I made it here in one piece.'

'Central London's a bit more complicated,' Abe cautioned.

'Just drop me near a bus stop and I'll wander around for an hour and head back.' He held Abe's stare. 'It will please Edie, too – next time I'll meet the tailors who are using our cloth.'

'Next time you'll have a baby to worry about, son. Life is not going to be the same for you.'

11

Perhaps it was optimism for the future that had made him find new daring as he now urged Sol to take him deeper into the city than originally agreed.

'We can go all the way together . . . come with me to the Row,' Sol tried yet again.

Tom had no idea where they were or how close they were to Sol's destination but he shook his head. 'No, I want you to leave me somewhere where I can see buses but also where I can easily find a gift for Edie, not for the nursery or the baby. Something just for her. Perfume, perhaps?'

'Piccadilly Circus is your best bet, but it's the busiest possible spot in London, Tom. There's traffic and noise and people and constant activity. I'd feel bad leaving you there.'

It felt like a challenge . . . a gauntlet. Yes, he wanted to see Savile Row but that would mean being babysat by Sol and he was determined to be alone. Edie would then never worry about him again. He could do it. Since waking up on the ship, he'd never felt more in control or more positive than he did in this moment.

'I lost my memory but I know I didn't lose my courage back on the battlefield.'

'No, son, but —'

'Drop me at Piccadilly Circus,' he insisted.

Edie was seated in her parlour with a towel wrapped around her shoulders. Flanking her was Delia and a tall, golden, sylph-like creature named Madeleine, who was brandishing a small but potentially lethal pair of scissors.

The room was filled with a reassuring scent of baking pastry that had fruit juice bubbling through cracks in the sugared lid. As Edie sat listening to her new companions, she wondered how Tom was getting on. Was he already on the bus home? Or had he decided to stay with her father overnight? Her mind raced on a wave of thoughts about how the sale went. Tom's pledge to her was extraordinary and so unexpected she could still feel the tingling thrill his words caused. Edie had never drunk champagne but she'd seen movie stars drinking it on the big screen and she was sure the bubbly fizz would be as intoxicating as Tom's determination to give her a salon of her own.

'You've never tasted champagne?'

'Pardon me?' Edie said, coming out of her thoughts.

Madeleine was staring with a languorous sapphire gaze, scissors still clicking ominously in her right hand. She wore rouge and lipstick even though it was the middle of the day, on the fringe of Epping Village. To Edie she seemed exotic and dangerous. 'Did I hear you right?'

'Did I say that aloud?'

Her friends laughed and Madeleine shifted her weight onto one hip. It was such an effortless pose, oozing confidence, arrogance even, and definitely sex.

'Champagne, Eden, is the nectar of the gods,' Madeleine crooned in her seductive accent. 'Of the French gods,' she added with a wink. 'Now, about these tresses of yours.'

'I just want —'

'Eden,' Madeleine interrupted, dragging her name out lazily but the clacking scissors attested to her irritation. 'You have a most beautiful name and yet you allow everyone to reduce it to something that makes you sound like Delia's grandmother's best friend's aunty.'

Delia blinked but Edie followed and laughed. 'I've always been called Edie,' she admitted.

'But Eden is so exotic. It's all woman, my girl.' She leaned close to Edie. 'It's sex.'

Delia coughed.

'Check the pie, Delia,' Edie suggested, uncertain of where Madeleine was headed with her curious conversation.

The Frenchwoman was not to be deterred. She was perhaps a decade older than Edie and she wore her hair cut not much longer than a man's. It looked like a helmet to Edie but she didn't dare say so. It shone, silky and blunt-edged, with a curiously short fringe. It would be severe on most women but on Madeleine it looked right – no, sensational. Her lips were painted a cherry-red pout. She wore black, despite the season, and while Madeleine shook her head at Edie's hair, all Edie could think about was how amazing Madeleine would look modelling clothes. Her clothes.

'Eden would do "elfin" so well,' Madeleine finally drawled, pushing away from the sink and snipping at the air.

Delia closed the oven door. 'Not quite ready.'

'Elfin?' Edie repeated.

Madeleine nodded. 'Shorter than mine.'

'Oh no! Absolutely not!' Edie said, standing.

'I know what will work for you, Eden,' Madeleine said sternly.

'My husband will die of shock . . . if he doesn't die of heartbreak first. No, no, no! I agree my hair needs styling but I am not allowing you near me with those scissors until we agree on what I want.'

The women waited.

'Here,' Edie said, marking the length she'd allow.

Both looked dismayed.

'Neither here nor there, as you English say,' Madeleine replied.

'Well, it's here or nothing,' Edie shrugged. 'I want the bob but the wavy version. Short will make me look like a boy.'

'She has a point,' Delia said. 'Start slow, Mads.'

Madeleine sighed a soft curse in French. 'Let's get started, then.'

―――――――

London began to crowd around Tom and the bubble of invincibility that had wrapped itself around him all morning began to deflate as the sounds of people, traffic and the press of the city began to mock his fragility. With a sinking heart, he tapped Sol's arm.

'Set me down here, please.'

'This is Green Park. Piccadilly is just down —'

Tom took a deep breath that he knew his friend noted. 'Here's best, Sol. I'd like to sit in the park for a while.'

Sol slowed the wagonette and looked at Tom. 'There's no shame in calling it quits, mate. You've already achieved so much in one day.'

'One more test. I need to find my way home.' As Sol opened his mouth, Tom added. 'Alone.'

A pause stretched between them until finally Sol nodded. 'The bus stop you want is there,' he pointed. 'I'll write down the number . . . just in case.'

Tom knew he didn't want to say, *Just in case you forget*, or *Just in case you go and lose your mind again*.

'I'm going to sit in this park for a few minutes, then take this number bus home. You sell my cloth and make us all a handsome profit. And remember, Sol, it's for Edie. I want her to have this money, so don't let them bully you.'

Tom shook Sol's hand before lifting a hand in farewell as he stepped nimbly down to the pavement. The vast expanse of verdant parkland was a balm for him. He sat down on a bench to take stock and to calm his anxiety. He reassured himself that he'd done it. He was in the big smoke and, while he had lost his nerve to go further, he felt his breathing slowing and the previous sense of happy adventure returning.

A dapper old fellow who'd been approaching sat on the other end of the bench and lifted his hat to him.

'Hope you don't mind if I join you?'

'Not at all. I was enjoying the peace for a few minutes before I was on my way,' he admitted.

'I come here daily,' the man said, pulling out a scrap of newspaper he'd fashioned into a bag. 'Like to feed the birds and watch all you youngsters hurrying along in your busy lives.'

Tom smiled. 'Do you live nearby?'

The man nodded. 'Mayfair. I live alone, though, so this way I get to see some folk, talk to people like you.'

'I live in Epping.'

'From the country. Marvellous! Although with the way our city is growing and housing going up all over the place, I doubt it will remain that sleepy hamlet for long. Always lived out that way?'

'I can't remember.' He tapped his head. 'The war stole something from me. I'm Tom.' He deliberately shared no surname.

'Edgar. Pleased to meet you, Tom. I'm glad the war didn't steal your life. What it took may yet return or at worst you can replace. Look at it this way . . . you have a clean slate, which is more than I can say for your chin.'

Tom laughed. 'No good?'

'Makes you look shifty, son. As though you're hiding something. Doesn't your lovely wife complain at its roughness?'

'Not once,' he admitted. But Edgar's notion got him thinking. 'Really? Shifty?'

Edgar gave a small chuckle. 'I used to be a lawyer. Retired years ago. But I never fully trusted a man with a beard, unless he wore it to cover a scar, or it was his religion.'

Tom pondered this and Edgar continued feeding the birds.

'Is there a barber around here?'

With no surprise in his voice, Edgar gave directions. 'It will take you three minutes . . . go out of that gate, turn left, first right, and you'll find it.'

'Thanks, Edgar,' Tom said, standing and offering his hand.

Edgar shook it. 'Don't mention it. I'm sure your wife will thank me. Best present you ever took home from the city, eh?' He tapped his nose and chuckled again. 'Goodbye, Tom. Nice meeting you. Oh, and don't say too much to him if you cherish your privacy – and I suspect you do. He's a nosy fellow.'

After leaving the gate with a final wave to Edgar and following the directions, he caught sight of a red-and-white striped sign in the distance.

A shave suddenly seemed the perfect gift for Edie. As he walked towards it, flitting through his mind came the thought that this was originally the sign for bloodletting, signifying the blood and the bandages, reminding him that barber surgeons had once been so important to the military. He bent his thoughts to this sudden and seemingly momentous decision to shave his beard off after resisting it for so long.

What a joy it would be for Edie, who had never once asked him to remove it, but he knew it was only her patient nature that overcame her natural curiosity to see the man she loved truly emerge from hiding. And he had been in hiding. If today was about change and going forward, then it was time to confront the real Tom.

Tom stepped inside the shop lined with white tiles and nodded at the white-coated barber, who was just finishing with a client in his chair, adding a final slick of pomade through the man's hair.

'Good morning, Sir . . . a trim?'

'Short back and sides and a shave, please,' Tom replied.

'Full shave, Sir?'

'Please.'

The barber smiled and gestured to a waiting chair behind. 'Take a seat. I'm Eric.'

Beneath the deft and speedy ministrations of the barber the hidden visage of Tom Valentine emerged. Revealed was a face outlined by a square jaw, evenly set features with a forehead a similar width as the distance from brow to the bottom of his straight, Greco-style nose, and again from there to the point of his ever-so-slightly cleft chin.

Keeping Edgar's warning in mind, Tom distracted the chatty fellow away from all information that he construed as personal and instead directed their conversation towards a general discussion on everything from England's weather to menswear and the new penchant for three-piece suits with pleated, cuffed trousers and homburg hats. Tom found he could discuss styling easily after life with Edie, and the barber seemed to have an opinion on the trend towards brighter colours.

'Haven't you noticed the pastel shirts the gents are wearing?'

Tom nodded, just to keep him talking through the process. His companion was poised to shave above Tom's lip.

'Pencil moustaches are becoming fashionable,' he offered.

'Thanks, I'll stick with clean-shaven.'

After the man removed the hot towel Tom stared at himself silently.

He'd had no idea that he had dimples, which now indented as he trialled a smile on his new clean-shaven face.

'Been a while, Sir?'

Tom nodded, not quite ready to speak; he looked so different and he was now concerned whether Edie would recognise him, let alone approve of this gift he was bringing home from London. He explained to the barber that his wife had never seen him without a beard.

'I wouldn't trouble yourself, Sir. Look at the handsome fellow you see in that mirror. No woman could resist you.'

'There's only one I care about.'

'Fair enough. But she's going to love the new man in her life. Besides, beards are for old men. How old are you, if you don't mind my asking?' Eric dried off Tom's face and slapped something that smelled bright and citrusy against his cheek and jaw, which stung like merry hell.

'Er . . .'

'You can't be more than thirty if you're a day, Sir,' Eric continued.

Tom smiled, relieved. 'Today's my birthday,' he lied, ignoring the man's query. It seemed appropriate to call today his birthday. It was like a rebirth of sorts, after all.

'Truly? Well, happy birthday to you.'

He rubbed at his strangely smooth chin. 'I should celebrate it while I'm here, shouldn't I?'

'Oh, you can't go straight home now, Sir,' he said. 'Take in the sights, even if you just go sit on the steps at Piccadilly. Then you can pick up something for your lovely lady from one of those fine shops. You sound like you can afford to walk into Fortnum & Mason!' He gave Tom a playful nudge.

Tom felt that his bravado was now intact again, and his confidence rising. It did sound like a fun plan and, besides, he would privately brand himself a coward if he didn't face his demons and at least test his will against the noise and traffic of one of the busiest spots in London. Perhaps he could also take something home for the baby?

He emerged from the barbershop in Mayfair looking like an entirely new man but disappointingly no clearer about the mystery of his past.

Sitting on the steps below Eros, Tom wondered again at his naivety, or was it stupidity? He'd felt relatively calm following Eric's directions into the mad throng that was Piccadilly Circus. But no, he realised now he wasn't ready for this. The mass of activity – just the blur of colour as people moved around him – set his pulse racing and Tom realised as he tried to focus on the cool stone of the steps that he was not in control.

Immediately he became aware of his breathing and deliberately inhaled and exhaled slowly as Edie had suggested. It worked initially. He felt no immediate panic, although he was certainly alarmed by the intensity of noise, action, colour, smells and sounds. Feeling his pulse pounding as it was, Tom knew that the next stage was indeed a panic attack.

The traffic was like a sea and he was on an island in the middle of it. He tried to focus on one vehicle, an old van, but as it was swallowed into the ocean of vehicles and he lost sight of it, Tom's confidence fled and he began to feel the familiar sensation of entrapment. A frantically busy road surrounded him and black cars circled, chased by big dark monsters in the shape of buses, squealing and belching fumes. He was being reminded of the dark stuff of war. He couldn't focus on those memories because they were too misty, but the smell of women's perfume soured in his headspace to a smell of gas while the roar of traffic became the demonic sounds of bombs and gunfire. Beads of perspiration formed on his forehead and his shirt began to feel damp beneath his jacket. He'd felt so hopeful – cocky, even – but the reality was he couldn't cope . . . not yet.

Tom hung his head between his knees, which he hoped would ease the dizziness, and sucked in air that tasted of fumes. Memories rippled strongly, riding on that smell of petrol, disturbing because they spoke of darkness . . . of being stalked . . . of gaping wounds and broken men . . . of death and, always, of suffocation.

Periodic shouts or gusts of laughter reached through his escalating alarm and at the rim of his mind, where there was still some rationality, he knew it was hopeless. He was slipping into confusion. Tom tried to stand and wondered if he was swaying or whether the world was tipping. He tried to say something but didn't know if he slurred or perhaps had not uttered anything. He thought of Edie and the baby, tried to regain some measure of control by forcing himself to look up and read the signs around him.

He saw *Bovril* in huge letters on the top of one building. He moved the letters around in his mind and came up with *Boil*. Instantly he experienced a fleeting glimpse of blood bubbling up from someone's chest that had been blown apart. He blinked in terror and shifted his panicked gaze to the big clock above the large jeweller's shopfront. The clock cheerfully yelled in big lettering 'Guinness Time'; *Guest*, he saw immediately, and thought of his presence in the Valentine home. Then he saw *Nest* – what he'd made with Edie in Epping. And he felt a surge of hope that he could find his way back to their cosy cottage, but then he saw the word *Mine* form itself and distantly he heard a bomb as a van backfired and he cringed. The letters rearranged themselves before his eyes: he saw *Stem* and again he had a vague notion of pressing down on a terrible wound but the blood was leaking through his fingers. A young man barely out of his teens cried beneath, begging Tom not to let him die. The letters he stared at reformed into *Mist* and a smell of killing gas wafted across his senses. He experienced a brief, vivid vision of soldiers hurling themselves over the top of a vast trench but being cut down and falling back into the grave immediately, himself amongst them, and that image flared in horrible, sharp colour but disappeared just as quickly to leave him breathing fast and frantically.

Tom felt stone beneath him, realised he was seated again. Had he fallen back? Was that him making that strange whimpering sound?

'Hey, Mister,' came a voice through the tunnelled vision that was all he had now. He must have raised his head, saw a boy, but in his hand was a pistol. *Gun!* Tom thought with deep dread. Machine-gun fire echoed in his mind, bullet casings, damage, shrapnel, wounds, blood . . . always blood.

'Bang!' the little boy yelled gleefully and he pulled the trigger on his toy gun. The hammer slammed home and in his mind Tom heard a deafening explosion. He launched himself from the shallow steps beneath the statue of the god of love and out into the sea of vehicles that began to honk their horns. He caught horrified expressions from drivers, waving fists and curses at him although he heard no words. He startled a small coach-load of passengers, their mouths suddenly gaping holes of silent screams.

Tom had lost all understanding of where he was and the direction he was headed. He bounced off a lamppost onto a wall, back into a road and perhaps someone helped him back onto the pavement; he didn't know. If he could have watched himself, he would have seen a man lurching forward, at times holding his head, weaving a zigzag path, banging into the walls of buildings and knocking his knees painfully when he fell down. He clambered his way back to his feet and staggered on, his trousers torn, hands grazed, and all the while aware of bullets whizzing past his ears and a low, animal-like scream that he knew was his.

And suddenly hands were upon him. 'Hey, drunkard!' he heard.

'Help me, please,' he thought he murmured, but Tom was vaguely aware of whispering and low laughter; fingers rummaging through pockets. He thought he heard 'Stupid sod' as he was thrown backwards but the words were lost as he lurched on and away from the battlefield of Piccadilly Circus, machine-gun fire and blood chasing him.

He hurried. Away from guns and explosions. *Find the trench!* Tom carried in his mind. He broke into a run. *Get to the dugout!* The surrounds were definitely quieting – perhaps he had cleared no-man's-land? His breathing was ragged and he was nauseous and dizzy; was he choking? Was it poison gas? His limbs were so numb now that only the pins and needles in his fingers and around his neck assured him he had any feeling at all. His vision had reduced to a tiny circle and even that was blurring now. At least he couldn't hear the battlefield any longer. Everything had become quiet, save odd, polite voices punching through his disorientation.

'I say, old chap, are you all right?'

'Good heavens, man! Whatever is the matter with you?'

But the words strung together and sounded like they were coming from the bottom of a grave, as though everyone was buried alive, the corpses trying to speak to him, warn him that Edie was waiting. He had to get back to Edie. Their baby was due. Abe wouldn't forgive. His fears would be confirmed.

Should have married Ben Levi.

Tom's body was running with perspiration, his shirt clung damply to him. An afternoon wind gleefully blew her cool breath and he began to shiver helplessly.

He heard one last voice.

'Hey! Look out!'

He had a final thought – a single word that came to mind. *Eden.* He saw a garden of safety that he lurched towards. Tom felt one final blow as he staggered in the direction of his haven.

The driver of the vehicle that had just entered Savile Row saw the drunk, swerved to miss him but the back of the big, solid Crossley 20/25 clipped him, spinning him and propelling him into a nearby lamppost. The taxi driver looked back in horror to see the man hit his head against the iron and bounce off to collapse alongside the Victorian iron fretwork fence on the pavement outside Poole & Co.

And in that moment, Tom died.

12

Edie heard the slightly unpleasant scraping sound that accompanied the tugging sensation on her hair, which had been combed out to sit at her shoulderblades. Deep down she wasn't scared of having her hair cut; the truth was she wanted it desperately because she knew how fashionable it was, but she was anxious at how Tom would react. She had seen that the short bob cut had not only transformed the appearance of American women but she knew it would forever change the clothes they wore.

Short hair was the immediate future and meant so much more than simply a new style. It spoke of a new freedom coming for women and it was not only a release from the long skirt and tight bodices but would also show itself in eye-poppingly daring haircuts that released women from their pins and clips, buns and ponytails, ringlets and rags. Suddenly women could look tomboyish if they chose, but they could style that short hair by night to be dazzlingly elegant with diamante headbands or pearl decorations; they could crimp it, wave it or wear it in a daringly elfin way.

'You're sure, aren't you, Edie?' Delia asked with a sudden attack of doubt.

'Too late, *ma cherie*,' Madeleine chuckled and Edie felt a hank of her hair give. She stole a glance at the offcuts on the floor and saw in them the death of Edie Valentine, and in her soul felt the surge of her hidden self – the more daring, driven and exotic Eden Valentine pushing through.

Madeleine made a few more dramatic cuts before she squeezed Edie's shoulders. 'All gone,' she murmured close to her ear, but not unkindly. 'I have to tidy it up yet,' she warned, straightening from where she had been bent, scrutinising the sharp line at Edie's nape. 'But here. Take a look at yourself with short hair.' She gave Edie a hand mirror.

And as Edie saw the stranger appear in the glass to stare back at her, she felt as though her heart stilled. It became momentarily difficult to breathe. This was how Tom would feel when he found the courage to shave. This is what he was afraid of – seeing a new person . . . or, more likely, remembering an old one.

In that moment she felt a pain alarming through her.

'Say something,' Delia pleaded, her expression filled with worry.

'Something's happened,' Edie whispered in shock, reaching for her belly. She couldn't explain it. But it had felt as though the world at that moment had, in that desperately painful heartbeat, fallen out of kilter for her. She was aware of her companions frowning at her but she couldn't find the right words. After waiting, they both began speaking at once, while she struggled to draw a frightening breath.

'What are you talking about?'

'Is it the baby?'

Edie shook her head. 'I . . . I don't know. I feel strange.' She clutched her hand to her chest.

'Are you ill, Eden?' Madeleine asked, crouching before her. Suddenly Madeleine's cool blue gaze felt calming; no longer gently mocking but solid and dependable.

Delia had hurried to pour Edie a glass of water. 'Drink, Edie. You look like a ghost walked over your grave.'

'I think it did,' Edie admitted, gulping down the water to moisten her throat that felt suddenly dry and choked.

'You can grow it out,' Madeleine offered, her expression softening with concern.

She shook her head. 'It's not my hair. I can't explain it. It just felt as though my heart skipped a beat or stopped . . . it hurt.'

The women exchanged a glance.

'Heart? Have you been ill recently?' Delia wondered.

She was returning to normal, could think more clearly. 'No. Something's happened . . .'

'Your baby —' Madeleine began, sounding scared for her. 'Is it perhaps a first sign of labour? What do they call those warning cramps?'

Edie suddenly froze in fear. 'He's . . .'

Her friends shared another worried look. Madeleine put the scissors on the floor and they both waited. 'Eden?' she murmured, her expression tense.

'He's all right,' she suddenly breathed out in a shaking voice. 'He's kicking. It's not labour. My waters haven't broken. There's no pain.'

Delia's hand flew to her chest to cover her own tripping heart.

'Your child is fine,' Madeleine said calmly. 'Your hair is lovely. Your pie is beautiful,' she continued and Edie half laughed, half wept. 'All is well,' Madeleine steadied. 'You just panicked, perhaps in your dismay, to see your hair gone, but it suits you more than you can imagine.' She grinned.

'That's right,' Delia soothed.

'Don't you just look so amazing?' Madeleine said, holding up Edie's mirror again. 'Look!'

Edie blinked back the worry. She didn't want to go with her thoughts, which desperately wanted to lead her to Tom in London . . . alone. 'I do love it, Madeleine,' she admitted truthfully. 'And everyone will have to get used to it.'

'Well, they have no choice now, do they?' Delia remarked, sweeping away Edie's hair.

Edie found a small but genuine laugh. 'Put the kettle on, Del. I'll make some tea.'

Madeleine tutted. 'Delia can make the tea. I haven't finished with you yet. I want you looking ravishing tonight for that handsome man of yours.'

———

People hurried to the fallen man.

'He staggered into my path,' the taxi driver bleated, his complexion grey, voice unsteady.

'I saw it,' someone reassured. 'It was not your fault.'

There were only two women in the huddle and they both looked distraught, one dabbing at her eyes with a lacy handkerchief.

'Oh, Geoffrey, he's dead.'

'Now, now, dear. We can't be sure.'

'Make way, please. I am a doctor,' came a voice from the back. A man pushed through. His fiercely white thatch of hair, precisely trimmed, distinguished him from the rest of the fine folk straining for a peek at the dead man.

'Oh, I say, Sir, you're half dressed,' said Geoffrey.

'I'm with my tailor having a suit fitted at Poole's, if you don't mind,' he countered, sounding indignant. 'I'm Dr John Cavendish of Harley Street. Now, please, if you good people would not mind giving this man and me some air.'

'Is he dead?' someone asked.

'It's what I'm trying to establish,' Cavendish snipped.

Tailors began spilling out of the salons with measuring tapes strung around their necks; one carried a long ruler, another still had pins in his mouth. All were dressed in either dark grey or black and the cut of their clothes was unmistakably fine, even though they had arrived in shirtsleeves.

'Dr Cavendish, Sir?' one man said now. His moustache, which looked as though it had been drawn over his top lip by a stroke of charcoal, twitched in worry to see his client kneeling on the pavement in his yet-to-be-finished evening suit.

Cavendish had his fingers to the victim's neck, straining for the silence he needed. Finally he nodded. 'The fellow's not dead. He's been knocked unconscious.'

There were sighs of relief all round.

'Who saw what happened?'

Several people began explaining at once and Cavendish looked pained as he tried to make sense of it. 'On the lamppost, you say?' he repeated.

A man nodded. 'Charles Rainsford,' he offered. 'I work in the city. I was just leaving Gieves & Hawkes when this man, clearly drunk, staggered around the corner, bumping into me. I called out to him, wanted to give him a piece of my mind. The cabbie swerved to miss the blaggard but unfortunately it caught him on the shoulder and he spun as described, hitting his head on the post. I couldn't see whether it was chin or forehead, to be honest.'

'Thank you,' Cavendish said. 'But this man is not intoxicated. I smell no liquor on him.'

A murmur rippled through the onlookers.

'What the hell was he doing lurching around like that, then?' Rainsford demanded.

'Well, that's what I aim to establish,' Cavendish said in a clipped tone. 'George, do you have any smelling salts in the shop, please?'

A youngish man in shirtsleeves and waistcoat nodded. 'Yes, of course, Doctor. Back in a jiff.' He hurried away and up the small stairs into one of the tailoring doorways.

A distinguished-looking man with a fashionably thin moustache had shouldered his way to the front of the small crowd. He had a military bearing with precisely cut dark hair lightening to silver, like steel wool. He opened his mouth to speak, when George returned with a squat dark-brown bottle of Mackenzies salts.

'Here, Dr Cavendish,' he said, eagerly.

Cavendish unscrewed the lid, pulling a tight face as he tentatively smelled from the open bottle. 'Yes,' he coughed. 'They're fresh.' He waved the open bottle just beneath the prone man's nose. 'Come on now, my good fellow. Inhale.'

Everyone waited.

'Excuse me, Doctor,' a new voice punctuated the tense silence.

Cavendish looked up at the man with silvered hair and thin moustache.

'I was just passing, Sir, but I am Percival Fitch.' When the doctor blinked, the man continued. 'Er, from Anderson & Sheppard,' he said, pointing vaguely over his shoulder. 'I recognise this gentleman.' He nodded towards the fallen man, who at that moment groaned, coughed and twisted his head away from the offending vapours.

The onlookers uttered small gasps of relief.

'Steady now,' Cavendish soothed. 'You've been knocked out. We're trying to help.'

The man's eyes opened and his expression was wild at first, then grew frightened. His look turned quickly to dismay as he took in his surrounds.

'What the hell happened?' he croaked.

The doctor repeated what they knew briefly. 'How do you feel?'

'Embarrassed,' he said, looking around, pushing himself up on his elbows. 'Hello, Fitch. Help me up. There's a good sport.'

'I think you should —' Cavendish began.

'Nonsense. I took enough hits in the trenches to be able to bounce back from tripping over in Savile Row. How bloody ridiculous I must look. I'm sorry for the nuisance, everyone. I'm fine, just a bit bruised,' he assured, rubbing his shoulder before touching a spot beneath his chin. 'Please, no more fuss.'

'As you wish. I'm Dr John Cavendish,' he said, pushing himself up to stand, grimacing at the crack from his knees as he watched the man brush himself down as people began to lift their hats in farewell and drift away now that the drama was over. 'How many fingers am I holding up?' Cavendish said.

'Four,' the man replied, sounding bored.

'Both hands, please,' Cavendish prompted.

'Seven,' came the reply in a slightly more irritated tone.

'And you can remember your name?' Cavendish asked, as though moving through a stock series of questions.

The man glared at him, straightening his tie. 'Yes. I don't think that's beyond me, Dr Cavendish. I'm Alexander Wynter.' He nodded at Fitch. 'Whatever are these clothes I'm wearing, Fitch? I never wear navy.'

'No, Sir. But I did not make that suit for you, Mr Wynter.'

'Really?'

Fitch gave a small, apologetic shrug. 'No, Mr Wynter, although even from a distance it looks finely made, perhaps a bit snug, if you don't mind my saying so?'

Wynter nodded. 'But you make all my suits, Fitch.' He frowned.

Fitch gave a polite shrug. 'We haven't seen you in years, Sir.'

The man stared at him, perplexed, as though Fitch had just said that it no longer rained in England.

'The war changed business for us, Mr Wynter.' Fitch sighed. 'So many of our clients never returned. I thought you might have been one of the lost.' He blinked rapidly and cleared his throat in apology. 'Forgive me.'

'No, no, don't mention it. Er . . . what date is it?'

'September 30, Sir.'

'Ah. Good. Er . . . and the year?'

Both men stared at him with astonishment.

Cavendish spoke first. 'It's 1920. Why don't you know this?'

Wynter grinned but not before the doctor saw shock dance through his expression. 'Feeling a bit befuddled, I suppose, from the knock,' Wynter admitted. 'Maybe I should get myself checked.'

'Come with me now, Mr Wynter. I'm on my way to Harley Street directly. I was going to take a taxi.'

'I have my own doctor, Sir. Lloyd Rathbone usually looks after our family.'

'I know Lloyd,' Cavendish nodded. 'He's away on a tour of Europe, as I understand it. Let me satisfy myself by giving you a proper examination in my rooms, or I will not feel comfortable letting you leave my care.'

Wynter sighed dramatically. 'All right, if it would make you sleep easier tonight.'

'It would.'

'Fitch, this suit is rather untidy now and I've just noticed a small tear at the knee.'

'I noticed it too,' Fitch said carefully.

'I don't suppose you'd have —'

'Well, Sir, in a curious coincidence, I do happen to have a suit for you. You had one measured up in 1915 just before you left and told me to have it ready for your return. I won't be long, you said to me,' Fitch quoted sadly.

'Five years,' Wynter murmured.

'It will fit you, Mr Wynter, of that I have no doubt. I don't believe you've put on an ounce in the time you've been gone; if anything, you look a bit leaner.'

'Only you would know, Fitch. You have a suit. How marvellous.' Wynter sounded delighted.

'On your account and still hanging in its suit bag; I always hoped you would collect it, Sir,' Fitch said, and then cleared his throat lest he sound emotional. 'Er, forgive me. Too few have returned.'

Alexander Wynter defied his name and beamed Fitch a summery smile before turning to Cavendish. 'Indulge me, Cavendish. Let me change out of this stained and damaged suit.'

'Of course. I'll hail a taxi and meet you in Old Burlington Street.'

Wynter nodded his thanks and followed Mr Fitch to the tailoring haven of Anderson & Sheppard, which had clearly once been a grand home in a previous century, and probably doctors' rooms before being infiltrated by the tailoring community. All the surgeons had fled from the crush of clothiers into Harley Street and now this whole neighbourhood of London was given over to the wardrobing of gentlemen and royalty.

As they approached the store, Wynter appreciated the warren of tailoring shops and salons that had clustered into the tiny region of London, all with their specialties. Some started out as helmet and hat makers – like Thomas Hawkes, who formed the partnership of Gieves & Hawkes at Number One Savile Row. Others began as providers of hunting silks and pinks or ceremonial dress for royals and other dignitaries.

They comprised mainly three-storey houses with a garret and a basement. Mr Fitch's tailoring home sprawled through all three levels. Wynter knew that seamstresses were in the garret, where the daylight was good for the buttonholing and finishing jobs that required small, nimble hands and a deft touch. Meanwhile the basement usually housed the cutting team and patternmakers, where plenty of sunlight filtered down into the tiny courtyard below street level and through the tall windows directly onto the cutting table.

The familiar plum-coloured brick beckoned and Wynter used the pretty iron railing to steady his climb up the short flight of stairs into the tailoring salon. He didn't really want to admit that his head was still feeling 'fuzzy', which was the only way he could describe it.

Panelled timber walls and a marble fireplace welcomed him into the club-like interior.

'Ah, that's better,' Fitch said. 'Elton?'

A younger man appeared. 'Mr Wynter, Sir!' His eyes were wide with astonishment and delight. 'How wonderful to welcome you back into the salon!'

Their visitor stood with his back to the unlit fireplace. 'It's damn good to be back, Elton. You made it home as well. How are you?'

'Oh, as you see, all in one piece, Sir, thank you.'

'Where did you end up?'

'In Italy, Sir. But it's good to be home. I married my sweetheart, Sally. She's expecting our first any minute. You must be just as pleased to be home too.'

'Good lad,' Wynter said, not wanting to admit he had no idea what home felt like these days.

'Mr Elton, would you fetch Mr Wynter's suit, please, and ask Yardley to bring something warm to drink. Tea, Sir?'

He considered it. 'Better not,' Wynter said, reaching for his fob that wasn't there. 'Odd,' he murmured. 'Um, Dr Cavendish is waiting.'

'Oh, yes, of course,' Fitch replied. 'Mr Wynter, if you'll follow me, we'll get you out of your clothes in the back room.'

Within minutes, Fitch had him re-dressed in a dark charcoal-coloured suit of impeccable cut. Wynter knew he had a long torso but so did Fitch and that was reflected in the perfect image he saw in the mirror as Fitch swept a brush across his client's shoulders.

'Excellent, Sir. I'm thrilled. Of course, back in 1915 you were something of a visionary with suiting and knew this styling, though daring, was the future. Your splendid father came with you that day. Do you remember, Sir?'

Father? 'Ah yes, of course,' Wynter said, as pre-war memories began to flood back into his mind. He took a slow breath to stop himself feeling overwhelmed. He was suddenly desperate to see his father, Thomas Fineas Wynter.

'Your father was having his new morning suit measured and I don't know if you recall how horrified he was by your choice.' Fitch chuckled and Wynter had to follow. 'Anyway, Sir, for your next suit we'll be putting cuffs on the trousers, wider lapels, I suspect, and the jacket will go double-breasted.'

'Really?'

'You always liked to stay at the front of the new cuts.'

'Whatever you say, Fitch. Thank you for the shirt and tie, too.'

'Don't mention it, Mr Wynter. We selected everything before you . . . um, at the last fitting. And this looks extremely sharp, if I may say so. Plus the colour is very you, Sir.'

Wynter smiled. 'Well, I'd better dash, old boy. Thank you again. Er, payment?'

'Already paid, Sir.'

'Excellent. Dr Cavendish will be getting impatient, I suspect.'

'Um, what about the old suit, Sir?'

'I have no need for it.'

'I shall repair it and give it to the poor house, if that's all right with you? There are plenty of men in need.'

'Of course,' Wynter said, covering his embarrassment that he hadn't thought that far himself. If Fitch only realised the truth, he'd know that his client was barely thinking at all. The world felt like a horribly strange place and it was all he could do to just keep track of this conversation. It was 1920! What had happened since 1917, when he had been standing in a trench trying to bolster the spirits of demoralised men?

'I'll see you out, Mr Wynter. Please visit again soon. I'm sure you'll be wanting some new garments for autumn, perhaps even a new winter coat?'

'Oh, absolutely.' Wynter lifted a hand to Cavendish waiting in a taxi.

'I hope that's not the one that hit you, Sir,' Fitch remarked, making a good attempt at a parting jest.

'Indeed.' He shook the man's hand. 'See you soon, Fitch.'

'You will, Sir. Thank you.'

He clambered into the car. 'Thank you, Cavendish.'

'Not at all. It wouldn't sit easily on my conscience if we didn't do this. Harley Street, please,' he said and tapped his walking cane on the window between them and the driver. 'Hope this isn't the same fellow who clipped you,' he mumbled.

———

Later, in Cavendish's rooms, the doctor frowned at him.

'So, what's the verdict?' Wynter asked.

'So far, so good; you're in sound physical health, although I notice a limp?'

'Shrapnel,' Wynter offered wearily, taking a guess.

'Where were you?'

'Ypres.' He chuckled with no mirth. 'The generals liked to break it down into battles. For us in the trenches it was just one long war. But for the purposes of bureaucratic accuracy, I sustained this injury in what the military called the Third Battle.' He'd guessed at the last bit – it seemed obvious enough, although he wished he could remember more than simply that it was close to the end of 1917, there was constant shelling, a determined press to take the town of Passchendaele, and clay soil that had turned their lives into an endless mudslide.

The doctor reached for his stethoscope, which he placed

around his neck in a fluid motion. 'Go on,' he encouraged as he began setting up some equipment from a shiny oblong tin box.

Wynter frowned as he recalled the images. 'We were running in formation across no-man's-land; a shell exploded nearby and the blast hurled me into a ditch.' His gaze narrowed as though he was trying to see it all over again from the horizon of his mind. 'It was extremely deep and littered with corpses and dying men; awful sounds of pain, pleading for their mothers; most of them so young.'

The doctor nodded as he set up his blood pressure contraption.

'Shrapnel and bullets were whizzing overhead and the ground was shaking with constant shelling. I didn't expect to survive beyond the next few minutes anyway and thought I'd claw my way out and at least get off a few more rounds with the brave lads on top.'

The doctor put a finger to his lips as he put his stethoscope into his ears. Wynter listened to the cuff wheezing to full inflation and felt the slightly numb sensation in his arm. Cavendish continued listening, seemingly content with what he'd heard, and began unravelling the cuff. 'Please continue.'

Wynter shrugged. 'Nothing more to tell. I . . . well, I think there was another enormous explosion, another direct hit on the trench. I don't know how I'm here to tell the tale, to be honest, but I suppose I was knocked out for a while as I can't remember much more of that day.'

'Indeed, you are a fortunate fellow,' the doctor agreed, giving a sigh. 'Blood pressure's up but that's to be expected. All in all, you seem in jolly decent shape. You'll have a bruise there tomorrow,' he said, pointing beneath his patient's chin, 'and I suspect it will feel rather tender for a while.'

'Ouch!' Wynter complained.

'Mmm, sorry about that.' He frowned. 'And your shoulder is obviously painful. It's not broken or dislocated. Time will heal it.'

Cavendish blew out a breath. 'So, Wynter, I can work out everything that happened to make you unconscious in Savile Row, I just can't work out what happened immediately prior. Care to enlighten me?'

Wynter stared back at him unblinking. 'I'm afraid I cannot.'

The doctor's expression was one of confusion. 'Why can't you remember?'

He shrugged. 'I'm at a loss.'

Cavendish's gaze narrowed. 'What's going on, Wynter? Tell me. I will help.'

'That's just it. I can't remember anything to tell.'

'I don't understand.'

'I remember nothing else . . . except the grave. After that . . . nothing much at all until now.'

The doctor stared at him over his glasses. 'Are you telling me you can't remember coming home?'

He shook his head. 'Nothing since I saw dear old Johnny Four Fingers explode into mist where his body had formerly stood and only minutes earlier had made me a mug of tea . . .'

'Good heavens! Complete memory loss?'

He nodded. 'Probably. Is amnesia common?'

'There's no stigma in calling it for what it likely is, Wynter. Shellshock is far more common than people realise in our brave returned soldiers.'

Wynter shrugged. 'Frankly, I'm astonished to find myself here. It's as though I've lost a chunk of my life. My last clear memory is the trench during the battle. After that, nothing.'

'How intriguing,' Cavendish said, in spite of his concern. 'So we have no clue as to why you came to be in London or in Savile Row?'

He shook his head. 'I have no idea what I'm doing back in England, Cavendish! Why am I in London? Why am I staggering around when you can tell I haven't been drinking? My family home is in Sussex but I've no memory of being there.'

'You can't remember your family . . . I mean, seeing them?'

'No. And to be honest, it was only when the tailor mentioned my father that I realised the last time I remember seeing him was hugging him on the steps of Larksfell.'

'Oh, of course, Larksfell Hall,' Cavendish remarked, frowning. 'I believe my cousin may know your family. Richard Bosworth.'

Wynter grinned. 'Dickie Bosworth? He and my father go back.'

'So, which date is your last memory?'

'October 12, 1917 is the day I recall. We were sandwiched between the Anzacs – New Zealanders to the left of us, Aussies to the right – with a mind to assault the Passchendaele Ridge and capture the village itself. There were thickets of barbed wire stretching out either side of us, thirty-feet deep. Behind them German machine-gun posts populated the area and deeper into the valley were concrete strongholds of Germans spotting the ugly marshland that both sides were giving up a generation of our young men for. In truth, the Anzacs had already relieved most of our Tommies in the front line. We desperately needed some relief from the onslaught. My men were spent, morale was as low as it had ever been, numbers were shockingly depleted, food was appalling and weather conditions more hellish than anyone back home could even dream in their worst nightmares.'

Cavendish watched Wynter's gaze drift as though seeing an image far away and his tone turned dreamy. 'The winds had escalated during the previous evening. It was as though hurricanes were battering us as storms lashed across Flanders. The troops were exhausted and this extra beating from the weather felt like the final straw. Our boys trudged along the duckboard tracks we'd constructed so we could cover the boggy ground faster. Without them we'd sink halfway to our knees.' He shook his head. 'I assured my lads that the edict from above was that attacks would only be pressed when the weather favoured it. Experience should have taught us once and for all how futile it is to throw the men into full assault under unfavourable conditions. Men get isolated, bogged, exhausted twice as fast, disoriented quickly as vision decreases; they get trapped in hopeless positions with no advantage . . . whole units get wiped out,' Wynter recalled passionately.

Then his voice turned toneless. 'Of course, that was the agreement in principle, but the reality was that our generals pushed ahead despite all of the experience and hard-won knowledge . . . and all the pointless deaths of bright, brave young men. The pressure was on to take the village after years of trying.' He gave a choked laugh. 'I think they rather hoped that the enemy's vigilance would be disrupted by the violence of the storm and that in some fairyland of their thoughts, they really believed that the Germans might be taken unawares.'

Wynter blinked, coming out of his memories. He shook his head as though he didn't want to continue speaking. Cavendish stared at him silently, enthralled.

'We dug in but digging into water is a contradiction in terms. Stiff from the freezing cold, our men never had much of a chance. Pitch dark, our superiors wanted us to leap over the top, pre-dawn, into a raging wind, while they drank brandy probably and pored over maps like schoolboys pushing around their tin soldiers!' His tone had turned to full disgust. 'Germans had the high ground. It was all so pointless. We didn't even know they'd brought in fresh divisions. The men and I did our duty and most died for it. I got lucky again. I was one of the first over the top, heard the spray of machine-gun fire, kept running far longer than I thought I might, and then there was an almighty explosion.' He rubbed his face as if trying to wipe the memory of it. 'And then I told you how I was buried alive. Don't ask me how they found me. I was losing consciousness again so I wasn't aware of drawing any attention to myself. I have no idea precisely how long I lay there in the mud, slowly suffocating. I genuinely have no memory of time – it seemed to all happen in a few heartbeats. Everything is lost to me from that explosion; actually that's not true. I have a hazy recollection of a surgeon, drugs and fever. And I'm sure I recall somewhere in my stupor overhearing about the slaughter.'

Cavendish nodded. 'One of our darkest days. I followed the war closely. Two of my best friends were at Passchendaele.'

'Did they make it?'

Cavendish closed the equipment tin. 'You can roll down your sleeve, get dressed,' he said. 'Only Clifton returned. I was in one of those field hospitals supporting the Western Front. I saw much suffering and fully understand what you're describing, but that battle was one of the worst, according to Donald. Nearly half a million lives lost. The Australians and New Zealanders were worst hit; the Aussies lost nearly twenty-six thousand of their young braves in just one month, although Don said the Anzacs were incredibly courageous, as were the Canadians.'

Both men remained silent momentarily, lost in bleak thought.

'Nothing else coming to mind?'

Wynter shook his head truthfully.

'Well, I think we should get you reunited with your family. I don't see any immediate medical complications from today's events but you need some quiet and rest. Concussion is a strange thing; you may feel fine but you could feel vaguely unwell for days – weak, too, perhaps.'

There was a soft knock at the door and Cavendish's assistant appeared.

'Yes, Miss Appleyard?'

'Forgive me, Dr Cavendish, but a Mr Percival Fitch from Anderson & Sheppard left a note and this small envelope. One of his delivery boys just dropped it off.'

Wynter swung around. 'Is it for me?'

'Perhaps,' the woman said. She handed the small package to Cavendish.

He put on his glasses and read the note aloud. '*I presume Mr Wynter has his wallet and other private accoutrements but I took the liberty of checking all the pockets of the suit he left behind. In the inside security pocket I found this, which I am returning. I do hope we have not missed him. Sincerely, Percival Fitch.*' Cavendish took off his glasses again and handed an even smaller envelope to Wynter.

Wynter looked confused as he broke the seal and looked inside. His frown deepened as he pulled out a small, red handkerchief. He blinked and unfolded it to reveal a heart-shaped gap in the middle.

Miss Appleyard had to stifle a smile. 'Excuse me,' she said, and quietly left.

'Good grief, man. Doesn't that mean anything to you?'

Wynter shrugged. 'Nothing. Why ever would I be carrying that around?'

'Well, it certainly points to being specific.'

'I have never carried a red handkerchief in my life.'

'Well, clearly you have been walking around with one and its heart is missing.'

Wynter cut him an unhappy glare.

'Too sentimental for you?' Cavendish quipped. The doctor took the handkerchief and stared at it. 'Neatly done. The edge has been sewn to prevent fraying. All quite deliberate.'

Wynter nodded as he pulled on his jacket. 'It's still meaningless.' He felt in his pockets. 'Heavens! I have no money . . . I have nothing, in fact, to pay you —' He looked mortified. 'Wandering around with no money, no identification at all and a red handkerchief cut with a heart shape? I must be going mad.' He gave a sound of half disgust, half despair. 'This story becomes stranger by the moment.'

Cavendish waved his words away. 'I'll organise it all. We can settle up anytime.' He pressed a button on the desk. 'Miss Appleyard?'

She reappeared. 'Yes, Doctor?'

'Can you organise a driver, please, on my account to deliver Mr Wynter back to his address in Sussex?'

'Now, Doctor?'

'Ready to go home, Mr Wynter?' Cavendish asked, sensing the difficult crossroads his patient faced.

'I have nowhere else to be,' Wynter admitted. 'Thank you for your generosity.'

Cavendish nodded at his assistant and she closed the door. 'Come and see me again. With your own doctor away, I'll be glad to assist anytime, especially if you remember what has occurred. I think it would be helpful to get to the bottom of what prompted your arrival in Savile Row. If nothing else, it will surely provide some insight as to where you have been these last couple of years . . . and why you have that handkerchief; why you were wearing a well-cut suit you didn't recognise and so on.'

Wynter ran a hand through his dark hair, smoothing it back from where a hank had fallen forward. 'It would be very good to learn where I've been for the last few years, Cavendish. But not yet. I need to cope with where I am now and what's ahead.'

'Small steps. I completely agree. You must give yourself time, Wynter.'

He shook hands with the doctor. 'You've been extremely kind.'

The man tutted. 'Nonsense. It's my job. And you're an intriguing case. I . . . er, I hope the reunion is not too daunting. Here, Wynter, take my card. Stay in touch.'

13

Edie paced, distraught. Abe had given up trying to soothe his daughter over her husband's tardiness; he was offering all the right placations and yet he grudgingly accepted that a couple in love share intangible rhythms. He couldn't explain it – perhaps a biologist, or even one of those new types of philosophers or theologians who called themselves psychologists could. It didn't need explaining, though. He'd experienced it with Nina himself.

In Edie's case she was murmuring repeatedly, 'I just know something is wrong.' Abe was now resigned that perhaps she did know, and given they understood so little about Tom's background, perhaps no one should be entirely shocked by a disappearance.

It had been hours and Shabbat had begun; Abe didn't doubt that this man adored his daughter and fully respected her faith. Tom would not be late for Shabbat, even if he was a gentile. Abe liked to think Tom even wore a beard to emulate the preferred masculine appearance for his adopted family. He pursed his lips in sorrow to see his daughter suffering as she stared out of the window once more in what he was fast becoming sure was a vain hope for sighting her husband.

Since Tom had come into her life Edie always had a ready smile and laughter was itching to erupt. Even a look across a room from Tom could amuse Edie; they needed no words. She had made herself a new wardrobe of clothes for her pregnancy, all beautifully styled and cut. Abe imagined she probably had a drawer full of baby clothes she'd been sewing as well. The little one would be the best-dressed baby in England, he was convinced of it.

His grandchild. Abe's heart sang at the notion. A new generation of Valentines; he hoped it might be a boy, after their Daniel.

In the doorway a tall Frenchwoman unobtrusively made pots of tea, never partaking of the seemingly endless cups she'd poured since Abe had arrived at his family's cottage at four p.m. The statuesque woman walked as though she floated across the flagstones.

'Can I get you anything, Mr Valentine?' Madeleine asked.

'No, dear, you've been most attentive.'

She gave a small sigh. 'I prefer to be busy.'

'How long have you known my daughter?'

'I met her only today. Do you like her hair?'

'It was a shock. I prefer her long hair, like her mother's.'

'But you don't dislike it?' she offered with a slight smile.

'No, I don't dislike it.' He wanted to say he didn't understand it. 'I can't dislike anything about Edie.'

She nodded. 'I believe she and I will be good friends. I like honest people. Eden is true.'

He frowned. 'So you don't know Tom?'

Madeleine shrugged. 'I have never seen him. I don't live on this side of Epping, although it's pretty enough. Maybe I should move.' She smiled lazily as if teasing him. 'She couldn't even show me a wedding picture of them.'

Abe muttered a curse. 'One of those unlucky things. They had some lovely memories recorded.'

'What happened?'

'A fire at the photographer's studio,' Edie said, back inside and on another pacing circuit of the cottage. 'We lost all the film and Tom refused to have any more taken.' She sighed. 'He's agreed we'll have some photographs with our child when he or she arrives.' She rubbed her belly absently and moved away from them.

The clock on the mantelpiece – one of Abe's wedding gifts to his daughter – ticked past nine p.m. but only now twilight was surrendering. No one had eaten and Abe had said private prayers for Shabbat over a piece of bread and butter, which was all he was prepared to eat despite Edie's weary encouragement. Meanwhile she refused anything but the odd sip of tea.

Abe stepped outside into the mild evening, made cooler only because it was so clear, and a dome of dark velvet, still a burnished pink at its furthest reaches from the scattered sunlight, looked studded by diamonds. He privately marvelled at the night sky in the country, which gave a gift of the heavens often so hard to see against the concentrated artificial lighting of London. He had to admit, he understood Edie's joy of this place.

Edie was in and out of London regularly – at least twice a week – to be briefed on various jobs, do some shopping and pay visits to the community that missed her; he had her work delivered by horse and cart but he wondered now how life would change once the baby arrived. He saw movement ahead. His attention snapped fully to the shadowy figure approaching. Was it Tom? His heart leapt with hope and the thought that his son-in-law had better have a good reason for keeping them all so worried.

Abe had accepted his new son-in-law with grace, commiserated with the Levi family, shaking his head, shrugging, sighing, apologising far too often for his daughter's seemingly outrageous decision to marry out of her faith. Samuel accepted as Samuel always would, but he suspected Dena was unforgiving, while Ben refused to discuss it. And so they hadn't talked about it again. They were all polite but the sense of family that years of friendship had achieved was lost when Edie had accepted Tom's marriage proposal and thus refused Benjamin. Edie's refusal was at every gathering; it haunted every conversation he shared with Ben or Dena and yet each wore smiles, asked politely after Edie – but never Tom – and even went through motions of congratulations when he had been forced to yield the information of her pregnancy.

Even though it had been the wisest decision for Edie to leave the neighbourhood, he loathed that his precious daughter had left Golders Green. Nevertheless even on his first visit to this tumbledown cottage he could feel the love within it and sensed how much Edie enjoyed her new-found nesting instincts. She'd turned the cottage quickly into a home: running up curtains, covering old furniture he'd given them and making them look new again. She'd made bedspreads and sewn bright tablecloths. Yes, he was the first to admit that his daughter had never looked happier or more content since her wedding to Tom. A needle of familiar remorse pricked that he'd ever made his beautiful girl feel such guilt over Benjamin Levi.

Edie and Tom had been so eager to marry that the engagement had been little more than formality. Abe had always dreamed of his daughter marrying beneath the *chuppah*, but that would never be permitted. Instead, Abe had needed to wrap his mind around his daughter being married in a registry office. Given the sorrows of that night in November, Abe just wanted the sad fracture of friendship and faith behind him. By January he had accepted that Edie had never looked brighter or happier, and he was not prepared to lose his only remaining child because of her modern attitude. Yes, he wanted his beautiful daughter surrounded by elders beneath the sunlight, but only Solly attended to witness the marriage, and yes, he'd looked forward to seeing Edie being led around her husband-to-be seven times as blessings were spoken. He had also wanted to see her husband stamp on the glass beneath the linen and break it. However, despite being denied all that, it didn't stop him setting aside his misgivings and murmuring, '*Mazel Tov!*' in congratulations when the civil ceremony declared Edie and Tom to be formally married. Abe had also cast a silent prayer that Tom would not break Edie's heart but remain true to her, for she had now given up her community for him. There was no dancing, no songs or party . . . just a simple celebration feast for the four of them above the shop as plans were made to leave Golders Green.

Abe pulled himself from his memories as the caped figure on a bicycle drew closer out of the darkness and into the thin light that Edie's open doorway afforded.

'Edie,' Abe called over his shoulder. 'The police constable is here.'

14

The taxi had left London behind a long time ago but they had moved off the main London-to-Brighton road and had been driving down country lanes for probably half an hour; Alex Wynter had lost track and had no watch. It was almost exactly how he remembered it, with tall hedgerows and narrow roads. A patchwork of meadows crisscrossed either side of them with softly undulating hills. They had passed woodlands with drifts of dandelions and rolled through villages with pubs that had yet to put their lights on because the days were so long now and the evenings so deliciously warm that men were drinking their ales outside.

'Beautiful part of the world,' the driver remarked. 'Not that I've seen much north of Liverpool or south of Brighton,' he quipped. 'How about you, Sir?'

'Oh, yes, I've travelled rather widely. The war made sure of that, but before the war I was certainly fortunate to see much of Europe before it was bombed.'

'I was told to take you to Larksfell Hall. That's right, isn't it?'

'Correct.'

'You may have to guide me. I know London like my own face but I'm not so reliable here. Are you familiar with the directions?'

'Certainly. I've lived there all my life. There's a sharp bend up ahead and then we'll be entering Larksfell land. The main gates are about half a mile in.'

'Righto, Sir.'

Once they rounded the bend all the surrounds became achingly familiar and Alex felt as though he'd never left. Even the English laurels flanking their path felt the same – no bigger or smaller, no bushier, but thirty-foot high sentinels that closed off the light of dusk and reminded Alex that he would be disturbing the family settling down for the night. He wondered who might be around . . . A new anxious thought occurred as the gatekeeper's cottage came into view: What if his brothers had died during the war? Douglas had been stationed in London when Alex was leaving for France – he may have been posted somewhere and suffered. Despite his youth, Rupert definitely would have enlisted. It was expected of the gentrified families. So many of the good young lives lost came from families like his . . . a generation of landowners and potential industrialists wiped out.

Larksfell Hall suddenly appeared as they cleared the laurel hedge, and Alex felt his heart thump once so hard he caught his breath. Home. A huge stone and gabled monument to Elizabethan architecture loomed ahead and Alex was instantly transported to the long, galleried reception rooms he'd ridden his tricycle through as a child. He could see the swallows swooping and wheeling above the house, getting ready to settle beneath the eaves for the night, and the sky was a brilliant deep blue, dying to purple, as their backdrop. The Wynter house looked magnificent – lights were glowing gently behind Renaissance-style small leaded windowpanes and his gaze searched for his suite of rooms. Far left on the first storey. Those rooms remained stubbornly darkened.

The emotion of seeing it again felt suffocating for that heartbeat and his throat choked momentarily. Boarding school, the fishing lodge in Lancashire, which he considered a second home because it prompted the happiest memories of being with his father and brothers and an uncle or two, and then the trenches were his only other places of abode.

Suddenly a shed in a small garden filled with old roses flashed into his mind and he blinked in surprise. The image was gone but in that bright moment, overriding the fragrance of rose perfume, he'd tasted sewing-machine oil, of all things. He knew that smell from his old Nanny's nook, as all the Wynter children had called her tiny wing near their nursery. Nanny sewed on her treadle machine for them, delighting in making pinafores for his sister and shirts for the boys. Nanny – with her sausage-like fingers – bathed them and fed them and comforted them whenever their parents were not around . . . and sometimes even when they were. He had loved Nanny as he had his own mother, never grasping until much later that she wasn't blood. But she was family to him . . . right up until the very day her kidneys failed and she was stolen from them. But it was not Nanny now who stuck in his mind. He shook his head in surprise at the unfamiliar picture that had lingered with the machine-oil smell . . . he then glimpsed a leather satchel, an old bicycle, women's shoes, a different sewing machine, a dressmaker's wax mannequin. He had no idea what it meant.

'What time is it, please?' The image snapped shut in his mind.

The taxi driver glanced at his watch. 'Nearing eight, Sir.'

Light was fading. 'Just pull up at the lodge, please. You can leave me there.'

'Are you sure, Sir? I'm happy to drive you all the way to the house.'

'No, I feel like a walk. Thank you so much. Er, will you be all right for getting back?'

'Yes, Sir. Don't you worry. I know my way now. I'll just keep my eyes peeled for hedgehogs and badgers.'

'And deer,' Alex warned as the car slowed to a halt.

The driver jumped out and opened the door for Alex, politely touching his hat. 'Goodnight, Sir.'

'Night,' Alex called and watched the car turn around laboriously before it rumbled off down the path of laurels.

The door to the gatekeeper's house was suddenly flung back.

'Who is it?'

'Clarence?'

'Name yourself, please. If you're a scavenger hoping for food, there'll be none to have tonight. Tomorrow, perhaps.'

'Clarrie, it's me.'

The elderly man squinted into the low light. 'Me? I don't know you from that stone pillar over there. You'll not be getting let in tonight, whoever you are,' he cautioned. 'The family is not entertaining.'

'Really? I never knew the Wynters to turn away family,' he quipped. Clarence looked like he'd aged more than a decade. His hair was wild and white, and pushed out of place from where he'd probably been napping in his faded armchair, which carried an imprint of the old fellow's backside. Where had that stoop come from? His hip appeared to be injured, judging by the way he limped, and Alex was reminded of his own limp, now so much a part of him he barely remembered it.

'Family? No guests tonight. And if you were closely associated with the family, you'd know that tonight of all nights is sacred to them.'

'Why is Friday so special?'

'Good grief, man. Get on with you! You're an insult. Leave them in peace. I'll fetch my shotgun if you're not careful.'

Alex laughed. 'Clarrie. For heaven's sake, man. It's Alex . . . Lex.' He sighed. 'Wynter!'

He watched the man's slightly rheumy gaze falter and guilt washed over him to see Clarrie's chin tremble.

'Captain Wynter?' he whispered.

'Oh, what's all this captain stuff, eh? I'm Lex to you, Clarrie,' he said, taking a stride and clutching the man into a bear hug. 'Mmm, still smoking Savinelli English Mixture, eh? I thought you were going to give up your pipe?'

Clarrie moved back to stare at him open-mouthed in the lowering light. 'Mr Alex . . .' he choked out in a shaking voice and Alex suddenly worried the man might suffer heart failure. He looked ready to crumple from shock.

'It's me,' he assured.

'Back from the dead,' Clarrie whispered, filled with disbelief.

He found a grin. 'Yes. You don't get rid of a Wynter that easily.'

Clarrie broke down and it hurt Alex's heart to see his dear old friend – a person he'd loved since early childhood, someone strong and gruff but always kind – weep on his behalf.

'Don't, Clarrie. I'm back now. Everything is going to be fine.'

'No, Master Alex. You're too late.'

'Too late?' He helped the old man to straighten, forced him to meet his gaze in the twilight. 'Too late for what?'

'For Lord Wynter, Sir. Your dear father passed away, and was buried yesterday.'

It was as though Clarrie had picked up a club and whipped it as hard as he could into Alex's belly. He gasped, as if needing to suddenly suck in a lungful of air. Alex lurched away to lean on one of the tall stone pillars that flanked the grand gates of Larksfell.

'I'm sorry, son.' Clarrie reached out, limping to him as though he was still uncertain whether or not the man bent and groaning before him was a ghost. 'He slipped away peacefully. The family was around him. No pain.'

'Why? Was he ill?'

The man shrugged. 'I believe he died of a broken heart, Master Lex, but that's likely not the official reason.' He cleared his throat. 'He was proud of his sons going off to war but he never came to terms with losing you at Ypres. He didn't say much to the family, Sir, but we had our quiet moments walking the property and . . . well, anyway, age finds us all out one way or another. I'll not be long behind him, I'm sure. And perhaps I don't want to be, now that Mr Thomas isn't around. We were boys together, you know . . . good friends, just born on different sides of the bed, if you get my meaning.'

Alex nodded, straightening but still wearing a haunted expression. 'My mother?'

'She's up at the house, grieving with the family.'

'My brothers are safe?'

'Oh, yes. Mr Douglas and Mr Rupert are well. Mr Rupert was injured but he's fully convalesced now.'

Relief shot through him, overriding the sadness of his father's passing. There would be the right time for grieving. All he wanted to do right now was hug the family that had survived the war. 'Oh, that's so good to hear,' he said. 'I'm sorry to bring more shock,' he said, speaking more to himself than to Clarrie.

'No, Sir. Your return is just what this house needs. Your father has been ailing for years. I'm sure Mr Bramson will fill you in.' Clarrie seemed to have gathered his wits and his voice sounded gruff again. 'Shall I let him know you're here, Sir?'

'Yes, please.'

'Would you like me to accompany you, Master Alex?'

He shook his head and squeezed the gatekeeper's shoulder. 'No, Clarrie. Just let Mr Bramson know ahead and I'll walk up slowly.'

'Right you are, Sir.' He grinned. 'So good to have you back, Master Alex.'

'Clarrie, one more thing. I'm in no hurry to meet everyone except my mother. Would you indulge me and hold off making the call to Bramson for a couple of hours?'

'Sir?'

'It's hard to explain. Tell Bramson to expect me but not immediately. When does everyone turn in?'

'Not for hours normally, Master Lex. But in this week of grieving I gather there have been no communal meals of an evening. Most are living in their rooms out of respect for your mother's mourning in particular.'

'What time is it, Clarrie?'

The old man checked his fob watch, holding the lantern over it. 'It's nearing eight-thirty, Sir.'

'I'll wait until ten.'

Alex sat on a favourite old tree stump and thought back over the strange day. He was glad to have this peace in the dark to arrange his thoughts and emotions. His father was gone. Where had he, the eldest son, been while his family gathered around as Wynter Senior took his final breath, believing his son lost in Ypres, buried beneath many feet of mud along with tens of thousands of other innocents?

There was nothing to be gained thinking like this. No amount of soul searching would bring his beloved father back. The main thing was that he was home now – better to push his energies into rebuilding the family and continuing its fortune-making than focusing on the past.

Easy to say. It felt impossible at this moment not to tease at whose life he'd been living since the injury. He had begun to think of him as the invisible man that would accompany him into every room he entered. And each time from here on that someone laid eyes on Alexander Wynter, they would also unknowingly gaze at the stranger and ask the inevitable question, 'Where has he been the last few years?'

But for now the man whose life he had been leading was mute and couldn't answer their query. And if there was one thing that Alex Wynter enjoyed unravelling, it was a mystery. He'd irritated his siblings by working out their magic tricks or finding them much too fast during a game of hide-and-seek, or spoiling the conjuror's show at the circus because he was always watching for the sleight of hand. It was hard to surprise him, too. Girls had been complaining since his teens that they could never give him anything that he didn't already have. They whined that he never showed delight at their gifts of silk scarves, or tickets to the ballet, or ludicrously expensive bottles of cognac.

'They should just give you a five-thousand-piece jigsaw puzzle, Lex,' his mother had once offered in her traditionally sardonic way. 'Hours of glee for you.'

His mother knew him too well, for everything money could buy was attainable for him – she also knew that people rarely impressed him either, especially by what they owned. Alex had to sadly admit to himself now that the array of glittering, gorgeous young things that vied for his attention tended to blend into a single pair of lips and a single slimline body sporting perfectly coiffed hair. Such women bored him because in general they were spoiled, used to having their own way and pouting to get it, remarkably heedless of the needs of people less fortunate.

'When you meet someone who surprises you, Lex, then you'll fall in love with her.'

'But where is she, Mother?'

He recalled how his still-beautiful mother had cut him her aqua gaze and shaken her head. 'Not in the circle you move in, darling.'

How right she was. He'd gone to war an eligible bachelor, despite one close call with Jemima Bartleby, where he had nearly agreed to settle down with a gorgeous woman who'd give him equally gorgeous children and be the perfect partner in every way except the one way that he needed, which was to be in love with her. He didn't desire a woman who wanted nothing. He wanted an equal, someone with ambition for herself and dreams of her own, someone with skills to admire and conversation that drifted from the hottest new luncheon spot to be seen in.

'I want that exhilarating feeling of love,' he'd once said to his mother. 'I'd jump off the cliff from boredom with Jemima.'

'Oh, darling, that's cruel. She can't help that she's dull. Look at her mother. She's a mouse. At least Jemima has tried to stand out. She's very beautiful.'

'Yes, but vacant. I spend days with her, and can't remember a thing she's said.'

'Money can't buy you that perfect chemistry, my darling. At least you've shown the courage not to settle for second best. I don't mind if you cast your wild oats far and wide, Lex, but do not be a man who cheats on his wife once you make your decision. That I will not tolerate. So once you have that heart-stopping moment of falling in love and knowing it's the right person, chase her, commit to her wholly.'

She was a formidable woman, Cecily Wynter. And she married a formidable man whom she adored; he envied them their relationship. And now that man was gone. He couldn't imagine how she was coping and yet he knew she would be the one displaying the composure that would set the tone for the rest of the family. She would be its strength. No one could ever accuse Cecily Wynter, née Gilford, of being anything but poised in every situation.

He wished he had his watch. Where could it be? Perhaps left beneath that same mud in a field in Flanders where he'd left his mind?

Alex sighed. Whatever the time was, he had put off this moment long enough. He pushed himself off the stump in the main grounds and approached the grand hall, hearing the soft crunch of his shoes on the sweeping gravel drive, on which he remembered spinning the wheels of his Harley-Davidson motorcycle, presented to him by his father on his twenty-first birthday in 1912, and for completing his studies at Oxford.

A few years later and he'd been twenty-five, a captain leading a unit of men – many younger, most older than he . . . all of them counting on that same bravado, all prepared to follow their good-looking, fearless officer, but he'd learned a horrible lesson by then that no man was invincible, no matter how young or brave . . . or rich.

In between university and heading off to war he'd emulated his father with a keen nose for enterprise, learning everything he could about the diverse family business. Thomas Wynter had invented himself as a business magnate, taking the family fortune made from wool and textile manufacture and moving into everything from agriculture – 'People will always need to eat, Lex,' he remembered his father saying – to shipping, to investing in the railways. It was Lex who had urged his father to put money into what he claimed was the future – motor vehicle production – and into the burgeoning shipbuilding industry.

Wynter and Co. Ltd had its fingers reaching into most of the profitable growth areas in Britain and abroad, and even the wily old Thomas could see that his eldest son possessed an inherent talent for seeing opportunities and making money. Alex's youth made him take risks that a more mature man might not.

'Just learn from your poor decisions and capitalise on the good ones,' Thomas had told Lex.

Everyone in the family accepted that Lex was the eldest and thus heir to the Wynter throne, and he had earned the right, having displayed all the appropriate talent for business and management, to keep the family empire profitable.

Alex heard dogs barking and grinned at the familiar sound. Gin and Tonic. They'd be old now. Ginny would have to be nearly fourteen. The dogs would have roused suspicion especially as Clarrie would have alerted Bramson by now. As Alex considered this he saw new lights winking on.

He let go of thoughts of the family firm, although he did wonder if Douglas still felt overshadowed. 'It's hard being the middle brother, darling,' his mother would explain. 'Easy being you – the dashing and talented eldest. To Dougie it would seem as though you got everything.'

'But what about Rupert? I don't see him carrying on.'

'And it's also very easy being Rupert. He's third in line, with little expected of him, and, being the baby, he has never had designs on inheriting the throne. Besides, he's spoiled, adored, has your looks in spades and he's reckless with himself and money – plus, he's so easy to love, isn't he? Women adore him. What more could a rich young man want?' She'd smiled. Alex loved his mother. She saw her three sons clearly and loved them individually; he didn't think Dougie, no matter what private demons he wrestled with, could ever accuse their mother of treating him any differently.

The door opened and Alex was dragged into the present. Silhouetted in the doorway was the familiar shape of Bramson.

'Mr Alex, Sir?' He'd never heard Bramson sound so tremulous. 'Is it really you?' he said softly into the darkness.

'Yes, it's me, Bramson. I'm back.'

The tall, lean butler, who had started with the family as a houseboy and grown with it in stature, was immensely liked by every family member. He had been the Wynters' butler since Alex had been packed off to boarding school aged eight. Now the still spry head of staff skipped down the small flight of stone stairs and uncharacteristically hugged the eldest son.

'Er . . .' He cleared his throat. 'Forgive me, Sir. I am overcome to see you alive.'

'Nothing to forgive, Bramson.'

'You're going to make your mother so happy. Her spirits . . . well, I'm sure you understand. I wish . . .'

Alex saved him. 'Does my mother know I'm returned yet?'

'No, Sir. I had to come and check for myself. I couldn't believe what Clarrie was telling me.'

He nodded. 'That was wise of you. Let's go see her, then, and cheer her.'

'I'm so sorry about Mr Thomas.' Alex swallowed the pain as Bramson spoke. 'Mr Wynter was – well, almost a second father to me, and as his former valet . . .' He didn't continue the thought. Instead he brightened his voice. 'Your return is going to help ease the pall that's shrouding this house.'

'Thank you, Bramson.' Alex was glad his voice was steady. But although he wanted to say more the words clogged in his throat as he began to imagine a world without the towering strength and knowledge – and that booming laugh – of Thomas Wynter.

'I'll wake the family, Sir.'

'Er, no . . .' He grabbed Bramson's elbow. 'Best not, old chap.'

'Sir?'

'Bramson, this is all very difficult for me. I regained consciousness this morning after falling over and hitting my head. Apart from the splitting headache it delivered, it also returned my memory. You can't imagine how odd this all feels. I've lost years somewhere, no idea where. I am trying to piece it all together but it's not coming easily. Not coming at all, in fact.'

'Oh, Master Alex. It never occurred —'

'How could you know? Please don't feel bad. But to wake everyone and have to field their questions tonight, well . . .' He blew

188

out a breath he felt he'd been holding in since London. 'I can wait a few more hours for that. I need to . . . um . . . acclimatise again. They'll all still be here in the morning.'

'Yes, Sir. Your father's will is being read tomorrow afternoon.'

'I see. What ghastly timing I'm showing.'

In the darkness, they paused and Alex was sure they were both thinking the same thing about how his return now changed everything that the family thought was likely to occur, particularly for Douglas.

It was Bramson's turn to clear his throat. 'I believe your mother is still awake, Sir; Effie took up a small tray of cocoa and biscuits just half an hour ago.'

'Let me go up. I haven't forgotten the way.'

'Of course, Sir. Can I get you anything?'

'I'm famished, now you mention it. I can't remember when I last ate.'

'Leave it to me. Um, your old room will be a bit musty, Sir.'

Alex paused on the steps and grinned. Dim light leaked out from the reception hall to illuminate the men. 'I could sleep on the floor, I'm so weary.' And he saw that Bramson looked hardly a day older than he recalled, save the gentle silvering around his hairline, and in that moment felt reassured.

It was as though everything familiar was pulling him into a collective embrace – from the soft smile of Larksfell's butler to the waft of beeswax polish that drifted out through the open doors from its grand reception hall. It reached around him affectionately and clutched Alex to its intangible bosom and told him he was safe now . . . He was home.

He took a slow, deep breath and entered his house. Only small low-lit wall lamps were on so the reception felt uncharacteristically gloomy, but it was appropriate for the grieving household. The house was also unnervingly silent, save the massive grandfather clock that had been chiming away the hours of the family's life since before Alex was born. He walked up to it now, running his fingers over the magnificent inlaid pattern, and facts filtered into his mind: rare George III, made by Christopher Goddard of London, in the mid-eighteenth century, with Roman hours and Arabic five minutes. The mechanism was made by clockmaker Jennens & Son, also of London, with nine bells for the quarter hour and a beautifully deep and mellow gong that struck the hour. Alex shook his head. How could he remember all of this detail about a piece of furniture and not know where his life had been spent since the end of the war?

'Master Alex?'

'The clock prompted happy memories.'

'I can imagine, Sir. I took over your role of winding it when you left. You always took the chore seriously.'

Alex smiled. 'I begged Grandfather for years, but he said only when I was tall enough to turn the key without a stepladder to reach the winding mechanism.' He shrugged.

'You were fifteen, Sir.'

Alex turned to regard the gently sweeping staircase. 'I presume my mother has not vacated the Lapsang Souchong rooms?'

Bramson chuckled quietly at the childhood jest. 'No, Sir, she has not. The Oriental Rooms are still her private suite.'

Alex cut him a grin. 'Wish me luck.'

'You shan't need it.'

He nodded, and began climbing the stairs, but then took them two at a time, recalling how he used to race up the flight. On the first landing were his and his parents' rooms. He glanced to the right, where his suite had been located, looking out over the walled garden of his childhood. Upstairs were his brothers' rooms and a host of guest rooms. Servants lived above those in the garrets, reached by a second series of stairs that the family never used.

He glanced to his left, steeling himself to ignore his father's suite and the haunting aroma of pipe tobacco that clung to this part of the hallway and perhaps always would. He pushed past the memories and walked to the end of the corridor, where an arrangement of funereal lilies stood on a marble plinth before the grand mullioned window. He knew tomorrow morning that window would permit this corridor to be flooded with soft morning light, which had nonetheless faded the exquisite Chinese silk carpet upon which he now stood.

He took a deep breath and, facing the door of his mother's suite, knocked gently. From behind it he heard muted voices, recognised his mother's and felt his heart leap.

The door was pulled back and there stood Effie, now in her early forties but still cutting a much younger figure, with narrow hips and blonde hair. She did not know him in that instant but he didn't blame her. The light was low, and like the rest of the family she had long presumed him dead.

He could see his mother's straight back. She was seated before her dressing table and it was as if time stood still for Alex for several heartbeats. She had been massaging cream onto her hands as she did each evening before bed and Alex was glad to see that routines were keeping his mother composed. The reflection in the mirror that regarded him across the distance of the room looked sunken and haunted – far too thin and as though the entire grief of the Wynter family had been borne by Cecily. He hoped it was the very low lamplight playing tricks, because his mother looked as though the years of his absence had been cruel.

He heard her soft gasp as she swung around on her stool. A mother recognised her child in all of his incarnations. There was no doubting that Cecily Gilford Wynter knew him now.

With wide, disbelieving eyes, she struggled to stand. 'Lex?'

Now Effie turned back to gape at him. 'Master Alex!' she whispered, echoing his mother's shock.

And then he was crossing the room, oblivious to his surrounds or the lack of manners in barging into a woman's boudoir at this hour.

'Yes, it's me, Mother,' he choked out and swept her into his arms. She felt like a bird, fragile and light enough that he was sure he could lift her up into his embrace in a single movement. Beneath that hug he heard a wrenching sob.

'Lex,' she repeated, her voice trilling with alarm. 'Is it really you?'

He pulled back, trying to effect a roguish grin for her but he knew it must look lopsided as he tried to keep a lid on his emotion. Years of memories crowded in, from the first glance of the mainly blue Chinoiserie of the room's decor to the perfume of violets that drifted around him.

He watched her face, bared of any make-up, crumple as she gave way to tears that his mother was not known for.

'How? How? How?' she kept repeating.

Alex held her, nodded behind his mother at an equally emotional Effie, and made soothing sounds.

'I shall explain everything that I can. But tell me about Father.'

She pulled away to look at him, tried to say something but choked on it. 'I'm so sorry he missed you,' he thought she said.

15

Edie hadn't slept. Her father had tried to keep her company, as had Madeleine, who refused to leave. When Edie periodically emerged from her own frightened thoughts and the tense stupor she had slipped into, she realised that Madeleine was moving around her home like a silent angel, taking care of everything from answering the door – sympathetic visitors held at bay – to ensuring her father was fed. Here was a true friend at last, and definitely when she most needed one.

Police Constable Ball had been as good as his word, making the near six-mile round trip twice through the evening to reassure her that enquiries were 'in motion'. The night had closed in and Edie's eyes were wide open and her demeanour one of someone in shock by the time the larks first began to sing their elaborate mating song on the wing, high above Epping.

Madeleine was pressing something into her hands. Edie blinked, once again torn from her beautiful, reassuring memories of being held by Tom, teased by Tom, kissed by Tom, only to return to the present and the disturbing realisation that it had no Tom in it. Her father dozed in Tom's armchair, whistling softly as he snored by the hearth.

'You kept the fire going, thank you,' she murmured, her tone polite but disinterested. 'You've been very good to me, Madeleine,' she added, only now comprehending that yet another steaming mug of tea was in her hands.

'Don't spill it,' her friend warned. 'I couldn't leave you,' she admitted.

'We hardly know each other.'

Madeleine regarded her after a brief glance at Abe's bent head. 'We know each other,' she assured. 'Drink up.' Madeleine cut a glance back at Abe. 'He doesn't look so well.'

'What?' Edie replied. She'd been drifting again.

'Should we get your father into a bed?'

Edie shrugged. 'He won't want to leave me.'

'Then perhaps you should also —'

'He's not coming home.'

'You don't know that, Eden. He may have —'

'I do know it. I know Tom.'

'Something may have happened. An accident or something.'

'Yes, but whatever's happened, Tom's not coming home. I feel it.'

'Stop talking like this.' Madeleine was crouched by Edie's knees as Edie began to leak silent tears and shake her head gently. 'Don't give up hope,' her new friend pleaded.

'I won't. Not ever. But I can feel it.' She shrugged. 'Instinct, sixth sense. I don't know what to call it but I know Tom's left me.' She watched Madeleine's eyes widen in surprise. 'Not intentionally, perhaps. But he's gone. I knew we were too happy. This is my punishment.'

'You are *not* being punished.'

'Yes, I am. I know I am. And my punishment is just beginning. First Tom.' Madeleine stared at her, frowning. 'And I can't feel the baby. He hasn't moved since last night.'

'Shock can do that to you.'

Edie nodded, distracted, bored by the placations. She stood. 'I suppose I'd better tidy myself for Constable Ball.'

As if an invisible stage director had pointed a finger, there was a knock on the door. Both women jumped and Abe was startled from his sleep. Madeleine moved first.

'Hello, Constable Ball. Come in, please.'

The policeman walked in with his helmet removed, bicycle clips keeping his trouser ends from flapping and his buttons shiny enough that Edie was sure she might see her own reflection in them. She turned away from the policeman's sombre expression and watched her father straighten his clothes and wipe dried spittle from the corner of his lips. His normally immaculately groomed hair was tousled and she felt her breath catch with sadness for all of them.

Constable Ball cleared his throat.

'Anything?' Edie asked, already knowing the answer.

He shook his head. 'Nothing at all, I'm afraid. It's as if your husband didn't exist, Mrs Valentine. My colleagues at Golders Green have spoken to Solomon Bergman, who saw him last, but Mr Bergman dropped Mr Valentine off at Green Park in the city.'

Edie frowned. 'Why Green Park?'

Ball shrugged. 'I'm sorry, Mrs Valentine. I thought it may mean something more to you.'

Abe spoke up. 'I might be able to help there, Constable.' He turned to Edie. 'As I told you before, Tom wanted to test his new-found confidence. He decided not to head home immediately but to go on a little with Sol.'

She nodded. 'Did Sol say whether Tom was nervous?'

Ball glanced at his notepad. 'No, I don't believe so.'

Madeleine brought a mug of tea and some biscuits for the policeman, who looked profoundly grateful. It occurred to Edie that Constable Ball might not have had any sleep either and now that the notion arrived, she could see the telltale whiskers poking through his jaw, and his eyes, though alert, looked red.

'Pardon me?' Ball said.

Edie hadn't realised she'd spoken aloud. 'Er, I said that Tom wouldn't do this knowingly.'

'Knowingly?' He gulped his tea.

Until this moment she hadn't put Tom and the word 'disappeared' together in her mind. And the truth of her worst fears fell into her mind like a door closing with a slam.

'I m—mean,' she stammered, blinking through the tide of emotions that threatened to drown her. 'Tom is lost.' Everyone waited in a frigid silence. Edie blinked again and found a fresh strength. 'Tom was lost when I found him.'

'What are you saying, Mrs Valentine?'

Madeleine was at her side, a soothing hand on her arm. 'She's saying something's obviously happened again to Tom.'

Abe looked back at Edie as if he was in pain. 'You mean, he's lost his memory again?'

Edie began to tremble uncontrollably. 'No, Abba. I think he may have found it this time.' She let out a sob of anguish and with it came a terrible, chilling feeling of release. A needle of pain shot through her body, beginning low in the hip. Another rode hard in on it.

Madeleine was helping her to sit down. Edie could hear her father's concern and was aware of the dark uniform of the policeman hovering on the rim of her vision, which was rapidly clouding. What was happening? The needles of pain had changed into cramps. She thought she was imagining it; wanted to believe this was not her baby beginning its labour. *Not without Tom! Please, no . . .*

'Eden . . . Eden?'

Edie squeezed Madeleine's hand.

'How can I help you?'

'It's happening.' She blinked, tried to clear her view of the world. Madeleine's angular features became more focused. Her grey-green eyes searched Edie's face with a question. 'The baby,' Edie whispered and let the pain carry her. It seemed so appropriate to ride agony when loss was her companion.

Tom will break your heart. She heard her father's words echo in her mind now as she galloped away from the cottage's sitting room into the darkness of despair. Abba's words followed her, though, chasing her through the mist of hurt.

I imagine sooner or later Tom will discover the truth about himself.

Edie was vaguely aware of leakage and the cramps intensifying. Hands were pulling at her, shocked voices were filtering through on the fringe of her mind, and not only had her father's words been prophetic – that she would lose Tom to his memories – but she was suddenly certain that divine punishment was taking place and his child was being ripped from her too.

It had been a long, strange night for Alex. He had sat in his mother's rooms, held her hand and told her everything he could remember about his life since he'd last seen her. Effie had quietly come back into the chamber, where they sat and laid out a supper for him that he had greedily enjoyed, the hot cocoa especially, with a slug of brandy in it.

'To help you sleep, Master Lex.' She grinned and he could still see the amazement in her eyes that he'd returned.

After the door closed his mother had raised an eyebrow.

'I know. The servants' quarters will be abuzz with gossip before the main house wakes,' he admitted.

'My darling, that's nothing to what your arrival is going to do to poor Dougie.'

'Am I an ill wind, Mother?' he'd said, winking.

'Far worse in his mind, I suspect.'

'Surely he'll be pleased I'm alive?' he sighed.

'Lex, Dougie loves you. There's no question that you were a trio of brothers who were close; it was something your father and

I were quietly proud of . . . our finest achievement. But before the war each of you had his place in the family's structure. Dougie, though he often whined about it as a child, understood he was the middle son and would always have a slightly tougher path.'

'I know that's why you always took his side.'

She smiled sadly. 'I tried to stand back but it's hard not to sympathise. Your father insisted he work it out for himself.' She stroked her son's cheek, still in shock that he was sitting before her, needing to touch him so the mirage didn't disappear. 'And then suddenly your disappearance changed everything. Dougie became a "firstborn", for want of a better term. And unfortunately, darling, this revelation coincided with his marriage to someone who perhaps doesn't offer him the counterbalance that most marriages require.'

'Dougie's married?' Alex said in wonder.

'Oh, yes! Huge society wedding – everything your father and I privately loathed. But we performed spectacularly on the day for Dougie's sake.'

'Who's the lucky lady?'

'Guess,' she demanded with a wicked giggle.

'Helena James?'

'Oh, come on. You can do better than that.'

'Not Daphne Kirkham-Jones.'

She winced. 'Over my corpse,' she muttered. 'But you're getting warmer, darling. Go back to Dreadful Daphne's circle and think of the hardest-working socialite of them all.'

'You jest,' he said, his voice ringed with disbelief as dawning hit. 'He married Frantic Fashionable Fern?'

Cecily Gilford Wynter dissolved into helpless giggles. 'I shouldn't be laughing when I'm supposed to be grieving,' she said, looking desperately guilty. She began to weep softly. 'Your father was gravely ill for a long time. It really wasn't a surprise. Forgive me.'

'Mother, if there was one aspect of you that Father loved more than any other, it was to hear you laugh. Laugh and hope he can hear you. So, Frantic Fern is now a Wynter, eh?'

'Stop it, Lex. You're going to see her in a few hours.'

'She's here?'

'Of course! Nothing could keep her from the reading of your father's will – which reminds me, I have to phone Gerald.' Alex was once again faced with a woman of sorrow. 'I do miss him.'

'Gerald?' he offered, reaching for that lightness. He recalled the family lawyer and close friend of his father.

She admonished him with a glance. 'What will we all do now without Thomas?'

He took his mother's hands again. 'You know, I missed him bitterly when I left but as the war years drew on, I realised he'd equipped me to be alone. All the important building blocks were in place and I didn't panic. I knew others were depending on me just as he'd always said one day they would.'

She looked at him with affection. 'Your father was deeply proud of you, son. Or should I say Captain Wynter?'

'You should not. My point is, Father will have equipped you to live life without him too. The age gap was always —'

'Don't, darling. The inevitability of his death doesn't stop the sense of loss or make the mourning any easier.' She gave a sad shrug.

'I knew about his death before I walked in. I was outside for several hours just getting used to the idea that he wasn't going to be here. I began my grieving out there on the stump where he and I used to sit and talk about the estate, the family . . . my responsibilities.'

'And you're just like him,' she said.

'Am I?'

Cecily nodded. 'Your father never dwelled on anything he couldn't control. I can tell you've already set your grief aside, realising that you had no control over his passing.'

'Not aside, Mother; it's just private now. I can't turn time back and —'

'You're doing it again, darling.'

'What?'

'Disappearing . . . or at least drifting from me. I refuse to lose you again. It makes my insides twist like coils to realise you've been likely lying around in hospitals for years. The army assured us they had looked for you.'

He blew out an audible breath of frustration. 'Sorry. It's just something about that subject of not being able to turn back time.'

She gave a soft laugh. 'Oh, I think we'd all do that if we could.'

He covered her hand with his.

She sighed. 'I must call Gerald.'

'Really? At this time?'

'You did hear what I said, didn't you, darling . . . I mean about reading the will? You're back. Everything changes.'

His expression dropped.

'I thought you weren't cottoning on fast enough. Dougie is not going to enjoy waking up to this news. He's no longer the senior Wynter male, with all the prestige that affords him, and he's no longer inheriting what he'd planned.'

Alex gave a nod of understanding and his spirits deflated. 'I feel like a leper.'

She shook her head. 'Don't you dare. This is your rightful place.'

'And Frantic Fern is going to like my presence even less!'

'It's not your problem.'

'You know, Mother. I could just walk away.'

'Don't be ridiculous!' she said, sounding deeply offended.

'No, think about it. Right now everyone's settled. Even you said Dougie had become accustomed to his new role in the family as senior son. Why disrupt everyone? The family is grieving . . .'

'All the more reason to celebrate your return.'

'Are you sure it's something to celebrate?'

'Well, I am! You saw Effie's face. I can only guess at Bramson's delight – and Clarrie must be hugging himself. Charlotte will be over the moon – your sister loves you more than that new motorcar of hers!'

'Dear Charlie. Still a tomboy?'

'I'm afraid so. Her mother's girl she is not,' she said, but with a twinkle in her eye. 'She's fearless, Lex. She lied about her age, got away to Europe as fast as she could to be part of the nursing corps. I can't imagine what she's seen.'

'I can. We should all be hugely proud of her.'

'Your father was. He didn't say much but deep down, he was astonished and pleased by her behaviour.'

'Anyone in her life?'

'I think so. Nice fellow by the name of Phelps. Good family. She doesn't like to talk about it. You know Charlotte: hates to admit to being in any way a normal girl.'

Alex grinned affectionately.

'By the way, Cousin Penny's here too.'

'Really?'

'Your father always had a terribly soft spot for her.'

'She always was a sweet little thing.'

'Not so little now, darling.'

Alex's thoughts were already running to his favourite sibling. 'How's Rupert doing?'

'You all over again . . . just more reckless. He was wounded.'

He frowned. 'I heard that he's got no lasting injuries, though.'

She shook her head. 'Rupert is a sunny person, as you know, but I sensed he was fooling everyone. Everyone but me, that is. He refuses to share what he experienced.'

'It's too painful, Mother. I completely understand. No one else can unless they were there.'

She nodded. 'He came home battered, wounded, but essentially in one piece. I felt lucky. Now I am surely blessed; all of my sons are returned.' The lines of age on Cecily's face suddenly crinkled, like delicate parchment, folding in on themselves around her forehead as she frowned. 'Perhaps I should feel guilty.'

Alex hugged her gently. 'I don't think so. What's the time?'

Cecily reached for a slim wristwatch on the dressing table, where they still sat, backs to the mirror.

'Good heavens, darling, we've been talking for hours! It's past midnight.'

'To bed, then. Big day tomorrow.'

'Not until I've phoned Gerald.'

He looked at her with pain. 'Leave things as Father had them . . . please.'

'Lex, I hope your war injuries do not include madness,' she replied, her brow furrowing again with concern despite the sarcasm.

He sighed.

'Your father's last breath was about you. Thomas was not prone to regrets but his one deep regret as he died was that he wasn't able to pass the reins of his sprawling business to one Alexander Wynter. He'd groomed you for this moment and you had proved to him many years ago that you were the one to take the family towards the next century.'

'Dougie —'

'Don't, Lex. I'm fully aware that this must all seem strange and unsettling right now, but your personal issues aside, you have a duty to your father . . . to the family.'

Lex took a slow audible breath.

'You don't forget how to do business, like you don't forget how to ride a bicycle or kiss a beautiful woman, son.' She blinked, surprise ghosting across her features. 'What does that look mean? Did someone walk over your grave?'

He shook his head. 'Memories being tripped, I suppose.'

'Who have you been kissing, I wonder?' she said archly, amused.

Alex thought of the handkerchief with a heart-shaped cut-out missing. Who owned his heart?

———

Abe Valentine sat in the draughty corridor of the local Epping Infirmary – as it was known – located on the plains of Essex. Next to him was a poised Frenchwoman whose looks attracted double glances from doctors and nurses alike, but right now Abe was barely aware of the beauty at his side. All he wanted was for normal life to return. If he could just turn back the clock one day . . .

In truth, Abe would turn back the clock to 1919 and choose not to send his beloved daughter to Edmonton Hospital for a fitting on one day and a delivery the next. She would never have met Tom, never have moved away from home, not be going through this trauma. She would be married by now to Benjamin Levi and pregnant with Ben's child. It would have been enough. Tom had brought complications and anxieties an old man did not need at this stage of his life. He'd always known Tom's background would catch up with them.

Edie had been a gift from the heavens and this child of hers and Tom's was to be a new beginning. The family was growing . . . It was active again. Edie had always promised him several grandchildren and she'd wasted no time conceiving her first. And now he had a grandson, born a few hours earlier as his mother's distress had brought on his premature birth. Would either survive, though?

Abe felt a cool hand touch his. 'Mr Valentine?'

Madeleine pointed out a doctor and older nurse approaching. Abe struggled to his feet, accepting his companion's help.

'Abraham Valentine?' the doctor asked.

Abe couldn't speak.

'This is Mr Valentine, yes,' Madeleine answered for him. 'I am a friend of the family. Miss Delacroix.'

Abe noted that the nurse had pulled her hair tightly into a bun so that her hat could sit primly atop it. She wasn't looking directly at him but at a point just past him. He knew it was bad news . . . felt it in his heart.

'Mr Valentine, your daughter is sleeping but doing fine.'

His gaze flared back to life as he gave the doctor his full attention. 'She's going to be all right?' he choked out.

The doctor's sombre expression didn't change. 'Yes, I believe she is out of all danger. She is weak now, and is going to need some bed rest and quiet.'

Abe shifted his gaze to Madeleine, who offered a watery smile. She squeezed his hand, sharing her joy at the news.

The doctor cleared his throat. 'I am afraid it's not all good news.'

Abe swallowed, not sure he'd heard right. He waited.

'I'm afraid to say that the child is not very strong. And there's not much we can do. One of the sisters firmly believes in the new-fangled incubator, but frankly I don't. It would be giving false hope to suggest that the weakling, barely thirty-six weeks, if I'm correct, can survive without much strength to feed from his mother.'

Abe blinked in shock, but a glance at Madeleine's suddenly lost expression confirmed that his hearing was still precise.

The doctor hurried on, filling the terrible silence. Abe heard placations. His daughter would be able to have more children, start again. It was all just words and more words – meaningless – while he wrestled with the realisation that yet another precious Valentine was about to be taken from him.

Punishment. Why? He'd been a faithful husband, a loving father. He'd provided for his family and looked after friends. Why, why, why!

'. . . lots of sunshine, good food to get her health up – she's a bit thin. Right now rest is what I'm ordering.'

Abe heard it but the words flew around him like dark wasps attacking. He could hear their drone, and the doctor's voice became one long buzzing sound at the back of his ears. The stinging turned to a fist around his heart, squeezing the life and laughter from him. Shocking pain erupted to take away his breath and he could no longer see the doctor or his prudish nurse.

The last sound he heard was a woman gasping in surprise and then he was falling, holding on to Nina's hand. His wife was at his side and she was leading him somewhere with urgency. She was smiling, though. 'Come, Abe,' he heard and he was happy to follow.

Madeleine had no family in England, few enough back in France and perhaps an old uncle in Algiers who might still be alive, but over the course of this day she'd found a new family. There was a connection with Eden Valentine – she'd felt it the moment she'd met the young woman with a name to match her beauty.

One glance around Eden's cottage and she could see the girl had immense style. And after an hour looking through her wardrobe, which belied her circumstances, Madeleine also knew she was in the presence of someone with a gift. Eden's ability as a seamstress went beyond anything Madeleine had seen . . . even in Paris.

This young woman had vision. Her styling, so sharp and tailored, with moments of shockingly beautiful flamboyance, had taken Madeleine's breath away. None of the villagers knew that the Frenchwoman in their midst had once been a model for Callot Souers. The four Callot sisters had learned their skills from their mother, a talented lace-maker, and were known for their simple but exotic designs that Madeleine, their favourite model, showed off brilliantly from her angular frame.

And Eden, like Marie Callot, the head designer at Callot Souers, was a jump ahead of most other fashion houses. Madeleine could tell from Eden's clothes that her new friend had the ability to see the future of fashion, perhaps had the inherent sense to predict what women would like to wear . . . *should* wear.

Talking with Eden, she'd been impressed to hear the young designer say that women should wear what they want, what they like, rather than what a fashion house dictates. But someone has to provide the designs to trigger their desire.

They'd both laughed at that.

'And you may be just that woman, Eden,' she'd said, still not ready to explain her background.

Madeleine's mother and aunt had cut hair for a living. Growing up around these two women a girl could hardly miss out on absorbing some of the skills. Epping had provided a sleepy hamlet, away from Europe, where she could hide from a violent man. Escape had cost Madeleine her reputation and living as a well-known Parisian couturier's preferred model, but she had never regretted leaving France. She knew Pierre believed she'd run away to Morocco or Algeria, perhaps even into Switzerland or Belgium. He would never think to look for her in dowdy England.

And so she'd been cutting hair, making ends meet by helping out Delia at the pub and quietly getting on with building a dull but new life for herself that was safe in its boring regularity.

But Eden Valentine changed that. In a few hours she'd not only fallen in love with a new friend but had seen a fresh life opening up, especially with Eden's plans to open her own salon. Madeleine knew she could help – more than that, she knew she could be Eden's ace up her sleeve for how to sell to women effortlessly.

And then, in as many hours again, Eden's life had unravelled.

Abe had reminded Madeleine of her grandfather, his presence solid and dependable, but suddenly he was falling away from her. She still had hold of his hand, squeezing tightly as bad news was delivered, but then she'd gasped as he'd dropped from her grasp, crumpling heavily to the green linoleum floor.

The block of a nursing sister, with thick calves and a pinched expression, moved with surprising speed and efficiency, opening Abe's tie and collar. The doctor was instantly tearing off the perfectly made striped shirt to reveal a wrinkled, grey-haired chest upon which he placed a stethoscope, while the sister quickly ensured the old man's airways were clear.

They waited while the doctor listened.

Madeleine held her breath, covering her mouth with her hands.

Finally the doctor sighed and took the listening device from his ears. He looked up at Madeleine and shook his head sombrely. 'I'm sorry, Miss Delacroix. He's gone.'

'Oh, Eden,' she whispered, shaking her head slowly in disbelief as her thoughts immediately fled to Abe's daughter and how to tell her she'd potentially lost her entire family in the space of one day.

16

Douglas Wynter strolled to the ornate credenza and inspected the morning offerings. Breakfast had been laid out under Bramson's supervision and the butler now flanked the buffet, welcoming the Wynter brood as each family member arrived downstairs. He was not surprised to see Douglas appear first with his social-climbing wife of four years, who seemed to relish every visit to Larksfell more than the last. Perhaps because with each stay Fern Wynter, née Duffield, felt herself inch ever closer to the prize of becoming Lady of Larksfell Hall. *What a rude shock awaited her this morning*, the butler thought wryly.

As Bramson watched, Douglas and Fern Wynter poked at the food with their habitually greedy attitudes. It struck him that if Alex and Dougie Wynter stood side by side, few would pick them as relatives, let alone brothers. They possessed such an entirely different build and colouring that they could have originated from separate families. Douglas had thinning, mousy-brown hair that was receding to reveal a long, shiny forehead. Intense, small-ish blue eyes were sentinels to a curiously wide nose, while a pencil-thin moustache of indeterminate colour hovered above thin lips that didn't help to hide a chin dropping sharply away into a loose fold of his neck. It was a clue to the fact that Dougie Wynter was also slipping away well before his time into a middle-aged paunchy body. He sniffed a hard-boiled egg for no apparent reason and plonked it into a china eggcup that he balanced on his plate.

Bramson smiled to himself at today's breakfast, which was deliberately simple by Wynter standards: no rich scrambled eggs with butter and chives or eggs Benedict with smoked salmon. Today, Mrs Dear the cook had presented a spare choice of creamed oats followed by boiled or poached eggs with toast and braised spinach. Bacon, onions, mushrooms and tomatoes were noticeably absent, as Douglas lifted various tureen lids, clearly hoping to find more.

'Thin pickings today, darling,' his wife said with a twist of blood-red lipstick and mocking eyes of a lacklustre brown that matched her hair, neatly tied in a loose bun. Fern's clothes were unremarkable in colour but her olive and beige outfit was clearly well made in expensive lightweight fabrics. Her shoes were sensible flat brogues in chocolate brown but again made in the softest of kid leather. She reeked of money but in such a drab way. She reminded Bramson of a female blackbird, always working hard to please her family but so easy to miss amongst the bright, loud peacocks that she now lived amidst.

'Hmm. Not having sausages isn't going to bring back my father or make any of us feel any better,' he muttered.

'Worse, if anything, darling, eh?' the lady blackbird snipped alongside. Her husband grabbed some toast and two whorls of butter and drifted away to the main table. Fern dutifully followed.

'Good morning, Bramson,' breezed a new voice. It was Charlotte, who looked flushed. 'Thank you for the lovely bed you had made up for me. I don't realise how much I miss this big old place until I come back and sleep in my own bed. Ooh, yummy, poached eggs. What a treat.'

'Coffee, Miss Charlotte?'

'Please,' she said. 'Where's Rupe?'

'Never far away,' Rupert said, arriving right on cue with a shining smile. 'I know we're all supposed to be sombre today but I'm sure our father would be mortified to see his family so desperately grim. Let's not be maudlin, eh?'

'Morning, everyone.'

'Hello, Pen. Oh, why can't I do that?' Charlie bleated.

'Do what?' the newcomer said, looking herself up and down self-consciously.

'Well, it's not even eight-thirty and yet you look effortlessly gorgeous and breezy with perfect hair and perfect outfit for the occasion.'

'Perfect Pen, that's our new nickname for you,' Rupe said, blowing his cousin a kiss.

Bramson smiled at the newcomer. Like his employer, he was fond of the Wynter cousin, related distantly and called cousin because no one could work out how many times removed she actually was. 'Coffee, Miss Aubrey-Finch?'

'Thank you, but I don't take breakfast these days,' she said, beaming him a smile.

'Watching your weight, Pen?' Rupert quipped as he seated himself.

'Are you joking, Rupe? She has the most adorable figure. I'm envious,' Charlotte remarked, sighing as she regarded her full plate of food. 'Look at me. Eating for two.'

Douglas looked up from his eggs in horror.

'I'm joking, Doug.'

'Where is that darling man of yours anyway, Charlotte?' Fern asked.

As Charlotte made excuses for where Julian was and why she didn't have a ring on her finger yet, Bramson checked his fob watch. Mr Alex would be down shortly. He'd spoken with the soon-to-be head of the household early this morning and agreed that he should wait for his mother, who liked to take her breakfast daily at 8:45 a.m. sharp. One minute to go.

He smiled inwardly as he heard footsteps approaching. He couldn't help himself and turned to see Master Lex with the newly radiant Cecily Wynter on his arm on the top landing, about to lead her down the stairs.

Bramson felt his heart swell with happiness. All would feel right again soon with Master Lex back in the house, taking over. He glanced again at Douglas, helplessly relishing the moment of surprise that was coming. He didn't dislike Master Douglas, but the staff adored Alex Wynter . . . always had. Poor Dougie, Bramson thought.

Fern had turned the morning's discussion back to the subject of herself. 'Well, Douglas and I can't wait to start our family. I want plenty of children. Of course, you will all be most welcome at Larksfell with your families, and it doesn't matter how many children we have. Your mother will be welcome to —'

'Welcome to what, Fern, dear?' Cecily interrupted as she swanned in. 'Look at what the postman delivered home,' she beamed, not even waiting for Fern to reply.

Bramson held his breath and watched five pairs of eyes widen with shock. He felt sure even the air around the three Wynter siblings had solidified. Fern had fallen neatly into the trap her mother-in-law had unintentionally laid.

'Good morning, Cecily. A new guest?'

Cecily chuckled. 'Close your mouths, my darlings, and welcome back your big brother.'

Although Alex was the tallest of the brothers, Bramson thought he appeared to loom more powerfully than he recalled. His smile beamed a fresh brightness into the room that had been sorely lacking for years. 'Hello, everyone. Sorry for the dramatic entrance. I only got in very late last night,' Alex said, his tone disarming.

Suddenly chairs were being pushed back and all the Wynters were on their feet, with Fern looking the most confused, while Penelope's normally apricot-blushed complexion had blanched.

Charlotte rushed at Alex and threw herself into his arms. She was already weeping her hello.

'Oh, come on now, Charlie. There, there, I'm safe and sound,' Alex said, holding her back. 'Look at you! You are gorgeous.'

'I can't believe you're here, you're alive!'

'Lex . . .' It was Rupert, in a voice devoid of its usual amusement but filled with delighted disbelief. 'What the hell happened?'

'Long story, old chap,' Alex said, pulling his youngest brother to his chest. 'I've missed you, though. Lots to catch up on.' He turned his focus to Douglas. 'Dougie. How are you doing?' Alex said, striding up to Douglas and reaching for his hand, pulling him into a hug. 'It's great to see you.' He stepped back and held out his hand to the bewildered woman at his brother's side. 'And you must be Fern. Congratulations, you two. What a handsome couple you make.'

Douglas blanched. 'From where the hell have you sprung, Lex?'

Everyone made soft noises of admonition while Bramson caught the wink that Cecily Wynter threw at him. 'I have quite an appetite this morning, Bramson,' she whispered.

'I'm pleased to hear it, Lady Wynter.'

'Alex,' his mother called. 'Cousin Penny is here too.'

Alex swung around and although Bramson had always known that the young lady had a soft spot for the eldest, it had not occurred to him that as she had matured, so had her affections. But he could see it now in the way her gaze hungrily drank in the sight of Alexander Wynter like a person parched beneath a hot summer sun being offered a chilled drink.

'Penny!' he called, seemingly oblivious to her torture, and walked over to hug her, lifting her so her feet left the ground, and spinning her around. 'Good heavens, Cousin Penny. You're all grown-up and delicious to boot!'

He set her down and she self-consciously straightened her clothes. 'I prefer Penelope now.'

'Really?'

She shrugged. 'Actually, Pen's fine.'

'Well, well . . . you certainly are a sight for sore eyes, cousin.' And then he swung back to address the still-shocked room. 'Again, I'm sorry to return unannounced like this but I'll explain everything over breakfast. I'm starving, Bramson. Load up a plate, would you?'

The butler smiled. 'I'd be delighted to, Lord Wynter,' he said, and couldn't resist stealing a glance at Douglas, who was hiding his distress reasonably well under the circumstances.

'Now, now. Enough of that, Bramson. I'm Mr Alex to you and that's how it shall remain.'

'So . . .' Fern began, helplessly thinking aloud and looking at her husband with dismay. 'So . . . you're back and that means you are . . .'

'Yes, Fern dear,' Cecily joined in. 'Our darling Alex is back, the line of inheritance is righted and most importantly, I have all of my brood gathered safely. Thomas can rest in peace; his family is intact.'

As Bramson set down a plate of food in front of Cecily, she beamed him her thanks. 'Now, while I have everyone's attention, you should know I spoke with Gerald in the early hours of this morning to alert him to the obvious change that Lex's return brings.' Fern's mouth was still slightly open with shock, her food congealing on her plate. 'Your father took the sensible precaution of having a codicil to his will and I think we have Cousin Penny to thank for that, as she convinced Thomas to never give up hope that his eldest heir might walk through that front door one day, which is exactly what he did last night,' she said, placing an affectionate hand on Alex's arm. 'Anyway, Douglas, my darling, let's talk quietly after breakfast; there are matters you and I must discuss. This is what your father would have wanted.' She gave her middle son the briefest of sad smiles. 'I'll let Lex tell you his story.'

As Mr Alex began to relate the events of what he could recall since leaving Larksfell, Bramson believed that two people at the Wynter breakfast table were not paying attention. Mr Douglas looked as shellshocked as the men his brother was describing in the trenches of Ypres, while Miss Aubrey-Finch appeared mesmerised by her eldest cousin, as though he were an apparition sent from the heavens.

———————

Edie startled awake, her eyes opening and not registering anywhere familiar. Harsh sounds echoed of metal on metal, heels clicking on cold floors and distant voices. She was lying in a hard bed, could feel rubber squeaking somewhere beneath her, and now as her thoughts assembled, she remembered passing out at home.

She dug rapidly and could only come up with blurry images of nurses prodding at her, talking overly loudly into the vacuum she felt like she'd slipped into. She'd drifted into and out of a deep sleep that was sometimes painful, sometimes numbed. She couldn't remember anything else, not even why she'd fainted in the first instance.

Edie blinked and swung her head around to recognise Madeleine.

'*Bonjour, cherie*,' she whispered.

Edie gave a wan smile. 'Am I in hospital?'

Her friend nodded. 'How do you feel?'

'Weak,' she admitted.

A nurse arrived, prim and starched but friendly. 'Hello, dear. Any pain?'

'Nothing much,' she admitted. 'The baby?'

The two women at her bedside shared a glance.

'I'll leave you alone,' the nurse said. 'Call if you need anything. She'll probably be thirsty.'

'Where's my child?' Edie demanded, her voice ringing with sharp anxiety.

'Your son is weak but he has courage. He made it through the night and today. All good signs. The nurses are holding high hopes. Be calm. Here, drink this,' Madeleine said, and helped to lift Edie's shoulders from the bed so she could sip the water, then her friend dropped back onto the pillow with relief at the news.

'I ache but I want to see him.' She watched her friend nod before the Frenchwoman took a deep breath, as though she were hurting too. 'Madeleine?'

'Eden . . . listen.'

And then Edie remembered. 'Tom!'

Her friend shook her head. 'There's no more news.'

Edie felt her pain intensify.

'Eden . . .' Madeleine hesitated and looked so pale and distraught that Edie frowned and understood that Tom's disappearance clearly wasn't the only bad news.

'Just tell me,' she demanded. Eden watched, almost as if she were an observer, rather than a participant, as Madeleine took her hand.

'Now, listen to me. I have things to tell you that are painful. But I'm here and I will not leave you.'

Edie swallowed hard.

———

The will of Thomas Wynter had been read to the gathered family and with the codicil's influence it was precisely as was expected, since the four siblings were old enough to understand about inheritances. All were well set up for the future. However, for Douglas, and especially for his wife, it was as neither had expected.

This was obvious to all and Alex especially sympathised. While Fern was sobbing in their suite and hurriedly trying to pack up their things, Alex found his brother sitting in the plum orchard, looking deeply glum.

Douglas bristled at Alex's quiet approach. 'Come to gloat?'

'You don't believe that for a moment, surely. You know me better than that, Dougie.'

Dougie sighed. 'That's what's so intolerable, old man. Everyone finds you impossible to dislike, including me. You and Rupe always were like that, always will be.' He tossed away an unripe plum he'd been rolling around his palm. 'Another month . . . end of August . . . and this place will be dripping with fruit ready to be jammed or jarred,' he remarked wistfully, staring up into the crowded canopy of fruit trees, laden with bounty for the Wynter kitchen.

'You always liked it here.'

His brother nodded. 'I used to get bellyache from all the plums I plucked.' He sounded melancholy and Alex understood that although his middle brother was opposite to him in so many ways, he had never forgotten their closeness during childhood. By their late teens Doug had discovered a streak of bitterness towards Alex's luck, often remarking that he'd rather have been born last than in the middle. Alex could hear in his brother's wistfulness a yearning for the simplicity of childhood days.

'You know Dougie, I didn't plan for this. I wouldn't deliberately hurt you, ever.'

He nodded. 'I know. It's a shock, that's all. We'd all come to terms with the notion – that you'd been lost – and I did grieve for you, don't doubt that. But I'd got used to the idea that I would be the head of the Wynter empire and . . .' He gave a sad gust of laughter. 'Fern had made meticulous plans for the redecorating of Larksfell.'

Alex cut him a bewildered glance.

'Don't blame me, old boy,' Dougie continued. 'I would leave it just as it is. I'm as sentimental as any of you three, but Fern has always felt no one in the family truly likes her.'

'So she hoped to sweep us all away with her new broom?'

Dougie shrugged. 'Something like that. I do love my wife, Lex, despite her sharp edges. You know, after you'd gone, it was our father who suggested I hold off volunteering.' He shook his head. 'You even got to be the hero. Father allowed Rupe to join up, too – said it was definitely his role and yours. Mine was to stay back and help him run things here, especially on the farms. "Essential food for the boys in uniform." I bought into it, Lex; really felt I had a role to finally play.'

Alex sighed, only now fully tapping into what must be a lifetime of pain for his middle brother.

'Anyway, one day I had to go into Eastbourne to run some business errands for Father and there was a parade on. Another jolly bunch of men off to war being cheered on wildly by their adoring wives and girlfriends. I paused to clap them on – I felt proud of them and in that moment I wished with all of my heart that I could be one of them. I was so distracted that I had no idea some woman had come up and tucked a white feather into my breast pocket; I only realised after she left my side with a sneer. I learned later it was part of a revolt called the Women of England's Active Service League. Its sole objective was to urge their men, even shame them, into joining up. If that meant publicly labelling them cowards, so be it.'

Alex heard his brother's voice crack and his heart went out to him. 'I had no idea, Dougie.'

'It wasn't my last. I've kept the three feathers I earned for my cowardice and it was only after a frightful argument with Mother and Father that I was finally allowed to join up.' He gave a mirthless gust of breath. 'I'm not even that sure if either of our parents didn't rig the test – you know, pull some strings so I wasn't permitted to head to the front.'

Lex nodded. 'You were talking about Fern,' he said gently, needing to get his brother away from talk of war.

'Yes . . . I was. She was the only woman I met who didn't raise her eyebrows that I wasn't seen to be part of the fighting effort. She understood that some men had to remain behind to run the country, the factories, the farms —'

'You don't have to convince me.'

His brother swallowed back another tirade. 'Anyway, I'm not a dullard, old chap. Fern can be avaricious but she's never had much and her parents used to put on a good show of pretending they did, trading off the family name. There are no assets, though. It couldn't have been easy for her growing up. I put it down to her shock at suddenly being able to afford just about anything she wants; I keep hoping she might run out of energy for acquiring stuff. All her sisters have had to make strategic marriages. None of us know what that feels like. But she and I are lucky because I know in our quiet times that Fern loves me for the right reasons . . . as well as for the wise reasons.'

'I'm not judging you, Dougie. I do understand. If I'd come home on time or even if I'd genuinely died in action . . .' He sighed. 'After seeing Mother, all night long I thought about just walking out and forgetting about Larksfell and the inheritance and —'

'Don't be bonkers. It was always your rightful place. I knew that. It's just a drag that it was so very nearly mine . . .'

Alex gave him a soft look of pain. 'I've forgotten so much. All I have is family as my life raft now. It's a hollow feeling not knowing where I've been since the end of 1917.'

'How bad was it?'

'I don't believe I have enough words or even the right ones to describe life in the trenches. Words . . . well, they're just not adequate. The physical pain of wounds are the least of it.' Alex tapped his head. 'The nightmare is in here. It's the emotional agony that is the worst. Fear of what's coming. Fear for one's families – so many of the brave Tommies I was responsible for were family men, their hearts breaking just a little more each day for the children they knew they'd not hold, or the wife they'd not sleep next to again, the parents they'd never got around to telling how much they loved. And it was all so pointless, Dougie! Our generals have a lot to answer for. An inestimable number of dead and wounded on both sides – in the hundreds of thousands – and for what, I ask you? An obscure village in Flanders on the tip of the Ypres salient! An emotionally disconnected decision-maker at a desk somewhere clearly thought it was a mile or two worth claiming . . .' He didn't finish, but gave a sound of growling disgust instead.

Dougie watched him closely. 'I saw no action, did Mother mention?'

Alex lied, shook his head. 'I'm glad. You don't need to share the sort of nightmares I have.'

'No, Lex. I genuinely wish I could. Finding out my health wasn't up to it was like being publicly emasculated. Everyone from King's in my year saw action. It's actually more traumatising to admit you're a pen-pusher than to be one of the cheering, rosy-cheeked mob rushing off to be killed.'

'But that's the point. It was like a bloody game. My blokes used to toss biscuits and fruit cake across to the German trenches. They'd fling back their goodies in similar spirit. And then some wit was sent a tennis ball and a new sport was invented called "Beat the Boche" and that ball was thrown around across no-man's-land during the rare quiet times. There was cheering and even bloody scoring! I also heard somewhere that one captain decided he'd lead his men over the top by kicking a rugger ball as far as he could. Hell of a kick, apparently, and he took a riddle of bullets while his men were cheering it into Touch.' He leaned forward for emphasis. 'Don't you see, Dougie? None of us had a clue what we were letting ourselves in for. It was just our duty to defend King and Country, we thought. None of us were trained. I heard a fellow officer quip that the only qualification for officer status was that we could conjugate our Latin verbs and bowl a good off spin.'

Dougie looked back at him, perplexed.

Alex pressed his point. 'It was nothing to do with ability or even suitability; the army preferred "gentlemen" to professionals: which club you belonged to, how decent your bank account, whether you could quote bloody Keats. Leadership is not an acquired skill – people like us are apparently born with it,' Alex said, giving a disdainful sigh. 'Just like we inherently know which knife to use!'

'You had leadership in spades, Lex.'

'That's not the point! I would have been made captain without it and I could have got a cushier job away from the front line. We were young, wide-eyed boys, fresh from punting on university lakes, who were leading butchers and bakers, miners and postmen to certain death, with absolutely no idea what it was all about. No one was checking on us for our leadership in the field, no one tested our abilities or even reviewed our decisions or professionalism. We were *gentlemen*, therefore we would surely conduct ourselves accordingly. Except war is not fair or gentlemanly, Dougie; it's not even vaguely sporting.'

Alex stopped speaking to give a harsh laugh. 'It was damned unsporting for the Germans to keep our tennis ball overnight and send it back with a small rock hidden inside, which killed one of our Tommies.' He stood and paced. 'As for the rank and file, they were ordinary chaps dying in the hundreds daily in front of me.

I refused to let myself get close to anyone because I knew most of us wouldn't survive more than a few days.'

'But you did. You came home.'

'Yes, I did and I don't know why. The guilt is overwhelming. I tried damn hard to die, or so it felt at the time. Don't hold it against me, Dougie. I have nowhere else to go. And after what I've seen and experienced, I don't want to be anywhere else but Larksfell, or believe me I'd leave you and Fern to your title and parties and your enormous bank account, and disappear again. I've never had time for any of it – you know that. I'd give it to you but Mother would revolt and I know, and so do you, that Father wanted it this way.'

Dougie nodded, and looked back at his brother with pain in his face. 'That's it, though. I hate that you don't care and still you get it all.'

'Not all, Dougie. And I was groomed to run the Wynter interests, to take over where Father left off. The family can be sure I have the skills to broaden an already strong empire. You and Fern should get on with that family I hear she wants so much. You will want for nothing.'

'Nothing except everything that you have, brother. But then what's new, eh?' he replied. Dougie shook his head. 'I wish you no ill. I also wish you hadn't come home. For the first time in my life I felt I was a man in control of my destiny.'

'Sorry, old chap.'

Dougie nodded, looking resigned. He stood and shook his brother's hand. 'Bye, Lex. I suppose we shall see you for Christmas.'

'No doubt.' Alex sighed and watched Dougie walk away, squelching on a plum that hadn't made it through to maturity. And as Alex regretted the pain his survival brought to his brother, he smelled the sweetish fragrance of the squashed fruit with that familiar muskiness he recalled from his happy childhood, and wished with all of his heart he could go back to those days.

17

OCTOBER 1920

Edie sat on the double bed she'd shared with Tom and stroked the soft fabric of the padded chintz eiderdown. It had been one of their wedding gifts from the Levis. Ben's mother knew the colours that Edie loved; no pinks or lilacs or fairytale hues. No, Dena Levi knew that Edie loved greens and charcoal greys, hints of scarlet or a burst of yellow. Dena had chosen well with this bedspread – a floral design, predominantly sage green with accents of fuchsia and white. She'd loved it immediately but even now she had not lost the notion that with this gift the Levi family were delivering a message. It was likely a paranoid notion but Edie knew they wanted her to always appreciate their sentiment that she was sharing her bed with the wrong man. And the Levi presence would always hover above her marital bed and remind her of this. Although Tom had scoffed at the idea, Edie knew Dena, and maybe Ben's mother had somehow cursed her marriage. Is that why Tom had disappeared? Was this her punishment for following desire rather than duty?

He will break your heart, her father had warned.

Yes . . . Tom was breaking her heart.

'Where are you, my darling?' she whispered as she laid her head down on his pillow and pressed her face to where his had once been, smiling back at her.

She'd remained in hospital for six weeks but had been moving in a stupor, learning to cope with the loss of both her beloved father and husband while fortunately her son strengthened, surprising everyone but Edie.

She didn't know when she'd agreed for Madeleine to move in with her but Edie accepted now that the Frenchwoman was a divine gift like her son, both of them delivered into her life to keep her sane.

'Look at this dear little mite,' Madeleine said, gliding into the bedroom. 'Getting stronger every day,' she said, holding out a tiny bundle of blankets to Edie. 'I took him for a walk around the cottage, but he's hungry and desperate for his *maman*,' she said, her voice surprisingly tender as she gazed at Edie's son.

Edie made herself comfy against the pillows. 'Come here, darling,' she said, taking her son and putting him to her breast. 'I'm sorry, I was drifting off,' she admitted, trying not to weep again.

'Eden, you're grieving. I understand, but there's too much pain at once. You need to get away from here – from its memories – so you can look at it all from a distance for a while.'

Dear Madeleine, practical as ever.

Edie gazed at her son's tiny head with his thatch of dark hair. He was perfect. Strong of heart, like his father, she thought, determined to win through and beat the odds that said he wouldn't make it, presumably as Tom had in the battlefields of Flanders.

'Why haven't you given this child a name yet?'

Edie shrugged to mask her guilt. 'The hospital gave him such little chance of survival.'

'But Matron never gave up on him,' Madeleine reminded.

Edie recalled the stout woman's determination. 'We've lost a generation of sons to war. I refuse to lose another child without throwing my own war at the enemy,' she said as she'd helped another nurse drag a special box she called an incubator into Edie's ward. 'Think mother hen sitting on her clutch of eggs,' she explained to Edie. 'It's going to keep him constantly warm and protected. And you, my girl, are going to stare through this little glass window and pray for your son to hold on and live. You'll hardly touch him but he'll know you're there and he'll feel your love.'

And that's how it had been; day after quiet day in hospital, she'd wept for her father, despaired over Tom and had watched the rapid rise and fall of her son's sparrow-like chest as he rallied and somehow defied the doctor's prognosis. Days had stretched to weeks until Edie noticed a season change as the soft and golden afternoons of summer surrendered to the crispy sounds and sharper, whiter light of autumn. Edie had walked her infant around the hospital gardens, smothered in layers, ever fearful of the danger of winter's onset but equally determined that he inhale the fresh, bright air into his tiny lungs.

His early arrival gave him a somewhat ghostlike presence. Madeleine had summed it up one afternoon as they walked together near the small duck pond.

'He's so quiet. I thought babies cried for everything.'

While Edie had never wanted to say it aloud, she had been thinking identically that her son was near silent. She often wondered if he sensed her grief.

Matron had reassured her. 'Be grateful, dear. Soon enough you'll be begging him to stop asking you every question, from why the moon rises to whether an ant thinks.' She'd patted Edie's arm. 'You're both doing so well. Look at how he thrives. You'd know if anything was wrong.' She tapped her heart. 'I have a huge respect for a mother's instinct. He's a baby who was only meant to be born later this week. He's doing a great job after four weeks to be here, getting stronger. He needs time and understanding. He'll let you know when he's beginning to catch up to his peers. He deserves a name,' she'd added with a firm look.

'I love you, Matron.'

'Well, I'd be lying if I didn't admit that I have a special place in my heart for the Valentines. I do hope you'll visit and let me watch this little fellow continue to thrive.'

They shared a smile. 'Our family is now non-existent. Perhaps we might make you an honorary aunt.'

'Aunt Tilda it is,' Matron had beamed. 'He'll be small for a long time,' she had warned. 'I've seen it before. Most don't make it but your family is blessed and that boy is a survivor, so cheer for him always . . . even when he walks late or toilet trains long after your friends' children. And when he's not winning the races at school or learning his times tables as fast, be sympathetic and remember this moment. He'll need time and understanding to catch up.'

And now here was Tom's son in her arms, sucking greedily at her breast, and she could feel the weight he'd put on; Matron was right. Her boy was beginning to thrive. If only Tom could see him now.

Her mind drifted to that morning, that last kiss, how she'd lost sight of him when he'd turned the corner and left her life.

'Can I get you anything?' Madeleine interrupted her thoughts.

Edie shook her head, gave her friend the pluckiest smile she could muster, but knew it was a sad one. 'I was trying to pick through our last morning together. But I've been over it repeatedly in my mind for signs. There was nothing, Mads. Nothing at all to suggest anything was amiss.'

'I know, *cherie*.'

Edie gave her a soft look of apology.

'Listen, Eden. I've had an idea. Let us go to Paris.'

'What?' Edie looked at her friend, perplexed, searching for a vague hint of amusement that her remark was a joke.

'Paris will help heal you, darling,' Madeleine said. 'I have a plan. I know you won't take a grand tour or anything like that, but I'm talking about just a few days. I've heard you English say that a change is as good as a rest and I believe it. I think if we change the scenery for a short time, you'll come to terms with what you need to.'

'Mads, you don't just get over this with a snap of the fingers or a trip across the Channel. I'm hurting . . . so deeply. I have moments where I just don't want to wake up and face another day. If not for him . . .' She gave her baby an affectionate glance, stroking his downy dark hair.

Her friend gave her a look of warning. 'But what good does all this moping do you, Eden? Will anything you do bring back the men you've lost?'

Edie gasped. 'Don't.'

'Answer me.'

'You know it won't.'

'But do you know that? You can grieve for the rest of your life but it doesn't mean you don't have to get on with a life. Let it be about you and the child now.'

'Mads —'

'Grieve, by all means, but do it in here,' she said, pointing at Edie's heart. 'Don't make your son pay the price for your heart-break in the same way you've hinted that your father made you bear the burden for his sorrows.'

Edie felt the truth of Madeleine's words stir her courage. Just for a beat of her heart it felt like she'd stepped out of the shadow of despair and into some sunlight of rationality. For a moment, even though her unhappy world made no sense, Madeleine did, pushing her to grasp that she alone could shape her future. Madeleine was still talking: '. . . as for Tom, the fact that you've had no news could be taken optimistically.'

Edie shook her head. 'Tell me how, Mads?'

Her friend lifted a single, angular shoulder. 'No reported injuries or deaths. That means your husband is out there somewhere.

He's going to turn up. Now, you could kill yourself searching in vain, or you can trust Tom's love for you is stronger than whatever it is that is keeping him from you. So, pick yourself up, Eden Valentine, and start your life again for this little boy's sake. Get strong now. Everyone's parents die. Your father lived a long life.'

'But he died thinking his grandson would not make it!' she replied in a surge of bitterness.

'Well, nothing's going to change that now,' her friend said. It was brutal but Edie was used to Madeleine's candour.

The Frenchwoman bent down before her, earnest grey-green eyes regarding Edie with such intensity that she dared not look away.

'I didn't say this would be easy, but let's plan to go to Paris sometime soon – just for a few days . . . bring your son, of course. There you'll be able to contend with the decision about your father's shop and home that you're avoiding; you'll be able to actually talk about what to do with the cottage here in Epping too. I know the thought of living in London again is frightening. I'll help you every step of the way, Eden. I'll babysit, I'll change nappies – we'll do it together. Don't give up the dream of the salon. Be true to Tom – be a good mother to his son and be a good wife who follows through on her promise to be the most exciting young designer London has seen in a long time.'

Edie smiled softly as she lifted her baby's tiny frame gently to help him burp. 'I thought you said you'd never go back to Paris?'

Madeleine could see that a sparkle had entered Edie's gaze. 'Never say never, Eden.'

Edie frowned and it was obvious she was seriously considering the offer. 'I would feel as though I'm running away from my problems . . .'

'And what harm is there in that? Stand back from it all and your problems lose their size; you get a sense of everything else around them.'

Edie nodded. 'I have the money from the sale of the cloth,' she agreed. Tom had set up an account for Edie, specifically for her new salon.

'You could sell your father's shop too.'

At Edie's wounded gaze, her friend hugged her. 'Be realistic, Eden. No man wants his suits made by a woman. Not yet anyway, but a man who knows your father's reputation may well urge his wife to come to your salon.'

Edie audibly gulped. 'You make it sound so easy. What about him?' she said, looking down at her sleepy child, warm and snuggled against her breast.

'Don't make it too difficult in your mind. You have help. We can hire more if you need. He's portable right now and such an easy boy . . . and Tom has provided for you both. You won't have to sell the cottage either. I know you won't want to do that but you can move into the city and with the proceeds of your London home and father's shop, you really can set up in town.' She hugged Edie. 'What do you say?'

Edie remembered the money in the leather satchel and how Tom was determined she realise her dream, but family was also part of his dream. 'We'll go next spring. He'll be stronger – strong enough to make that journey. I'll come with you to Paris next April,' she answered, visibly trembling with her excited decision.

Madeleine nodded as though she'd won a victory but had no intention of gloating.

Edie looked into the yawning expression of her child and she saw his father reflected in the gesture. 'I'm calling him Tommy. Thomas Daniel Valentine.'

'*Bravo, ma cherie*,' Madeleine replied, leaning in to kiss the baby. '*Bonjour, Tommy, tu es si beau, mon petit.*'

18

APRIL 1921

It seemed impossible to Alex how quickly time had slipped away. He had deliberately kept himself frantically busy. There was so much catching up to do on the company's business dealings and that made it easier not to confront the painful truth: that he'd escaped one no-man's-land to run the daily gauntlet of another. Life at Larksfell, though privileged and ordered, felt as empty of hope as the trenches had. He realised he had no right to be feeling like this, of course, and he berated himself through each interminable night of restless sleep that if he just persisted, it would get easier and he would feel connected to this life again.

But the notion that he may have belonged to someone else nagged in its darkly silent way. It hunched in the shadows of his mind like an unspoken accusation that had taken form . . . and yet it was shapeless. It had no face, no name, no voice, just a sound. The sound was of heels clicking on stone but it was always leaving him; had he been with someone who abandoned him? He'd had a lover, of this he was sure. The red handkerchief attested to that, and so he carried it like a talisman wherever he went, hoping that maybe one day its secret would be revealed and he would be there to discover it along with the truth about his past few years.

In the meantime he'd made a private pact with himself that he would not torture the rest of the family with his angst. Why shouldn't they believe that he was deliriously happy to be returned to the bosom of the family, proud to take up the reins of his father's empire, and with a full heart that he was home at Larksfell and the world was at peace?

And so Alex Wynter had thrown himself into picking up the threads of where his father had left off and acquainting himself with the entire reach of the Wynter industrial and corporate empire. It had meant relentless meetings with the firm's accountants, lawyers and bankers as well as travelling east to west, mainly up north, to visit all of the manufacturing locations. Manchester was where he invested a lot of time and Alex was also pleased to attend several football matches to cheer on his family's favourite team. He gave up most of his hours getting to know the managers who were busily running all the various strands of the diverse organisation that Wynter & Co had become, ensuring they felt safe that the son was going to be as supportive as the father.

He had admitted to his mother the previous evening that he felt ready to start making strategic decisions.

'I wonder if you might also feel ready to rejoin our lives?' she pondered, as though thinking aloud.

'What does that mean?'

She fixed him with her cool, pale gaze. 'You're here in person but not in spirit, Lex. My conversations with you are always tinged with the sadness that I have you back, but not fully.'

He shook his head, baffled. 'What am I missing here, Mother?'

'It's been eight months since your return but it feels to me as though you're on a frozen lake, skating over the top, taking the fastest route to the other side, hardly daring to look left or right.'

He indulged her. 'What's on the other side?'

'Old age, my darling. You've passed through autumn and winter barely noticing them and here we are welcoming spring and I bet you can't even tell me when you last took a day to notice anything about it.'

'Make a point, Mother.'

'I thought I had. Stop working so hard and start enjoying your life. It's important, Alex. You've had a ghastly few years and I don't want you to look up and realise another year has passed!' His mother shook her head as though she could see right through to his churning thoughts. 'Tell me where you go to in that troubled mind of yours.'

He hadn't been able to give her an answer, preferring not to confide his sense of dislocation. Alex shook his head as he'd shrugged.

She'd risen, squeezed his hand. 'I'm going to bed, darling. Tomorrow, promise me you'll rejoin life. If an opportunity presents itself, give it a chance.'

He'd frowned, but was glad to be let off the hook of her pale-eyed scrutiny.

Eight months! Alex stretched, heard the soft crack of complaint in his spine and considered that he'd been here all morning without shifting from his seat. He glanced out of the French windows and could see the early bulbs in bright roar – jonquils and snowdrops were leading the charge with the merry colours of Clarrie's croci not far behind. Soon the Wynter gardens would be a splendid meadow of spring cheer.

To be fair, he argued silently, the time had also given the family a chance to settle into its new shape and for Dougie to accept being the middle son again, although Alex was deliberately shifting greater responsibility to his brother. The brothers met regularly now to share their ideas for the future and for Dougie to update Alex on various projects that he was now spearheading.

Alex returned his attention to the latest file of paperwork requiring his signature, but his thoughts distracted him. He wanted to get these back to London by tomorrow. He dragged the nib of his fountain pen across his blotter but was irritated to realise he was out of ink. As he began the process of refilling the pen, there was a knock at the door that startled him. The plunger snapped back and ink splattered predictably in a brief and localised rainstorm all over his precious red handkerchief lying nearby. He stared at it, horrified.

'Damn!'

'I'm sorry to disturb you, Master Lex,' Bramson said as he half appeared around the door. He took in the scene immediately and sensibly waited while Alex got the lid back onto his bottle.

'Something wrong, Bramson?'

'Not at all, Sir. Um, you have a visitor. Miss Aubrey-Finch is here to see you.'

He frowned. 'Me? Is my mother in?'

'No. Clarrie has run her into Hove today to see some friends. She won't be back until this evening.'

'Ah, yes, she mentioned something about that.'

'Miss Aubrey-Finch seemed to know about that too, Sir,' Bramson said.

Alex looked taken aback. 'She surely can't be here to see only me. There must be a mistake.'

'No mistake, Sir,' he replied dryly. 'I have shown her into the orangery.'

He sighed, glanced at the stained handkerchief and felt strangely sickened that it had been tarnished. He could see tiny spots of ink had bled onto that fine stitching around the heart. He was surprised how much it hurt to see it. 'Well, I suppose it must be about time for a coffee,' he offered, distracted.

'Already ordered, Master Lex.'

'I'll get down there, then,' he said and winked at his butler, hoping he was covering his angst well enough.

Bramson's expression didn't shift. 'I'll let your guest know.'

Alex emerged from his father's study – his study now – and drifted across to the warmer side of the house, which caught the morning sun. His mother's pride, the orangery, was aglow with the sharp spring light, twinkling through the panes of glass that formed a ceiling and arched beneath a cloudless blue dome. Corinthian columns soared like alabaster sentinels and around them spread the dark, shiny leaves of figs and palm trees. At lower levels ferns added a softer background for Cecily's breathtaking array of orchids with their complex, fragile arrangement of petals, while simple-veined leaves were a foil for the gregarious blooms.

Alex saw Penny admiring an exquisite, trumpet-like flower that was neither pink nor white but had a blushing quality to it. Alex couldn't help but notice the neat figure and curve of his distant cousin's breasts as she bent over the bloom.

'Beautiful, isn't it?' He startled his guest and grinned. 'Mother is very proud of her vanilla orchid. So few gardeners can grow it outside of subtropical regions.'

'I didn't hear you coming. The war must have taught you to tread silently.'

He nodded. 'You're right there, Penny . . . Sorry. It's Penelope now, isn't it?' He strode across the black-and-white chequered floor to peck her gently on both cheeks.

'Pen is fine,' she said easily and then surprised him by blushing. 'Hope you don't mind me dropping in?'

'Not at all,' he lied airily, keen not to offend. 'You've brightened an otherwise dull day. I mean, a dull day in the office; it looks jolly decent out there.'

'Well, why don't you enjoy it?'

'What do you mean?'

'Join me on a picnic.'

Alex was astonished. 'Er . . . I have to sign —'

'Oh, come on, Alex. I've been dying to talk to you properly,' she said, risking poking him in the chest. 'I've held off for months because you never seem to be available.'

He looked back at her, perplexed. 'Pen, I've been overloaded with a lot of —'

'I know, I know. Your mother, Bramson . . . everyone tells me how bogged down you are in work but you have to come up for air sometime or you're going to miss spring altogether.'

'Now you sound like my mother,' he said, wondering if she had anything to do with Penny's visit.

'You need a life, Alex, or what was the point in coming back?'

He grinned helplessly. 'Are you sure?'

'About what? The picnic, you mean?'

'No, about coming to see me? I thought you were just being polite because my mother wasn't in.'

Did he detect a ghosting of guilt in her expression? 'I deliberately came to see you. I've just told you I've been trying to catch you for weeks and weeks with no luck. I knew Cecily was not available today. She's seeing the Smyth-Carters,' she added at his silence.

'So I gather. Um . . .'

'So, shall we?' she said, gesturing to a basket. 'I came prepared.'

'So you have.'

'Come on.' She ushered him out of the glasshouse. 'Get out of that stuffy tie and jacket, pull on a jumper and let's go. And don't say you've got work to do because no one should be working on a day like today.'

She was right. And in the spirit of cooperation with what his mother had been lecturing him about, he decided he could give himself a day off. The paperwork would wait. No one would die. Nations wouldn't fall. 'Give me a couple of minutes.'

Madeleine stretched her long limbs and Edie noticed with amusement that her friend's body ran the full length of the French bed with her feet hanging over the edge. Crooked in her arm, Tommy gurgled and Edie could tell that she was deeply in love with this child too.

'Neither Britain nor France is built for me,' Madeleine drawled.

'Mads, we're like a married couple, aren't we? Living together, travelling together, raising Tommy together.'

'Careful,' the Frenchwoman yawned. 'People will talk.'

'I don't care.' Edie leaned back, her head on the pillow of the twin bed nearby. 'I feel quite changed.'

'How so?'

'These last few months have shown me that I must stop yearning for Tom to walk back into my life and . . .'

Madeleine waited.

'And save me.'

'From what?'

'Oh, I don't know. My whole life has been dominated by men. My father, my brother, the elders, Ben . . . even Tom, although Tom at least viewed me as his partner in everything. Now it's up to me. I don't need a man to achieve anything.' Edie reached across the space between their beds and put her finger into Tommy's hand and smiled as his small fist clamped around it and immediately raised her finger to his mouth. 'This is the little man in my life and he's entirely dependent on me. He *is* my life now. Him and the salon.'

'And Tom?'

'I haven't given up hope. But the last time I saw him was a hot August day. Here we are . . . a new spring . . . and in Paris.' She lifted a shoulder. 'I have to let go of that need to scour every street for a glimpse of him. I find myself staring into buses, peering into taxis. Any tall, dark fellow gets scrutinised. I can't live like that any more. Tom wouldn't have left me knowingly, and as there is no sign of him, no record of anyone like him in a hospital – or morgue – then my only conclusion is that my greatest fear has occurred.'

'His memory returned,' Mads finished for her. 'Odd, if it's true, that he can't remember you at all.'

'The doctors had told Tom how contrary the mind can be with head injuries compounded by the shellshock of war. For all we know, his memory of who he was returned but took with it his memory of who he had become.'

'You're making me dizzy,' Madeleine admitted.

'It circulates like a nasty merry-go-round in my mind too, and it's time I got off.'

Madeleine sat up to face her friend, cradling a wriggling Tommy, who was stretching and yawning. 'That's a big change, Eden.'

'You and Tommy are my family now.' She took her child, who broke into a gummy smile. 'Look at those two little pearls,' she said proudly, pointing to where tiny teeth were pushing through at the front. 'He never complains.'

'Tommy's calm and easy, that's for sure,' her friend agreed.

'Just like his father, who I realise is here through our son. It has to be enough. If Tom comes back, we're blessed, but my heart can't take the pain of yearning any more. I'm going to throw everything into the salon and raising Tommy. That's it.'

'*Bravo*, Eden,' Madeleine said, reaching over to hug her.

Edie smiled sadly. 'You've saved my life, and bringing me here has already given me perspective.'

'Eden, my darling, *you've* saved your life by having the courage to face it.'

'And here we are,' Edie said, standing. She planted a tender kiss on her son's dark head. 'Paris,' she said, dreamily. 'You're a lucky boy, Tommy. Travelling to far-flung places already. Gosh, what a rush that was. Can't believe we nearly missed the train. I've never run like that in heels in my life. I thought my hat was going to blow off.'

Madeleine began to chuckle at the memory. 'We must have looked very amusing – like two famous movie starlets skipping down the platform, hissing at the porter to hold the train . . . and our child! Anyway, next time we'll be wealthy enough to take the British Pullman and do it in style . . . and they will hold the carriage open for us.'

'Next time, Mads, Tommy and I are going all the way to Istanbul on the Orient Express,' Edie assured.

'Now you're talking. For now, we make do with a boat train and a stay at my ageing friend's apartment.'

'Yes, who is Monsieur Faubourg? Don't say a former lover.'

Madeleine raised an eyebrow. 'He was a lover, once.'

'I know you say things like that to shock me. It doesn't work any more.'

'You are a changed woman.'

'I am,' she sighed, joining Madeleine at the window, shielding Tommy's eyes from the piercingly bright shaft of sunlight. 'I feel as though I've lived several lives: the life as my father's daughter and brother's sister, then the life as my father's companion and carer, his friend and partner in the business.' She paused. 'And then my life as a woman in love . . . a wife, now a mother.' Her voice shook momentarily. 'Don't worry. I refuse to get maudlin in Paris!'

'Eden, I'd be more worried if you bottled it all up. I prefer emotions to be shown. It's very French, too.'

'Well, I can see why you chose Paris. It's so effervescent here. Even this place; I can't imagine how much it's worth.'

Madeleine turned back into the apartment. 'A cool fortune, as you English say. Nothing in this neighbourhood comes cheap.'

'These parquetry floors are so beautiful,' Eden said, kicking off her sandals to feel the soft timber beneath her feet. 'In fact, everything about this apartment, from its gilding to its gorgeous, romantic shuttered windows, speaks to my design sense.'

'Good, then use it!'

'When are we meeting Mademoiselle Veronique?'

'Tomorrow at ten. So today is ours to roam. Are you both up to it?'

'I couldn't bear to waste a moment in sleep. Besides, I don't want to dream. Tom waits there.'

'Then we shall sleep when we're dead,' Madeleine announced and they dissolved into amusement.

'Mads, you are good for me. And thanks for arranging the pram.'

'Don't mention it. All of my old friends owe favours anyway. Come on, let's change into our finest and take a promenade around the Luxembourg Gardens. Tommy will love the fresh air and you are going to think you've died and gone to heaven. Actually, no, that's how you'll feel when you see Versailles. Hurry! Tonight we might be able to hear Kiki sing.'

'Kiki?'

'Model, singer, cabaret artist. The Belle of Montparnasse.'

'You know Kiki?'

'Know her? We spent some of our childhood together. And I believe I did some nude modelling with her!' She gave a dramatic pause and Edie gasped for her benefit.

'I'd better put through a call to Ben first. I promised I would.'

'I'm glad you've renewed that friendship. He seems fond of Tommy.'

She nodded. 'Too fond, in fact.'

As Edie and Madeleine discussed him, Benjamin Levi sat in his office, not far from The Strand, and gazed, fixated on an image in the morning's newspaper that had taken his breath away. The steaming cup of tea delivered by his assistant had cooled, untouched.

Unaware of the traffic sounds, the slow tick of the clock on his mantelpiece or the distant clatter of typewriters beyond his office door, he stared at the face of a man with the potential to ruin his life . . . again. Was it him or just his imagination?

Ben took a painful breath and moistened dry lips, realising that his hair felt as though it was standing to attention and the warmth from the grate could not touch the chill he was feeling. The name sounded like a klaxon in his mind as he read it repeatedly . . .

Alexander Wynter, new chairman of Wynter & Co Ltd, took over at the helm following the passing of his industrialist father, Thomas Wynter, in August 1920. Pictured here, Mr Wynter is giving a speech at the opening of the firm's new bottling plant in Wigan.

Ben looked away from the copy and gazed at the features that he feared had once been hidden by a beard. For several long minutes now he'd dithered between believing his assumption and then telling himself it was pure fancy. He couldn't know for sure and yet his instincts suggested there was no doubting those eyes, or that haunted expression. Could it really be penniless, broken Tom? Tom, the war hero. Tom, the usurper. Tom, the thief who had stolen Edie from him. Tom, who had little to offer his bride but a ramshackle cottage out in the sticks and piecemeal work as a bookkeeper?

He couldn't be sure. But he also couldn't take his eyes off the dashing figure with the rakish smile.

The solicitor let out a ragged laugh. Had poverty-stricken Tom with the grand ideas and fine manners turned out to be one of the nation's wealthiest sons from a family of enviable pedigree? It horrified him. Alex Wynter had everything to offer Edie Valentine. Jealousy of this stranger cut through him, hard on the heels of his quickening anger. Maybe he wasn't a stranger.

Had Edie seen this morning's newspaper on her way to Paris? If so, then his quest to rekindle her affections might already be lost.

There had never been anyone else for him and the only way he would ever forgive her for her public betrayal was if she were to accept his offer of marriage when he made it again. His mother had admitted to wanting to spit on Nina Valentine's grave for birthing a daughter who had brought such shame to the Levi family, but Ben's obsession for Edie was as strong as it had ever been. He had remained politely detached from all eligible partners until even a determined Dena had given up her campaign to see her son married to a different girl.

Tom's disappearance had brought Ben such pleasure he was embarrassed by it, and couldn't risk looking upon Edie for a fortnight afterwards until he had his glee under control. And then he'd begun his new campaign. Slow, gentle, clinical almost, as he'd shown what a stand-up fellow he was in letting the past remain as old history, not to be revisited. Ben made twice-weekly trips to Epping Hospital, bringing fashion magazines and flowers for her, clothes for the boy. And if his feelings for Edie could be termed obsessive, then his fascination for the child had become consuming. A son. Everything he dreamed of, everything his parents wanted now out of life. He wanted that child to be his. He would give him a home, his name, and never let who sired him enter his consciousness. He would only look for Edie's qualities in the child, ignoring anything that might echo his real father.

It irked that she had called him Tommy, but if he won Edie back he would find a way to convince her to call him by his middle name. Daniel was Jewish. Daniel Levi worked, in his mind. But for the time being Ben made no demands. He'd known that first he must restore Edie's trust and then their friendship until she leaned on him, laughed with him again. Then he knew he must support her endeavours, show her that he was a different man – even though he loathed her modern thinking and her need to earn her own income while somehow juggling motherhood.

He'd also worked hard to pass whatever tests her French friend had set for him. Madeleine now seemed less challenging around him; accepting that he was re-emerging into Edie's life. Madeleine wasn't jealous of him, but she was protective of Edie. The ace was that Madeleine had never met Tom, never been seduced by the charm and attraction that had swept Edie from him.

He sat back, staring at the smiling photo of Wynter.

'Is that you, Tom?' he murmured at the stranger. The delight looked genuine enough in Wynter's expression and yet Ben believed he could see behind it to the ghost trapped inside. If Alex Wynter was Tom Valentine, then he surely couldn't be thinking about Edie, or he would be at her side right now. So what had happened? No one in their right mind would leave Eden Valentine behind. If Wynter was Tom, then he had forgotten her.

Ben gave a low sneer. Oh, he was so close now. Edie was more than just his friend again. She was opening up to his affections; she'd let him hold her hand, hug her in the way that people who are more than simple friends hug. Soon he would find the courage, and the moment, to kiss Edie and declare his love. But all of this would collapse if she even suspected that Tom was accessible.

Edie's future looked achingly bright if she could completely let go of Tom, and it was here that Ben was suspended with indecision. He wanted the bridal salon to help Edie move beyond her hurts but not to the point where it gave her such confidence that she believed herself independent enough that she may not consider Ben's proposal. He felt himself trapped, privately despising her growing independence and yet needing to be seen to foster it if he was to win her back. What's more, he was going to have to ignore the fact that he believed Tom was alive or he would be breaking the law by marrying Edie . . . if she'd have him.

He gave a low growl, ripping the page of the newspaper he hadn't realised he was suddenly holding so tightly that his knuckles had turned white. The phone rang.

'Yes!' he snarled.

'Forgive me, Mr Levi, but I thought you may want to take this call from Miss Valentine. She's ringing from Paris.'

'Yes . . . yes, of course,' he said, blinking in embarrassment. 'Thank you.' He waited, listening to the instant silence and then a series of clicks.

'Go ahead, please,' his assistant said and he heard a final clunk.

'Hello, Edie?' He felt sick. It was as though she knew he'd been plotting. He flung the paper aside, as though fearful she could somehow see it, suspect his cunning.

'Oh, Ben, hello!' Her low voice in a new breezy tone gushed. 'Sorry. I hope I'm not disturbing you.'

He swallowed. 'No, no . . . not really. Er, you sound as though you're calling from the bottom of the ocean.'

'I know . . . horrible echo, too. I won't stay, I just wanted to let you know we've arrived safely.'

Was that all? 'Oh . . . good. Excellent. I've been wondering. You know, you and Tommy are never far from my thoughts, Edie.'

'I do, Ben. You're very sweet.'

'How is my little man?' He held his breath. Was he pushing too hard?

'Perfect. He made the crossing without a whimper. It's cool but gorgeous here. No rain. We nearly missed the train, though. Had to run for our lives to make it.'

'Really? No chance to grab papers and magazines to read on the way, then?' He winced at how obvious he sounded.

'No chance to grab anything but our hats and run down the platform. I'm assuming there's no news worth worrying about?'

'No, Edie.' He breathed relief. 'All very boring and nothing at all like the time you're going to have in Paris. I do hope you have fun.'

'Thanks, Ben. Well, I'd better dash. Mads is waiting – we're in an apartment on the Left Bank and we're heading out to

Montparnasse this evening. She's got a friend to babysit Tommy. A lovely older woman who lives in the apartment below.'

'Perhaps one day you'll show me your Paris.' *On our honeymoon*, he added silently.

'*Au revoir*, Ben.' He imagined her smiling as she spoke his name.

'Be good,' he joked.

'Always. See you in a few days.'

'I'm taking you to dinner when you get back. Make sure Madeleine can babysit.'

'I'll hold you to it. Must go.'

He heard the click as the line went dead and found justification in his heart that what Edie didn't know, she didn't need to learn from him. With his confidence restored, he decided to risk another call.

With a drumming heart Ben picked up the phone again and asked his assistant to connect him to a new number. He waited nervously until the phone jangled and startled him.

'Yes?'

'I have Mr Wynter's office for you.'

'Thank you.' He waited, dry-mouthed.

'Hello, Mr Levi, this is Alex Wynter's secretary.'

He knew his secretary would have mentioned his city law firm's name. Wynter's secretary shouldn't be too hard to get past. Ben cleared his throat. 'Is Mr Wynter available please? It's . . . a personal call.'

'May I ask you to hold the line for a moment, please?'

'Of course.'

Breathe, he told himself as he waited and heard odd clicks and buzzes, and the distant echoes of voices that were tripping over phone lines.

'I'll put you through now, Mr Levi,' she said, sounding suddenly loud in his ear.

'Hello, this is Alex Wynter,' came a familiar voice. Ben felt his throat tighten. No doubt now. It was Tom.

'Mr Wynter. I'm um . . . Benjamin Levi,' he said, saying his name carefully and listening for the reaction. He gave his firm's name. Wynter didn't interrupt. 'I believe my father knew yours and as my old man hasn't been well,' he lied, 'I thought I should make the effort on his behalf to convey our family's condolences at your loss.'

'That's very kind of you,' Wynter said, although Ben heard a note of soft irritation in his tone. 'Coming up for a year ago now, Mr Levi.' It sounded like an admonishment.

Ben had to think fast. 'Yes, forgive me for raising it. It's just his name came up in conversation and my father mentioned his regret at not passing on the family's wishes at the time. I . . . er, well, I felt I should. Forgive me for calling, Mr Wynter, perhaps I should have written to you instead.' Wynter said nothing on the other end and Ben licked his lips with the tense sound of silence punctuated only by the clicks and whirrs of the connection. 'I don't wish to press on a wound but my other reason for calling was to express my firm's desire to offer our legal assistance should you ever require them,' he said, finding himself on the more familiar turf of selling the firm's services. 'As our fathers go back well before the war, I thought it polite to ensure this generation kept the connection. No pressure, of course. I presume you have your legal counsel in place, Mr Wynter, but should you ever have the situation arise where you might wish some independent advice, please don't hesitate.' He blew out his breath silently, relieved that he had navigated his way through this treacherous path relatively well.

'Thank you,' Wynter replied, his tone more accommodating. 'I'm sorry that I don't recognise your family name. I was . . . well, away for the war and then was rather late in returning to my family, actually.'

'Of course,' Ben said. 'I do wish you every success at the head of Wynter & Co.'

'I appreciate that. Goodbye, Mr Levi.'

'Goodbye, Mr Wynter.' *Good riddance, Tom.* Ben permitted himself a smug smile after he took a sip of the tea, ignoring the notion that it tasted as cold as his heart felt.

Their first day rushed past Edie in what she could only describe as a tornado of colours, sounds, sights and tastes. Tommy was understandably exhausted and was now sleeping beneath the watchful eye of Madeleine's old friend, Madame Charlotte.

Madame Charlotte was like a fat mother hen but she oozed style and wore scarlet without shame at sixty. She had her granddaughter, Juliet, staying for a couple of weeks and the twelve-year-old was enchanted by Tommy, keen to play and patiently feed him his evening meal.

Edie had observed the newcomers with her son and finally at eight, after watching him drift happily to sleep, she felt ready to leave.

'*Alors*, shoo!' Charlotte had chortled, waving her jewelled hands at Edie and Madeleine.

'Tell her we shan't be later than ten-thirty.'

Madeleine gave her a soft push of exasperation but still translated it.

'*Oui, je comprends*,' the woman said, nodding her understanding.

Edie hugged Madame Charlotte, blew a kiss to Juliet and allowed Madeleine to bundle her out of the top-floor apartment overlooking Rue de Renne and into the cool Parisian night. Edie looked back up at the soaring pale sandstone Haussmann building of the Left Bank where artistic folk liked to haunt the brasseries and bars of Montparnasse. She admired its elegance of delicate iron balconies curving around tall decorative windows, which punctuated the pale sandstone features. The street was alive with people and traffic and Edie had the notion that everyone looked as though they were enjoying themselves, whereas London traffic always felt urgent and distracted – people just headed from A to B. Paris appeared to move at its own unhurried pace, as though its inhabitants understood that this city's beauty should not be rushed. She sighed with pleasure at the glittering streetlamps throwing a glow around the first-floor window boxes and pooling soft light on the wide boulevard she and Madeleine had stepped onto. Edie decided that Americans, who were easy to pick out, seemed surprisingly at ease amongst their French hosts and she caught herself smiling at the twang of accents far from home.

'Americans, especially penniless poets and writers, love Paris,' Madeleine remarked, sensing her interest. 'Now, I want to take you to Bobinos tonight.' She lifted an eyebrow. 'Very "in", as you British say.' Edie laughed, feeling her spirits lighten. Paris had been an inspired idea. 'But first,' Madeleine continued, 'I know an excellent bar,' and she grinned conspiratorially.

'Everything in Paris is about style,' Edie marvelled later at La Closerie des Lilas after hearing Kiki sing, waving a chocolate-covered fork at her friend. It was approaching ten p.m. and cold, but spring and being abroad made them daring. The girls sat outside, ignoring the chill, with their backs to the windows of the café, watching Paris go by as they sipped on a black coffee and ate cake 'to kill all other cakes', as Edie claimed. 'I mean, look at this. It's chocolate cake, but Parisians elevate it to something cosmic. I almost can't bear to eat this exquisite swirl of brittle chocolate. Imagine what skill to shape it as the treble clef? Even the cream tastes different.'

'Chantilly,' her friend replied, amused, lighting a long, thin cigarette.

'Gold and silver leaf on one cake!' Edie exclaimed, then waved an arm again. 'How could you leave all of this?'

'Perhaps if you were facing what I was, then you could understand how easily I ran away. I do miss it now, though . . . now that I'm back here and seeing it through your eyes.' She saw her companion's expression falter. 'No, Eden, fret not, I will not let you return to London alone. I live there now and we have big plans together.'

'We're really going to do it, aren't we?' Edie replied, easing a final small fork-load of heavenly, dense sponge into her mouth.

'We are going to open Valentine's and you are going to cater to the cream of London's society . . . balls, engagements, weddings and beyond. Everything the modern woman needs in her wardrobe, you can design and tailor for her.'

'And if you model the clothes, no one will be able to resist my designs.'

'Let's drink to it. I wish I could share a glass of *la fée verte* with you but it was banned almost a decade ago for being too dangerous. I have tasted it and it is a curious liqueur.'

'What does it mean?'

'The green fairy. Absinthe. Dangerously high in alcohol and said to bring on hallucinations and changes in behaviour.'

'Good heavens. What is it made from?'

'Wormwood, whatever that is. Let's have champagne instead.'

'All right.' Edie looked unsure. 'Just a few sips. I'm not used to this sort of living.'

'Then get used to it. You're going to be a mad success, Eden. Haven't you noticed that every woman in this café eyed off your clothes as we walked in?'

Edie shook her head.

'Oh, please stop being so dreamy. They all want to be in them.' She grinned. 'But they all want to be you.'

Edie watched Madeleine order their drinks, flirting with the waiter as she did so. He brought two flutes and some petits fours, on the house, that he delivered with a wink.

'What shall we drink to?'

'To new beginnings, Eden. For both of us.'

'Absolutely,' she said with a sigh that spoke of sorrows that would never leave but tinged with an element of anticipation. 'To new beginnings,' she repeated and this time her voice didn't waver.

They drove in Pen's car with Alex at the wheel, along country roads with tall hedgerows that coursed between the Weald of Kent to the north and the rugged South Downs. He could smell the mineral aroma of salty marshland, drifting over from the Pevensey Levels, and while it did vaguely remind him of the bog he had often stood knee-deep in at Flanders, this was a more familiar and reassuring smell of childhood.

Alex inhaled. 'I love Sussex,' he said and cast a smile to his passenger. 'Nice wheels, by the way. Your father's?'

'How dare you!' she said, feigning horror. 'This is 1921, Lex Wynter, not the dark ages. This is my recent birthday present. Dad finally relented,' she laughed. 'I wanted an AC – open top, two-seater. But I was given this instead. Mummy said it's more sedate for a young lady.' She gave a moue of disdain. 'One day I'll buy my own roadster and I'll drive it fast enough that my hair whips out horizontally behind me.'

'How old *are* you?' he asked.

'I'm hurt you don't recall.'

'I recall piggy-backing you at a gallop to the main house when you'd been stung by nettles. I remember pushing you on the swing down by our river. I remember diving for pennies that you threw into the swimming pool and your squeals when I splashed you. You were always that tiny golden-haired angel, always laughing, ever fearless as you tried to keep up with us.'

She nodded. 'And you were always my dashing, dark hero,' she said, in a breathy voice, clasping her hand theatrically to her heart. 'I'm twenty-two, Lex. More than old enough.'

It was his turn to cut her a look of mock horror. 'For what?'

She glanced at him with barely concealed dismay. 'For absolutely anything I choose to do. I refuse to follow in Mummy's footsteps and do exactly as her parents told her, and then as soon as she was married, and given away by Grandpa, do exactly as Dad told her. Good heavens . . . a life of obedience is not for me. I want to break that mould.'

He chuckled. 'A modern woman, eh, Pen?'

'I hope you believe me,' she said with determination as they approached a T-junction.

'I do. Anyone from our neck of the woods who calls their father "Dad" is a modern woman. Turn right, I think,' he murmured.

'Dad says it's thoroughly middle class but I think he secretly likes it. He finds a lot of my friends intolerable . . . . I think I do too. All daddies' little girls. Where are we going?'

'I seem to remember there was a rather splendid stretch of woodland just down here.'

'I have a horrible sense of direction so don't count on me,' she admitted and as Alex deftly cornered, they saw the dark canopy of trees ahead of them. 'You're right. Clever you. Who said your memory was damaged?'

Alex parked on the verge, opened the door for Pen and she fetched their picnic basket from the boot. 'Oh, this is beautiful,' she said, stretching.

He wasn't sure if it was a deliberate gesture or just her complete lack of affectation but Alex was treated to a lingering look at

Penny's surprisingly generous, yet perfectly shaped breasts on her lean frame. He had to admit that the little Penny he'd once carried on his shoulders was today a gorgeous vision in pastel yellow with curves that demanded his attention.

'Lead me, then,' she said, unashamedly taking his hand. 'Take me to your secret spot.'

Alex couldn't be sure that he wasn't the one blushing – was his cousin flirting with him? 'Er, through here, then. We do have to cross a low stile, if I'm not mistaken.'

'Oh, I'm sure you're strong enough to lift me clear of it,' she said.

No, he wasn't imagining it. Penny Aubrey-Finch was flirting with him! She even waited as they approached the stile for Alex to take her basket and place it on the other side. She made no attempt to clamber over it herself. Alex dutifully and easily lifted her over and as he took her by the waist he was reminded, just for a heartbeat, of doing this very action in a countryside setting . . . but not with Penny. Not even with a blonde.

'What's wrong, Lex?' Her smile faltered.

'Nothing . . . just . . . no, nothing.'

'A memory?'

'Mmm, possibly.'

'What did you see?' Pen asked, smoothing her narrow, drop-waisted frock.

'It wasn't so much an image,' he admitted as he picked up the basket, 'as a feeling.'

'Deja vu?'

He shrugged. 'It's gone, Pen.'

'I suspect this is going to happen often. You'll get used to it and perhaps there will be some feelings that stick and turn into real memories.'

'I hope so.'

She casually took his hand again as though it was perfectly natural to do so, and just in that moment he was comforted by the contact of her soft, gloved palm against his. 'Do you? Why not let the past go?'

'I wish I could.' He nodded. 'Over here to the clearing.'

She followed, happy to be led. 'You can. Just let go. Whatever happened was part of the war, its isolation, its traumas. Leaving it behind and all of its memories, including even the lost ones that don't need to be found, are part of the healing.'

He stopped to regard her. 'Are you really only twenty-two?'

She chuckled. 'I've always believed age is irrelevant.'

'Now, if we push past this clump of trees . . .' he murmured. 'Ah yes, here we are.'

'Oh, Lex, I remember this place!' she said in wonder and he grinned, delighted by the pleasure in her tone. 'We came here one spring, didn't we . . . I mean all of us – with our parents?'

'We did indeed.'

'A carpet of bluebells,' she exclaimed.

It was a good description, he thought, glad that he'd remembered this picnic spot that had always felt like magic woodland in his childhood. A stunning contrast of the fiercely lime-green leaves of beech trees acted as a foil for the swathes of violet flowers that stretched into the distance. They had only the birds for company.

'It's a most romantic spot. Thank you, Alex.'

Romance had not been his intention. 'I used to say the sight of bluebells in this woodland could make me turn to writing poetry – and I'm no poet.'

'Oh, I don't know. I seem to recall you were always a sentimental sort.'

He pondered this as he looked around for a suitable spot to throw down the car rug. 'I really don't want to crush them,' he thought aloud.

'The flowers stretched for a hundred miles, I was sure,' she said and he nodded in amusement as he unfurled the rug. 'I seem to recall you telling me that fairies lived in the bluebell cups and I believed you.'

He offered her a hand and helped her to sit down. Pen kicked off her flat shoes and removed her small straw hat with its matching butter-yellow satin ribbon and sat back effortlessly on her knees, unheeding of her fine dress. She raised her chin to where a shaft of sunlight bathed her in a radiant glow of gold. Her hair shone and tiny insects showed up in that light as though paying homage to an angel in their midst. It was warm and the only sounds were the blackbirds and thrushes, singing their hearts out. Again this simple sound, which could probably be heard in most English gardens, was deeply comforting. The war was behind him. His new life beckoned.

'Even your freckles have gone,' he remarked.

She threw her driving gloves, which she hadn't needed, at him. 'Thank goodness. I hated my freckles. You always teased me about them; you said they'd grow bigger as I did.'

Alex laughed. 'You remember a lot about me, don't you?'

Her gaze suddenly intensified, as though shaping itself into an arrow and spearing him. 'I forget nothing about you, Lex.'

He heard the passion in her voice, refused to acknowledge it and instead changed the subject. 'So what have we got in here?' he said, pulling her basket closer.

'Chicken and walnut sandwiches; some madeira cake. I've got some cherries too that I picked from our orchard . . . and this!' Pen said, pulling out a bottle of champagne.

'Good grief! What's the occasion?'

She shrugged. 'You are! I've wanted to celebrate your return since that morning you turned up at breakfast.'

'Really? But that was ages ago, and you barely spoke to me.'

'I was in shock,' she said. 'Plus . . . you were surrounded by family. I thought it best to let your nearest and dearest have you to themselves.'

He frowned. 'You didn't stay for the reading either, did you?'

She shook her head.

'Why? Father included you in his will. I'm glad you got that painting. Penny Farthing, he used to call you. You really were so tiny.'

'No, you lot were just hideously tall. Even Charlotte walks on stilts. I was terribly fond of your father, Lex. I do love that painting and I shall always think of Uncle Thomas whenever I look at it.'

'Funny, that portrait always troubled me.'

'Why?'

'Because she looked so sad.'

'Not sad. Wistful,' Pen said and gave a self-conscious smile. 'I always related to the girl who sat for that painting, whoever she was.'

'Why?'

She sighed. 'I can't tell you the truth of why, not yet anyway. However, there are two reasons and the second is that I'm an only child. It has its benefits, I readily admit. But you can't imagine what it's like to have parental attention focused solely and wholly on you every moment of your growing up.'

He began rolling up his sleeves. It was a deliciously mild day, even beneath the cool of the glade. 'I guess not.'

'Please,' she said, offering food. 'I made everything myself.'

He gave her a look that said he was impressed.

'Mind you, you were the one being groomed . . . in the spotlight.'

'Indeed,' he agreed, taking the triangular sandwich she offered, which had its crusts neatly cut off.

She paused, fixing him again with a similar intense look. 'He was heartbroken, you know . . . I mean, when there were endless months of no news.'

He swallowed, remembering his father's serious but ever-kind face – its lines and wrinkles that attested to years of listening rather than speaking, to acquiring information rather than offering advice, to thinking long before he spoke. Strangers often thought that Thomas Wynter was deaf, or perhaps rude, because he rarely answered a question immediately. Those who knew him well understood that he was genuinely considering each response. 'I can imagine my father was the last to give up hope.'

'Actually, no. I think your mother and I both agree that your darling father finally sickened and passed away when he gave up on you ever being found – alive or . . .' She smiled away the word she didn't want to say. 'But there was one person who never gave up, Lex.'

He guessed what was coming. Pen had matured but there was one quality that had not left her since childhood, he noted, and that was her open expression. He recalled now how easy she was to read.

'I never gave up hope that you'd return.'

He cleared his throat softly. 'I'm grateful for that.'

'Are you?' He felt his skin compress beneath the cool palm she laid against his arm. He looked at where her unblemished hand, with its pale complexion, neatly proportioned fingers and manicured nails sat upon his naturally darker skin. There was something terribly intimate about her gesture. He wished she wouldn't and yet it felt helplessly pleasant. She knew it too, and he saw the realisation of that intimacy glimmer in eyes that seemed to echo the violet of the bluebells. She was passing a message and wanted him to make no mistake in understanding it.

And now those eyes misted slightly. 'I began in Scotland,' she said.

'Began what?'

'Looking for you.'

Alex was sure that little could shock him these days but her remark made his mouth open in silent surprise.

She nodded, giving a thin smile. 'Everyone said I was mad – including both our fathers, but I think Uncle Thomas admired me for it. He admitted to me before he died that because he was so busy comforting your mother, all he did was utter plac-ations that sounded horribly empty. He said that he counted on me to be the one true believer beyond himself that you had somehow survived and would return. It's why he made that codicil to his will.' She dabbed at a tear with a lace handkerchief but didn't appear self-conscious about weeping in front of him. 'My parents tried endlessly to talk me out of the search but I wouldn't be per-suaded, Lex. I had to find you, if you were to be found. I worked my way down through all of the military hospitals and any public hospitals that were taking returning soldiers. I lost count of how many heads of nursing I spoke to.' He looked at her in dismay. 'And I lost count of the weeks I spent trawling the hospitals. In fact, the day I discovered the hospital you'd been in, you'd —'

His shock spilled over and he cut her off. 'Bloody hell, Pen! What was in your head?' Alex ran a hand through his neatly combed hair, disturbing it so a lock fell forward.

He knew she noticed it. 'Love, I suspect,' she reacted, fixing him with a liquid gaze.

Although he'd let himself in for that remark, it didn't temper his shock at the easily spoken words. He stared at her uncomfortably.

'Well.' She broke the silence and gave a watery smile. 'I'm glad I can surprise you.'

'Oh, Pen.'

She refused to look at him now, busying herself in the picnic basket. 'Is it so far-fetched that I could be in love with you? That I always have been? That I always will be?'

He didn't know what to say and was aware of shaking his head slightly.

She rescued him, letting her gaze find him again. 'Did you not know?'

'No.'

She laughed sadly. 'Lex, you're pathetic. I've been crazy about you since I was about seven years old.'

'What?'

'I was that age, I think, when our families started meeting regularly; you must have been what – about fourteen then? And you became more dashing with each year. Didn't you wonder why I was always angling to spend the holidays here?'

'I thought it was Charlie's friendship. I mean, you are a cousin, after all.'

'Tosh! That was something the adults found convenient. Yes, we are related but so distantly that I'm probably a closer cousin to your gatekeeper!'

'I'm sorry, Pen.'

'For what?'

'Not realising.'

'I hid it well. To tell you the truth, I was terrified that you'd guess.'

He shook his head. 'I thought you found me intolerable.'

'Quite the contrary!' She laughed and he had to admit he found her amusement most attractive. 'I was so nervous that I might be wearing my heart on my sleeve, that you could hear it pounding harder whenever I was near you, or that I'd faint if you touched me accidentally. I did avoid contact as we grew older. Silly little girl that I was.'

'No longer a silly little girl, though.'

She shook her head. 'Far from it. And forgive me for being so direct but it's best you know that none of my girlish crush has waned. If anything, it's deepened. You're every bit and so much more than the handsome, charming, funny Alex Wynter I recall.'

'I am shocked.'

'I can tell. But when you left, I was just fifteen and —'

'Podgy.'

She slapped him playfully.

'Didn't we call you Podge?'

'Very unkind it was, too.'

'Well, well. You certainly didn't live up to it. You are such a catch now, Pen.'

'I don't want to be a catch for anyone, Lex. I want to be yours.'

Every ounce of breath was trapped in his lungs because each time he tried to divert the conversation, she dragged him deeper. She grinned disarmingly. 'Moving too fast for you?'

He scratched his head, feeling unnerved. 'Yes, a little. Leaping over the top of a trench with machine guns firing at me and bombs dropping all around me feels easier to navigate than this minefield.'

She edged closer and took his hand. 'I won't rush you, but I made a promise to myself that if my prayers were granted and you walked back into our lives that I would not waste a minute before telling you how I feel. I'm sorry to ambush you but I have to say this right now or I'll never find the courage and probably not have this opportunity of us being alone in a totally romantic bluebell field again.' Alex knew she wanted to sound witty but instead it struck him as so intense that he wanted to stop her saying any more, but she pushed on. 'So here it is. I have loved you since I was old enough to understand the difference between how I loved my pet rabbits and how I love my parents. You were in my life – romantically, I mean – like a burning meteorite from my eleventh birthday and in my mind you have never lost your fire. I told you I searched for you the length and breadth of England and that is no word of a lie. Even your mother begged me to stop, feared I was going mad.' She shrugged. 'She was right. I surely did go a little mad. I was convinced that you'd made it through and that you were injured somewhere and didn't know how to get home.'

'That probably sums me up.'

'I refused to believe that the man I secretly loved – the man I'd never been able to look in the eye and tell him how I'd felt for years – was gone. I had to find you, Lex.'

Without thinking through the potential repercussions, Alex lifted her hand to his face and gently placed it against his lips. He made no attempt to kiss it, but even in that gentle act of affection, he knew he risked the young, passionate Penelope Aubrey-Finch reading so much more into the gesture.

'Thank you for not giving up.'

'Oh, Lex.' She threw her arms around his neck and hugged him. He could feel her body trembling and even though he didn't dare hold her close, he stroked her in a brotherly way.

'Come on, now. I'm home.'

She pulled away and damp eyes regarded him. He knew she desperately wanted him to kiss her but he found himself in a strange mindset, one he couldn't explain yet. He wasn't sure if this potential relationship was wrong but just now it certainly wasn't right.

'Let's get that champers open, Pen. We need to celebrate, surely?'

She moved closer to kiss his cheek gently. 'I'm so grateful to the angels who guarded you and kept you safe. I'll be patient but not for much longer,' she whispered, before returning her attention to the champagne bottle. 'Will this do?'

He glanced at the label: *Veuve Clicquot Ponsardin*.

'Brut,' he pronounced with relish, trying to ignore the kiss and her warning.

'Stole it from Dad's cellar. He won't miss one,' she said with a conspiratorial wink.

Alex deliberately popped the cork so it exploded in a cascade of bubbles. He poured the frothing pale golden liquid into two glasses.

'Here's to your safe return,' Pen said, offering her glass in a toast. 'I'm celebrating that you're back in my life,' she said, more directly. 'I'm going to say it, Lex, no matter how it shocks you. I know I must be patient while you come to the conclusion that you also want me to be Mrs Alex Wynter.'

Alex's hand, raising his flute, froze mid-air.

'There, I did it,' she said, more nervously than she'd said anything today. 'No one will ever be able to accuse me of skirting the issue or falling into that terribly British trap of not actually saying what one means. I prefer to be candid.'

'You certainly do,' he breathed.

'I hope that doesn't scare you?' she frowned.

He shook his head, half amused, half baffled. 'You're extremely refreshing.'

'Good!' she said, eagerly. 'I think I've scared off most other suitors because of it.'

'Really?'

'Well, that and the fact that the only man my heart was beating for never knew how I felt. Now he does,' she said with a determined nod. 'Will you drink to honesty?'

Alex raised his champagne. 'To honesty.'

'Will you always be honest with me, Lex?'

'I promise you I will.'

They clinked glasses and sipped. 'Mmm, that's delicious. Now, shall we keep eating?'

He laughed. 'You are quite a girl, Penelope.'

'I am. I hope I'll continue to impress you enough that you'll truly believe it. My family has more than enough that I shall never have to worry about money, you know that.' She blinked. 'So I'm not Fern. Furthermore, I certainly don't need the Wynter surname to give myself social status, or security.'

'No, indeed,' he said, chewing on another sandwich although

the food felt suddenly too thick in his throat to swallow.

'I am not interested in anything that belongs to the Wynters . . . other than you. If you suggested we elope to South America and turn our backs on everything, I'd say yes and not flinch. I know I'm young, and I can see in your perplexed expression that you are still struggling to see me as anything but your "little cousin". But I want you to accompany me to the ballet next week and just give me a chance. I'm asking for nothing more than your company and let's see how we are together.'

He blinked, watching her carefully.

She frowned suddenly. 'Oh, Lex, I've been so insensitive . . . is there someone else? A girl in France, or Belgium, whom you need to go back for? Perhaps there's a nurse you met while in hospital?'

He sighed. 'I don't know, Pen. Have I lived as a monk for the past few years . . . or has there been someone special in my life?' He thought of the heart cut out of the handkerchief. 'I don't know. I fear there may have been.'

She looked instantly downcast. 'And?'

'I just can't remember. These are confusing days for me.'

'Do you feel anything for someone else?'

Alex shrugged. He chose to be honest. 'I feel nothing. A void.'

She gave him a look of genuine sympathy. 'The photograph of you in the newspaper a few days ago didn't prompt any calls?'

'None. Well, unless you count a lawyer offering his services and using my father's death and family connections as an excuse. He didn't mention the article but the timing struck me as too obvious.' He gave a sound of disdain. 'And the police did call and say a barber in the city might have recognised me and phoned his local station, but when questioned further became less sure and had little to offer in the way of information anyway. He didn't know the name of the customer, where he was from or where he was going – only that he recalled someone who looked like the man in the newspaper article which he glimpsed over a client's shoulder. All he could tell police is that the man came in on his birthday and that he was going off to celebrate. That's all he knew. Their conversation was so general he recalled nothing important from it.'

'Well, then. It definitely wasn't you. Your birthday is February, if I'm not mistaken.'

'You're not.'

'More importantly, you don't like celebrating birthdays.'

'You know me too well. Just a coincidence.' He sighed. 'Mother has demanded that I let the past be just that.'

'I can understand that, Lex. She's got you back. To her, what else matters? And surely someone significant would have recognised you and come forward. Perhaps you need to allow that there is no great secret? You were in and out of hospitals, you were ill, you may have been cared for by a family, but it doesn't necessarily mean that there's anything to fear.'

He let his shoulders slump. 'You make it all sound so easy . . . as though I can just get on with my life.'

'Why not? No one's come forward. Just get on with being Alex Wynter, returned soldier.'

He thought about this and all the sense she was making. Truly, for a youngster, Penelope Aubrey-Finch was impressive in her maturity. And he would be lying if he didn't admit that she was beautiful and fun to be around.

'You are good for me,' he said with a sigh.

'Then . . . will you give us a chance?'

Alex smiled softly. 'I'll certainly accompany you to the ballet.'

Her troubled expression relaxed and she beamed him a smile of pure pleasure. 'It's a beginning.'

'Let's drink to new beginnings,' he said and meant it.

19

AUGUST 1921

The two women stood back by the door of the salon and said nothing for a long time.

'You've done it, Eden. It's perfect.'

'Are you sure?'

'*Absolument!*' Madeleine exclaimed. 'It is as though I have walked into a top Parisian fashion house. You have captured its spirit. And yet it's very you – very *now*. I know of no fashion salon in Paris that looks anything like this.'

'Meaning?'

'The stark, bold, clean lines. There's not an ounce of . . . what's the word I need? Um, you know when you whip egg whites.'

'Meringue?' Edie offered, bemused. 'Froth?'

'*Oui!* Yes! There is nothing, how you say, frothy about this salon.'

Edie adored Madeleine's accent. 'Well, perhaps because there is nothing "frossy" about me either.'

'This is true. I love it, Eden. And so will your clients.'

Edie still wasn't convinced. 'The colour scheme . . .?'

'So you were right. I will never question your taste again. I know I said go for tropical colours, which everyone seems to be favouring, but your restraint works. What do you call this?'

'Monochrome.' She had to repeat it when Madeleine returned a perplexed look. 'I've never been to New York but I've seen photographs and I wanted to achieve that look.'

'Ah, one day we shall both go there and celebrate your eye for style. In the meantime, it is perfect. The mirrors are divine. They make the salon look twice as big.'

'Don't they?' Edie hugged herself.

'I suspect women are going to come here just to see the salon and be able to say to their friends that they're engaging London's latest designer. It's bold, Eden. I've modelled for enough houses to know that a lot of these places aim to create a sense of a woman's *boudoir*. But you . . .' She shook her head.

'What?' Edie asked, eager to hear it all.

'Valentine's looks like a place of secrets but also a glimpse of the future.'

'Let's hope it's not too bold; I don't want to scare potential clients away.'

Madeleine shook her head. 'Everyone will want to see it.'

'Perhaps I should charge a fee to walk through the doors.' She giggled. 'And recoup Tom's money.'

'Not Tom's. Yours,' Madeleine said gently but with a firm glance. 'It's been a year, Eden.'

She nodded. 'I forgot to tell you. Tommy took his first steps last night.'

'I missed it?' Madeleine sounded genuinely disappointed.

'I didn't expect it so soon.' She shrugged. 'Last night in the park he was on the grass by my side, crawled to a bench and, blow me down, Mads, he dragged himself to his feet and stood there unsteadily for a few moments. I was so shocked I couldn't move. And then he turned and gave me such a victorious smile all I could then do was cry.'

Madeleine shook her head with a baffled expression. 'I can only imagine how it is to be a mother with all this endless emotion swirling for one's child.'

'He reminded me so much of Tom in that moment of triumph. Same infectious grin. And then, when I called to him, he let go of the bench and although it must have felt like miles, he tottered across to me, falling down only as he reached me.'

'I wish I'd been there.'

Edie squeezed her friend's wrist. 'You were. You're always with us. There's no stopping him now, of course. Poor Louise, she's got her hands full.'

'Oh, your babysitter loves it; she told me she was dying for when he could walk,' Madeleine said, pushing herself away from the door to adjust the hang of a scarf in the window.

'Lulu, as Tommy calls her, is a saint. I thank my lucky stars the day Tilda put her in touch with us. She's crazy about Tommy, you know.'

'I've noticed. Hard to imagine she's been part of your circle for almost a year now.'

She gave Madeleine a soft smile. The last time she'd held Tom in her arms was this time the year before. It seemed impossible. There were days when it felt like yesterday. And then there were times, like now, when she pulled back from her busy life and all of its distractions to realise that weeks, even months, had flown past, without her crying herself to sleep or spending a day hiding her sorrows.

'Tommy's a happy little chap. That's all that matters. And I love my work.'

'Couldn't be happier?' Madeleine said dryly.

She couldn't fool her best friend. 'I wish I had a photograph of him,' she murmured, 'because with each day I think his features blur a little more in my mind.'

'That's a good thing,' Madeleine said. 'Perhaps now you'll let Mr Levi back into your life.'

'Poor Benjamin. He's a saint too.'

'No, he's not, Eden. He's just a man in love. And he's shown extreme patience with you.'

Edie nodded, frowning slightly. 'Yes. Ben's changed, though. Not so long ago he believed my place was in the nursery or behind the stove.'

'Oh, come on. I think he's handsome, eligible, and clearly smitten.' She linked an arm with Edie and they walked back the length of the salon, Edie running her fingertips over the day bed that she had designed herself, choosing the fabric and then having the piece of furniture made. The round seat that looked like four leather club chairs in a circle was her favourite piece and she'd sewn the cushions herself, using tiny pearl buttons as decorations and as a nod to the brides who would sit here and watch Madeleine model gowns.

'Well, he's extraordinarily proud of what you've done here . . . Give him a chance, Eden.'

She couldn't help but wonder if Ben had put her friend up to this. 'When was he here, anyway?'

'The day you finished the spring–summer collection and went home early. Same day you were furious the curtains hadn't arrived and Tommy vomited on your purple dress.'

Edie laughed. 'How can I forget that day!' She picked up a folder tied with ribbon. 'It feels as though my whole life is in here,' she admitted, undoing the ribbon to leaf once again through the sketches. 'All of my dreams right here in pictures.'

'They're exquisite on paper, Eden, and once you make them up, women are going to flock here.' She smiled. 'I do love this one,' she said and pointed.

'The party went better than I could have hoped,' Edie sighed.

The unofficial launch of Valentine's, at the eastern end of King's Road at Sloane Square, had offered an opportunity for the wives and wives-to-be of London's most well-heeled to attend a cocktail party and 'play' with fabrics, designs and colours, and to watch some of the salon's wedding gowns walked across its stunning black-and-white geometric carpet by the inhouse model, Madeleine Delacroix.

'Tom chose this site so well,' she continued. 'At first I thought he was barmy to tuck the salon away beneath the giant shadow of Peter Jones.' She shook her head. 'I see now his choice was inspired. Peter Jones is the main stomping ground for the women of Belgravia, Knightsbridge and Chelsea; Tom must have understood that no matter how tiny I was, those keen shopping eyes would not fail to notice Valentine's as they swarmed in and out of the department store.'

'I'll admit, your husband was smart.'

'*Is* smart, Mads. I'm not ready to put him into the past tense. And with one of my favourite haunts of Petticoat Lane just up the way, it all feels familiar. My father used to buy a lot of his raw materials from Petticoat Lane,' she said, a slightly wistful tone in her voice. 'The button-makers and importers of silks offered me instant credit because of his reputation.'

'I'm sure he would want you to trade on it, Eden, especially with your official launch only weeks away.'

The official launch would bring together some magazine publishers and newspaper editors with a few of London's socialites. The plan was that this event would garner valuable attention for its new owner and 'avant-garde designer', as Eden Valentine was described by *Vogue*'s editor-in-chief in a newspaper feature on trends. Far more important to their success, however, would be word-of-mouth passed across luncheon tables, swapped between bridge quartets, discussed during cocktails before the theatre and at supper clubs after it.

British *Vogue*'s editor described the salon as 'a seriously cool oasis in a desert of British fashion innovation' and went on to say that the 'angelic-looking designer behind the label, together with the French-born goddess who models her clothes, are set to make heavenly fashion for brides of the new decade.'

Eden chuckled as Madeleine read that last sentence from this morning's newspaper yet again.

'Try telling me you're not on your way now, Eden Valentine,' her friend glared with mock fury.

'It all depends on the proper launch, when my designs are on display in the editorials and people start to make up their own minds.'

'How many clients do we need, do you think?'

Edie lifted a shoulder and dropped it again. 'I honestly believe it's about quality, not quantity. Tom used to have a catchphrase that perception is everything. I understand now what he was getting at. I think all we need is a handful of wealthy, influential clients who move in the circles of Queen Charlotte's Ball and are on the lookout during the "coming out season" for husbands for their girls and it will gather its own momentum.'

'You said Miss Fincham might say yes.'

Edie grinned. 'Her wedding is next April. She'll have to hurry and make a decision.'

Madeleine looked delighted. 'Tell me it was because I put on that gorgeous cream and gauze silk shift.'

'Of course it was! The problem is she wants it in white.'

'Better in ivory.'

'I couldn't agree more, and neither could her head bridesmaid, but her mother wants her in white and Lady Fincham is not to be countered.'

'The client is always right, Eden.'

'That's a myth. Besides, every bride is a representation of my design. I want that gown to be first seen in the ivory satin it was designed with.'

'The Fincham bridal gown and trousseau, as well as her ten bridesmaids and mother-of-the-bride's outfit, will help to put us, how you say, "on the map"?'

'It would, but I can't compromise before I've even had a chance to launch, not after *Vogue* has set me up for such high expectations.'

'I guess it's a balance of your *esthétique* values versus income.'

'I just want to establish my place, Mads. People need to know that if they buy a Valentine it will have a certain look about it. And we both know the gown that Miss Fincham wants is my signature gown for next year. It must be worn in ivory or not at all.'

Madeleine raised a worried eyebrow. 'Well, I hope your persuasive powers are up to it.'

'I've agreed that some of the sketches can be published, in the *Sunday Times*, particularly this one,' she said, flicking a hand at the Fincham gown.

'She won't mind?'

'She'll love the attention and, besides, a sketch and a finished gown are a lifetime apart. Once she's worn it, a client can ask me to produce it in sky-blue and pink with purple ribbons for all I care. But appearing in the *Sunday Times* will create the groundswell of interest – another of Tom's phrases – and then I'm guessing we'll take orders for at least a dozen new spring wedding gowns that I am aware are up for grabs.'

'And a host of bridesmaids, a queue of mothers' frocks, a frightening array of honeymoon wardrobes, including one enormous order for Lady Pippa Danby, no less.'

'I want that order for the Danby gown, Mads. I already know what I would like to dress Lady Pippa in.'

'Eden, if all goes to plan, how are we going to do this? I mean, I can help sew on buttons, even answer the phone . . . but —'

'I'll tell you what we're *not* going to do, Mads. We're not going to get anxious. We're not going to doubt ourselves and, unlike my father, I *am* going to hire staff. Lots of staff, in fact; I know plenty of skilled seamstresses who would appreciate the work. But first we need to order all our silks and voiles, our threads and sequins, our lace and satins.' Edie rubbed her eyes. 'Gosh, I think I will probably have to spend a week just on the fabrics.'

'Well, there go my nice, quiet Sundays,' Madeleine moaned. 'And I had visions of spending them in bed with Mr Quinn.'

Edie swung around. 'And who is Mr Quinn? I thought you were seeing someone called Fallon.'

'I was. He became rather dull. It's Quinn now, although I have my eye on Jonathan Gamble.'

'The jeweller?'

'So much more, Eden. Five shops now. But it's not the rise of his jewellery salons that interests me,' she said, baiting her friend.

'Doesn't work any more, Mads,' she said, but laughed all the same. 'Surely the sparkle of diamonds do, though?'

Mads smiled, a sense of the wicked in her gaze.

'Don't give up your Sundays. We must have one day of complete rest from the salon – a chance for both of us to get away from it and everything connected with fashion. I think next Sunday I'll have everyone around for Tommy's birthday. I can do some baking at long last. You can bring Quinn or Gamble or whoever is currently escorting you around London's fashionable haunts. I can't keep up with you, Mads.'

Madeleine groaned. 'A birthday party? This Sunday morning I want to sleep.'

'Then do it. Eat breakfast at teatime with us – so long as it's cake, I don't care when you eat.' She laughed. 'I'll ask Tilda, Louise, of course. Delia might be in town that day. My neighbours love Tommy too so I'll have them over. It will be fun. And I want to spoil him.'

'As if you don't already. Speaking of dinnertime, aren't you meant to be meeting Ben?' Madeleine reminded, glancing at her wristwatch.

'I am.' Edie began packing up the sketches. 'I'm taking these home.'

Madeline gave her a soft glare. 'Why?'

'I want to do some final adjustments to the Fincham gown and bridesmaids for the feature.'

'What about House of Ainsworth?'

She shrugged. 'I don't fear the competition. *Vogue* said our designs would set trends. That means everyone else follows.'

'Well, be careful with those precious sketches!'

There was a tap at the door. They both swung around and there stood Benjamin with a bouquet of flowers.

Edie smiled at Ben. 'Sorry, not open yet.'

'Let me take you both to dinner,' he called through the glass.

'I am no one's raspberry,' Madeleine drawled and made Edie suffuse with laughter. 'What?'

'It's gooseberry.'

'Go on. I can close up. Kiss Tommy for me. Tell him I'm very proud of his walking.'

She kissed Madeleine. 'Thank you, darling.' Edie turned to Ben. 'I'll just get my coat,' she called.

'You'll need it. It's the coldest October I remember.' They walked out arm in arm, and Ben pointed at Sloane Square. 'Let's head towards the Star & Garter,' he suggested.

The streetlamps were already glowing as they walked beneath the endless canopy that stretched out from the deep red brick of the Peter Jones shopfront that soared above them.

'Do you know, you can walk into this department store now and buy everything from linoleum to a squirrel?' Edie exclaimed, marvelling at how far down the street the Peter Jones empire now sprawled.

Ben took Edie's hand and guided her across the broad road, dodging horses pulling their wagonettes and cars rolling slowly behind. 'How's the little man?'

'Tommy's wonderful. I'm very lucky to have Mrs Miller look after him whenever I need to be alone in the salon. I've realised I can do all my design work from home and Mads can run the salon if we have no appointments. And I do the sewing at night and she watches Tommy while he sleeps. It's a juggle but it works. Oh, I haven't told you. He's walking!'

'Oh! I can't wait to see that. Now your problems begin, I presume,' he grinned.

'I think you're right. I'll have to keep making adjustments as he grows. It's not ideal but for now I've got good support and Tommy's happy.' She could tell Ben wanted to say something about that final remark and she imagined he would be all too happy to offer his support – financial as much as physical – in a more official capacity, but Edie deliberately swung around to stare at the shops. 'I really must think about what to get him for his birthday. He never seems to want anything but cardboard boxes and wooden spoons to make noise with.' She laughed, trying to deflect Ben's thoughts.

'I've got him a train set.'

'Oh, Ben, how sweet that you remember!'

'I can hardly forget holding that boy for the first time last summer. I knew his birthday was close. August 17?'

'Nineteenth,' she corrected softly. It was a bittersweet date for her. 'But a train set? That's a little extravagant for a one-year-old.'

'Perhaps. But I wanted a train set for years and years. I think I was ten before I got my first. Who else am I going to spoil if not you two?'

Edie smiled but had to look away. That searching question was not one she wanted to answer. 'Well, he's a lucky boy,' she deflected again, before once more switching subjects. 'I thought we were going to the pub?'

'No, you deserve far better than a noisy pub. There's a new restaurant I'd like to try. Apparently the Dover sole is its star dish.'

'The flowers are beautiful,' she said, inhaling from the bouquet and balancing her folder. 'Perhaps I should have left them at the salon, though.'

'No, they're for your new flat.'

'I love living in Chelsea. And we're so close to the park.'

'Well, I love that you're back in London proper. Means I can see more of you.'

It began to shower and they were instantly scurrying with the rest of London into doorways and shops, and in their case to an early dinner at a dining room that Edie didn't even catch the name of.

She began shrugging off her lightweight stole, with its fur trim.

'You look very beautiful, Edie,' he murmured as he unwrapped it from her shoulders and gave it to the cloakroom assistant.

'Thank you,' she said, already knowing the organza and ivory lace handkerchief dress would steal attention. She had a bridal version of this in mind and was trialling the look as a frock first before she invested so much expensive fabric in a gown.

'Excuse me, Miss. Do you want to leave that here?' the girl asked, gesturing at Edie's folder.

Ben glanced at her enquiringly. 'Go ahead.'

'No, thank you. Much too precious.'

'Oh?' he said, intrigued, casting a smile at the waiter welcoming them. 'I have a table booked in the name of Levi, please.'

While the man checked his reservations book, Ben looked back at Edie indulgently. 'Secret salon business?' he asked, glancing again at the folder.

'My sketches. My life,' she said with mock drama in her tone. 'The competition would love to get its hands on these and make my salon fail before it even opens its doors.'

'I'm sure it's safe here, right, young lady?' Ben said, barely glancing at the cloakroom girl. He quickly moved away to speak with the maitre d'.

The girl was clearly used to being ignored because she didn't answer Ben and fixed her eyes on Edie. 'It will only be released with this, I promise,' she replied, handing Edie a ticket. Edie relented and exchanged the folder for the cloakroom ticket. 'You don't have to worry. I will take very good care of it. My name's Sarah.'

'Thank you, Sarah.'

The girl smiled and it lit her face. Edie turned back to where Ben stood with the head waiter.

'Very good, Sir. Please, follow me. We have a lovely table by the window for you.'

After excited chatter about the salon's opening day, and a main course of Dover sole, Edie licked her lips. 'I'd forgotten how good butter tastes. It seems like such a treat to be able to buy it whenever I want . . . or sugar, or coffee, or white bread that hasn't been stretched with coarse grains.'

He smiled. 'I love watching you eat, Edie. I always have.'

'What do you mean?'

'Your tiny mouthfuls that seem to incorporate a taste of everything on your plate.'

'Father's training. He was always so strict at the table.'

'I know you miss him.'

'I do. But the strange thing is, Ben, ever since . . .' She blinked. 'I have had to become extremely independent and I'd be lying if I didn't say I love the freedom that it's brought.'

'Actually, I envy you.'

'Why?' Edie reached for her glass of wine.

He shrugged. 'Is it not obvious? I live with my parents! Still do as my father requests, still privately quake at the thought that my mother may tell me off for spilling something on my shirt . . .'

Edie laughed. 'Then leave home! You're far too old to be under your parents' roof.'

Ben looked suddenly energised. 'Well, I'm excited to tell you that I have been looking at houses. In fact, I think I've found one.'

'Really? Where?'

'Not far from here, actually. In Chelsea.'

'Oh . . .' Edie tried to hide her private dismay at how close he would be by gushing, 'That's wonderful.'

'Yes, now I can walk you home, or take you out more often – both of you, I mean. I'll have a car permanently in London now.' Ben's words were spilling fast and Edie sensed he was selling her on this idea. 'I'm no longer going to be a man who lives with his parents and nurses a broken heart that still beats for the girl he's always loved.'

His words silenced her. Edie felt instantly smothered and reminded of past days, but neither was she shocked. She'd felt his proposal coming for weeks. Since allowing him to steal quietly back into her life as the good friends they'd always been, it didn't seem surprising that he might rekindle his hope for a future together.

He passed what appeared like a nervous, long-fingered hand through coarse black hair. It stayed in place as though made of wire. It gave Ben a luxuriant look. He would never go bald, Edie thought. But then neither would Tom, and she knew whose dark hair she would prefer to feel against her skin. Ben watched her through chocolate-dark eyes carefully. Had he rehearsed this? She felt instantly sorry for him, still as boyish in his looks as his moods; still looking for her approval, still wanting to impress her and yet at the same time own her, control her . . .

'I'm sorry,' he said, realising she wasn't going to fill the awkward silence. 'Nothing's changed for me.' He daringly took her hand, looking concerned at her silence. 'Forgive me, Edie. I wanted to help you celebrate, not make you feel uncomfortable.'

'There's nothing to forgive, Ben. You've always been very sweet to me.'

'Ouch!' He let go of her, reached for his wine and sank a big gulp. 'I hate being thought of as sweet. Anyway, now there's a little boy to worry about. You know how much I enjoy him. He needs a father. I want to —'

'He has a father.'

'I mean, your son needs a man in his life. He's surrounded by women.'

Edie forced herself to breathe despite how suddenly suffocated she felt. 'His name is Tommy. You never say it.'

'Tommy,' he replied.

'You don't like it, do you?'

He shrugged but she saw the guilt as he dropped his gaze quickly. 'You couldn't blame me for it not being my favourite name. But his middle name I like enormously.'

'Ben . . .' He looked up. 'I hurt you. I loved another. I still do.' She noticed a different, unreadable expression now ghost across Ben's usually open face. Edie shook her head. 'What?'

'Nothing,' he said, clearly smiling with an effort. She detected the false note in his bright tone. 'Sorry, I was just thinking about the old days and how boring I must have seemed. I did so love you, though, Edie, and impossible though it seems, I think I love you even more now. I let you go because I had to. But I don't have to any more. I need you to know that I don't care that you were in love with another man.'

'That I married another man,' she corrected.

'Tom's not coming back, Edie,' he said carefully, searching her face.

Edie twirled her glass, staring at the sparkles of colour the candlelight cast in the crystal. She made a helpless mental note to remember them for a design using crystal beads that was flitting around the rim of her mind. 'I'm not dense. I'm just stubborn about accepting it.' She looked back up at Ben's earnest expression.

'I don't believe he's dead. I think I would know it in here,' she said, touching her heart. 'That's my problem.'

'Well, if it's any consolation, I have long ago accepted that you did love Tom. And there was no room for me once he arrived into your life. But now that Tom's gone . . .'

She couldn't respond, refused to join him in this conversation and instead let the silence hang between them.

Ben cleared his throat softly. 'Yes . . . now he's gone. And you're still the same gorgeous Edie I was always in love with, except now there's Tommy and he needs more. I know you're lonely even though you have a child and Madeleine and a host of new acquaintances. I know you're still the same Edie in here,' he said, touching his chest. 'You want Tommy to have a brother or sister. You still like the idea of being part of a family. You still believe in marriage.' He shrugged. 'You're still Jewish. No one understands you better than I do, or can offer you what you need more than I can.'

Now she had to correct him. She opened her mouth but he held up a hand.

'Wait, Edie. Just let me say this. I've come to see all that you are, all that you want to be, and I realise I made errors before in underestimating you and your needs, your dreams. I'm different now.'

Are you, Ben? She didn't believe him; if anything he was becoming more embedded in the ways of the older generation – his occupation alone pushed him deeper into tradition. Edie suspected the idea that women would very likely win the equal right to vote alongside men in the next decade privately disturbed him. He did have a fascination with Tommy, though – she had sensed that long ago – and his fondness for her child was as hard to dispute as it was to fathom. Of all children to love, why would he fall for the child of the man he loathed? Perhaps because Tommy was captivating in an innocent and helplessly sunny way, or maybe it was just another way to exert control. Tom's wife, Tom's child . . . trying to make them both his. And her son was everyone's friend. He gave his affections with great ease and Ben had obviously been as seduced as Madeleine or Lulu. And he was a boy – that would be important to a traditional man like Ben. Tommy was dark and small. Was Ben convincing himself that Tommy could pass as his son? Edie felt sorrow ripple through her; it didn't need much imagination to see that if echoes had shapes, then Tommy was an echo of his father and would grow as tall and strong as the next boy.

Ben was still talking. 'I want children too, but we have time.'

'I would like Tommy to have a brother or sister . . . or both,' she sighed and saw his hopes lift. She shouldn't have shared that.

'Edie, I can hire the help you might need so that you can have family and career. I know you want to go to New York . . . we can take a transatlantic cruise for our honeymoon.' His eyes were shining with eagerness in the candlelight and Edie could tell he'd been planning this all carefully. 'I won't rush you. Just please say you'll consider what I'm asking and not ignore the fact that we're both lonely. I can make you happy, Edie, if you'll let me.'

'You forget I'm still married, Ben.'

He shook his head. 'And you forget I'm a solicitor. There are legal ways to deal with your situation. I can legally adopt Tommy. I can give him my name.' She tried not to shrink back when he took her hand. *Tommy Levi?* Or would he want that name changed to *Daniel Levi* once they were married? 'Just think about it, Edie.'

She nodded without commitment but with no intention of Tommy being anything but Valentine. 'Tell me about Sol,' Edie said, shifting subject as smoothly as she could.

'It's not good. The cancer has spread.'

'I wish he'd said something to my father.'

Ben shrugged.

'I've been remiss in not seeing him. He was my father's close friend.'

'Sol understands.' He cleared his throat. 'He's never fully forgiven himself for Tom's disappearance.'

'There's no blame to be laid. However, perhaps saying it aloud – offering forgiveness – is something I can give him before he passes away. I think I'll take Tommy on the bus and visit him tomorrow.'

'I'd come with you but I have to drive my parents to Brighton.'

'No need,' she said before smiling, remembering it was every late August that a most important birthday occurred. 'Great Aunt Esther?'

He nodded. 'You see, you do belong in our family. Her ninety-second. Mother says she'll live forever.'

She could almost hear the cogs in his brain turning and before he could offer up the inevitable invitation, she gave a small, embarrassed yawn. 'Wish her well from me. Now, I'd better go,' she said, taking out the cloakroom ticket from her clutch bag. 'I said I'd pick Tommy up by seven. Thank you for a most lovely evening. Actually, can you get this for me?' she said, handing him the ticket. 'I'll just powder my nose.' She rose from her seat, glad to make her escape.

When Edie returned Ben was already at the doorway with her coat and folder. He hailed her a taxi and after the expected expressions of good luck for her long-awaited debut, he surprised Edie by placing a gentle but perhaps overly familiar kiss, aimed deliberately for her mouth. 'Think about what I said,' he murmured into her shock. 'Not for a day since November 1919 have I ever stopped being in love with you.'

'Ben, I don't —'

'Nonsense,' he said with such confidence it felt like a reprimand. 'We were so in love before you lost Daniel, before Tom came along. You've just forgotten.' He grinned and banged the top of the taxi. 'See you very soon. My love to Tommy.'

Edie felt lost for words at his condescension and knew her expression must have looked equally as blank. She dug deep for a smile but came up wanting and instead forced herself to nod, not sure what other gesture to give. And as the taxi eased away from the kerb, Edie was highly aware that Ben's kiss felt as awkward now on her lips as it always had.

20

It was Saturday and Alex trailed after his mother in the orangery, holding a small basket she'd thrust into his hands fifteen minutes earlier. It was now filling with dead leaves that her sharp garden snips and equally sharp gaze had dealt with.

'Mother?'

'I heard you, Lex.'

'Well?'

She straightened and eyed him. 'What do you want me to say?'

'That you approve, perhaps.'

'I suppose I do.'

'But?'

She sighed, pulled off her gloves and threw them into the basket with the snips. 'Put that down. Let's have some coffee. It's too cold for this today anyway.'

Cecily led her son into the morning room, where comfy armchairs hugged a small but merrily dancing fire. She pulled on a long tapestry ribbon that rang a bell in the bowels of Larksfell and told the staff that the Wynters were ready for their coffee to be served.

'Well?' he said.

'Let's wait for our refreshments. How's everything? I haven't seen you in what must be a fortnight. Bramson said you'd been up north? I swear you're avoiding me.'

He shook his head. 'I was checking out our investments in the steelworks at Newcastle. Shipping of the passenger kind is the future.'

'Really, darling, you should know your father's business dealings didn't hold an iota of interest for me and yours don't either. Is that rude?'

He laughed. 'Your candour is.'

'Oh dear, and I thought that was what my Wynter men liked best about me.'

He leaned in to give her a kiss as he helped her to her seat. 'It is, Mother. To answer your question, *everything* is fine.'

They made some small talk about the family; whether or not Phelps was indeed the best match for Charlotte, the fact that Fern was coming around more often again and that Rupe needed distraction of the work – rather than social – kind. They both agreed to go ahead with the scholarship in his father's name that one of the universities was hunting and to make a large donation to King's for its new library.

The coffee tray duly arrived and Bramson supervised as a maid laid out the cups on saucers and a tall pot.

'I've warmed the milk as you like, Ma'am. Would you like me to pour for you?'

'No, that's fine, thank you, Elsie. My son enjoys waiting on his mother,' she said and the shy girl grinned back before she left.

Bramson nodded at them both and left. Alex poured the coffee, enjoying inhaling the aroma of the infusion from the African beans his mother had roasted to her specifications in Hove. But with the intoxicating smell came a memory of yearning.

'I think I would have run across no-man's-land naked for a cup of real coffee in my darkest days.' At his mother's unhappy expression, he added: 'I can't help it. The most simple experiences can trigger a memory,' Alex said.

'You must try not to remember, darling,' Cecily said, surprising him. 'We all know it must have been awful but everyone is looking to the future now.'

'The future isn't easy, Mother. The boom following the war has been short-lived and stocks are crashing all over Europe. It hasn't affected us Wynters, for reasons I shan't risk boring you with, but people are doing it very tough out there in the real world . . . people like Elsie.'

'I think we look after our staff rather well,' Cecily said, accepting her coffee. 'Better than the Favershams treat theirs, for instance.'

'I used Elsie simply as a metaphor for all the working families of Britain. Times are going to stay hard for most of the population. Unrest will be next, as the workers begin to get rankled at conditions, lack of pay rises, the usual problems, and after all the suffering they feel they have a right to expect more from employers.'

'Alexander, I could reel off a dozen fine families to you right now who have all lost two or more male members of their family. I think our level of society paid just as high a price as Elsie's lot, as our men felt obliged to head off to war and lead.'

'I know, I know, Mother. I was one of them, remember?' He gave her a soft look of apology. 'This wasn't what I wanted to talk to you about. It's about Pen.'

'Hmm, Pretty Penny,' she said and sipped at her coffee. 'Ah, that's hitting the spot.'

Alex frowned, his gaze drifting to the flames.

'Lex?'

He seemed not to hear her.

'Alex, are you all right?'

'Forgive me,' he said, sounding worried. 'Something you said . . . it . . .'

'What did I say? We were talking about Penelope Aubrey-Finch, weren't we?'

It was gone, whatever it was. 'Yes . . . um, yes, we were.'

'Darling, are you sure about this?' his mother asked, sounding tired. 'Is she really right for you?'

'Do you mean her age?'

'Her age, her history with us . . .'

'Except she's not a blood relative, Mother. And I would have thought her family, pedigree, everything about her, in fact, would suit the Wynter aspirations perfectly. She's young, I agree, but she's surprisingly composed.'

'I do know what you mean,' Cecily admitted. 'And I would be lying if I didn't also tell you that I have more time for Penelope than I do for most young women I meet. But are you ready for marriage? Ready to really settle down? Perhaps you need more time . . .'

'I find her utterly charming and if I refuse her now . . . I may hurt her enough to lose her.' He drained his coffee. 'She told me last night that if I choose not to marry her – and she's fully accepting that I may not – then she's going off on a transatlantic voyage and then a grand European tour. She may even choose to live in America permanently.'

'Good grief,' she said with appropriate shock, but then skewered her son with a look. 'Do you really care?'

'What an odd remark.'

'I don't think so. A mother knows her child. You can trick the world but you can't trick me.'

Alex now inhaled visibly with exasperation. 'What do I have to do? Burst into song? Do a tap dance?'

'Be quiet, Lex. Now listen to me. When I asked you to engage with life and take up social opportunities, I did not mean for you to marry the first girl who caught your eye.' She held up a finger to stop him. 'Hear me out. Penny is a favourite of mine, and your father loved her like a daughter, so you can be confident nothing would have made him happier than to see the two of you walk down the aisle together. But!' She leaned forward, placing her cup and saucer on the table beside her but not allowing him to wriggle off the skewer she had him on. 'She deserves so much more than being a convenient means to an end for you.'

'That's grossly unfair.'

'Is it? You don't love her, Lex, do you?'

He lifted a guilty shoulder and looked at his hands. 'She's waited a long time, Mother, carried a torch around for me when most would have given up. She's proved her love. I can learn to love her, can't I?'

Cecily's lips tightened.

'I will be very attentive.'

'But absent.'

'No. I'll make a promise to you now that if —'

'I mean in here,' his mother said, covering her heart.

Alex took a long, deep breath that was full of sadness. He shook his head. 'I can't let it go. I've tried throwing myself into work – thinking distraction would help. I've tried attending all of Pen's social engagements but I loathe them. I went fishing in Scotland – hoping isolation and silence would open up my mind. And I just felt lonely. I've even taken up gardening – have you noticed?'

'Clarrie showed me your new roses.'

'I don't know why but I see old roses in my mind and I thought maybe planting new ones and cutting their blooms might trigger something. But nothing's coming. I'm now of the belief that I have to start from scratch. It's not the life I yearn for but then I don't know what it is I'm yearning for. So I shall build a new life and make that work, or I might as well be dead in the trenches with the rest of the Tommies.'

'Don't say that.'

'I'm dead in here, Mother,' he revealed, echoing her gesture by covering his heart, and could see her grimace at his honesty. 'I can't explain it. I don't love Pen as I imagine I'm supposed to but I am terribly fond of her and I know I can bring her happiness if I agree to what she wants. And she is extremely determined to be my wife. I have no defence against her. To say anything but yes is to hurt her deeply and I have no alternative. So why not? I can make it work.'

'You could also ruin her life.'

He shrugged. The gesture looked helpless rather than heartless.

'What greater insult is there to a woman than unrequited love?'

'What do you want me to do?' he snapped suddenly, standing and moving to lean on the mantelpiece, glowering at her. 'I'm trying to please everyone. Marrying Pen gives some structure – a framework to build upon. I have to start somewhere.'

'And not please yourself,' she said in a terse voice.

'I can't please myself because I don't know how to. This pain has got to stop.' Alex withdrew from his pocket the red handkerchief.

Cecily frowned. 'What's this?'

'This is what I'm reaching for. But don't ask me what it means.'

His mother blinked at the red square with a heart shape cut out of its middle. 'It could mean nothing.'

He nodded and sighed. 'Or everything.'

'But no one has come forward in the past two years.'

'Exactly! That's why I've let Pen get close.'

Cecily pulled a face of resignation.

'I suppose I've reached the conclusion that I could spend the next few years wondering about that lost chunk of my life,' he said, his finger tracing the shape of the heart, 'or I could just get on with living. Penelope offers me that chance.'

'You make it sound so clinical.'

'But with Pen it doesn't feel that way. We're good together.'

'I suppose you want my blessing?' she asked.

He leaned over and kissed his mother's cheek. 'How does a May wedding suit you?'

She smiled and he hated that she looked as sad as he privately felt. 'Well, darling, I suppose Larksfell always does look its best in spring.'

––––––––––

Tommy sat on Edie's lap as they rode the bus.

'Hello, gorgeous,' the conductor said to Edie as he ruffled Tommy's hair. 'You sure you're not meant to be taking a taxi?'

She smiled, realising she probably did look conspicuous, but this was conservative dressing for her. At least the styling was; perhaps the tangerine of her otherwise plain dress was loud enough to attract attention, and clashing it with a fuchsia ribbon on her summer hat certainly didn't reduce its bright effect. 'Golders Green, please.'

'Great day to be up here,' he said, looking around the empty top deck. 'Bit early for most, though, on a Sunday.'

She smiled politely and took their tickets. 'Yes, I thought Tommy would enjoy it.'

Finally new people stepped aboard. 'Have a great day, you two,' he winked.

She nodded, hugging Tommy closer. 'Everything all right with you?' she whispered, kissing his warm, plump cheek.

He nodded happily. Tommy was not a great talker but she'd accustomed herself to his quiet way. Perhaps he takes after his father's side, she sometimes wondered.

She put her cheek alongside his and stared at what Tommy seemed mesmerised by: the buses and cars grinding alongside. 'Horsey.' He pointed.

'Big, isn't he? And strong like you,' she said, losing count of the tiny teeth he could now smile widely with. He was growing so fast.

Tommy nodded. He turned around on her lap to follow the progress of the horse and she stared at his bright, open expression and experienced a familiar sense of melting, a cleaving of hearts. *I wish you could see him, Tom,* she said silently. 'You know something, Tommy? You make me want to be better at everything.' He didn't understand and he was straining to catch a final glimpse of the horse. His breath smelled of sugar from the three jelly babies she'd allowed him to choose and put in his pocket, encouraging him to say the colours aloud as he'd selected them with focused precision. Red, green and yellow, which he'd pronounced 'Lello'. That was what she was going to call the canary she planned to give him for his birthday. Next year, maybe a puppy.

'Are you looking forward to your party?'

He nodded shyly, and surprised her by planting a long, wet kiss on her nose that she was sure tasted of jelly baby.

She felt a sting of happy tears. *And so much more enjoyable than a kiss from Ben,* she thought privately.

Edie was aware that an old grief had her in its maw as she watched the dying man sleep. Sol's complexion looked grey and he'd withered to half the person she recalled. He lay in the bed looking frighteningly small and if not for the weak, laboured rise of his chest, she could believe his spirit had already fled.

'Wake him,' Irena had urged. 'He would want to know you're both here. I'll make some coffee. Come on, darling, you come with Aunty Irena.' Sol's wife had gestured for Edie to proceed into the bedroom as she steered the little boy into the kitchen, but it wasn't awkwardness she was feeling; it was fear. Fear of being reminded of her previous life – the one she'd worked hard to distance herself from.

She needed to find the courage, though. 'Sol . . .' she whispered. Edie moved closer and took his hand. It was dry and his skin looked as thin as onion skin. 'Sol, it's me, Edie. Edie Valentine.'

He stirred. 'Edie?' he croaked and his eyelids fluttered.

'Yes, I'm here.'

Sol turned. 'I thought I was dreaming. Hello, beautiful.'

She smiled at the affectionate nickname, and the inevitable tears fell for a good man and old friend.

'No crying for me, Edie. It's not so bad, love. No pain.'

'Oh, Sol. I'm so sorry I haven't been to —'

'Hush now. You've made my day.' He frowned. 'Is it day?'

She gave a watery laugh, glancing at the windows that had their heavy curtains drawn. 'Yes.'

'The light hurts my eyes. Shame. I'd prefer to go looking out at the sky.'

'Don't, Sol,' she murmured.

'Irena told me all about how you're getting on. You'll make us all proud.'

'Hope so.'

'I'm sorry I lost him, Edie,' he croaked, reaching for her hand.

'Me too. I miss Abba every day.'

He smiled sadly. 'I meant Tom,' he said, sounding so frail she wanted to call his wife, bring Tommy in quickly so he could see her fine boy, but didn't dare let go of his hand or shift attention. 'I've wanted to say that to you for a long time.'

Her tears began to flow freely and she gave up trying to dab at them.

'He just wanted to buy you a gift.'

She caught her breath. This was the first snippet relating to Tom's disappearance she'd heard since that terrible day.

'Really? You didn't mention it back then.'

Sol struggled to breathe as he spoke but was determined to say what he had to. 'I forgot. I thought Abe would have mentioned it. We're old men, Edie. Our minds aren't what they used to be. Tom said he was feeling strong. He had plans to go to Piccadilly Circus but as we approached he realised it was too much and so I set him down at Green Park.'

'I heard that. I never fully understand why he didn't go to Savile Row with you. Why he was dropped off. I assumed he was scared and decided to head home on a bus out of central London, but it all became too much.'

'He should have stuck with me. The Row is quiet.'

Edie nodded in agreement.

'I dreamed of Tom not so long ago.'

She sniffed. 'I dream of him all the time. Tragic, aren't we?'

Her son peered around the door. She caught sight, beckoned to him, whispering.

'Sol . . . this is our little boy. I called him Tommy.'

'Tommy,' he repeated in soft wonder, his voice gently rapturous.

'Say hello to Solly,' she whispered.

'Hello, Solly,' the little boy mangled with a slight lisp.

Sol chuckled. 'Wow, Edie. He's a Valentine all right, but I see Tom.'

'Me too. I'm glad you do.'

'I remembered something after my dream. It was as if I was there again. It was all so clear I could believe I could reach out and touch him, bring him back to you.'

Edie caught a sob in her throat; refused to crumple into tears.

'You have to find the old man.'

'Old man?' she repeated, her voice shaking.

'The one Tom was speaking to.'

She blinked. 'I didn't hear anything about an old man.'

'I didn't remember him at the time. It was all so . . . so . . . frantic when the police were making their enquiries.' He stopped and gulped. 'And losing Abe. I felt so responsible, Edie. I don't think

I was thinking straight. But in my dream I saw him, an old man, approaching Tom. I've seen him before when I've done deliveries. I think the old fellow feeds the birds at the park.'

Edie squeezed Sol's hand. 'Remember again. Tell me everything you can recall. Every tiny detail, Sol.'

———————

The weather, though unseasonably wet, was also hot enough to send most people scurrying to the closest seafronts. Alex had booked a table at The Grand Hotel in Brighton and whisked a delighted Pen in Rupert's new car to the coast in a roar of petrol fumes.

'Glad I borrowed this motor. Mine's far too sedate. I shall definitely have to get myself one of these,' he yelled to her over the growl of the engine.

'I shall race you to the purchase,' she challenged, holding on to her hat, her face flushed with happiness.

After a laughter-filled lunch and a flute of champagne to add to the effervescence of the afternoon, he suggested a stroll on the promenade.

'I have to tell you, Pen, you somehow manage to look as cool as ice-cream in this outrageous heat, and just as delicious.'

She grinned. 'There is a saucy response that comes to mind with that remark.'

He laughed, delightedly. 'I can work it out, I'm sure.'

She slapped him. 'You're a tease. I should be blushing.'

'Really?'

'I wish it wasn't a tease,' she said and gave him a sidelong, searching glance that he couldn't hold.

They stopped and leaned against the dark Victorian lacework balustrade that separated the promenade from the shingle beach and enjoyed the balm that the very soft breeze brought.

'Thank you for bringing me out today. It's wonderful to hear you laugh,' Pen said.

'I actually had a question to ask,' he began, frowning. Was this the moment he let go of his life to this point? He could feel the presence of the red handkerchief in his inside breast pocket, fancying that it was pressing against his heart, pleading with him to stay true. Whoever she was, she was looking for him. And as Pen turned towards the wind to catch its taunting relief, Alex heard it bring with it a plea. *Find me*. Damn it! That voice. It blew through his mind, disintegrating as fast as it came, so he was reaching after tendrils of the smoke it sounded like. The voice in his mind made him think of a garden. A tranquil, perfect garden of safety. Is that why he was suddenly gardening? Was her name Rose? Is that why he was growing magnificent perfumed roses over an arbour near his study window?

'Ask away,' Pen said brightly. 'If I can help with something, I'd be glad to.'

Alex braced and smiled. He could do this. Had to, if he was to have any chance at normality again. 'It is something I could use your help with, Pen. You see, I think I need a wife.'

Her head snapped around and she regarded him in wide shock; if this was what she hungered for, then she hadn't seen it coming and he liked her all the more for that. He watched now as her normally violet eyes seemed to reflect the summery blue of the sky to match her dress. She'd never looked more gorgeous, and he couldn't help but love seeing her speechless for once.

'Do you mean it, Alex?' she whispered, all amusement gone.

'Care to marry me, Pen?'

Her shriek of joy managed to eclipse the music and squeals from the funfair rides on West Pier but even though it was noted by passers-by, all they saw was a woman oblivious to all around but the man she stared at so intently.

'In a heartbeat,' she gushed, clasping his hand and pulling it to her heart.

How could anyone resist her? 'I'll take it that's a yes, then?'

'Yes, oh, yes, I want to marry you with all my heart.'

'May I kiss you?'

'I'll die if you don't.'

Elders taking a seafront walk nearby hissed private disgust while younger people whistled as the couple on the Brighton promenade kissed and sealed a new society engagement that would set tongues buzzing wildly in London.

Meanwhile Alex could smell the perfume of roses and heard a woman's heels walking away from him in his mind as a robin sang.

21

Edie stared at the newspaper with a dulled glaze in her eyes. The buttered toast appeared damp and lifeless to match her expression, while smudges of white had appeared on her already pale cheeks like night cream she'd forgotten to smooth in. Madeleine stood in unnerved silence, hands on hips, watching Edie.

'Say something,' she finally murmured. 'Let it out.'

'I'm not one for histrionics.'

'Translation please.'

'I don't go in for screaming and tearing my hair out or slamming doors . . . but I feel as though I'm doing all of those things in my mind.'

'How could this have happened, Eden?'

'I'm not imagining it, am I?' she begged. 'Those are my sketches.' She looked up at her friend as though pleading to be contradicted.

Madeleine visibly swallowed. 'They're not your sketches but they are your designs. Unmistakably.' She shifted to stand behind where Edie sat, numb, in the salon. 'How? You protect that folder like a child.'

'It hasn't left my possession.'

'Where is it now?'

'Here. In the office. I carry it everywhere.'

'Wait. I'll fetch it.' Madeleine disappeared and then re-emerged, carrying the folder. She handed it to Edie, who undid the ribbon and opened it.

Sifting through the sheets, she searched for her sketches of the designs that were on display in the newspaper. Edie shook her head, making a soft noise of despair as she flicked through the drawings once more. 'They're gone. I didn't notice before because they were finished and I've been working on the others. The three gowns featured in the article are missing,' she said. 'They were the most dramatic, my best work, but also effortlessly simple. The thieves could have them made up in days by an accomplished team of seamstresses.'

There was no passion in her voice at all. Madeleine laid hands on Edie's shoulders. 'You sound too calm. What's happening?'

'Calm? I feel dead, Mads.' She flung the newspaper aside and stood, her arms clutching her elbows as if holding herself in pain. 'Steadily, everything I love has been taken from me. I have told myself that there are people around me who have lost more . . . I've got Tommy, friends, I've got some money, and I've got my dreams. I've made all that enough – forgive me, Madeleine, I don't mean to demean you.'

'You're not. I understand.'

Edie shook her head. 'When Tom disappeared and then I lost Abba, I felt as though my life was over.'

Madeleine nodded. 'Natural enough, but with Tommy needing you, you've picked yourself up and faced it all.'

'Sometimes I cast out the words "Find me, Tom!" and convince myself he'll hear it somehow and come back.'

Madeleine couldn't hide the despair she felt on her friend's behalf.

'But this . . . this feels like the end for me, Mads. I'm tired.'

'Eden, someone stole your designs. Get angry, get a lawyer . . . but don't give up.'

'I have a lawyer in my life.'

'Then ask Ben what you should do.'

'It's House of Ainsworth's word against mine. I can't prove those are my designs!'

The phone rang. Madeleine answered the call. 'Valentine's, good morning. Ah, Lady Fincham, good morning. We're not officially open yet but we'll be happy to —'

Edie was back unfurling the newspaper and staring again at the sketches that were being described as 'a new wave of bridal gown designs that herald the arrival of the jazz and cocktail age'. They appeared in the weekend feature on spring bridal wear in the *Sunday Times*. Edie hadn't seen the newspaper until this morning as she'd spent Sunday listening to Sol recall in sudden vivid clarity about the afternoon she had lost Tom in London. Unbeknownst to her, by the time she'd returned to her flat in Chelsea, Sol was already slipping away from his family, released now that he'd spoken to Edie about that terrible day. She shook her head, still blankly staring at her designs with no clue as to how anyone could have taken them from under her nose. *Only Mads had access*, her mind screamed. But she dismissed the treacherous thought in a heartbeat and besides, the sketches had been in her care this last week.

Madeleine put the phone receiver down and looked at Edie, unsure. 'That was Lady Fincham.'

Edie could guess what was coming. She made it easier for her friend. 'I'm guessing she's taking her business to House of Ainsworth.'

Madeleine hesitated. 'She said they will make up the gown in white.'

'Of course they will. That's because they have no taste,' she said in a bitter tone. 'Did she at least wonder at how that bridal house could possibly have the same design to offer her daughter?'

'She didn't mention,' Madeleine replied but Edie could hear the lie, knew her friend was protecting her feelings. Lady Fincham had probably accused Edie of copying someone else's designs. It hurt. But she had no more tears to weep for herself.

The phone rang again. 'That will probably be the Danby order,' Edie murmured. 'I guess Pippa Danby is having her gown made at House of Ainsworth too. I'm going out, Mads. Will you take care of it?'

'Yes, of course, but . . .'

'I just need some air.'

Her coat was hanging near the door or she would have left without it, despite the snap cold that had come with the rain. She didn't have her bag and suddenly her folder of precious designs didn't matter any more. Her bubble had been burst.

Edie walked without purpose, pausing to stare blankly into the windows of Peter Jones, where autumn fashions and even a few Christmas decorations were sneaking in. Fairy lights would go up in London in the next month or two and people would get into the festive spirit. She would have to bring Tommy out at night to enjoy them. But Edie didn't feel like any of it right now, believing she had nothing to celebrate and nothing to look forward to but the misery of a collapsed dream.

She thought of Ben, curiously enough, and his desire to support her in her career, but perhaps his former attitude had been right. Maybe what she needed to think about now was security, being married, having a future with someone, starting again with trying for a new family . . .

Ben wanted to marry her. He wouldn't care that her business had failed before it had even begun. He would handle the paperwork ending her marriage with Tom. Ben offered life beyond all of her suffering. Back to Golders Green regularly, although she could still live in Chelsea apparently. Back to synagogues, Shabbat, being a dutiful wife. No more sketching, no more dreaming. She could probably take up sewing for some of the tailors of Savile Row . . .

She saw her reflection in the window, noted the tear stains that she swore she would avoid, but mostly she noted the daringly mannish soft suede coat of grey that ended in a thick hare-fur trim to lend femininity. She admired the rich purple ribbon that embellished the pockets and lapels, complementing a matching silk lining and the ribbon around her charcoal cloche hat. It was a striking ensemble. Would she dress like this as Ben's wife? She doubted it. Ben was so conservative, she was sure he barely understood her clothes. He'd not even asked to look at the sketches she was so proud of that evening in the restaurant.

The restaurant! Eight days ago! That was the last occasion she'd let the folder out of her sight. Friday had passed in a blur of activity and she hadn't touched the folder. Saturday likewise. Sunday she'd been at Sol's house. In fact, the last time she even opened the folder had been Thursday morning.

Edie turned on her heel and hurried back to the salon.

'Mads!'

Her friend looked up from the small counter. She looked grave. 'Four cancellations, Eden. I won't lie.'

'Never mind that now. We can't change it. But we can find the culprit.'

'What do you mean?'

Edie explained.

'Wait,' Mads said, her tone ringing with admonishment. 'You think a cloakroom girl has stolen your designs and sold them to House of Ainsworth?'

'It was the only time I let that folder out of my sight! Can you think of another explanation?'

Her friend shrugged sadly. 'It's logical, perhaps, but surely —'

'Why? Doesn't a girl working in a cloakroom have dreams too? She may have been curious because I seemed so reluctant to hand my folder over. Perhaps she stole a peek inside, realised they had some value . . .' She shrugged. 'Maybe she is interested in fashion, follows the stories in the penny newspapers about where skirt lengths are headed and the arrival of the jazz age.'

'But how would she know what to do with them?'

'I don't know, Mads. I'm just trying to find an answer. I can cope if I know what happened.'

'All right. Do you remember her name?'

'Sarah. I don't know the name of the restaurant, though,' she continued and ignored Madeleine's look of soft despair. 'But,' she emphasised, 'I know exactly where it is, at the bottom of Sloane Square.'

'Right, let's go, then.'

'Now?'

'Got anything better to do, Eden? We don't have any more clients on the books at present and I am guessing that you're not going to be making up the Fincham gown in ivory or white.'

Edie shook her head ruefully. 'I hope it turns out dreadfully.' She gulped. 'I didn't mean that, did I?'

Madeleine took her friend by the arm. 'You know, sometimes it's healthy to be . . . as we French say, *méchant*.'

Edie sighed. 'And after that?'

'Well, let's agree there's no point in prosecution.'

'Isn't there?'

'What's to be gained? Not your name, your reputation, not your designs . . .'

'The damage is done?'

Madeleine nodded sadly. 'It simply draws more attention to a situation that requires no more kindling to the flames. Let the fire burn out, Eden. No one can steal your talent.'

'Start again?' she said, wearily. 'I want to punish this thief.'

'Stay optimistic. The editor at *Vogue* loved your designs. All you need to do is replace the designs you've lost.'

'But those sketches were my best! They were so fresh and new.'

'Eden, if I've learned anything, it's that fashion waits for no one. Design something even more spectacular!'

'For whom?' she said glumly. 'We have no clients.'

'Oh, come on, the season is just beginning. There's got to be a society engagement out there. Some disgustingly wealthy man has just proposed to an equally disgustingly wealthy woman, bringing together two disgustingly wealthy families who are prepared to spend a disgustingly enormous amount on their wedding.'

Edie laughed. 'Where is she, Mads? Where's my disgustingly wealthy fiancée?'

'Out there, looking for you right now. She won't want to go to House of Ainsworth, which everyone is talking about. That would be de rigueur for our girl. She'll want you, Eden. You just have to let her know you're here and waiting for her.'

'I love you, Mads.' Edie hugged her friend. 'But I want to look that thief in the eye so she knows I know.'

Madeleine sighed. 'Nothing to be gained. I'll walk with you and you take the time of the journey to think it through and change your mind.'

It was while walking to Sloane Square that Edie began to tell her friend of Sol's dream and his vivid recollection of the old man in the park who may have spoken to Tom, perhaps seen which way he headed . . . might even have exchanged a few words.

The King's Road led into Sloane Square and Madeleine paused at the pub on its corner.

'Forget Sarah. We've already decided there's nothing to be done.'

'She can't get away with it.'

'But she already has. Put your energies into Tom instead. Let's go find this old man. We'll go right now, to Green Park.' Madeleine turned to gaze back at the clock tower above Peter Jones. 'What time of day did Sol say he dropped Tom off?'

'Just before noon.'

'Well, it's not quite ten-fifteen. Let's make our way to Green Park. At worst it will be a pleasant morning out in the fresh air; we can visit Savile Row – which you're always saying you want to do – and then we can return with clear heads to work out some new designs and make a pact that Valentine's is going to be the big success story for London's bridal scene in 1922.'

Eden took a deep breath.

'She hasn't ruined your life. Sarah – if it was her – has just set you back a few weeks, Eden.'

'I was taught to turn the other cheek.'

'Abe raised you wisely, then. Come on. An afternoon in the park beckons.'

———

Alex had finished making the Aubrey-Finches 'the happiest parents in the world', according to Pen's mother, who pecked Alex's cheek. 'Go on, you two. We'll join you later down by the duck pond. I'm sure you'd appreciate some time alone,' her mother said, waving them away, still dabbing at her eyes as she glanced with a watery smile at her husband, who drew her close with an indulgent smile.

'I'm sure I don't need to ask you how it went with Dad,' Pen admitted, linking her arm around Alex. 'I'll bet my mother's the one who wants to be alone because she can't wait to share the gossip.'

Alex grinned to cover the unsettled feeling that the news would now move through the country like a fire out of control. They wandered in comfortable silence into the small copse surrounding the Aubrey-Finch property that sat on countless acres of stunning, fertile land around Rye in Sussex.

'Do you remember the duck pond? We used to swim in it,' Pen reminded her fiancé.

'Of course I do.'

The duck pond came into view, a contented pair of ducks drifting over its softly rippling water.

'Lex, this is the happiest moment of my life,' Pen said. 'Right alongside the moment you came back from the dead, and the moment you asked me to marry you in Brighton. All of it, because my dream has come true.'

'I'm sensing a "but" coming,' he sighed, finding a comfy spot on the grass.

She joined him. 'But . . . do you know through all of this dreamy happiness, you haven't once said you love me?'

Alex had been expecting this.

'I . . . I'm not even insisting that you say it,' she added, her tone pensive. 'I just worry a little that I'm not enough.'

'What do you mean?' he said, shifting to meet her gaze, hating that he was the cause of the soft injury in it. And still she was being the generous one.

'There are moments when you're physically present, but your mind is absent.'

'Pen —'

'I know . . . I know. I promised myself I wouldn't take you to task and yet here I am, treacherously jealous monster that I've become, doing just that. And I don't even know what I'm jealous of.'

'Ghosts. Nothing more,' he uttered but heard the lie echoing through his mind to the tip-tap of heels on a stone pathway.

'I hate myself for sounding pathetic and needy,' she continued and he suddenly wished he could stop this merry-go-round that he was now clinging to as it began to spin faster. The smiling horses were blurring into one sickening motion of speed but going nowhere, except round and round in circles.

Red handkerchief, clicking heels, sewing machine oil, a well-made suit, roses, garden shed, leather satchel . . . a heart. Always a heart.

'It's just, I love you so much, Alex. So much that sometimes I can't breathe for the happiness that you're safe. But I don't want to trap you in my love. I don't want it to be just my love that binds us. I worry that you're going along with this whole wedding thing because you don't have any other better offers.'

'That's not true . . . nor is it fair.'

'No,' she said, blushing slightly at his admonishment. 'It's probably not fair at all to expect you to love your bride.' Her searching gaze found him again and nailed him where he sat.

Alex cleared his throat. 'Listen, Pen. My life of late has been strange, to say the least. It's impossible to explain to you how awkward I feel at times.'

'Awkward with me?'

'No, not with you . . . but with life itself, and that does include you. But listen to me now,' he said, taking her hand and kissing it. 'It's the confusion that makes me appear odd and it doesn't reflect how I want to feel. I can't think of a more suitable wife . . .' As alarm flared in her eyes, he squeezed her hand. 'Or someone I would more want to spent my life with. I don't know how to love just now. I have flashes of memory, but not images, just feelings. Anything tangible is still out of reach.'

'Aren't the doctors offering any advice?'

'Nothing that helps.'

'A specialist, then?'

'Look, I may see Cavendish again. He's the doctor who assisted me at Savile Row. But, Pen, do you really want me to learn any more?'

She laid her head on his shoulder and he obliged by putting his arm around her, which he knew she needed. 'Lex, I love you, but I want your happiness first before your ring. I don't need you to look after me or provide for me. I just need you to adore me.'

Alex was disgusted that he found it so easy to beguile her. 'I think this mood will pass. We shall be married and be hideously happy.' He needed to believe it.

She turned to gaze at him. 'I hope you mean that.'

'You make me feel safe, you make me want family, you make me want to be the Alex Wynter my father expects me to be. Above all, you make me proud.'

She smiled. 'Proud?'

'Proud for the women of this country . . . you're an amazing role model. This family needs you . . . I need you, Pen. Is that enough?'

Pen looked up at him with soft eyes and kissed him long and gently. 'For now,' she murmured.

22

Edie and Madeleine had taken a bus and found themselves huddled in the breeze on a bench in Green Park, hoping to see 'an old man'.

'Apparently he feeds the birds,' Edie remarked.

'We've been here for nearly two hours. I doubt he's coming.'

'We could have missed him . . .'

'He could be dead.'

Edie threw Madeleine a sharp glance. 'It could just be too blowy today. It's not exactly pleasant.' She looked up. 'Rainclouds gathering too.'

'Right!' Madeleine stood. 'Well, no luck here and my thighs are numb, so I need to walk.'

'Savile Row?' Edie suggested.

'Let's go. Are you going to be gloomy again?'

'No. But maybe I'll come again sometime. I don't care about Sarah any more. I don't even care about the sketches. It's not the end of the world.'

'I am proud to hear it.'

'Thanks. Let's go ogle some handsome, wealthy gents.'

'Many of whom have eligible spinster daughters,' Madeleine said, tapping her nose.

They walked briskly against the wind, past a barber's shop.

'My father liked to come to this salon for a haircut and shave when he was much younger. I think the son has taken over now,'

Edie said, staring into the window. The sign told her the shop was closed and she had no reason to go in there anyway. 'Perhaps Tom looked into this window that day,' she said, touching the glass.

Madeleine pulled on her arm. 'Come on. Don't get soppy or you'll see clues everywhere where they aren't. Take me to Savile Row.'

Edie confidently guided her friend down Piccadilly towards St James's Church. The pair turned into Sackville Street, hanging on to their hats as the gusty weather wanted to snatch them away, while the tall grey stone buildings created a wind tunnel that made them shriek from the cold blast.

They hurried and skipped into Vigo Street, where London turned quieter, and it led them into Burlington Gardens, where the wind didn't burn so viciously. 'This way.' Edie pointed across the road and they cut right. 'This is Savile Row,' she said with a note of triumph and the sounds of traffic and people in a hurry instantly disappeared.

Madeleine gave a low whistle as she stared at the imposing, handsome building with a brick frontage that was at least three windows wide. Round arched windows and doorways sported elaborate brick trimmings, and the main door was set back into an arched recess with plain stone imposts.

'This is Gieves & Hawkes, gentlemen's outfitters. Three storeys and a basement. I've been in and out of this tailoring salon so many times I've lost count. Abba was a favoured supplier of its master tailor.'

'Why?'

Edie smiled. 'Abba had what the tailoring people called the Rock of Eye.' At Madeleine's frown, she explained. 'That's a phrase used for someone who is skilled enough to ignore the rules.'

'Rules?'

Edie took Madeleine's arm and began walking again. 'Most tailors or seamstresses cut to patterns based on a set of meticulously taken measurements. Patterns and tailoring is mostly about mathematics to get the cut perfect on the client. Abba could cut by instinct. He had patterns but the truth is he never needed them. It's a gift. It's called the Rock of Eye.'

'You have that! I know you only measured me because you felt obliged. Admit it, you sized me up and could cut that first dress from nothing more than a sketch.'

'I suppose,' Edie said, strolling on.

'I knew it! Eden, I've never known anyone in my career to have that talent. You are every inch your father's daughter.'

Eden nodded. '"The tailor's girl" is how they knew me as a little child around here,' she admitted. Then she smiled, pointing. 'Here's Anderson & Sheppard, another of Abba's admirers. And there's its head tailor – a lovely gentleman called Percival Fitch.'

Fitch had stepped outside to check the colour of some cloth in the thin grey daylight. 'Good grief. That isn't you, Edie Valentine, is it?'

'It is! How are you, Mr Fitch?'

'Come here.' She was surprised by the genuine hug she received. 'It's been far too long. Oh, look at that ring; Abe always said you'd marry Benjamin Levi. Congratulations.'

Edie blinked; she didn't want to go into the truth with Mr Fitch and it really didn't matter now.

'I heard about Abe,' Fitch continued. 'I'm terribly sorry for your loss.'

'Thank you.' There was so much more she could say but she swiftly moved on. 'Mr Fitch, this is my closest friend, Miss Madeleine Delacroix.'

'*Enchanté, Mademoiselle*,' he said, smiling gently.

'*Merci, Monsieur Fitch*.'

Fitch grinned. 'Eden, did I hear that you've set up a bridal salon?' She nodded.

'Well, well. Everyone on the Row will be proud of our little tailor's girl.'

Edie gave Madeleine a sideways grin. 'Thank you. And how is business for you, Mr Fitch?'

'Oh, much the same. Our loyal clientele keeps the workflow steady.'

Edie turned to her friend. 'Mr Fitch always said a gentleman comes here to have a suit made but also to get away from nagging women and all other noise. Discretion is currency on the Row.'

Fitch demurred, looking embarrassed. 'We like to keep it peaceful. No excitement if we can help it.'

'Isn't that dull?' Madeleine wondered.

He knew he was being teased because he smiled genuinely. 'Dull is how we like it. Not so long ago one of our most valued clients got knocked down in Savile Row by a taxi. Caused such a stir, it took days for the talk to settle down.' He shook his head and tutted.

Both women laughed. 'I hope your client is recovered, Mr Fitch?' Edie offered.

'Oh, I'm relieved to say he wasn't injured beyond being dazed momentarily. We hadn't seen him for years but we still had a pre-war suit of his that I could give him, as his own navy one was torn. I heard later from another client – a doctor – that he pulled up surprisingly well and was on his way home that evening.'

'Well, that does sound like an unusual day.' Edie was reminded of Tom's navy suit, a daring colour she always loved him in.

'Indeed. Especially as he was a returned officer who —'

'Excuse me, Mr Fitch.' A young man appeared, hovering behind him. 'Your two o'clock appointment will be arriving half an hour earlier. Is that all right with you?'

Fitch frowned, took out his fob and tutted again. 'I suppose it must be. Sorry, ladies. Duty calls,' Fitch said.

'Not at all.'

'Mademoiselle Delacroix.' He gave a gallant nod to Madeleine before giving Edie's arm an affectionate squeeze. 'Good luck, Edie. I'll watch your progress with fond interest.'

The women made their way up Conduit Street, towards Regent Street and a bus to take them closer to home.

'He could have asked us in to warm up,' Madeleine complained.

'Anderson & Sheppard is not a woman's place, Mads. Savile Row isn't either, but I'm glad you've seen it.'

'You don't have to tell a French person about discretion. It's second nature to us because everyone's having affairs!' Madeleine said in a dry tone.

'The tailoring shops of Savile Row are the old guard, but ultimately changes will come as younger blood arrives. Ready-to-wear is on our doorstep, Mads, which is why if I can get a few brides into the salon, I can start thinking about my first collection beyond bespoke. Buying ready-made clothes is the future.'

The family had gathered once more in the drawing room at Larksfell; Fern was noticeably absent, and Alex suspected she wasn't yet ready to face the entire Wynter clan again when clearly something formal was afoot.

Afternoon tea had been served and Elsie had just finished cutting a sugar-dusted jam sponge into slices.

'Will that be all, Ma'am?'

'Thank you, Elsie,' Cecily said.

Bramson remained at the far end of the room, away from the warmth of the fire but never so far that he couldn't be the eyes and ears of the household that Cecily Wynter depended on . . . and always had.

'So, Mother, what brings us back together so quickly and

demands I rush up from London?' Rupert said, adding a spoonful of sugar to his tea.

'On such a cold Monday afternoon, no less,' Dougie added.

'Yes, really, Mother,' Charlotte bleated. 'Julian and I were hoping to spend a few days together.'

'I'm sorry, darlings, but we have some rather startling news to share.'

Her words were accompanied by groans.

'Oh no,' Charlotte said. 'No more bad news, please.'

'It's good news, actually,' Alex cut in, taking over the conversation as he shot a look of assurance to Pen, who was sitting as quietly as Bramson stood.

'Are you paying us a new dividend or something, Lex? Spit it out,' Rupert urged.

Alex grinned. 'No, old chap. We asked everyone here today to announce that I shall be getting married next spring.'

Cups were clattered onto saucers, mouths opened and gasps were heard before all the Wynters began speaking at once.

'You're so recently back! How can you be announcing an engagement?' Charlotte squealed.

'Hurrah for that! It takes the heat off me!' Rupert jested.

Dougie, after his initial groan, said, 'You can't be serious!'

'Darlings, please,' their mother appealed. 'I'll get one of my headaches.'

'Who's the lucky girl, brother?' Rupert winked at Pen.

'Well, you see, everyone . . . you all know her rather well.'

'Good heavens!' Dougie exclaimed. 'Pen, can you shed any light on this? I'm afraid Alex is being deliberately obtuse.'

Alex noticed that Pen didn't quail beneath the Wynter stares that suddenly regarded her.

'I can, as a matter of fact, Dougie. I happen to know the very happy girl extremely well,' she said, helplessly smug. 'It's me.'

Later, after the initial shock had worn off and the questions had adjusted to offers of congratulations, Rupert departed and Dougie was not far behind.

Alex accompanied his middle brother to the door. 'No problems with her being distantly related?'

Dougie shook his head. 'Keep it in the family, I say, but to be honest, Lex, I thought you were just being brotherly escorting Pen to various events. We all did, I suspect. It's not as though you are . . . er, well, overly affectionate.' Alex visibly inhaled at the soft rebuke. His brother gave a small laugh. 'You're full of surprises, Lex. But this is the best yet. You are sure, aren't you?'

'Pen's a great girl.'

'That sounds incredibly romantic,' Dougie replied, unable to disguise the sarcasm. 'I don't know why I'm shocked. I've always known Pen had a desperate crush on you, but I thought she'd grown up.'

'She has. I suppose the crush has changed to love.'

'Yes, but I'm not hearing love in *your* voice.'

'Just be grateful you have it with Fern and don't judge others. I'm doing my best, Dougie.'

Bramson blinked as Alex returned to the drawing room and he had no idea what the gesture meant. Alex hoped it was approval.

'Well, I'm glad that's over,' he said, refreshing his cup with a fresh pour from the pot.

'You must allow for the shock, Lex,' Charlotte soothed. 'It's odd, I won't lie to you both, but I think you're extremely well matched and I hope you are very happy,' she added, taking Pen's hand.

'Well said, Charlie,' Cecily said. 'The boys will come around. Rupert can now officially be called the Wynter playboy and Dougie is just a fraction jealous. You're a catch, Pen dear. No two ways about it. Alex is a lucky fellow.'

'So . . . your dress!' Charlie exclaimed. 'Your gown will be the talk of the south.'

'I'm afraid so,' she admitted. 'Only child, only daughter – it's going to be a big one, Lex. I'm sorry, Aunt Cecily. I know you prefer more low-key affairs.'

'Nonsense, darling. This is going to be the biggest day of your life and your mother is perfectly entitled to make it as loud as she chooses.'

'Pen, I don't think I could bear the full-on society wedding . . .' Lex began.

'You may have to,' Pen said with apology. 'I did give you an opportunity to marry me on Brighton Pier but you turned me down. So grit your teeth and bear it. I promise beyond the wedding I shall never put you through any more pomp . . . not even for the christening of our children, which I'll be very glad to hold in the Wynter chapel.'

'Not so fast,' Charlie warned. 'I want to know about your gown. White, of course.'

'I thought ivory, actually,' Pen said.

'I saw in the weekend paper that House of Ainsworth has released a daring new range of designs for next spring,' Cecily noted.

'Oh, I saw those too. Very exciting,' Charlie gushed. 'You must go there.'

Pen shrugged. 'I'm not planning to, actually. You know I'm Nicola Fincham's number one for her wedding?'

Alex looked bored already and threw a look of plea to Bramson to rescue him. 'I refuse to talk matrons-of-honour and bridesmaids' fluffery.'

'Fluffery? Is that a word, darling?' his mother baited.

'Er . . . Mr Alex, could I have a word with you, please?' Bramson said, taking the hint. 'Forgive me for interrupting.'

'Of course,' Alex replied gratefully, swallowing his tea. 'Excuse me, Mother. I won't be long.'

The women barely noticed him leave.

'Go on,' his sister said, eager to hear more.

'Good heavens, Charlie,' Cecily said. 'I've never known you to take an ounce of interest in clothes, let alone bridal wear. Should we expect wedding bells from you and Julian soon?'

Charlie blushed and Pen gave a squeal. 'Really?'

'You and Alex stole my thunder,' she admitted.

'Oh, darling!' Cecily said, reaching for her daughter. 'How exciting. I'm thrilled for you.'

'Julian's in a bit of a rush, I have to say, so I'm quite pleased you two have got in the way. I can slow things down. I do want to say yes to him, and Father did like Julian, didn't he?'

Her mother nodded. 'Very much so. And I do too. I approve without reservation, so whenever you're ready, you give that fine young man of yours an answer.'

'Thanks. I was going to speak to Lex about it soon. Anyway, Pen, don't think I'm cross because I'm relieved. But I am interested in your thoughts about the gown. Will you help me?'

'Only if you'll be in my bridal party. I want a Wynter on both sides!'

Charlie grinned. 'I'd love to.'

'Well, anyway, Nicola originally visited a rather amazing new salon that's opened in Chelsea, called Valentine's. Not only is the salon frightfully daring, the owner – Eden Valentine – is stunning and her sketches are breathtakingly original. Everything we look at in the American or French magazines she's already channelling, but better.'

Her listeners looked impressed.

'Then why are they now using House of Ainsworth for the bridal party?' Cecily wondered.

'Beats me, but I'm going to stick with Eden Valentine. I think she's fabulous and her model could make a bag of rags look spectacular. I shall definitely be dressed by them.'

'Well done, Pen. Then I will too,' Charlie said. 'She sounds exciting.'

'As we've ruined your few days with Julian, do you fancy coming up to London with me and we can meet her?'

'Yes, you two. Away to London. You can stay at the Belgravia apartment if you need, Charlie.'

'Perfect, Mother. We can walk to the salon, no doubt?'

'Absolutely,' Pen said. 'I may use the telephone now and make an appointment.'

Alex strolled back in. 'Oh, you're not still talking about satin and lace, are you?'

'Just finished,' Pen said. 'Will you drive us up to London tomorrow, Lex?'

'I don't see why not. I need to see my own tailor, anyway. Time to get that spring wardrobe sorted.'

'And a Morning Grey for the wedding, darling,' Pen reminded.

Although they were as close as sisters these days, Edie and Madeleine had opted not to share their accommodation, even though it made sense. Edie had offered to look for a three-bedroom apartment but Madeleine had been wise enough to point out that such an arrangement had the potential to fast become a thorn in Edie's side.

'I stay up late, I smoke, drink champagne when I can afford to and I like entertaining men when the mood takes me. And I play jazz very loudly on the gramophone while we enjoy each other. I like to walk around in my dressing gown; better still, naked.' She'd smiled lazily at her friend. 'I've lived alone for too long, *cherie*.

I love you, I love Tommy, but I live by a set of my own rules that are not ideal for raising a child.'

So while Madeleine had moved into a rented apartment at Thurloe Square in South Kensington, Edie had made her home in a tiny two-bedroom flat in Flood Street, Chelsea, that she was able to buy. It was so convenient for her salon, she could cut down into the Kings Road via the embankment and at the end of the street was The Coopers Arms, where she and Madeleine could share a meal when they were too tired to cook. Or if Edie was missing her cottage garden in Epping, she could spend a happy hour in the Chelsea Physic Garden at the end of her street, and Tommy had somewhere to play.

A lady from the neighbourhood whom Edie had spent time finding and interviewing was a retired teacher who was happy to earn some shillings, and between her and Tilda, the two provided all the grandmotherly love that Tommy could want. Mrs Miller had Tommy for a few hours most days and Eden took Mondays off to be at home just for her little boy and Wednesday afternoons when she did her chores with Tommy in tow. The fourteen-month-old was thriving in the care of several women and soon would be ready for nursery school.

Buses plied the busy King's Road but Edie preferred to walk it, passing by its shops, getting a feeling for the streets and the people moving through them and what they wore.

Madeleine usually opened up, as Edie was rarely in before quarter past ten, after settling Tommy with Mrs Miller. Madeleine walked into the 'wardrobe', as they called it, to view the gown that Eden had been working on. Eden had kept a cloak of secrecy around it, even from Madeleine. She was apparently frightened of seeing looks of disapproval as she took an even more daring path.

And as the French model unbuttoned the soft cotton bag that protected the fragile gown and watched it fall away, she gave a soft gasp of pleasure.

It was exquisite. Flying in the face of the trend towards shorter hemlines, Edie had dropped the length back down to the ankles of the mannequin upon which she'd hung it. Madeleine knew it had been made to her height and sizing, and also instinctively recognised that this was her friend's most inspired creation to date.

She remembered Edie's words after the Fincham fiasco: 'I think a bride in a short dress, no matter how young she may be, appears somehow undignified. For a start, the length becomes immediately unbalanced with a veil and train.'

And here was the result. Madeleine caressed the gently drop-waisted dress in the softest of organza and ecru *crepe de Chine*, with its elaborate embroidery at its base studded with pearls. Sleeves of gossamer Duchesse Brussels lace gave the gown a sense of the provocative without any vulgarity. The flesh of this bride would be seen, but sheathed. 'Oh, Eden, you are a sorceress with the needle,' Madeleine whispered. 'No woman could resist this.'

The phone rang and Madeleine glanced at her watch. It wasn't even nine-thirty yet. She ducked out of the wardrobe and back to the office.

'Valentine's, this is Madeleine?'

'Oh, good morning, Madeleine. I don't know if you remember me but my name is Penelope Aubrey-Finch and I came into the salon with Miss Fincham.'

Madeleine hesitated as she took her mind back to the warring Finchams.

'Ah, yes, I modelled the bridal and bridesmaids' gowns for your party,' she said, taking care to keep all bitterness from her tone. 'I do hope you are not enquiring after Miss Valentine's sketches . . . they curiously went missing.' She let the accusation hang.

'I saw the newspaper feature. I did wonder about the gown and whether it really did belong to House of Ainsworth. I'm so sorry at what must have occurred.'

Madeleine sensibly hesitated in responding, suddenly curious but also vaguely embarrassed.

'You see, I am getting married too . . . er, we're in a hurry. Oh, dear, that sounds terrible. I've just loved this man since we were children and finally he's noticed me and I refuse to give him a chance to change his mind!'

Madeleine smiled, her heart warming to Miss Aubrey-Finch. 'Congratulations.'

'Oh, thank you. I'm so happy I think I could just explode.'

Madeleine chuckled. 'How can Valentine's help you, Miss Aubrey-Finch?' she said, although she could now guess.

'Well, I adored Miss Valentine. I adored her salon and her sketches, and the gowns we viewed were the most exciting designs I've ever seen. I want to ask her to make my bridal gown and my bridal party's gowns.'

Madeleine's breath caught.

'I also want to know if Miss Valentine would consider making a new wardrobe for me. You see, I could tell she's a woman of immense style. I wanted to rip that gorgeous tweed suit right off her and claim it as my own,' Pen said and chuckled. 'You must think I'm mad, sorry. I'm intoxicated by happiness. It will settle.'

'I don't think you are mad at all. Eden Valentine is my friend but in spite of my bias, I believe she is going to create a storm of interest.'

'Oh, so do I! And I want to be one of her first brides.'

'You would be her very first, Miss Aubrey-Finch.'

'All the better. And I want to get her name moving in the right circles if I can lend any assistance.'

'*Zut, alors!*'

The client chuckled. 'I did some of my schooling in Paris, Madeleine,' she said in flawless but still conversational French.

Madeleine appreciated hearing her own language and used it to speak candidly to her new client. 'Thank you for bringing your business to Valentine's, Miss Aubrey-Finch. I would be lying if I said we have been anything but glum since the sketches were discovered missing and published under another design house's name. But Eden is choosing to leap over the obstacle and start again. Forgive me, but it was easier to make such an exclamation aloud in French.'

'I understand,' Pen continued, then shifted back to English. 'Gosh. She's a saint.'

Madeleine returned to her adopted language. 'What she is, is immensely talented and if what she's replaced her signature gown with is anything to go by, I believe Eden is going to emerge with an even stronger look. I think she would be delighted to dress you for your honeymoon and beyond.'

'You've made me very excited and I desperately want to see the new design now!'

Madeleine smiled. 'Are you in London, Miss Aubrey-Finch?'

'I will be tomorrow. May I come into the salon the day after?'

'Of course. Shall we say eleven a.m. on Thursday, then?'

'Perfect.'

'Are you accompanied by anyone?'

'Yes, a Miss Charlotte Wynter. She's to be my head bridesmaid.'

'Excellent. And your mother?'

'No. I'll be making my own decision about my gown, Madeleine. Mummy can see it at the first fitting.'

Madeleine smiled to herself and cheered inwardly at the good news awaiting Eden. 'We shall look forward to seeing you on Thursday – *à bientôt*.'

'You're quite sure?' Edie asked.

'It's one minute past. And it's drizzling, Eden. She's coming, I promise.'

'Oh, I hope so. I asked around about Miss Aubrey-Finch. Serious socialite, Mads. Parents fantastically wealthy . . . old, old money with French connections, apparently.'

'Well, I have to say she sounded delightful on the telephone. Ah, here she comes. That's her getting out of the car on the other side of the street.' She flapped at her friend. 'Go out the back, Eden. You need to make an entrance.'

'What?'

Madeleine hissed and shooed her away.

Edie couldn't see but had to listen to the gentle tinkle of the door being swung open and a woman's voice calling: 'Bye, Lex. Thanks again, darling,' and then two women laughing about scurrying in from the drizzle. *What happened to summer?* Edie wondered. Disappeared in a blink and now it was October already. She hoped Mrs Miller would be able to get Tommy out to the park . . .

'Miss Aubrey-Finch?' she heard Madeleine say.

'Yes, but do please call me Penelope. You must be Madeleine. *Enchanté.*'

'*Enchanté,*' Madeleine replied. 'And . . . Miss Wynter, I believe?'

'Charlotte. But call me Charlie, because everyone else does.'

'I shall call you Charlotte because it's a beautiful name, like its owner,' Madeleine said and Edie grinned behind the scene. 'Let me take your coats, ladies. Was that your fiancé, Penelope?'

'Yes. Alex drove us up to London yesterday and was far too gallant to let his favourite girls get wet this morning so he gave us his black brolly. I'll put it here, shall I?'

'I like him already.' Madeleine smiled. 'Let me take that umbrella and I shall call Miss Valentine. Can I get you anything?'

Eden straightened her dress as she heard the women politely decline, explaining that the man called Alex had also treated them to a slap-up breakfast that morning. She took a deep breath. She'd been very daring today, dressing in a masculine way, which she knew would challenge the notion of a designer for a giggling bride and her maid. The box-cut coat in navy wool and matching tailored skirt was a neat, simple autumn suit with its only embellishment the crimson tussah silk lining that flashed if she took her jacket off. It was how she'd styled it that might catch the most attention.

Madeleine arrived and nodded at her. 'Ready to do battle?'

'Get dressed into the new gown! We might as well go for broke.'

They hugged and parted, Madeleine already tearing off her wraparound skirt, while Eden lifted her shoulders and walked briskly into her salon.

'Miss Aubrey-Finch and Miss Wynter, how lovely to see you and welcome to Valentine's.'

Both women audibly gasped.

Eden had anticipated it and felt immediate relief. She'd already won them. 'Is something wrong?' she asked.

'No, not at all,' said the blonde with the dazzling smile who stood to greet her and who must surely be Penelope. 'Your tie . . . it's . . . amazing! Please call me Penelope.'

'Thank you. This will be all the rage shortly. I thought I'd lead the charge.'

'It's wonderful! The colour is . . . dangerous.'

Eden grinned. 'Well, in the depths of a British winter – which is surely coming at us faster than we'd all hoped – there is nothing so cheering as a splash of bright colour on a woman, don't you agree?'

'I do. Oh, you're a woman after my own heart, Miss Valentine. This is Charlotte, my bridesmaid.'

'And I'm Eden,' she said, for the first time embracing her full name for the power Madeleine always maintained it held. 'I can see from how you're dressed, Penelope, that I have little to suggest to you about enhancing your own beauty. I think you understand your body and you dress it with elegance.'

The blonde woman glanced at her friend in pleasure. 'Thank you. That means a great deal coming from you.'

'A bridal gown is arguably the most important, potentially the most expensive, often the most public, gown a woman may ever wear. Some women need more guidance about what might suit them best. I don't think you do, so I shall just let you tell me what you see yourself wearing. I gather it's a spring wedding?'

'End of April, yes,' Penelope began. 'But I don't want to go white. Ivory is my first inclination but I'm not sure it suits my hair colour. I was thinking a richer cream tone. Silk and lace, of course.' She shrugged. 'Which girl doesn't want that on her wedding day? As for styling, I'd rather hear what you think will grab just the right attention.'

From listening to Penelope, Edie already knew that her light ecru signature gown was going to be perfect on Miss Aubrey-Finch. She called for Madeleine and even Edie felt as though her heart stilled a moment when her friend glided out in her newest creation, which floated off her tall frame effortlessly.

Edie stole a glance at Penelope and noticed her client's mouth was open, her gaze wide and shining with awe. Yes indeed, this was the gown for Penelope Aubrey-Finch and the one that would put Valentine's on every new debutante's list of must-have labels.

'Oh, Eden, it's a dream,' Penelope whispered.

'Is it your dream?' she asked.

Penelope nodded. 'I don't even want to see anything else. It's better than the one you did for Nicola.'

Eden had to agree. 'I'm glad you think so. I would hazard that every bride you see next spring and summer will be in short sleeves, which came into vogue this year. But I think a bride should always hold on to a little modesty . . . it's far more seductive anyway to hint at the skin, rather than show it.'

The four women shared a knowing laugh.

'Now, let me show you on Madeleine how I think we can dress it for your big day.'

The next half-hour was spent in selecting the right veil and train. Edie teased at the froth of palest coffee-coloured silken netting that now formed a veil. Madeleine made a stunning bride and they could both see that their client was in raptures over the whole look. 'I think plain is important,' Edie continued. 'Your beauty is enough, Penelope. *You* wear the dress . . . don't let it wear you. So we must make sure that you shine through, and if we have too much . . . um . . . embellishment, it adds noise rather than elegance. If we keep it simple, then this veil will appear as a "glow" around you.'

Penelope nodded. She was yet to disagree with anything Edie had advised.

'Now, looking at the train, I thought we could have a little fun here. I was thinking about using a silk charmeuse in the same ecru toning so that it remains light, but not too floaty, and it won't drag on the wedding carpet when you're walking up the aisle. To add a little more weight and a bit of whimsy, we could line it with gold tissue silk and decorate with pearls.' She looked at her clients. 'Charlotte, with your colouring, the softest of greens or mauves would do the bride justice and the spring flowers for a bouquet would complement. Mother of the bride in dusky pink, mother of the groom in silver grey, or vice versa. Think spring flowers and don't be afraid of a —' she searched for a word, 'punch of bright colour, like a fuchsia or vermilion.'

'Going-away outfit?' Charlotte said, looking completely caught up in the excitement.

'Oh, a suit, of course . . . perhaps a matching coat and cape for spring. And I would suggest a cool colour. Pale blue or violet, to match your eyes, Penelope.'

The two visitors sighed. 'Well, Valentine's is hired, Eden. Please write out an order for everything we've discussed, including my mother, six bridesmaids, two flower girls and a page boy, if you could dress him too.'

Edie resisted the urge to glance at Madeleine or let go of the howl of joy that was bursting in her chest. 'Of course,' she said, studiously professional. 'I shall do that today for you.'

'Alex won't be able to resist me in this.'

'Why should he resist you?' Edie queried in a lightly arched tone, meant to amuse.

'Well, it's no longer a secret that I've been crazy for my fiancé since we were children,' she said, glancing at Charlie.

'Really? That's charming.'

Penelope shrugged. 'I had made up my mind privately that if Lex didn't come back from the war, then I was never going to marry anyone. There's never been anyone else for me but Lex Wynter.'

'Well, he did come home and he did ask you, so he clearly loves you too,' Edie replied but she saw doubt in Penelope's eyes.

'Charlotte is probably getting married in the next twelve months too, aren't you, darling?' Penelope hurried to shift subjects, or so it felt to Edie. 'I think you can count on another Wynter wedding party too.'

'Absolutely!' Charlie gushed. 'I'll let the dust settle on Pen and Alex's big day so maybe a late summer/early autumn wedding.'

Edie squeezed Charlotte's hand. 'That's lovely news. And of course I would be delighted to design you a bridal gown to make your father very proud to walk you down the aisle.'

Charlotte faltered. 'Er, my father has passed away.'

'Oh, forgive me,' Edie said, looking stricken, understanding how the young woman must feel. 'My father died not long after I was married. I'm sorry,' she said, laying a cool hand on Charlie's arm.

'You weren't to know,' Pen assured. 'It was very sad to lose Uncle Thomas when we did, just as Alex was coming back into our lives.'

Edie nodded, not sure what to say, feeling embarrassed by her slip.

'Oh, did you mention to Eden about the wardrobe for Europe?' Penelope interjected, looking at Madeleine.

Edie nodded. 'Yes, she did, but only vaguely. I'll have a series of sketches and fabric swatches for you to look at when you come in for your first fitting. I'll work on a spring wardrobe for Europe. Whereabouts are you planning to visit?'

'Lex is whisking me off to Paris and then we shall take the train across Europe to Istanbul.'

Edie gasped. 'That was always my dream, Penelope! My husband and I talked about making that trip.' She remembered a shared bath when Sunday bells were ringing in the local church.

'Well, I shall think of you as I sip my first champagne on the Orient Express out of Paris.'

'Actually, I'd love you to raise your glass to me in Venice as well. Tom and I wanted to rail between Paris and Venice together.'

'Tom?' Charlotte joined in. 'Thomas was my father's name. Granny called him Tom sometimes, though.'

Penelope stood and kissed Edie's cheek. 'Venice it is, I promise. And I shall kiss Alex as I think of you and Tom.'

23

Edie moved to the back of the salon and watched Madeleine show their new clients to the door, saw Penelope wave towards a fine car across the street. She squinted from the back of the salon to glimpse the man at the wheel who had so captured her client's heart from childhood. His arm waved back at Pen but his face was in the shadows of the car and then two buses rumbled up to block her view.

When they finally hauled away, Madeleine was standing in front of her. 'Now we break out the champagne, *non*?'

Edie sighed and hugged her friend. 'Thank you. You were marvellous!'

'Miss Aubrey-Finch had no other intention but commissioning Valentine's.'

'True. What a lovely person she is. So desperately in love too.'

'I always think it's a little frightening to love someone so much; didn't you hear the note of danger in her expression?'

'I admit I did.'

'Well, it's none of our business but I hope Mr Wynter loves her as much as she does him.'

Edie remembered the doubt in Penelope's eyes and felt sadness for her . . . and a sense of kinship. She'd always privately worried that her love for Tom was overwhelming, that one day she may lose him. And she had.

Her mind began to wander to the image of the man waving at Penelope, perhaps unaware of his fiancée's desperate need to love him and be loved . . . or perhaps he wasn't. She hadn't realised she'd become so thoughtful.

'Where did you go, then?' Madeleine asked.

'Sorry. I was thinking about the coincidence that Penelope's father-in-law was called Thomas.'

'Common enough name in England, I've discovered. Like Henri or Pierre in France. Anyway, I don't believe in coincidence.'

'No?'

'I believe in fate and the mystery of life. Coincidence is meaningless. It's a cynic's explanation when fate pushes you towards something.'

Edie giggled. 'Well, fate is definitely pushing us towards our official opening. And now we can face it with confidence, Mads. Two high-profile clients on our books and a lot of work ahead of us. By the way, you can hire that girl Monique. She can start after Christmas.'

'Excellent.'

'We're going to need her to assist you out the back as you'll be doing several changes for each client from now on, and I think we have to look at hiring a full-time staff member to help me with appointments and act as a go-between with clients and help with ordering fabrics. I'll put a sign in our window.'

The door opened and both women smiled to see Ben Levi.

'What are you doing here?' Edie asked.

'I had an appointment in Mayfair. Just stopped by to see if you'd have time for a coffee . . . er, if you'd thought about what we discussed over dinner.'

Edie refused to look at Madeleine, who she suspected was wearing an expression of intrigue.

'Er, well . . .'

'No more appointments today, Eden,' Madeleine said, only a hint of dryness in her tone.

'Come on – just a coffee,' Ben urged.

'Why not?' Edie relented, feeling cornered. 'I can't be long, though. We have lots on. We've just taken on a huge bridal job and another in the wings!'

'Excellent,' he said but without much enthusiasm. 'Grab your coat.'

Outside, she frowned. 'You didn't seem very happy for me.'

'Didn't I? Forgive me. I have a lot on my mind, work-wise.'

'Well, if you're so busy, why are you here, taking me out in the middle of the morning when we both have work to attend to?'

'Because I wanted to see you; I want to see you every day, Edie.'

She felt embarrassed for her harsh tone. 'Sorry, Ben. It's just this is a big event for me after what happened with the designs.'

'Yes, and it was insensitive of me not to show more pleasure for you. I am very happy. Who's the client?'

She cut him a look of mock horror. 'Shame on you. I don't ask you who your clients are, Benjamin Levi. Bridal designs and their clients are one of the most guarded secrets in society.' She grinned but it was short-lived. Her expression clouded again. 'Which makes the theft of my designs all the more sinister.'

'Theft is a harsh word. You probably misplaced them, Edie, and they fell into the wrong hands.'

'I did not misplace them. They were all together on the same day – the very day we were last out for a meal.'

'I know, I know. We've been through it,' he said.

'How would you feel if you lost an important file to a rival lawyer?'

'I'd be mortified.'

'That's putting it lightly.'

'It's not the same, Edie.'

'Oh, Ben, don't. You're making me furious all over again. I'm not finding you supportive about my business and it flies in the face of everything you promised.'

'Oh, please let's not argue about this. What's done is done. I . . . I wanted to talk about our future.'

Edie ignored him as she glanced across the street. 'I'm going back to that dining room and I'm going to speak with the cloakroom girl. It had to be her. I shall speak to the manager if I have to.'

She was shocked to feel Ben grab her arm, holding it tightly enough to notice the burn of his grip through her coat.

'You'll make a complete fool of yourself, Edie.'

She glared at him, wrenching her wrist from his hold.

'What's done is done. You can't turn time back, even if you could prove the theft, which I know you can't.' He sighed. 'Edie, darling. As your legal advisor I feel obliged to tell you that it will be your word against hers, and you have absolutely no proof . . .'

'What? She was the only one who had access to it.'

'But there was more than one cloakroom girl and any number of other staff with access. Sarah may have gone on a break. Anyone might have taken a fancy to your portfolio and decided to lift a few of the designs . . . realised they were more than just simple sketches and —'

'And what? Knew exactly who to sell them on to? My direct rival?'

'Well, how would Sarah know who to approach?'

'I don't know, Ben!'

'Well, until you do, I suggest you keep your accusations to yourself.'

Edie shook her head at the warning in his glance. 'Whoever did this set me back. It nearly stopped me in my tracks, Ben, but I'm fighting again.'

'Good for you,' he murmured and she heard the lack of sincerity.

The anger had burned away and Edie felt the cold nipping at her face. 'Why aren't you happy for me?'

'I am. But you could make me a lot happier if you'd answer my proposition, Edie.'

She stared at him and in that instant ran out of the strength to fight one of her most ardent supporters. 'All right, Ben,' she said, sounding suddenly wearied. 'You start the paperwork that makes me a free woman, and I'll give serious consideration to your proposal.'

She smiled faintly at the laughter that came back into his expression, hiding her reservation and a horrible, fresh new thought that had occurred.

'I will make you so happy,' he promised.

She nodded. 'Forgive me but I feel suddenly very cold and a headache is nagging. I won't have that coffee after all. I'll probably go home early and have the afternoon with Tommy.'

'I'll see you home —'

'No. I'll be fine. I've got a couple of things to do before I leave anyway. You get going.'

He frowned. 'Edie, promise me you won't speak with Sarah. The repercussions could be embarrassing.'

Yes, but for whom? she wondered, schooling her features to betray nothing of her new, disturbing notion. 'I promise.'

Later in the salon, she told Madeleine that she'd agreed to start proceedings for the legal dissolution of her marriage.

'I'm pleased for you,' Madeleine replied. 'I think.'

'Are you? I don't feel anything but empty. Tom's out there, I know it. He just doesn't know how to find me.'

'Ben thinks you could love him.'

Edie groaned. 'Do I love him like I loved Tom? No. Never. Not even close.'

'Don't lead Ben on. He deserves better. He's a good man.'

'Is he?' Edie questioned, finally allowing herself to confront the potentially deeply damaging notion that had nagged at her since Ben's outburst.

'Isn't he?'

She pushed a hand through her hair nervously. 'I have to tell you something. I have no proof, so it's just speculation.'

Madeleine's expression clouded.

'That night, when I lost the sketches, Ben barely looked at the girl serving me in the cloakroom. He was really offhand. Ever since he made partner in the law firm Ben's developed an attitude towards anyone who serves him. He's filled with his own importance; apart from his family, he's frozen out a lot of his old friends since becoming a member at Swithin's Club in the city. I think for Ben it's vital he looks every bit the successful city lawyer.' She shrugged. 'He's moving into his own house, finally . . . in Chelsea. And now he needs a wife and children. He's prepared to swallow his pride and try again with me, but he struggles with the fact that I run a business.'

'What does any of this have to do with your missing sketches?'

'Well, because of his attitude he paid the cloakroom attendant who handled my sketches with barely a scrap of attention.'

'And?'

'During our argument in the street he named her; he called her Sarah. And I happen to know that's her name because she told me, but Ben wasn't with me at the time.'

Madeleine stared at her with trepidation.

Edie moved towards the mannequin that Madeleine had set up. She reached for a bolt of *crepe de Chine* and threw it open on the workbench. She began to drape the fabric on the model, losing herself momentarily in the familiar, safe ritual of noticing its weight, shine, how it fell.

'Ben collected my folder that night,' she said. 'But I saw his anxiety just now. He desperately did not want me to confront Sarah or the management.'

'You honestly now believe that Ben, the man who claims to love you, stole your designs and gave them to the opposition?'

'I think he had the opportunity, is all I'm saying.'

'And his motive?'

'Crushing my dream.' She leapt as she poked herself with a pin. A bead of blood bloomed on her finger. 'Damn!' She stepped back. 'He never wanted me to have this.'

'Eden —'

'No, hear me out. I think he is capable of this deception, Mads, because I hurt him. I hurt him very deeply in choosing Tom and the manner in which it all happened. He'd know how damaging the theft would be. He had the opportunity, he had the knowledge of who to take my designs to for the maximum effect . . . and all the while he could play the hero, helping me.' Edie sucked her finger as she pulled the pin-cushion off her wrist.

'Eden, stop! It doesn't make sense.'

'It does all suddenly make bleak sense to me.' She swung around to face Madeleine. 'Ben doesn't want me going to Paris or New York . . . he doesn't want me searching out new raw silks from China or dyed silks from Italy. He doesn't want me tripping across to Belgium for lace. He wants me in his house in Chelsea like a trapped bird, taking coffee at home with friends he would probably help me choose, with an infant balanced across my belly and another on the way. He always used to joke about us having an army of children. He wants me to be the ideal he has in his mind of what the perfect "Jewish woman" is. The first and only time I ever defied my father was in bringing Tom into our lives.

And then our lives were never the same,' she said, remembering with a soft ache their passionate first kiss in the alleyway. Her eyes became wide and her expression haunted. 'I have to find him.'

'Eden . . . we've —'

'No, listen to me,' she said, rushing to take Madeleine's hands. 'If this is a day to get all my crazy thoughts out of my head, then let me say it all.'

'All? What else is there?'

'Just some nagging thoughts that won't go away.'

'Tell me.'

'Do you remember Percival Fitch at Savile Row?'

'I do.'

'He told us of a man who had an accident . . . run down by a taxi.'

'Yes, I recall the story. Dazed, tore his suit and they had one from pre-war days that fitted like a glove,' she reeled off. 'Really, Eden. I do pay attention, you know.'

Edie licked her lips. 'But what about the fact that he was a returned officer – he was one of Mr Fitch's regular clients and then they didn't see him for years?'

'He'd gone to war!'

'Mads, that's three years since the war ended.'

'Oh, you poor child. You think the man could be Tom.'

'*Is* Tom. Yes, for several reasons. The timing sounds right. The fact that he was a returned officer who had been away for so long and then turns up without an appointment. Tom was in Green Park – a skip away from Savile Row. Perhaps he found himself there, got knocked down as Mr Fitch told us, came back to his senses and the knowledge of his past, knew who he was.'

'But had forgotten he was Tom?' Edie nodded. 'Listen to yourself, Eden. This is crazier than thinking Ben is trying to bring down your business.'

'Not bring it down. Just scuttle it,' she said, irritation in her voice, not even bothering to explain to her friend what the latter word meant.

Madeleine regarded her in soft annoyance.

'Mads,' she appealed, 'the man Fitch was talking about was wearing a navy suit.'

'And you're going to tell me that Tom wore a navy suit that day, aren't you?'

Edie nodded, eyes glistening with tears.

'Eden,' Madeleine began, raising a long, narrow finger so close that Edie could see the shine of her manicured nail. 'This is dangerous thinking.'

'Abba and I always thought Tom spoke with a cultured voice, I just didn't want to accept it,' she wept. 'I'm sure it's why I led him away from London to our quiet, isolated cottage in Epping where few people would notice or question him. They just saw a nice, young, educated couple. I told everyone Tom had been injured in the war and let their imaginations do the rest. Oh, Mads, don't you see? Tom could be that man from Savile Row and now he's returned to his former life, wherever that is. I've slipped through the crack in his life . . . me, his child, our life . . . it's disappeared.'

Madeleine took Edie by the shoulders. 'This all makes sense in your mind, Eden, because you want it to be the truth.'

'It's plausible!'

'About as plausible as Ben wanting to destroy you and yet marry you.'

Edie felt the sobs lurch in her chest. The darkness was rising again. She'd kept it at bay, even kept away the whispers that had begun nagging at her since talking to Percival Fitch of the tiny coincidences that added up.

'If Sarah confirms Ben's actions, will you believe me?'

'Yes.'

Edie blew her nose on a handkerchief. It was red to match her tie and she remembered the heart she'd cut out from Tom's handkerchief, which she'd given him on the day he left. She still had the scrap of fabric at home and made a mental note to carry it with her from now on.

'I can't confront her, Mads. I promised Ben.'

'Oh, so now you care about Ben and his feelings?'

'I care about keeping my promises.'

'Right,' Madeleine said, approaching the coat stand and pulling down her cape. '*I* shall go and find Sarah and I shall confront her. Let's put an end to this speculation.'

'What about Tom?'

'One drama at a time, Eden. That's all I can cope with.'

She marched from the salon and Edie was left staring at a red handkerchief. She had so much work to do but her mind was swarming with the possibility that Tom was within her reach. She picked up the phone and asked the operator to put her through to the correct exchange, which then connected her with Anderson & Sheppard. It took several minutes until a voice answered.

'Oh, good afternoon, this is Miss Eden Valentine from Valentine's Bridal Salon at Sloane Square.'

'Hello, Edie. This is Jonathan Elton speaking.'

'Ah, Jonathan, thank you. I was wondering if Mr Fitch might be available.'

'Mr Fitch? I'm afraid not. He's taking annual leave. I believe he's gone rambling in the Lake District for three weeks.'

'Oh, I see,' she said, a wave of disappointment crashing against her hopes.

'Is there anything I can do?'

'Er, you may be able to. I don't know if you recall but Mr Fitch was telling me about the gentleman who was knocked down in Savile Row a while back . . . one of your clients?'

He hesitated. 'I do remember, yes.'

She knew it was wrong to ask. 'Could you give me his name, please?' She could picture Jonathan's kind, boyish face twisting with concern. 'Actually, Jonathan, don't,' she countered, deciding in the heartbeat of his indecision that she was behaving without discretion for the man in question, or for Mr Fitch. She knew the code of Savile Row better than most. 'I know it's not right in our line of work to be that indiscreet, but perhaps you'd let me put it another way. May I ask, were you aware of the name Tom coming up in relation to that client?' She was grasping at mist. If she believed this man to be Tom, then he would hardly have mentioned his name and then ignored it. It was ridiculous to ask, but the question was out now. 'I'm sorry to sound so desperate, Jonathan, but I just have it my mind that I know this gentleman, but I knew him as Tom and he lived at Epping.'

He sounded relieved when he spoke. 'I can tell you that name was never mentioned and I was there when it all happened, Miss Edie. Definitely no Tom. No mention of Epping, either.'

She nodded, her heart hurting as another door slammed in her face. 'All right, sorry to disturb you. Thanks, Jonathan, and please give Mr Fitch my best.'

'I will. Goodbye, Edie.'

'Bye, Jonathan,' she said softly, putting down the phone and suddenly feeling vaguely ridiculous. What would she have said to Fitch anyway? *I think one of your clients might be my lost husband? No, I'm sorry, I don't know his name. I only knew him as Tom.* She winced, knew she was behaving irrationally, and now she'd put Madeleine into the thick of her crazy notions.

The bell rang at the door and she swung around to see Madeleine standing in the doorway with Sarah.

Sarah was blushing and Madeleine looked uncharacteristically nervous. 'Sarah has something she wishes to tell you,' she said, gesturing for the cloakroom assistant to move into the salon. 'Go on, Sarah. Tell Eden what you told me.'

24

Alex sat behind his desk at Larksfell and stared at his red handkerchief.

Cecily had suggested it. 'It's part of letting go, Lex. Get rid of it. Here, give it to me now – I'll burn it.'

Alex had leapt as if scalded. 'No. You won't burn it. But I'll put it away, I promise.'

'I hate that handkerchief. If I see it, Lex, I'll get rid of it. That red rag is holding you back.'

He laughed deliberately, needing to prove that he was not emotionally dependent on it. 'I said I'd put it away, all right?'

And he had, tucking it right at the back of his desk drawer. But now here it was in his hand.

He had been in the process of signing a cheque to pay for the honeymoon, and now the sight of the handkerchief halted him. The feel of it, however, disturbed all the drawers in his mind where he had neatly folded away thoughts of a lover, a girlfriend . . . even a wife who might be waiting for him somewhere. It had taken every last reserve of willpower to banish this mysterious, invisible woman to concentrate on his fiancée and their forthcoming nuptials. He'd made a pact with himself that he would: he owed it to Pen, to his family, to himself.

And he had been winning that battle in his mind, but a simple glimpse at the handkerchief and all the demons were back, opening up the compartments with glee, shaking out their contents and spilling his guilt with every tormented question that always spiralled down to the same few words: *Who Are You?*

'It's all moving so fast,' he murmured.

'What is, darling?' his mother said.

He hid the handkerchief in his lap. Cecily Wynter had a penchant for sneaking up on him but in a breezy way that could never be considered stealth. She stood before him now with a plate of food. 'Alex, if you are going to stand me up for dinner at home, at least promise me you'll eat,' she said with affection. 'Oh, you are cosy in here,' she added, moving towards the hearth, having placed a plate of sandwiches in front of him. 'Eat, Alex, or you won't have strength to give me my first grandchild.'

'Don't be vulgar, Mother, it doesn't become you,' he said dryly and she chuckled.

'Is everything all right?'

He reached for a sandwich and made a grateful groaning sound as the taste of still warm and sticky roasted chicken melted in his mouth.

'Is this Dearie's own chutney?'

'From our apples too.'

He nodded, ate hungrily.

'You see, you're famished.'

As she turned away, he pushed the handkerchief into his pocket and followed his mother to the fireside, carrying his plate. 'I forgot the time. I hate the thought of having to leave everything for four weeks.'

'Nonsense, Lex. Your wedding is still a few moons away, so why you're worrying about work already is beyond me. I want you to take gorgeous Pen away and make her very, very happy, and also make my grandchild.'

He gave his mother a look of soft despair.

'Why is it moving too fast for you?' she asked, ignoring his admonishment and returning to the original conversation that he hoped he'd left behind.

'Pen's in such a rush to be married, I can barely catch my breath on all the arrangements. Which society girl planning a wedding doesn't give herself at least a year for all the histrionics? Pen's pulling this all together in a matter of a few months. April first will be upon us in a blink.'

'She's not pregnant, is she, darling?'

Now he gave her a slit-eyed look of caution.

'Well, it is April Fool's Day.' She shrugged in defence. 'Are you having second thoughts?'

'Not second thoughts, just thoughts. Why do we have to be in such a tearing hurry?'

'Well, she clearly believes she's waited long enough for you!'

He sighed and it was a sound of resignation. 'I could do worse.'

'Oh, Lex. This is the rest of your life, darling!' Cecily's exasperation was reflected in a pained gaze at her son.

Alex swallowed the food in his mouth that seemed suddenly tasteless. He turned to stare at the flames and for an instant was reminded of flames in a sitting room . . . an elegant room, but not especially large or fancy. He was aware of an old man . . . but then the recollection danced away from him like a disturbed butterfly.

'Alex? What's going on?'

He could smell the orange blossom note of his mother's perfume, had seen the squat, oval-shaped bottle that held the citrusy cologne, so why was he envisaging a different bottle and a whiff of floral fragrances?

'I . . . I'm smelling a scent. I had a vague notion of violets.'

She shrugged. 'There's a perfume called "April Violets", I believe. Yardley or something. I've tried it but it gives me a headache.'

'Yardley,' he murmured, turning the word over in his mind because it sounded so familiar.

'It's on Bond Street, darling,' she muttered to prompt him.

'I'm sorry. I seem to be having more frequent flashes of memory.'

She blinked. 'I suppose it had to occur. And hopefully it brings you relief.' Despite her positive approach, Cecily looked doubtful.

'Yes, except there are people in the memories, Mother. Obviously people who can fill in the gap of time that I was missing.'

'You look so worried.'

'I am. What if I was . . . well, with someone?'

'The Yardley perfume-wearer, you mean? It's the red handkerchief again, isn't it?' She eyed him from beneath a peeved expression. 'You promised.'

'Someone made that handkerchief with care. The meaning is all too obvious. I'm sorry, Mother, but it seems callous that I disregard it,' he said, doing his best to ignore her expression of doubt that anyone who wore April Violets and cut hearts into handkerchiefs was the right 'social' material for a Wynter.

'All right, let's just entertain this notion for a moment, although after this I shall never discuss it again with you. I want this matter closed.' She took an audible breath. 'What can you do about it, even if you wanted to know more?'

Alex felt a boost of admiration for his mother, who, if nothing else, was fair.

'I've thought about that a great deal, and I've come to the conclusion there is only one place to go. I have to return to where it was found, I suppose. It's the only starting point I have.'

'You mean Dr Cavendish?'

'I mean Fitch and his staff at Savile Row.'

She shook her head. 'Needle in a haystack, Lex. And plenty of disruption as you plan to marry.'

'Mother . . . what if I am already married?'

'Oh, good heavens!' She looked genuinely shocked.

'I could be marrying Pen illegally. You surely don't wish bigamy to be part of the Wynter legacy?'

Cecily's normally good-humoured expression clouded with worry. 'No, absolutely not. Until now it hadn't occurred to me that you might have actually married someone.'

He swallowed. 'I was away long enough that I might even have children.'

Now Cecily looked back at her son with deep dismay. 'Oh, Lex,' she pleaded. 'Now you're just teasing. You know how much I want a Wynter grandson . . . and many more grandchildren too.'

He shrugged in guilt at upsetting her. 'I'm just saying. We don't know.'

'Well, I shall speak to Gerald in the morning —'

He stood. 'No. Let me handle this. If we get Gerald involved, it becomes something much bigger and more serious than it may have to be. I could be fearing the worst unnecessarily. A few well-directed questions might open up the pathway we need.'

'Very well. I understand your reluctance to send in the cavalry.'

'Cavendish and Fitch were both present when I recovered consciousness. I will begin there; ask them to remember absolutely everything they can of that day. Maybe I was with someone?'

'Didn't you say something about being dressed in an old suit?'

He nodded. 'It wasn't old, as I recall. It was torn – presumably in the fall – but the suit itself was very well tailored, quality cloth . . .' He shrugged. 'Not my colour, although the truth is, I'd just never thought to wear navy before.'

'What was in the pockets?'

'The pockets were empty. The only reason the handkerchief

escaped notice was that it was found in an inside private pocket.'

She frowned. 'Nothing in your pockets. Why? Where was your money?'

'My theory is that thieves got to me. I'd like to think I put up a fight but if not, why not?'

'Wait,' she said. 'You said the suit was well tailored. So a tailor made it for you, but not Percy Fitch, you say.'

'Definitely not.'

'Well, darling . . . which label was in the suit? Surely if you know that, you can track it back to the maker.'

He opened his mouth in wonder and then leapt at his mother, kissing both her cheeks. 'Oh, you clever thing! Father definitely didn't marry you just because you were so pretty.'

'I can assure you of that,' she replied. 'Can you remember a name in the suit?'

'No, but I shall be calling Percival Fitch first thing tomorrow.'

'What about Penny?'

'Not a word, Mother. This could go nowhere.'

She nodded, let him help her up to her feet and she gave a soft groan. 'A word of caution, Lex. I know Penny comes across as a breezy, modern woman but you see she's never had to face real adversity. The only grandparent she's known is still hale and hearty, and Penny has never had to yearn for anything but you, darling. She's not had to shoulder the lesson that working entirely off emotion is dangerous.'

'Unlike us, you mean?'

Cecily smiled sadly. 'Let's just say we've learned how to keep our emotions quiet.'

'It's not my intention to hurt Penny, but I have to do this.'

'Then I suppose I shall help you all that I can.'

After a restless night, Alex appeared at the breakfast table in a fidgety mood to face the simple bowl of porridge with honey and poached winter fruits.

A small jug was placed near his hand. 'Didn't sleep well, Master Lex?'

'Does it show?'

Bramson blinked his answer.

'I might be going up to London tomorrow, Bramson; I promised to meet Miss Aubrey-Finch in town.'

'The theatre, Sir? I heard that those American funny men, the Marx Brothers, are performing to happy audiences.'

Alex frowned. 'I'll leave all that to my fiancée, Bramson. I fear I've been a bit reticent about all the frantic preparations she's in the midst of. The least I can do is take dear Pen out for dinner after a hectic day of wedding shopping.'

Bramson chuckled. 'She must be terribly excited, Mr Alex.'

Alex shrugged. 'What is it with women and weddings, Bramson? Most men just want it over and done with, eh?'

The butler smiled indulgently. 'Mr Jones is back from his break. I'll ask him to get the car out. I presume you'll want to be driven, Sir?'

'Jones?' His mind tripped at the mention.

'You haven't met him, Master Lex, but he's one of the Wynter family drivers and has been since 1915. His brother's been seriously unwell and your mother gave him time to go visit. I'm afraid his brother passed away.'

'Oh, that's too bad. A soldier?'

'Complications from wounds, yes, Sir. Jonesy . . . er, Mr Jones, was close to his brother . . .'

Alex stared at Bramson with a haunted expression.

'. . . twin, I gather,' he finished. 'Master Lex?'

'What? Sorry.'

'Oh, you looked as though someone walked upon your grave, Sir. Are you all right?'

'Fine. Forgive me. I don't even know what I was thinking. What were you saying?'

'I was just explaining that Jones is a twin, so perhaps it feels harder to lose his brother. Um, are you sure I can't ask Mrs Dear to cook you up a full breakfast?'

'No, this is plenty, thank you,' Alex said, his mind still reaching after the jolt at hearing the nickname of Jonesy. *Why? What did it mean? And why was he thinking about a hospital?* He ate his porridge in comfortable silence, barely glancing at the newspaper near his wrist. He wasn't interested today in anything but the mission he was on. Even the events of the world could wait, he thought, spooning in porridge faster than his mother might think polite, but he felt its warmth and comfort hit his belly and soothe away the demons of the night and his restless dreams . . . none of which he could recall now.

'I wonder why dreams slip through our minds like quicksand, Bramson?' he thought aloud. He dabbed his napkin against his mouth and left the table.

'Indeed, Sir. But I take the attitude that Mother Nature might have designed us to remember them if she wanted us to. Our dreams are the travels of our sleep and meant to remain there, I suspect.'

Alex patted the butler's arm. 'Where is Mrs Wynter?'

'Here, darling,' she said, appearing around the door in her usual yet always surprisingly well-timed manner.

'Morning, Mother.' He kissed her cheek. 'Lots to do, I'm afraid. Enjoy your eggs.'

'Well, I can see you don't want your newspaper either, so I am claiming it. I was speaking to your sister last night on the telephone and she told me that Penny's bridal designer is interviewed today and I've promised to pay attention to it. Beautiful young woman,

Charlotte assures me. Quite the catch! She joked she hopes you don't ever meet her – certainly not before the big day, because she's every inch your sort of girl.'

Their butler cleared his throat.

'Oh, Bramson. I'm only joking.'

Alex raised a hand in amused farewell and disappeared into his study. Before long he was connected through to Anderson & Sheppard.

'Oh, good morning, Mr Wynter. How are you, Sir?'

'Very well, thank you, Elton. Certainly much better than the last time we met.'

They both chuckled.

'I'm very pleased to hear it, Sir. You had us all worried but extremely relieved that you are returned.'

'Indeed,' Alex said. 'Er, I wonder if Mr Fitch is available?'

'I'm sorry, Sir. Mr Fitch is on holiday.'

'Oh?'

'He likes to go rambling up north. Lake District, Sir.'

'Good heavens. Aren't they all snowed in up there?'

'Probably, Sir.'

'When is he back, Elton?'

'Next week, Mr Wynter. Can I help with anything?'

He toyed with the idea of asking young Jonathan Elton for assistance but the head tailor was a stickler for protocol and ran his shop like a military unit. 'Um . . . no, look I'll leave it, thank you, Elton. Tell Mr Fitch I'll be up in London next week. Is Tuesday all right?'

'Yes, Sir. He's back for Monday but not taking appointments until the following day. Shall we say midday?'

'Perfect. Thank you, Mr Elton. Have a good week.'

He put the phone down and bit his lip in consternation, aware that he had a flea in his ear now and wanted to do something constructive towards ridding himself of it. Alex took out the red handkerchief and smoothed it out on the desk, staring at it, urging it to give up its secrets.

He touched the hand-sewn edge of the heart, felt the soft bumps of the matching red thread and begged it to tell him whose hand had held the needle. Even to an untrained eye the sewing was immaculate: fine, regular, neat. He imagined a woman with needle and thread, sitting by a window to catch the best light, and could almost picture the handkerchief in her lap as she worked, watching make-believe fingers move around the cotton.

He wanted to know her! Wanted to look upon her! *Find me,* she called to him on the wind. Her heels walked away from him, leading him somewhere . . . somewhere safe and filled with love. Or was he simply imagining all this?

Alex suddenly snatched up the mutilated square of fabric, scrunched it into a loose ball and pushed it to his nose, inhaling. He wanted every clue he might glean from this tiny link to his past. This and the navy suit were his history. Alex closed his eyes, emptied his mind of the angst and smelled again, deeply this time, allowing his senses to let go and follow whichever path they chose.

Distantly teasing him came the softest waft of violets.

Was it the perfume his mother had spoken of? It didn't matter if it was – but he at last had something of this elusive woman. She had to be young, he reasoned; no older woman would craft such an obvious object of passion. He would have to buy a bottle of the Yardley perfume his mother had mentioned.

So, was she my lover? A mistress? Alex swallowed. *A wife?*

Edie nodded at Sarah and though she could see the cloakroom assistant was wearing a deeply anxious expression, it was Edie who blushed.

'Hello, Sarah. Do you remember me?'

'I do, Miss.' She glanced at Madeleine, who nodded. 'Very well, actually.'

'Come and sit down,' Edie offered, gesturing at the love seat. 'How is it that you remember me so well?'

Sarah perched on the edge of the bench, gloves clutched against the handles of an old but attractive bag. Edie could see that beneath a slightly old-fashioned-cut suit bristled a tall, slim woman with a firm young figure, desperate to unclothe and clamber into the finer garments about her, strewn on hangers, that she watched Sarah's gaze drinking in.

'Miss Valentine, I did not steal your sketches. I did not even look in the folder.' It came out in such an earnest rush that Edie blinked.

'I didn't say you did,' she replied.

Sarah took a deep breath. 'I remember you well, because . . . because you are unforgettable,' she half smiled, but coloured up with embarrassment. 'I noticed how beautifully dressed you were that day. I haven't been able to stop thinking about that stole. One day . . . well, I love clothes, Miss Valentine.' She shrugged.

Edie did look at Madeleine now, who was staring down from her full height, arms crossed with an expression that suggested she wanted to say to Edie: *So what have you got to say now?* Instead, she smiled at Sarah.

'Sarah, tell Miss Valentine exactly what you told me.'

And as Edie listened, she paled in front of the two women and her heart began to drum loudly beneath her ribs.

His mind felt bruised and scattered. Alex pushed the handkerchief into his pocket, grabbed a thick jacket and scarf and let himself out quietly through the French windows of his study. Cold air hit him and made him gasp; it was like running into the sea off Brighton Beach.

The smell of smoke from grates around the property felt homely and comforting. Even more soothing was the aroma from Mrs Dear's oven in full roar – the air was scented with plum puddings she was readying for Christmas.

Alex set off without purpose but nevertheless determined to walk away his mood of frustration. He skirted the orchards and pushed on, hands plunged deep into his pockets. He wished now he'd thought to bring gloves and he buried his chin into his scarf, breathing through the cashmere to ease the effect of the biting chill.

He found himself standing at the entrance to the Larksfell maze, which used to so enchant the Wynter children. He slipped into the northern end of the maze and, without having to think, made his way through the privet until he came to the stone bench at its heart. The bench felt like a block of ice through his trousers but he felt released to be alone and silent with only a robin for company.

'Hello there, little friend,' he murmured.

The robin surprised him by singing suddenly, and with that familiar sound came the memory of another robin on another day when he was seated on a different bench in a rose garden, searching for similar peace.

'Of course, the hospital!' he exclaimed, startling the robin. It flew off immediately and Alex leapt to his feet. He broke into a run, scurrying back through the corridors of tall privet hedge, vaguely marvelling that he hadn't forgotten how to get out of the maze and yet couldn't remember where he'd been a year ago. He burst from the northern entrance again and this time was running, hurtling past the orchard, rushing past the French doors of his study and moving around the building's exterior until he hit the gravel drive. He slowed but not enough that he didn't catch the attention of Bramson, who was deep in discussion with Clarrie outside the big house.

'Everything all right, Mr Alex?'

'Peachy, thank you,' he said and although the thought crossed his mind, he couldn't be bothered bringing Bramson into the problem. He kept moving towards the northern side of Larksfell until he hit the garages, where, predictably, he found a man polishing one of the many in the fleet of Wynter motor cars.

'Jones?' he enquired, gusting steam from his deep breaths.

'Yes, Sir!' the man replied, straightening. 'Er . . .'

Alex sniffed, was tempted to reach for the red handkerchief. 'Sorry, I ran,' he said, although he could see it explained nothing to the startled driver.

'Can I help you, Sir?'

'Yes . . .' He grinned, dragging in a deep breath to calm himself. 'I'm Alex Wynter,' he began and noticed the man's eyes widen. 'Did Mr Bramson mention I was planning to go to London?'

'He did, Sir. Tomorrow, I believe it is.' Jones looked nervous and Alex was keen to defuse his anxiety.

'Actually, Jones, how do you feel about a jaunt today? Not into central London; more like Middlesex.'

'Today? Of course, Sir.' He looked around at the clutter of buckets and sponges. 'Er, when, Sir?'

'How about now? We can take a flask, share a cuppa on the way.' The suggestion didn't appear to relax Mr Jones. Alex grinned. 'Come on, Jones. Let's live dangerously.'

A twitch of a smile ghosted across the man's expression. 'I'll just clean up, Sir. Is twenty minutes all right?'

'Take half an hour. I'll organise that flask of tea,' he said, lifting a hand. 'Back soon.'

25

Alex was enjoying the smell of the rich, burgundy-coloured leather that had warmed around him in the car, although it was still necessary to be wrapped up in a heavy coat. His gloves made a squeaking sound as he rubbed at the condensation on the window so he could look out at the passing scenery as the rural landscape gave way to more built-up areas. It seemed frostier here in London than at Larksfell.

'You know, Jones, your surname feels meaningful to me and it's somehow linked with Edmonton Hospital,' Alex remarked, as they rolled across what he realised was a bridge in their approach to the hospital in north Middlesex.

'Is that right, Sir?' Jones said over his shoulder. 'I can't imagine it – such a normal name as mine being important to you.'

'Well, that's it, you see. No doubt you've been told I lost my memory towards the end of the war, and apparently I ended up here at Edmonton – or so my fiancée assures me. They called me Mr Jones because they didn't know my name and neither did I. I suppose they called other soldiers in a similar situation Mr Smith or Mr Green . . . easy names for us to remember and answer to.' Alex felt a ripple of pleasure that he was at last in a position to explain some small aspect of his disappearance. Why hadn't he thought to contact the hospital? Even this felt like a triumph and he was determined today's journey would throw more light on his puzzle.

'I see, Sir,' Jones said, glancing into the rear-vision mirror and nodding. 'Makes sense. Do you recall any of this scenery, Mr Wynter? This is the Lea Valley Bridge we've just crossed, and now into Angel Road.'

'Afraid not, old chap. Although – wait a minute,' he murmured, his gaze narrowing as a vast red-brick structure came into view. He sat forward to look out of the front window while he strained to grab on to a thought. 'There is something familiar about that building.'

'That's the hospital, Sir. It was used by the military during the war.'

Alex shook his head in wonder as fragile tendrils of memory seemed to reach around his mind and take vague purchase. He felt sure that if he fed the images, then his memory might be nourished and those tendrils would grow stronger, just as Dr Cavendish had warned might happen over time.

Time is against me, though! he thought with fresh frustration, suddenly seeing himself standing by the altar filled with doubt as the wedding march was striking up and Penelope Aubrey-Finch was walking slowly down the aisle. He had to be sure about this other woman who roamed his senses – her clicking heels, her perfume and her red handkerchief.

'Why, Sir?'

Alex hadn't realised he'd aired his worry about lack of time aloud. 'Well, I feel I must fill in the blanks of my life quickly, or I shall go mad, Jones.'

'I can understand that, Sir.'

Alex was convinced that Jones would like to tell him to be grateful, that he was one of England's richest industrialists, and to stop his bleating. There was some truth in this sentiment, of course, but still the ghosts of his past nagged.

Edie's pounding heartbeat had been replaced by a new energy. She hoped the others could not see her shaking. And if they could, she certainly hoped it would not be interpreted as anything but the fury she was experiencing. She took a few moments to gather her wits, moving over to an ensemble she was working on for her newest client.

'What do you think of this, Sarah?'

The girl blinked, unnerved.

'It's lovely.'

'Oh, come on. You can do better than that. Could you improve it, if you were given the opportunity? Be honest. I shan't be offended.'

Sarah approached the wax mannequin, staring nervously at the dress while Edie studied her. She was quite sure that Sarah was so modest she had little conception of how pretty she was with her sweet, neat profile and button-shaped nose. When Sarah turned to regard her, Edie was treated to a front view of soulful brown eyes that seemed an odd match to the brightly golden hair that was worn short near her dimpled chin. Edie remembered how captivating the young woman's smile and warm chocolate eyes had been on the first occasion they'd met at the restaurant.

'I . . . I would consider turning it into a matching dress and coat,' Sarah said.

Edie turned to look at her design, presently only modelled up in bleached calico.

'Lightweight coat,' Sarah continued, surprising Edie as she suddenly sounded more confident. 'In a soft but daring colour for spring.'

'Which colour?' *Don't say pink, Sarah. Surprise me*, Edie urged privately.

'Oh, it has to be a brilliantly light, bright blue,' came the reply. 'Like the first thaw of spring . . . like the pictures of a glacier I saw in a magazine.'

Edie felt her heart lighten. 'Sarah?'

'Yes?'

'I want to apologise unreservedly for putting your honesty into question. Will you forgive any misunderstanding?'

'Of course. I'm glad we cleared it up, Miss Valentine.'

'But very importantly, I want to say why don't you come and work for me? We could so use a new assistant. We're advertising for one right now. I need someone to be my eyes and ears out here. Can you sew?'

Sarah nodded; she looked stunned.

'Well, think about it. Perhaps you —'

'I don't have to!' Sarah gushed. 'Think about it, I mean. Yes, Miss Valentine. Yes, please!' Sarah's expression changed from guarded as she unleashed a smile that sparkled through the depths of those dark eyes to glisten within happy tears. 'I'd work here for free!'

Edie was touched, felt the heat of Sarah's pleasure warm the frostiness that the girl's explanation had set inside Edie. She would confront that later.

Madeleine gave a lazy smile that was all approval. 'Well, you'd better go hand in your notice to the restaurant, Sarah.' She turned to Edie. 'Does she begin tomorrow?'

'Why not make it the day after? Then I can run up a beautiful black shift for you to wear as a uniform. Do you have some black heels, Sarah?' Three pairs of eyes glanced down at Sarah's feet. Edie noted the shoes were polished but old enough to be sagging, the creases testimony to years of hard wear of a person on their feet all day. 'Madeleine, give Sarah two pounds, please.'

Both women stared, slightly flabbergasted, at her but Madeleine moved towards the back office and the salon's kitty. Edie gave Sarah a reassuring smile.

'Spend tomorrow looking for a pair of black shoes with a T-bar and buttonhole ankle strap.'

Sarah's eyes widened. 'Oh, Miss Valentine, I've seen exactly those in Peter Jones! I don't know what to say.'

'If you're going to work here, you must look the part, so there's nothing you need to say. Consider this not only part of my apology but also necessary to help you fulfill your role. Gradually we'll build you an appropriate wardrobe but those shoes will go with everything through winter, early spring and autumn. We'll need to take some quick measurements but I want you to enjoy your shopping day. Oh, and Sarah?'

She turned. 'Yes?'

'Don't say anything to anyone yet about where you're working . . . just until the day you start here. Then you can tell everyone.'

Sarah beamed. 'Our secret.'

———

Alex stood at the front of the imposing triple-storey building. From a distance, in the car, it had triggered a memory, but now, from the drive in front of the main entrance, the hopsital felt meaningless.

'You look disappointed, Sir,' Jones said as he opened the door.

He gave a low sigh and it had nothing to do with the soft drizzle of rain that had arrived. 'I had hoped it would trigger a flood of memories, but there's nothing.'

The man closed the door gently behind Alex. 'Maybe you don't remember this entrance, Mr Wynter. If you weren't well, Sir, you were probably brought in without seeing much at all anyway.' He gave a cheer-up grin. 'Once inside it may seem more familiar.'

'Thank you, Jones,' Alex said and nodded at him to ensure the man knew he meant it. 'Wish me luck.'

'Good luck, Sir,' he said, touching his cap. 'I'll be waiting right here.'

Alex walked up the few steps into the cavernous lobby and was aware of his footsteps echoing on the hard floor. This reception area connected various corridors leading off to different wings of the hospital, but nothing struck him as familiar, except for the smell of strong disinfectant and carbolic soap.

'Can I help you?' the petite nurse behind the counter asked. She was one of three busy women in uniform behind the desk; not the prettiest of the trio, but he liked the welcome in her voice immediately.

Alex detailed his situation succinctly and her expression began to ease into surprise. She offered a smile that he was sure would ease many a sick soldier's heart. 'Oh, Mr Wynter, that's such a happy ending.'

'Well, yes, I suppose it is,' he said.

'I'm afraid I transferred to Edmonton only a few months ago,' she continued, 'but I'll see if I can find someone who may have been around when you were here. Do you remember anyone at all?'

He shrugged. 'A void, I regret to say.'

'Well, don't you worry. My father returned from the war a bit fuzzy,' she said, tapping her temple. 'He's much better now.'

He gave her an indulgent smile and wondered how nurses managed to stay so damn bubbly without being nauseating.

'So, now, let me just go and ask around for you. Would you like to take a seat?'

'Er, may I ask your name please?'

She grinned. 'It's Betty.'

'Well, Betty, I don't suppose I'm allowed to stroll around, see if anything bubbles up in my memory?'

She frowned. 'Er, I'm not permitted to let you do that, Mr Wynter,' but he heard hesitation. That probably meant that his 'dis-arming smile' was working its charm.

'Go on, Betty. How about I accompany you? Could you perhaps walk me through to where the soldiers recuperated?'

'Oh, very well, then. Can't hurt. Our job is to heal, isn't it?'

'Well said, Betty. I'll bet you're a favourite with the patients.'

She giggled, blushing slightly. 'I do my best, Mr Wynter. Doesn't cost much to be cheerful or kind.'

'Amen to that,' he said and fell into step alongside her.

As they strolled through the wing of the hospital he was disappointed to realise that the hollow feeling of his arrival was deepening; he recognised nothing and no one.

Betty – or Bet, as she'd since suggested he call her – looked as crestfallen as he felt. 'There have been so many changes since you were here, Mr Wynter.'

'Who is the oldest nurse . . . or, better still, a matron?'

That seemed to prompt a fresh idea. 'Sister Bolton! She's been here for centuries. But she's not in this part of the hospital. She looks after the sanatorium wing.' Bet appeared to lower her voice in the last few words.

'What happens there?' He frowned.

'Well, as I understand it, right now it's for people who are incurable and for patients who have dementia. I don't know how it was used during and directly after the war, though.'

'Can we find out?'

'Of course. I'll just let my colleague know that I'm taking you through.'

As Alex accompanied Bet into what began to feel like a more dilapidated area of the hospital, he also began to sense the first awareness of vague familiarity.

'Any bells ringing?'

He didn't want to say they weren't just ringing but clanging, so he nodded. 'Hopefully we're on the right track here,' he remarked.

Bet stopped a redhead with a jaunty walk who was tying a dark cape at her neck. Alex guessed she had perhaps a decade on Betty. Something trilled deep inside him when the nurse turned front on and regarded them both. 'Oh, Nancy,' Betty began. 'Excuse me. I wondered if I could ask if —'

'Jonesy!' the new nurse exclaimed.

Alex's insides felt as though they were somersaulting. 'Do you recognise me?' *Nancy . . . Nancy*, he repeated in his mind, and then suddenly it was as if curtains were drawn back in his thoughts . . . *Nan*? That's all he had. A name. But it felt right and it had resonance, he was sure.

Her face filled with delight, reddish golden curls escaping from her hat. 'Yes, yes, of course I do! I wouldn't forget that rakish smile anywhere.' Then her eyes narrowed. 'You didn't half cause a panic for us, Jonesy, the way you walked out on us on the day of the Peace Party. Can you remember that?'

He stared back at her blankly but she didn't seem to want his reply. 'Got me into so much trouble with Matron, you did.' She gave him a playful slap and it was in that touch that a fresh memory triggered.

'Nurse Nancy,' he murmured and distractedly rubbed his chin.

'I see you shaved at long, long last. Wow, but you're a looker, Jonesy . . . but then I'm obviously not that fussy because I always fancied you with your beard.' She giggled and nudged him. 'My, my, but you look fine and well.'

Betty, he could see, felt overwhelmed by Nancy's response and made a gracious escape.

'Thank you, Betty,' he said as she began saying her farewell and made a mental note to send her something with his thanks for her kindness. He returned full attention to the redhead. 'Nancy, I need your help.'

'Ooh, the hide! After all the trouble and heartache you put me through?'

He could tell she was still teasing him. 'My name is Alex Wynter. I found my family.'

'That's wonderful.' He could tell she meant it and realised suddenly, feeling instantly foolish, that not everyone read the London business pages. Nancy recognised him in a blink without his beard so maybe he should have put out a photo and request into *The Evening News*, which he knew had close on a million readers. Little yellow vans delivered it to the paperboys and everyday people read its eight pages – people from Golders Green to even here in Middlesex. It seemed so obvious now. Perhaps he still could, but visions of his mother and fiancée with sour looks shut down that option.

Nancy's expression was filled with relief for him. 'Mr Wynter,' she repeated as she stood back to get a better look at him. 'You wear it well. So I suppose that beautiful young woman found you at last, eh? Oh, what's her name? I can't remember but she had been up and down the country searching for you. She was so distressed when we couldn't locate you and of course the hospital was very embarrassed that it had lost you.'

'Her name is Miss Aubrey-Finch.'

'Ah, that's right. Is she your sweetheart? What happened?'

He was glad of her endless curiosity. He didn't want to discuss Pen, so he answered her final question instead. 'Well, Nan, that's why I'm here. You see, I don't know what happened. I'm hoping you can help.'

She frowned at him, perplexed.

'Let me explain. When I remembered who I was, I'd forgotten who I'd been. And you've just given me my first clue . . . you said Jonesy.'

She looked shocked at this news. 'Mr Jones. Yes.' She shrugged, embarrassed. 'We gave all our returned soldiers easy-to-remember surnames.'

Alex looked around. They were conspicuous in the corridor and it didn't make for easy conversation. 'Nan, can we sit down somewhere for a few minutes? Perhaps you're due for a break? I can buy you a pot of tea at the cafeteria or something?'

She laughed. 'At last, the date I'd always hoped for.'

He looked back at her quizzically.

'Oh, never mind. I was just off on my break. I can give you ten minutes, unless you want to meet and see that new film *The Three Musketeers* that's showing at The Palace?' she offered. 'Douglas Fairbanks . . .'

He'd seen the posters and grinned, but it was a sad gesture. 'I can't, Nan.'

'Are you properly with Miss Aubrey-Finch, then?'

He nodded. 'She's my fiancée.'

Nancy pulled a face of regret. 'That makes perfect sense,' she said. 'All right, a cup of tea it is, then, in the canteen.'

They found a small table in a nook by the window and Alex did his best to ignore the stares from other nurses.

'Oh, well,' she remarked, 'at least this will get their tongues wagging. They'll all be wondering who my handsome guest is.'

He smiled. 'Thank you, Nancy, for whatever you did for me. I'm sorry that I can't remember any of it.'

'Oh, that's all right. You were easy. So polite, charming, witty when you wanted to be, although usually grumpy because you felt so hopeless all the time.'

He got to the point. 'What do you remember about that day I disappeared off the ward? I was on a ward, was I?'

'Yes,' she frowned. 'That's right. You were in the sanatorium, but everything was as normal. You were a bit low and you hated the idea that we expected you to get dressed into a suit and attend the Peace Party.'

He smiled. 'Go on.'

She recounted everything she could recall about the day, including the arrival of Penelope and the ensuing panic it set off when it was discovered he was missing.

She took two swigs of her tea, thirsty from all the talking. He'd also paid for her to have a cake.

He nodded at it now. 'Go ahead. You could use some fattening up,' he said, knowing every woman loved to hear such a remark. 'Where was I when I disappeared?'

Nan attacked her rock bun with a fork and struggled to get a neat chunk into her mouth. She talked while she chewed and he tried not to smile. 'As far as I can remember, you were in the garden, having a smoke. You liked to sit outside the ward, always talking about the little robin that visited.'

He nodded, remembering the connection he'd felt with the robin inside the maze.

'Sister Bolton was the last person to see you, we thought. Oh, but she was furious with you – you'd said you'd see her at the party, and no one defies Sister Bolton!'

Alex coughed a laugh, sipped his cold tea. 'So I just walked out?'

She nodded. 'The side gate, where all the deliveries were made through; quite cunning of you, especially as you'd always struck me as being unnerved by what lay beyond the hospital grounds.'

'What do you mean?'

'I think you were offended that no one had claimed you and gradually became more nervous about facing the world outside, not knowing who you really were.'

She may be a simple enough girl but Nan was perceptive, and he was very sure she made a terrific nurse. 'Do you think someone helped me?'

'We don't know. The only visitors around the time of your disappearance were Billy Lockley, who was a regular delivery boy from the local greengrocer, and Mr Fairview, a visiting physician. Neither of them knew anything about you.'

'Nancy, I regained consciousness and the memory of who I was while wandering around in Savile Row in 1921.'

She gasped. 'You're joking!'

Alex shook his head sadly. 'I have no idea where I spent those years in between but I was certainly well fed, healthy, shaved, dressed in a quality suit. I must even have had money in my pocket, but . . .'

Nancy looked shocked. When he paused she raised an eyebrow in silent disbelief and swallowed the rest of her tea. Alex turned to gaze out of the window at the rain that was falling heavier now, running in rivulets down the windowpane to distort the images beyond them. He sipped again on the tea he didn't want. Its stewy flavour reminded him of life in the trenches, while the chatter and laughter of nurses sounded like a hen-coop above the din of steel cutlery clattering against plates. He recalled now how the hospital trolley would trundle down the corridors, wheels in need of oiling and a cacophony of crashing crockery and ringing cutlery above them.

And drifting above all the other sensory information came the unexpected sound of high heels on a pathway and the memory of Nancy and him standing by the window.

He swallowed, his throat suddenly parched. Alex realised that Nan was shaking his arm.

'Mr Wynter?' She sounded worried.

'I'm so sorry,' he said, her anxious expression coming into focus. 'Forgive me. This happens sometimes. I was chasing a memory that is just as keen to elude me.'

She smiled, unsure. 'Are you feeling all right?'

'Truly, I am. Little glimpses puncture through from time to time and are prompted by the oddest of events. I was having a memory of us standing by a frosted window and someone's heels clicking down the pathway, and you nagging me to shave.'

She frowned. 'Hmm, let me think. It was a very cold few days, as I recall, and I'd given my word to Matron I'd have you shaved . . . so it had to be around then – November. You had agreed to put on a suit for it and I'd brought one in for you, as it happens.'

'Had you?'

She nodded and swallowed another forkful of rock bun. 'And you had a favourite green jumper that one of the volunteer corps had knitted.'

A vague recollection bubbled up but before he could latch on to it, it burst and disappeared.

Nan frowned. 'I mentioned your posh accent and you said you may have been an actor, but I reckoned you were more likely a banker or solicitor.'

'Go on. Then what?'

'Then, nothing. We talked about the Spanish Flu, and probably the weather. That was it. The next day was much the same except you were determined to go and sit out in the cold like a grump.'

He thought about the maze at Larksfell that had helped him to recall a sense of his past. 'Was there a privet hedge at all?'

She nodded. 'It's still there. You liked sitting near it. You could watch your friend, the robin, and you told me you distantly over-heard people passing. The children's higher, louder voices were easier to distinguish, you said.'

'*I had a little bird. Its name was Enza. I opened the window. And in-flu-Enza,*' he chanted softly, amazed by the memory coming back so easily.

'Where did you get that from?' she asked, checking the time on her upside-down fob watch. That action helped him to cement Nancy into his mind. He did remember her now, not so clearly that he would have picked her out in a line of women, but there was much that was familiar, from her playful touches to that habitual glancing at her watch. 'I have to go, I'm afraid,' she said.

The rhyme was singing distantly around his mind, echoing on repeat.

'Nancy, might I call you if I remember anything that needs clarification?'

'If that means, would I like to go out with you sometime, the answer's yes!'

They both laughed. 'I may just have a question or two.'

'Of course,' she said, standing, and he followed suit. 'I'm glad to see you looking so very well.'

'You're the best, Nancy,' he said, and held out a hand. It seemed far too perfunctory, and given that he knew they had an audience, Alex leaned in across the table and kissed her cheek softly, holding her hand longer than necessary. 'Thank you for looking after me so well.'

She tittered, glanced around sheepishly. 'That should see them through a few shifts!'

'Well, I'll walk you out. Let's see if we can't start those tongues wagging immediately.'

It occurred to him to ask if he could see the old ward and speak to Sister Bolton but he'd already imposed on Nancy and didn't want to push his luck. He could always make a return trip.

Once back in the car, he was keen to dismantle everything he'd learned and see if he couldn't put it back together into some semblance that was meaningful.

'Where to, Sir?'

'White's Club, please, Jonesy . . . St James's.'

'Right you are, Mr Wynter. Will you be overnighting at White's, Sir?'

'I shall,' he said, distractedly. 'But you should head back to Sussex this evening. I won't need the car.'

Jones nodded. 'And did you get what you came looking for, Sir?'

'Not quite, but I believe I'm a lot closer,' he admitted, as a random memory dislodged itself from the pile of information gathered today and began to shout at him from the rim of his mind to notice it.

26

Swithin's Club, known affectionately and perhaps a little pretentiously by Benjamin Levi as 'Swines', was located in the city of London, not far from the medieval Anglican church of St Swithin. It was currently cloaked in a typical London fog that was yet to clear. Edie knew she'd find the man she was looking for during a busy breakfast seating; Ben took all his midday meals here, and enjoyed breakfast on a Wednesday because 'they did a mean haddock' and a cream of wheat that was apparently so much better than 'plain old lumpy porridge'.

It made her angry just standing across the street and looking at the building – a bastion of male domination that Ben was utterly seduced by. But nothing could reach the depths of her disappointment to ease the pain of what she'd learned. She was sure she didn't have all the facts and so she tempered her rising fury by taking deep breaths of the chilled London air and giving Ben his chance to explain it. However, she wasn't going to give him the opportunity to turn all lawyerly on her and have the time to build his argument.

Edie blew out her last deep breath and skipped across the road, preparing for her ambush.

———————

Bartholomew Hudson had been concierge at Swithin's Club since its inception just before the turn of the previous century.

He'd survived the war, Spanish flu, the arrival of the jazz age, coal rationing due to the mining strike and even the unthinkable admission of a woman into the club for the first time. But he'd consoled himself that Ivy Williams could be forgiven for trampling into such male territory because she came from a pedigree of fine lawyers, herself a quite brilliant lawyer and one of the first women to be admitted to the inns of court. Plus, her barrister brother, a member of Swithin's, gave his life fighting for his country.

However, he'd not for a moment believed it might set a trend and that women would wish to cross the threshold of Swithin's regularly, so it was with dismay that he watched the striking woman skitter across Cannon Street with intent. He'd been watching her for a few minutes; she was hard to miss in that plum-coloured coat and fur hat amongst the river of black suits that flowed around her. Hudson had assumed she was simply admiring the building, but now he doubted that. She clearly had designs to enter.

It was fiercely cold, though, despite the fog, and a gossamer mist made the dark-haired beauty approaching seem all the more ethereal as she emerged into full view and was now just steps away. He realised it would be churlish to forbid her entry into the lobby and he leapt for the brass door handle that he'd made sure was polished to a gleam daily.

'Er, good morning, Miss,' he said, as she eased quickly through the opening. Cold air rushed in with her slipstream. 'I'm sorry. I think perhaps you may be in the wrong building,' he tried.

'I don't think so,' she said and disarmed him with not only an attractively husky voice but a smile to warm anyone's bones. 'This is Swithin's Club, isn't it?'

'Yes, indeed,' he replied. 'Um . . . a *gentleman's* club, Miss . . . er?'

'Eden Valentine,' she said, holding out a hand gloved in black suede.

It would have been rude not to shake her hand but now he found himself unnerved by her confident intrusion.

'Bartholomew Hudson. I'm the Chief Concierge, Miss Valentine. Do you need directions to somewhere?'

She seemed to pay no attention to his attempt at deflecting her back out into the cold. 'I do. Thank you, Mr Hudson. I need directions to your breakfast room, please.'

He stared back at her, disarmed.

'From the smell of bacon, I'm presuming it's upstairs,' she said, pointing towards the thickly carpeted flight that swept up from the central back of the lobby.

Members passed and threw glances of confusion their way. His heart sank as he noticed two eminent barristers drifting down the stairs.

'Miss Valentine. Forgive me, but women are not seen at Swithin's Club.'

'I am well aware of that, Mr Hudson. Men are also not seen wearing my gowns but that doesn't mean I forbid them from entering my salon.'

While he blustered to find the right response, she moved quickly, and within a couple of heartbeats he saw her finely turned ankles hurrying over the fleur-de-lis carpet and disappearing up the stairs. Hudson felt alarm grip him and initially he tried to dash after her, but the swarm of men now descending the stairs obstructed him as the first breakfast sitting ended. He decided to use the telephone instead.

He rang the dining room's extension three times before it was answered but by then it was already too late.

———

Feeling herself to be swimming upstream like a salmon, she dodged around burly shoulders and ignored the looks of alarm and the buzz that rippled through the diners as they emerged from double doors at the end of a corridor.

'I say, young lady. Are you meant to be here?'

'I need to find a Mr Benjamin Levi.'

The older man looked perplexed.

'Is Mr Levi in the dining room?' she pushed.

'I saw him in there, yes,' said a younger man who winked at her. 'Gosh, are we letting in women members now?'

She dodged away again before poor old Hudson could catch up with her.

Edie burst into the room and scanned the wide chamber for Ben. Her sharp gaze was quick to pick up on style and elegance and registered only opulence. She noted gilt and chandeliers, carpet that deadened sounds so the tap of forks and knives were unobtrusive and conversation muted. She smelled leather and sweet tobacco conflicting with haddock and boiled eggs. Tall Georgian windows, looming out of vermilion flock-wallpapered walls, were like giant picture frames giving her a view down onto the city. White tablecloths dazzled, silver glinted and crystal winked at her; she couldn't imagine how bright it would all appear on a sunny day. Perhaps they drew those heavy, emerald velvet drapes, she wondered absently, as her gaze finally fell upon a familiar shape.

Ben was reading the morning paper, his back to her and yet to pick up the sounds of discomfort as men began to clear their throats, flap their newspapers with distress and clink a knife against crystal glasses to win attention.

She waited, fending off urgent and sometimes beseeching enquiries from waiters, and ignored the blinking, clearly confounded arrival of a tall gentleman in a dark suit with a withering glare. 'Madam,' he said, as though it was a word never to be uttered between these walls. 'I really must ask you to follow me . . .' She waited, determined for Ben to pay attention, her anger rising with each second that ticked in the back of her mind.

Finally, his awareness was pricked by the lack of all sound that had stilled to an awkward hush. He turned and blanched at the sight of her.

'Hello, Ben.'

'Mr Levi, forgive me for this intrusion,' the man began, his tone and expression one of mortification.

'Unhand Miss Valentine, Sir!' Ben snapped in his shock and the head waiter dropped her arm as if scalded. Ben stood, reaching for a napkin to dab his lips. 'She is my fiancée and would only come here in an emergency.' His shifting glance at Edie begged that this was the case. 'Are you all right, Edie, my dear?'

It was a pity that she only now realised – in this uncomfortable silence, with a few dozen pairs of eyes fixed on her – how handsome Ben Levi was. She'd never been able to see it. As he stood there, tall and outfitted in a fine high-buttoning dark suit with his new affectation of a bow tie, his forehead puckered with a concerned frown, his luxurious black hair slicked back to frame his still boyish dark features that included an infectious grin, Edie appreciated that Ben had become a handsome man. Looking at him objectively, he would have made a good partner for her, physically, financially, religiously, but certainly not spiritually or emotionally.

He had never called her 'my dear'; it sounded so patronising that Edie sighed and in that moment the fight she was sure she'd come here to have stepped away like a shadow parting from her. Her shoulders relaxed as the pent fury expelled in that sigh and Edie made yet another important decision. It was as instinctive as the first time she'd made it.

'I'm sorry to intrude, Ben, but yes, it is important . . . and urgent,' she admitted, glancing at the men who now ringed her, ready to bundle her out of the dining room.

'Step away please, thank you, Mr Barnsley,' Ben warned. 'Excuse me, gentlemen,' he said to the room, showing no signs of the embarrassment she knew she was causing him. 'Dearest, perhaps we could step outside?'

His entreaty was too polite for her to spit it right back in his face and she gave a small incline of her head in agreement. In doing so she felt the tension surrounding her relax. Men melted back to their stations, and the head waiter cleared his throat and turned crisply on his heels as Ben took Edie's arm.

'There's a private room just next door.' He said no more until he'd escorted her into a small salon and closed the door behind them. He let out a long breath. 'Edie, whatever are you doing here?'

'I'm here to tell you that I cannot marry you, Ben.'

She had expected anger, at least irritation, but his chuckle surprised her into momentary silence.

'Again? You're doing it to me again?'

'It was a mistake to agree to marry you the first time. I don't know what I've been thinking.'

'Edie,' he said, sounding vaguely exasperated as he looked at the watch hanging from his waistcoat. 'Less than . . .' He paused to calculate. 'Er, fourteen hours ago, we were discussing a date for our nuptials. What on earth has prompted this curious behaviour? Nerves, perhaps? Perfectly understandable.'

She admired how reasonable he sounded. But Ben rarely argued.

'I came here today filled with a sort of righteous rage and I wanted to cause a scene. I wanted to pick a very public fight with you.'

His puzzlement deepened. 'You did cause a scene. I'm sure it will be the conversational highlight of the club.' She heard mocking amusement.

'You've got broad shoulders,' she said by way of apology.

'I'll enjoy the fame it brings me,' he soothed. 'Tell me what's wrong? What's happened?'

'Sarah happened,' she said, holding his gaze with defiance but speaking softly.

'Sarah?'

'Don't, Ben. I deserve your respect.'

He looked lost. Either it was a fine performance, or Sarah had lied. Edie couldn't doubt herself now; she decided he was playing with her, using the time to rapidly think through the situation.

'Sarah,' she continued, forcing her tone to sound even, 'is the former cloakroom assistant at the restaurant you took me to on the evening my sketches were stolen.'

He shrugged, looked baffled. 'What has this to do with me?'

She looked away, helplessly disappointed, having hoped, just in that heartbeat, that he might be truthful with her. 'You've always been my best friend. Remember our pact that day we went with all your cousins to the fair and we rode the Ferris wheel?'

'I promised I'd marry you and always love you,' he said, before she could continue. 'And I wanted you to say it back to me.'

'That's my point, Ben. We also made a promise that we'd never lie. I couldn't lie to you then and give my word I'd marry you. But I know you are lying to me now.'

She wasn't ready for how quickly he moved to clasp the tops of her arms. 'What is it? What do you believe?'

Clever. It was his legal brain taking over. Rational, calm, cunning; throw the responsibility back onto her.

She took a breath. 'I am led to believe that Sarah is wrongly accused of stealing my sketches. That it was you who took them, gave them to my rivals. That it was you who humiliated me, tried to crush my dreams before they'd had a chance to take flight. And it was you who set out to undermine my business.'

She saw anger flash in his eyes. 'And how do you come by this information, Edie? I thought I expressly forbade —'

'Oh, Ben, you forbid me nothing!' she snapped, shaking herself free of his touch. 'You don't own me!'

He looked around as though worried their voices might carry.

'Forgive me,' he said, running a shaking hand, she noticed, through his neatly combed hair. 'That came out wrong. I did ask you not to stir this up.'

'And now I understand why.'

'How can you possibly take the word of a common thief against mine? I don't blame that girl, of course,' he condescended. 'She probably doesn't know how to pay her rent.'

She shook her head, holding his gaze. 'I'm sorry. I don't believe you, and that means I don't trust you.'

'Edie, please.' He reached for her arm but she shrank from his touch.

'I admired you for being able to put aside how I must have wounded you last time. You made me trust that true friendship can overcome all hurts. I do thank you for that, Ben. But, you see, I think you have been the cynical one here and whichever way I look at it, it makes me dislike you. I think you did decide to teach me a lesson but you went about it clandestinely. Either that, or you were determined to take a woman back to a darker age of servility to her husband. That was why I loved Tom so very much.' Her eyes watered to be mentioning him again. She hated having to raise his name to defend her position. 'Tom never treated me as anything but an equal. In truth, he put me on a pedestal and fuelled my dream, helped me make it come true, while you have done the opposite. Sarah told me that she never opened the folder and that no one but you touched it from the moment I gave it into her care. She said she watched you open it, take out some of the pages, fold them and put them into your pocket. And I believe her, Ben.'

'I cannot credit what you are accusing me of,' he sniped.

'What is done cannot be undone and I shall waste no further energy on the lost designs. I trust Sarah's explanation because she had the wherewithal to know where to sell them, the knowledge and flair for fashion.'

Ben gave a look of disdain. 'The case rests, surely?'

'Does it? For someone with this keen know-how comes a desire to wear that sort of fashion.'

'I'm sure she'll use the proceeds unwisely then and not pay her rent but buy herself some fancy new clothes.'

'Indeed, that's what most would think, myself included. So why, if Sarah is such a cunning opportunist with an unexpected windfall and a nose for style, would she still be walking around in old, unfashionable shoes, carrying a battered bag and a darned skirt?'

Ben reddened and gave no answer.

'I have made amends for your cynical use of Sarah as your scapegoat but I'm afraid I can't see a way for amends to be made to me, Ben.'

His expression finally changed, shifting from deliberately blank to openly sullen. 'I gave you a second chance to be my wife, Edie, to have standing again. I swallowed my pride and all that pain, and here you are, slapping the other cheek. What I did I did for our shared good. I couldn't have a wife who is, let's face it, just a slightly glamorous version of a shopkeeper and potentially making a fool of herself.'

She nodded, grateful. 'And so finally you've revealed the truth. I don't know what I was thinking, Ben, and I have no intention of signing any papers that release me from my marriage to Tom, the father of my son. I know you want Tommy to be yours. I think you'd even make a fine fist of being a good father. But not to Tommy. He doesn't need you.'

Ben laughed with cruelty. 'He's not coming back for you, Edie. Your father once told me he feared that if Tom could lose his memory, he could just as likely regain it . . . seems his words were wise.'

Edie stared at Ben's snide expression and the shock of his words made it feel as though the floor had just fallen away, creating an exquisitely sharp trill of anxiety. She blanched, suddenly feeling as though she were in a terrifying dark tunnel. Uncharacteristic perspiration pricked beneath her clothes that felt uncomfortably tight. She gasped with breathlessness.

'I can see that has your attention, my dear Edie. Poor you. Poor Tom. Or perhaps not so *poor* Tom.'

'What do you know?' she croaked, her lips numb.

'My advice is you forget him, as he has clearly forgotten you. It's very clear he's not coming back to your cosy little cottage in Epping.'

'You've seen him?' she asked. The words hurt to be spoken.

He shrugged. 'I read or maybe I was told something somewhere, while you were away.'

'But you didn't think to mention it,' she whispered.

'You were gone for a week. I forgot.' She knew he lied; could see it in the way his Adam's apple bobbed in his tight throat. 'He clearly doesn't remember you, or his life or the fact he's a father. So don't ask me anything else about him, as I paid little attention.'

'No, I won't,' she said retreating towards the door of the suddenly stuffy room they stood so awkwardly in. 'We shall never speak of Tom again, you and I. In fact, we shall not speak on anything ever again. Goodbye, Ben.'

Edie did not wait for a response. She turned her back and fled down the now deserted corridor and stairs. Bursting into the cold London morning, she hurried down Cannon Street, dragging in the air, hoping its tingling cold would shake her from her stupor and help her to think clearly.

She hurried past the Italianate-design Terminus Hotel that adjoined the Cannon Street railway station and made her way through the entrance and into the station proper, where she stopped and drew breath beneath the great semicircular glass and iron atrium. Pausing here to find her handkerchief and dry the tears she hadn't been aware of until now, she found herself beginning to laugh through her despair. And as she looked up past the glass to the overcast, near-white November sky, she felt her spirits lifting.

Tom was alive. And she would find him.

27

Alex jerked awake to the sound of a woman's heels retreating and was momentarily shocked to find himself slouched in a leather armchair. He had obviously yelled something aloud too because the other members were giving him glances that ranged from annoyance to amusement.

'Another brandy, Sir?' said a middle-aged waiter in a droll tone.

Alex glanced to the small drinks table at his side and the near-empty crystal goblet. 'Er, no thanks, Albert. Stir the fire, though. There's a good fellow.' He raised himself from his slouch, stifling a yawn, and felt someone slap his back.

'Hope you won!'

'What? Oh, hello, Denton. Still here?'

'I said, I hope she won, old chap?'

Alex looked up, confused. 'What the devil are you flapping about, Timothy?'

'Pretty Penny. Sounded like you rode her to the finish line.'

'Penny is my fiancée, you oaf,' he said wearily. 'Damn, I must have nodded off.' He glanced at the big clock over the club's smoking room mantelpiece.

'I know, that's what made it funny,' Denton continued in a jolly tone. 'She may be your fiancée, but Pretty Penny was also a great filly a few years back. Never lost a race. Someone must have made a fortune on her because she came out of nowhere.' He tapped his nose. 'I had my chance. Wish I'd taken it. Night, Wynter.'

Pretty Penny? Had he really yelled that? He'd never bet on a racehorse in his life . . . not to his knowledge, anyway. He groaned. And the sound of heels still echoed distantly.

Alex sighed, stared at the flames that had been enlivened into fresh action by Albert, and thought about tomorrow. Would the tailoring house offer any further insight? He reached for the goblet and the alcohol's vapours gave him a notion of fresh flowers and ripe apricots. He drained the dregs of the brandy and a smooth but fiery toffee flavour hummed gently through him. Alex made a decision. He knew he was living a double life – the one that was getting ready to take on a wife, set up a family life as a good husband, and then there was the other one, the darker one, that lived in the shadows and hankered after misty thoughts about a different woman he wanted to know again, needed to see again . . . Those teasing thoughts had the power to undo him, destroy his potential to achieve equilibrium and, finally, return to normality. Unless he learned who he had been, where he had been, he was concerned the doubts would never rest and he could potentially destroy any chance of his and Pen's future happiness. She deserved better than this half of a man. What was the significance of Pretty Penny and all the other tiny, seemingly meaningless items of flotsam and jetsam that might lead him to the owner of the red handkerchief?

Decide, Alex, he commanded silently as the flames danced and reminded him of another fire in a far smaller room that was elegant and cosy . . . and filled with love. He held his breath. He wasn't mistaken; memories were definitely edging closer. Was the amnesia losing its grip or was he a victim of his own desperation? Was any of it real?

Enough! How much longer could he tolerate his own dithering? Real or not, the wedding banns were just a few weeks away and he could hear the strains of the wedding march. Wasn't he too far down the aisle already with Pen? He loathed the indecision, frustrated by his half mind, half life, and the half man that he'd become.

As Alex stared into the flames he reached a pact with himself. If the meeting with Percival Fitch revealed not a single lead, then he was going to set this search aside, put it behind him and forge ahead with the life he had on offer with Pen. How many poor Tommies would give their souls for a shot at what he had – the second chance? How many times had he heard them mutter in the trenches, while preparing to go over the top, that they would give an arm or a leg for one last day with their loved ones? He felt sickened by his lack of gratitude. The planets had aligned for whatever reason to give him this second chance . . . why risk it?

Alex could have stayed at the family apartment in Belgravia but preferred the convenience of the club and climbed the stairs to the guestroom. He slept in his clothes, barely loosening his collar, and dreamed of a garden toolshed and a timber framework that looked to be an infant's cot.

Madeleine had been helping Edie drown her sorrows, listening to her friend's slurring, halting words.

'I've never known Ben to be cruel. That's what hurts.'

'Oh, people do strange things when they're in love, darling. He's not immune, nor is he a saint. He's a man, after all!' This amused Mads and she began to laugh alone to herself, then she focused on her friend with drooping eyes. 'Eden, I am so tipsy I shall have to sleep at your place tonight.'

Edie glanced over at the empty champagne bottle and chuckled, remembering her friend's advice: 'You never lament the end of a love affair, *ma cherie*. You simply toast the next.'

'Of course. Find a place and sleep,' she slurred. 'Mads, am I drunk?'

'I do hope so. Then it means I'm not the only one spinning.'

They laughed but Edie wasn't sure why she sounded so jolly because she was suddenly feeling deeply queasy. 'I've got to check on Tommy.'

'Tommy sleeps like a tree,' Madeleine replied and Edie couldn't be bothered finding the energy to correct her. 'But we must get our beauty sleep. You know the Aubrey-Finch party is in tomorrow.'

'Oh, no. Say it isn't so,' Edie groaned, burying her face in a cushion. 'What time?'

'Ten.'

'Well, I'm falling asleep right here,' she admitted, her voice drifting.

'Then I shall take your bed, darling, because I'm the one who must model her honeymoon wardrobe.' Madeleine blew her an unsteady kiss. 'I'll check Tommy. *Bonne nuit, ma cherie.*'

'Bonnie,' Edie slurred, fully believing she'd spoken perfect French, and drifted off dreaming of eating apple and blackberry pie in a bathtub with Tom, while church bells rang for a wedding that was his but not hers.

———

The sound of the kettle whistling hurt her head. Edie groaned softly as Madeleine ran in to turn it off, cursing.

Edie looked up from sunken, bloodshot eyes. 'If you ever get me tipsy again,' she began before suddenly lurching forward, making a gagging sound. 'Quick, out of my way!' She scraped the chair back, pushed Tommy's porridge bowl at her and ran for the bathroom.

Madeleine raised her eyebrows at Tommy as he sat patiently in his high chair awaiting the next mouthful. 'Here, beautiful boy.

You have a go with this spoon. That's it, clever Tommy. You'll be two soon and Mummy can show off how well you eat with no help. I'd better make her a pot of tea.' She began searching for honey and lemon. Tommy amused himself by drawing with his porridge, squeezing it through his small fingers and smearing it on the tray of his high chair.

When Edie returned, her complexion looked waxy and her normally lustrous black hair hung in damp strands. 'Tommy! Look at this mess.'

Madeleine sniggered. 'A sponge and water cleans that up in a wink. Stop worrying. He's happy, he's eating. Here, drink this.'

'Absolutely not! I will never drink anything that is handed to me by you again. Morning sickness was so much easier than this,' she murmured.

'Except this will pass, my darling,' Madeleine said, archly, returning with a warm flannel for Tommy.

Edie smiled. 'What would I have done if you hadn't come into my life? You're always picking up the pieces of my desperately bad choices.'

'Neither was a bad choice, Eden. But Ben has let you down. You've hurt each other. It's over.' She shrugged. 'Tomorrow may bring another man.'

Eden gave her a scathing look. 'I told you what Ben said. I plan to discover what he learned about Tom.'

'Perhaps he was lying,' Mads mused.

'No, he knew something. I'll start with the newspapers on Fleet Street. Maybe he read an article.'

'You have no name, no details. Where to begin?'

Edie shrugged. 'He's out there. I will find him. What is this drink, anyway?'

'Honey . . . sugar always helps with a hangover. The lemon is vitamin C – didn't your granny teach you that?'

'Yes, I was taught *zat*,' she mimicked.

'And a surprise ingredient that is the key. Nothing harmful,' Madeleine assured. 'Drink it and you will feel better in about half an hour.'

Edie tipped her head back and swallowed the liquid with a wince. She looked up at Madeleine in accusation and then her eyes widened with the new prickling sensation on her tongue that Madeleine knew would be turning instantly hot. 'What the —'

'Cayenne pepper, darling. Chilli relieves pain, believe it or not.'

Edie coughed, and then started to splutter.

'Trust my French granny's recipe,' Madeleine said. 'Now, it's not quite seven-thirty, and you need to meet Miss Aubrey-Finch at ten. That's plenty of time —'

Edie kissed Tommy's head before slumping again on the kitchen table. 'No, Mads,' she groaned from beneath her arms, which cradled her head. 'I cannot see her. Not in this state.'

'You will be fine.'

'I won't. I feel nauseous. My head hurts. I will be retching again in a moment. Isn't Sarah in today?'

'She is.'

'I'll call Mrs Miller to sit with Tommy for an hour until I can see straight. Can you both handle the fitting?'

'I'm sure we could, but Miss Aubrey-Finch will be disappointed. And what if changes need to be made, or she's put on three hundred pounds?'

Even though it hurt to, Edie laughed.

'Well, ring her now from here and change the appointment. Blame me. Tell her I'm sick.'

'Oh, Eden. She was going to pay the balance today, no?'

'Don't blame me. This is all your fault, anyway. Oh, make the call, Mads, please,' she urged, then dragged herself to her feet. 'I'll be resting in the bathroom this morning.'

———

When Madeleine returned from dropping Tommy downstairs to Mrs Miller, she found the salon's diary that Edie had brought home last night and looked up Miss Aubrey-Finch's number. She checked the time. It was just past eight.

A few minutes later she tapped on the bathroom door. 'Eden?'

'Mmm?'

'Do you need help?'

'That chilli burned all the way back up.'

'Then you'll need another slug later. Get into bed.'

'My bedroom feels like a million miles away.' She opened the door, dishevelled and with a bloodless complexion.

'I've rearranged the appointment for tomorrow.'

'Thanks, Mads.' Edie headed for her room.

Madeleine watched Edie fall into bed and pull the covers around her gingerly. 'And she said she'd have payment brought around today.'

'Told you it would be fine,' Edie yawned, eyes closed.

'Telephone the salon when you finally get up,' Madeleine suggested. 'Be well, Eden.'

She left her friend's top-floor apartment in Chelsea and took a taxi back to her own, where within an hour she emerged immaculately groomed to step inside a horse-drawn hackney to take her the short distance to the salon. She arrived moments before Sarah.

'*Bienvenue*.' She beamed. 'Welcome,' she added, to the girl's lost expression. 'First-day nerves?'

Sarah nodded. 'I feel sick in my tummy.'

'Well, so does Miss Valentine. She won't be in, I'm afraid.' She watched Sarah's shoulders slump.

'Oh? Nothing serious, I hope.'

Madeleine shook her head. 'Headache. She's taking a well-needed rest.' She put her head to one side. 'You look extremely lovely.'

Sarah had taken off her coat and now straightened her skirt self-consciously. 'Oh, I'm happy you approve, Miss Delacroix. And . . . I didn't really get the chance to thank you for coming to find me that day. You were like an angel sent from heaven. I hated my work at the restaurant, but this is a new world,' she said, admiring the racks of clothes covered in muslin bags. 'Is this the Aubrey-Finch collection?'

'Yes. Well done on remembering. But we shan't be unwrapping it today. However, there's always plenty to do. Do you want to try on your new uniform? It's going to do your darling figure wonders and go with those new shoes perfectly. Oh, and please listen out for a messenger who will be delivering payment for Miss Aubrey-Finch . . .'

———

Alex had woken with a distant, dull headache and remembered the brandy of the previous evening. The jangling phone made him grind his teeth and he sat on the edge of the bed, realising he was still in yesterday's suit. It was Pen on the line, asking a favour.

'I've already sent the envelope to your club with a driver. If you're out and about and could deliver it, it would save me some faffing,' she said.

'That's fine, I can deliver it for you.' He yawned. 'What about tonight?'

He listened to her ideas for their evening entertainment. 'I don't think I'm in the mood for a show,' Alex replied and waited for her inevitable soft grumble. He knew she'd wanted to head to the theatre but he couldn't face it, and offered an alternative. 'How about that new jazz club you told me about?'

'Do you mean Murray's?'

'That's the one,' he answered. 'We could have a drink there and then go on to the Cecil Hotel?'

'Fine with me,' she approved. 'Alex, I can hear how sleepy you are. Don't forget the payment. I promised.'

'I'll deliver it this afternoon,' he confirmed.

'Thanks, see you at seven, darling. I'll pick you up in the taxi. I love you.'

Alex put the phone down and blinked at her effortless expression of love, while he had yet to bring himself to respond in kind. He knew it wounded her but his mother had cannily summed it up: 'Penny has the patience of a crocodile.'

He picked up the telephone receiver again and made a call, confirming his appointment in Savile Row. It felt like an important day after last night's decision: a watershed. By midday he would be letting go of the past. After today's meeting with Mr Fitch and the likely news that there was nothing to lead him any further into his past, he would simply let it go and allow it all to drift away like a lost balloon at a fairground.

He sat back against the worn leather in the hansom cab and looked out upon another frigid London morning. It felt dry and cold enough to snow and he noticed Christmas decorations appearing in the shop windows. A new year beckoned, and hopefully a whole new life.

The horse clip-clopped into Savile Row and Alex spied the spot where he had woken up with people clustered around him. His cheeks reddened at the memory and he was glad when the cab slowed. Alex stepped onto the pavement and paid the driver. When he turned to face the frontage of Anderson & Sheppard, Percival Fitch was beaming at him from the top of the short flight of stairs.

'Good morning, Mr Wynter.'

'Morning, Fitch. Hope you've got a good fire going in there.'

Jonathan Elton returned from running an errand and followed Alex in. He shivered, blew on his hands. 'Brass monkeys out there. Cup of tea, Sir?'

'Good idea,' Alex replied and while Elton peeled off down the corridor, he followed the senior tailor into the main salon. 'Well, you look hale, Fitch. That country air clearly suits you.'

'It's true.' He tapped his chest. 'And my doctor likes what it does for my heart. I gather you're not here for a suit, Sir? Mr Elton said you needed to see me.'

'Well, now you mention it, I think you had better measure me up for a new suit. I'm getting hitched, Fitch!' They laughed at the rhyme and the tailor looked genuinely delighted.

'Oh, congratulations, Mr Wynter. That's wonderful news. So a new morning suit, new dinner suit, some travelling clothes, presumably?'

Alex nodded. 'April it is. We're honeymooning in Europe and going as far as Constantinople.'

'You'll need some linens, then.'

'I'll leave it all to you. The wedding's on the first of April.'

'April Fool's Day, Sir?' Elton commented, returning with a tea tray. 'I hope you're not joking,' he said with a grin.

Fitch cleared his throat. 'The tea, Elton, please.' He returned his attention to Alex. 'Spring weddings are always lovely,' Fitch remarked, 'provided the rain holds off. Well, we shall do a fresh raft of measurements, Sir, if you don't mind.'

'Of course.'

Elton arrived with the pot and started to arrange cups on saucers as Fitch set about measuring Alex's chest.

'I need to talk to you about that day I took my tumble in the Row,' Alex began.

'Oh?' Fitch said. 'How can I help?'

Alex sighed. 'I'm not sure, really. I want to know everything you remember about that moment I came to.'

'I'll do my best, Sir.' He wrote down some numbers and began recounting the events as he measured.

Fitch straightened. '. . . and I sent it straight over.'

'This handkerchief?' Alex said, pulling it from his pocket and noticing Fitch's discomfort.

'Er, yes, Sir. While perhaps not important now, given your approaching nuptials, I thought it necessary at the time to return it to you.' The tailor must have been wondering why on earth Alex still carried the red handkerchief around with him.

'Fitch, this is my only link to a past I can't remember. I have no idea who it belongs to or why I have it. You'd be the first to agree that the sewing is accomplished and fine. I know everyone wants to pat me on the head and suggest it probably came from a thankful girl from a brothel, but . . .' He shook his head. 'I just don't think so.'

'I can shed no light on this for you, Sir,' Fitch replied.

'Perhaps you can shed some light on the suit?'

'The suit?' His brow wrinkled and he put the measuring tape back around his neck.

'The one I was wearing before you kindly supplied me with a fresh one. I hoped it might shed some clues.'

'No, Sir, I doubt it. I emptied the pockets myself and found only that handkerchief. There was nothing else. It has since occurred to me that you may have been robbed.'

Alex began to pace, heedless of his tailor's need to measure him. 'Yes, precisely.'

'I'm sorry, Mr Wynter,' Fitch said, gently.

'What happened to that suit?' he asked.

Fitch blanched. 'You asked me to get rid of it, Sir.'

'And you did?'

The tailor's expression became mortified.

'I'm not blaming you, Fitch. I'm simply trying to backtrack along a murky trail.'

'I understand, Sir. But I'm afraid I did follow your instructions. Mr Elton here disposed of it. We, er . . . well, I think it went to the North London Christian Mission. Mr Elton doesn't live far from there and took it to the Mission himself as I recall, didn't you, Mr Elton?'

Jonathan put down the teapot and reddened, opening his mouth to agree and then closing it again.

Fitch blinked with consternation. 'Jonathan?'

'Forgive me, Mr Fitch. It was a very nice suit.'

Alex's heart leapt. 'Elton, do you still have it?'

'Not as such, Sir. Um . . . my brother's not far off your size, Mr Wynter, and he was trying out for a job with the Hotel Cecil, Sir, and needed to make a good impression.'

'And did he?'

'What's that, Sir?'

'Make a good impression in my suit?'

Elton grinned. 'Yes, Mr Wynter. He's doing very well in the private dining room as a senior waiter now.'

'I'm glad the suit helped. Do you think he might still have it?'

Elton nodded, glancing in apology to his superior. 'Probably. Er, yes, Sir.'

'Really, Jonathan,' Fitch breathed with exasperation.

'Please, Fitch,' Alex said. 'I'm delighted that it found good use and even happier to know it's still traceable. It may offer a clue to my past, you see. Elton, I know it's terribly unusual, but I wonder if I might just take a look to satisfy myself? Could we call the hotel, perhaps?'

'Mr Wynter,' Fitch said, 'I don't wish to interfere, but may I respectfully ask what you hope to find?'

'The label! I was hoping I could visit the man who made it. I'm giving it one last-ditch effort, Mr Fitch. Unless you've walked in my shoes, you cannot begin to understand how frustrating it is to know you've been leading a life somewhere but have no memory of it.'

The tailor nodded. 'I do appreciate your yearning for the truth, Mr Wynter, and I was going to say that I can tell you who made that suit. I could tell you without even looking at the label.'

Alex's heart leapt. 'Really?'

'Of course. That was an Abraham Valentine suit. He was a Jewish tailor who had his own shop in Golders Green but he used to do a lot of excellent work for many of the tailors around here. He was liked by all; I always thought he would open up a business on the Row but he lived above his shop and was happy being amongst his own community.'

Alex hung on his words. 'Anything else?'

Fitch shrugged. 'A very good tailor, Sir.'

'You said he *was* a Jewish tailor?'

'Yes, Sir. Abe died not so long ago. His was quite a tragic life – lost his wife early, then his son to the trenches, and never fully realised his potential, but he left behind a beautiful daughter whom we've all known since she was a little girl. She married into the community.'

'So the suits he put his labels on were only sold into Golders Green?'

'For the most part, yes.'

'For the most part?'

Fitch shrugged. 'Oh, I know he had odd clients here and there. In fact, I put him onto a director of one of North London's busy hospitals.'

Alex, who had been staring out onto the street, swung around. 'Which hospital, Fitch?' he demanded.

'Er . . . Edmonton, I believe . . . isn't that right, Elton?'

Elton nodded.

'Mr Fitch,' Alex began, feeling as though his throat was closing. 'Edmonton was the hospital that my family traced me to.'

'Good gracious, Sir! I had no idea. But what are you saying?'

'I don't know!' Alex shook his head helplessly, yet the tingling feeling that was crawling up his spine and across his shoulders made him feel as though it was a lead. 'Maybe I should visit Golders Green?'

'I doubt there's anything to find there, Mr Wynter. Abe's been dead for a while; the shop closed. I did see his daughter a while back; married a young lawyer as I understand it.'

The metaphorical flea that he'd had in his ear was now buzzing with new energy, desperate for freedom.

'Er . . . Mr Wynter, what about my brother? Should I telephone The Hotel Cecil?'

'No. Thank you, though, Elton. Let's get these measurements done, Fitch. I've an errand I've promised to run, and if I'm lucky, I may be able to make it to Edmonton Hospital.'

'Really, Sir? Is it worth it?'

He nodded. 'No stone unturned, my father used to say.'

'Right then, Mr Wynter,' Fitch said, whipping his tape in a whizzing sound from around his neck. 'Waist and inside leg and you'll be free to go sleuthing. Feel free to drink your cup of tea while I finish these measurements.'

28

Madeleine looked at the salon clock and sighed. Where was the day going? She wondered if she should ring Edie to tell her how Sarah had got on. It would be all good news. Sarah was catching on to all their processes quickly and had even introduced Madeleine to a new filing system for client collections that she'd used at the restaurant.

Sarah gave a helplessly proud smile from her heart-shaped face. 'I so want to impress you both for giving me this chance.'

Madeleine squeezed her wrist. 'You already have. Now, I have to go to the bank before it closes and make up the kitty for the coming week. I had thought the Aubrey-Finch money would be here by now but I won't risk waiting – maybe it will come tomorrow. Will you be all right looking after the salon? I'll be fifteen minutes at most.'

'What if a client comes in?'

'No one will. Clients of the calibre who want a Valentine gown will call ahead to make an appointment.' She arched an eyebrow.

'Like Miss Aubrey-Finch?' Sarah chuckled.

'Actually, she's one of the nicest double-barrelled names I've met.'

'Down to earth?'

'*Exactement.*'

'I understand. You go ahead.'

Sarah was absorbed in draping some bolts of cloth in a corner as a decorative sculpture when the bell tinkled at the door and she swung around to see a tall, dark-haired man closing it. Well-attuned to wealthy people, Sarah had seen their money paraded in front of her for more than a year in her role at the restaurant, and this man screamed money, although it wasn't just his fine tailoring catching her attention.

'Ah, good afternoon,' he said, his voice cultured, his grin easily stretching despite his obvious trepidation to be in a wholly woman's domain.

'Er, good afternoon, Sir. Can I help you?'

'Yes, are you the right person to talk to about settling an account?'

'Is this for Miss Aubrey-Finch, Sir?'

He smiled, broad and delighted, as though she were the only person in the world who had ever charmed him. 'Indeed. Thank you. It's intimidating to walk into such a secretive spot. My, my, what a stunning salon,' he said.

'We've been expecting you, Mr . . .'

'Wynter.' He held out a hand. 'Alex Wynter.'

'Thank you, Sir. I'm Sarah.' She was ready with the paperwork, aware that Madeleine had been sweating on the money's arrival all day. 'Here is the final account, Mr Wynter. Um . . . I think you'll see everything's in order and settles the bridal, bridesmaids, flower girl and page boy in total.'

'Excellent, thank you.' He handed her a cheque.

Sarah read the Coutts & Co. name on the cheque and noted the amount was correct. 'That's fine. Thank you for bringing it in.'

He shook his head. 'I was passing,' he said, absently, his attention back on the styling in the salon. 'This is such a daring and fun design,' he said, admiring the surrounds.

'Do you like it, though, Mr Wynter?' she risked.

'I do. It's exciting. The window dressing is delectable. I think it would make me want to wear those dresses.'

She giggled, enjoying his jest. 'Miss Valentine has excellent taste,' she remarked. 'I'm sure your breath will be taken away when you see your bride.'

'You sell Miss Valentine's talents extremely well, Sarah. Is she around for me to thank?'

'Oh, I'm afraid she is not in today, Sir. What a pity.'

'Oh, well, perhaps our paths will cross another time.'

'I'm sure. Do come again. I think she'd be impressed by any man daring enough to visit.'

He grinned. 'No wonder my fiancée enjoys coming here so much.'

'I am looking forward to meeting Miss Aubrey-Finch tomorrow, actually. This is my first day.'

'Really?' He looked surprised. 'Funny,' he said, replacing his hat and making a move to leave.

'What is, Sir?'

'I'm just on my way to find a suit that was made by an *Abraham* Valentine. The coincidence didn't strike me earlier. I'm afraid my head's a bit fuzzy today.'

Sarah had learned that the best response in most instances of small talk with wealthy people was silence and a smile, which she gave him now.

'Her father wasn't a tailor, by any chance?' he quipped.

She shrugged. 'I don't know, Mr Wynter. I have much to learn about the business.'

'Of course.' He raised his hat. 'Well, good day to you, Sarah, and enjoy working here.'

His broad shoulders blocked the doorway for a moment and

then Sarah spotted Madeleine returning, and the two appeared to share a brief conversation. Sarah sighed behind the scenes, hoping she might catch the eye of someone as dashing as Mr Wynter some day.

———————

Madeleine wondered if it was the champagne from last night or her age, but she was feeling the onset of winter far harder these days. She shivered as she hurried back down the King's Road, keen to return to the warmth of the salon and hopefully close up and head home for a long soak, and early bedtime. Food never seemed to enter her head; she ate only if she was famished and only then to fuel herself. But she would give a tooth for one of Edie's bowls of chicken soup right now. Healing, that's what they both needed. She was considering whether to buy a chicken on the way home when she just avoided bumping into the chest of a tall man who had the door open to the salon.

In surprise she spoke in her native tongue. '*Ooh, bonjour, monsieur.*'

'*Mademoiselle,*' he said, lifting his hat.

'Ah, forgive me. I was in a hurry.'

'I can see. Here,' he said, holding the door open. She side-stepped beneath his arm. 'Come in from the cold.' He grinned and she felt the effect of his easy charm ignite a flame that hadn't been lit in a while.

'Thank you. Madeleine Delacroix,' she said, introducing herself, and holding out a hand.

'Alex Wynter. I'm engaged to Miss Aubrey-Finch. She seems incredibly happy with how everything's coming along,'

Madeleine couldn't resist flirting. 'I can see why,' she said, her glance lazily taking in the full length of him.

Madeleine saw the compliment spark in his laughing gaze. 'I do hope you ladies will come to the wedding; watch your gowns walk down the aisle?'

'I'm sure we shall indeed enjoy seeing Miss Aubrey-Finch become Mrs Wynter.'

'Good afternoon, Mademoiselle Delacroix,' he said and she thought his smile faltered as if unsettled by her remark.

And then the handsome Mr Wynter was gone, raising his hand to hail a cab and lost to the busy comings and goings of the King's Road.

––––––––––

'St James's, please. I'd like you to wait and then take me to Middlesex. Would that be all right?' he said to the driver; this time he'd managed to flag a car.

'Be my pleasure, Sir. Money's money, eh?'

'Indeed. It's White's Club in St James's Street first, then.'

'I know it, Sir,' the cabbie said and Alex smiled as he caught sight of Valentine's salon again. Something tripped in his mind but the cabbie began talking about the Christmas tree that would be going up at Buckingham Palace and he lost the strand of thought.

'A few minutes,' he said, quickly slipping out of the cab and up the three stairs to the club entrance. He didn't want to stop, trying to avoid eye contact with the concierge.

'Oh, Mr Wynter?'

He turned. 'Yes, Henry?'

'Your table at Murray's is booked for eight o'clock this evening. Will you be wanting a cab, Sir?'

'Thank you. And no to a cab. I'm being picked up.'

'Very good, Sir.'

Alex quickly made his way to the first floor, where some private telephones were available. The operator put him through to Edmonton Hospital. It felt like he'd been hanging on for most of his life but his watch told him it was only six minutes. Finally another voice returned.

'Mr Wynter?'

'Nancy, is that you?'

'Yes, so you still remember me?' She giggled.

'Nancy, I need to see you.'

Her voice became deeper. 'I've wanted to hear you say that all my life,' she drawled, chuckling again.

'I just need a few minutes, really. A couple of questions.'

She sighed.

'What time does your shift end today?'

'Well, I've got errands to run —'

'If you meet me, I shall have a car take you home. How's that?'

'You're joking, aren't you?'

He put a hint of a simmer in his voice. 'I'm certainly not. It's very cold, threatening rain, and a lovely girl like you should be driven home in a comfy car.' He could imagine her smiling.

'I get off at three-thirty.'

Alex calculated his time. 'Nancy, I can pick you up at the hospital and have my driver take you wherever you need to go. We could talk on the way.'

'You really do just want to talk, don't you? Or were you hoping I might ask you in?'

'Just five minutes of your time, dear Nancy. But, the bright side is that you don't have to go home in the dark on a bus.' He looked up and although it was only three now, it felt like evening was already closing in.

'See you outside in half an hour, then.'

Within moments he had wrapped his scarf around his neck again and was dashing back down to the lobby.

'Oh, Mr Wynter, there's a gentleman —'

'Back soon, Henry. Six at the latest,' he called to the frowning concierge and was closing the door on the cab and giving the driver the address. 'Can we make it in half an hour?'

'Easy,' the driver said and pulled away from the kerb.

With Sarah's help Madeleine had not only been able to return to the bank and deposit the Aubrey-Finch cheque, but they had readied the collection for their client tomorrow and set up appointments for other bridal parties who had heard 'on the Chelsea wireless' – as Edie liked to call it – about the Aubrey-Finch choice of salon. They'd shifted furniture around in the salon and Sarah had done two of her fabric sculptures, which impressed.

'I have to say, Sarah, those look somehow lazily chic.'

The new assistant smiled. 'Do you think Miss Valentine will like it, though?'

'Oh, she'll love it. She'll be mostly impressed that you showed some initiative and daring. They'd make me want to use those fabrics for my gown.'

'I'm all for practicality, Miss Delacroix.'

Madeleine nodded. 'Good first day. Off you go, Sarah. It's freezing out there, and you've got a bit of a journey . . . to Lambeth, isn't it?'

She nodded. 'My family's house is just off Clapham Common.'

'All the more reason to be on your way. Hang your uniform up. It's best not to wear it home.'

Sarah went to the back room to change, and Madeleine turned on the small lights in the window that was dressed to present two vastly different bridal gowns. One spoke to the modern woman with a shorter mid-calf length, and was narrow and loose. The other dress was ankle-length and featured a richly adorned Belgian lace of a more traditional shape, with a bodice nipping in at the waist. Both beautiful, both costing more than Sarah's income for several months, but a mere splash to the well-heeled women who passed this window and lived in Knightsbridge.

Madeleine thought about Penelope Aubrey-Finch and smiled to herself, reflecting on the dashing Mr Wynter. What a handsome couple they made.

Sarah emerged from the back room in her heavy plaid coat, carrying her umbrella, hat pulled low and pulling on thick gloves. 'See you tomorrow. I loved my first day.'

'*Bon*,' Madeleine said. 'And it loved you,' she added, turning away from the main window.

'Mr Wynter commented on the window. He used the word "delectable".'

'That's what we like to hear. What else did he remark on? It's not often we get treated to a man's opinion.'

Sarah recounted his words.

'Funny, he struck me as a little hesitant about the wedding.'

Sarah shrugged. 'I couldn't breathe he was so handsome!' she said, blushing, and then burst into laughter.

'He is certainly that,' Madeleine agreed. 'Right, get your umbrella up.'

Sarah moved to the door but paused before opening it. 'He did ask me about the name of the salon. I mean, where it comes from. I think he said something like, did Miss Valentine have any connection to . . . oh, wait, what was that name?' She frowned. 'Ah, that's right, he asked if she was connected to an Abraham Valentine.'

Madeleine nodded. 'That was Eden's father.'

'Oh! I'm sorry. I didn't know.'

'Why would you? Anyway, it is of no consequence. He was a tailor —'

'That's right. He did mention that he was trying to hunt down a suit that was made by Abraham Valentine.'

'A suit?'

'That's what he said.'

'Odd. I'll ask Eden,' Madeleine said dryly.

Madeleine followed Sarah out of the salon, feeling a lot brighter for being busy but still seduced by the thought of a bowl of steaming chicken soup. She was sure she could remember the few ingredients, and she'd surprise her friend with a meal, some company and then she was definitely going home for an early night.

Nancy was waiting at the hospital steps when the car pulled up. She grinned and waved as Alex stepped out to hold the door open for her.

'Oh, my word, this feels so fancy,' she said.

Alex took her hand before helping her into the taxi.

'Thank you, Mr Wynter.'

'Please call me Alex. You've bathed me, after all.' Nancy giggled with delight and pretended to look coy. 'We're at your command, Miss Nancy,' he continued. 'Tell our driver where you wish to go.'

'Oh.' She sat forward and gave an address. 'How are you then, Alex? You're looking fine.'

'I am well,' he nodded. 'I am,' he said as though trying to convince himself. 'And you?'

'Oh, overworked, underpaid, picked on by Matron – you know how it is. But,' she let out a sigh, 'I love my work.'

He nodded. 'The patients are lucky to have you. And thank you very much for agreeing to this.'

'Who else gets to ride home after a long shift in a swanky taxi? So go on, then, what's the burning question?'

Alex immediately became intense. 'It's a crazy question, I know, but I keep having a repetitive dream . . . it's actually more of a notion, Nancy, because it's a sound more than an image.'

She frowned, nodded for him to continue.

'I hear heels, a woman's heels, and they're walking away from me. It's connected with the hospital.'

She looked baffled. 'Well, no one wears heels on the staff, obviously. Only visitors, and the visitors to your ward were few and far between. There were four of you. Three of the fellows were found by loved ones quite quickly. Perhaps it's someone to do with one of those families? Although, now I recall, each of those boys was discovered by their fathers and one by both parents. The mother was older, and unlikely to be wearing higher-heeled shoes.'

He sighed out of his nose in soft anguish. It felt like another door slamming in his face. He only had one more door that was open to him. Alex took a slow, inaudible breath this time – it was the last chance.

'All right, Nancy. I said I had a couple of questions. Here's the final one and then I promise I'll let the matter drop.'

'You look like you have a good life, Alex, and lots of men came home to sad lives, to learn loved ones had died, or they were too wounded to live full lives.'

He pushed on, despite her obvious warning that she felt he shouldn't be dwelling any further on this matter. 'I discovered that a tailor by the name of Abraham Valentine made suits for the hospital director who would have been in charge of Edmonton at the time I was a patient.'

She nodded. 'And?'

'We believe the suit I was wearing when I remembered my real name had an Abraham Valentine label in it.'

Nancy bit her lip. 'So how does this help you? What are you trying to find out?'

'Well, firstly, can you recall whether the suit you gave me was made by that tailor?'

She shook her head, smiling faintly. 'No. Nothing so fancy. If the head of the hospital wore a suit by that tailor, I can assure you

Archie Blundell, who wore it before you, certainly didn't go to the same tailor. The suit I gave you was worn, patched in places, and really very low quality.' She smiled wider. 'But you managed to make it look extremely dashing.'

Alex frowned. 'You're sure of that? The patches?'

'Yes.'

'The suit I'm referring to had no patches. It was navy in colour and was a high-quality cloth.'

Nancy shrugged. 'Definitely not the same one, then. Does this help you?'

'I don't know. It means I acquired a new suit. Unfortunately Abraham Valentine is dead.'

'Well, his daughter is probably still alive. She used to deliver the suits to the hospital. Why don't you track her down? You've got money and connections. I'm sure she can be found easily enough and would be happy to help a war veteran. You probably don't recall this, but you and I discussed her brother, who died at Ypres.'

'Did we?'

'Yes. I mentioned it once because she walked past the garden outside your window, and I think she returned the same day of the party to drop off his suit. Yes, she did. I saw her talking to Matron.' She glanced past his shoulder, dipping slightly to look out and gauge where they were. 'You take a left once over the bridge, please, driver, and then it's first right.'

'Certainly, Miss,' he said over his shoulder.

She sat back and smiled at Alex. 'Thank you for this. Would have been a damp journey home for me. I didn't bother with the errands. This way I got a longer drive in your fancy car.'

'Don't mention it,' he said, a loose thought nagging.

'Yes, right just here, please,' Nancy said. 'I'm sorry I couldn't be more help. I'd like to think of you being very happy, though, with your new bride, and maybe you can put the war and its troubles behind you.' She patted his arm and there was something achingly familiar about the gesture. He had a flash of Nancy giving him a cheer-up smile, and dressed in an identical uniform. Suddenly he could smell coal-tar soap and the notion of a tarnished mirror struck him, the sound of heels clicking away and the glint of a coin . . . a robin warbling and party bunting being strung up around the hospital, along a short pathway that led to a privet hedge.

'Here we are,' she said, brightly. 'It's number five, just by the green door.' She looked up at the darkened sky and the drizzle that had become insistent before turning back to Alex. 'Don't get out. You'll only get wet. Be safe, Alex . . . and, just as important, be happy.'

She turned and opened the door to step out onto the kerb but Alex suddenly grabbed her arm. 'Nancy, wait!'

She paused. 'What's wrong?'

'You said the only delivery people on the day of my disappearance were the grocery boy and a physician, didn't you?'

She frowned. 'Yes.'

'But now you've mentioned that the tailor's daughter was there too.'

'She was. That's right. She remarked on all the lovely decorations but wouldn't stay for the celebrations.'

'Nancy . . . did the tailor's daughter wear heels?'

She laughed. 'Yes. Always immaculately dressed too, she was. She was terribly pretty. Small, dark, lovely figure – and the clothes! She made them herself, I gather. Quite a fashion horse.' Nancy flipped up her umbrella and as she dashed away he heard her say 'Bye, Alex!' He watched her skip up the short path and disappear behind her green door.

Alex hadn't heard a word she'd said since she'd admitted that Abraham Valentine's daughter wore heels and wished now he'd asked Nan if she knew her name. He heard the taxi driver asking him whether he was to head back into London and he realised it was getting dark and late.

'Yes, please, back to St James's,' he replied and even shared a grumble at the weather, but Alex didn't register much at all other than his racing thoughts and a new conviction that the tailor's girl might hold the key to his past.

Questions collided until his head hurt. He had to find her! And given that Valentine was an unusual name, perhaps Pen's bridal salon owner might be a relative or may be able to point him in the right direction.

He took out the red handkerchief and stared yet again at the heart-shaped hole cut in its middle. Alex didn't know the driver was watching from his rear-vision mirror.

'From your valentine, Sir?'

And Alex's heart felt as though it skipped a beat.

29

Edie's guilt had been escalating since she'd dragged herself from bed mid-morning and finally taken a shower. As soon as she'd emerged from the steam her head felt clearer and the nausea had settled. But now as it closed on four in the afternoon she felt remorseful at having put Miss Aubrey-Finch's appointment back and regretted that Sarah had spent her first day alone with Madeleine. Edie stared out into the gloom and then back to Tommy, who was playing with wooden bricks . . . or at least with the cardboard box that contained them. A drift of loneliness had swum through her at the sight of the toy that had formerly been Daniel's, turning her mood from optimistic of the previous evening to fractionally melancholy. In spite of her anger at Ben, it didn't reduce her sorrow at cutting ties with a childhood companion.

'Shall we go to the park, Tommy?' she offered, even though it was darkening rapidly; they could be quick and she could use some fresh air.

'Park,' he repeated and blew her a kiss. Her son's sweetness was just what was needed to remind her she had plenty of love and affection in her life.

The phone rang. 'Go find your woolly scarf, Tommy. The blue one, like this,' she said, pointing to her cardigan. 'Blue. And your gloves,' she said, mimicking pulling them on. Her little boy lurched off eagerly on surprisingly steady legs. He was defying all the warnings about a premature baby's development. Soon he'd be running, she thought, and instead of exciting her, it made her even more gloomy. *Don't grow up and leave me too soon, Tommy . . .*

She reached for the jangling receiver. 'Eden Valentine?'

'Oh, hello, Eden. Forgive me for disturbing you at home when I know you haven't been well today.' She recognised Penelope Aubrey-Finch's bright voice, full of concern.

'Hello, Miss Aubrey-Finch.'

'Oh, do call me Pen, please.'

Eden smiled. She wondered if every person who met this girl fell in love with her. 'Sorry . . . Pen. Is something wrong?'

'Not at all. I was just making sure you are well enough and I didn't want you getting out of a sick bed just for me. You see, I want to invite you out to lunch at The Savoy, tomorrow, where chef Monsieur Escoffier will make you believe you've arrived in heaven. I'm having a get-together with a few friends – all on the brink of tying the knot and potentially new grist for your mill . . . if you get my drift.' She gave an intoxicating chuckle that reached down the line to fully dismiss Edie's glum mood. 'I am frankly tired of choosing flowers to adorn every room, and my mother's fussing over the menu or the gilt on the invitations!'

Edie smiled. 'Wedding blues?'

'I just want it to be over and done with.'

'Oh, surely not?'

'I do, Eden. Really. I don't require any of this ritual and fuss. Don't misunderstand me. I love my gown and I am having fun with certain aspects – especially Valentine's – but I can't bear the way this event is consuming my mother. It's just a lot of bother when I would be happy to say "I do" in a tiny church in Scotland or Devon and elope.' She gave a small gasp. 'Oh, now I wish I'd thought of that earlier! We could have run off to Paris together.'

'That does sound romantic.'

'It does, doesn't it. Alex came by the salon today to drop off the cheque. I'm sorry you missed him. I would so love for you to have met.'

'Oh, now I'm sorry too. He sounds like the perfect Prince Charming.'

'He is. He is my dream come true, Eden.'

Edie blinked. 'You sound a bit sad when you say that.'

'Do I? Yes, I suppose I do. Alex is a bit distracted at the moment. I think all the planning is wearing him down too.'

'Do try and stay bright, Pen. No doubt his own family is fussing also.'

'Oh, they are. Well, his mother is. She and Mother are obsessed with the guest list. I hate it all.'

'Society weddings are hard work, I'm sure.'

'I'll bet your wedding was far more fun and less frantic.'

Edie smiled to herself in soft, sad memory. 'It was the happiest day of my life. As you love Mr Wynter, I loved Tom. I still do.'

'I'm an idiot. I'm sorry. Now *you* sound sad.'

'It's an old hurt. I know how to put it back in its box and lock it away. I think you should let the wedding excitement wash around you and worry about only what you can control.'

'My wardrobe.'

'That's it!' Eden laughed. 'You are going to make Mr Wynter's eyes pop when he sees you arrive at his side, I promise. What's more, I've been drawing some designs for your wedding-night trousseau . . .'

Pen gave a short squeak. 'Oh, gosh, I hadn't even thought about that yet.'

'Well . . . lucky for you, then, that I have. You're going to love what I have in mind. But don't ask me to explain lace that is almost not there. Maybe that's an excuse for another trip to London.'

'I can't wait. You see, you always manage to excite me, Eden.'

'And you have cheered me too.'

Tommy walked up, trailing his blue scarf and gloves. 'Park,' he called.

'Is that your little boy?' Pen asked.

'Yes. I promised Tommy a quick play in the park. We've both been cooped up for most of the day and I'm sure I'll feel brighter for a walk.'

'I won't keep you, then. So you will join me for lunch? I want to show you off, my new and dear friend. And I'm sure my husband will want to kiss you once he sees me on our wedding night in your whisper-quiet outfit.'

'Gossamer,' Edie murmured. 'Thanks for your invitation – I'd love to join you.'

'Perfect! I'll pick you up at the salon at midday. Wear that darling red tie of yours.'

'Oh, no, I'll have to think of something far more theatrical.'

The women shared a laugh and another farewell before Edie put the phone down, and as she did so, Madeleine let herself in through the front door. 'Hope you didn't mind me taking the spare key. I only did so in case you called and I had to make a dash back to you lying prone in the bathroom.'

'Hello, Mads.'

'Well, you look perky.'

'Sorry about today. All go well? Can you hand me Tommy's duffel coat – we're just off to the park for a few minutes.'

Madeleine did so and Edie began struggling to fit her son's small arms into short, thick sleeves. *Maybe I should design a children's range?* she thought. *To make it easier for mothers . . .*

She refocused on Madeleine's voice. '. . . Sarah's an angel. And what's more, we took three new appointments,' Mads added, beginning to unpack groceries. 'I've brought stuff for chicken soup, but you look too well for it.'

'Never too well for chicken soup. Can you get it on?' Mads nodded. 'So, tell me about Sarah's first day.'

Madeleine prattled amiably for a few minutes, helping Tommy into boots and a hat, while Edie pulled out a jar of peppercorns from her pantry and inspected all the ingredients her friend had thrown on the table.

'Perfect,' she approved. 'Right. Off to the park we go,' Edie said, taking Tommy's hand.

'Oh, I must tell you,' Madeleine said, her tone full of intrigue as she walked with them to the door. 'I met Alex Wynter today, the soon-to-be husband of our client.'

'And I meant to tell you that I spoke with Pen moments before you arrived. She's invited me to lunch at The Savoy tomorrow.'

The Frenchwoman's mouth opened in impressed surprise. 'Did she invite me as well?'

Edie grinned. 'Afraid not, Mads. She should have! Apparently she wants to introduce me to a gaggle of girlfriends and is determined that Valentine's becomes *the* salon of the socialite bride.'

Madeleine let out a small whistle. 'Well, she's worth her weight in gold, isn't she?'

'Yes. And she has no airs or graces, that girl. I like her very much.' Edie stepped out onto the landing outside the door.

'She deserves her handsome groom, then.'

'Is he?' she said, pulling on Tommy's bobble cap. 'There, you're more handsome than Mr Wynter,' she said to her son and gave him a hug.

'Wynter isn't just handsome – that description is far too ordinary. *Non*,' Madeleine said, smiling to herself in memory. 'Monsieur Wynter sizzles!'

Edie grinned helplessly. 'Tell me about him when we get back.'

'Have fun, you two. Don't be late. I need to get home tonight.'

Holding Tommy's small hand, they crunched across the red-and-gold carpet that littered the pathways of the park, and as Edie let his happy chatter fall around her like the late autumn leaves, her mood lifted immediately.

After a game of chase, they caught their breath with an obligatory visit to the pond, where Tommy was happy to lose several minutes gazing into the depths to make sounds of delight as he spied the bright flash of an orange goldfish tail. Edie was once again reminded that she nearly had everything she could ever want in life.

'Your daddy's going to find us, Tommy. Did you know that?'

He nodded shyly, not looking at her.

Edie knew she could have just asked him whether he'd like to eat chocolate for dinner and he'd have given an identical response. It didn't matter. She wrapped her arms around her child because when she held him like this, her life felt safe and in balance. Despite Ben's betrayal, he'd inadvertently given her the one gift she longed for. He'd given her Tom. Now, she knew he was alive.

'And not tomorrow, because I have a lot to catch up on,' she continued, 'but the day after, I'm going to begin my hunt to bring your daddy home.'

Tommy squealed a soft laugh and her emotions surged at the sound. 'Da,' he prattled. It could have meant anything, but to Edie it meant *Daddy*.

'Yes, darling. We both want him back.'

———

They arrived back at the flat with Edie feeling a fresh sense of purpose and empowerment.

'You two look rosy-cheeked,' Madeleine remarked.

'Blew all the mists away in my mind.'

After dinner, Madeleine bathed Tommy and then read to him while Edie cleaned up in the kitchen and brewed some coffee. It was past seven and fully dark by the time she set down the tray in her tiny sitting room and Madeleine tiptoed back in.

'Fast asleep,' she said.

'Thanks, Mads. I made you some coffee.' Edie switched on a small lamp and turned up the heating. 'I swear I'm feeling the cold earlier this year.' She settled back into the couch, warming her hands around the mug of coffee. 'You were going to tell me about Miss Aubrey-Finch's fiancé.'

'Ah, yes, and then I must go. Where to begin, darling? He's tall. That's mandatory, right?'

Edie nodded and put a finger in the air to signify it was a fundamental.

'Very dark hair.'

Edie smiled and put a second finger in the air.

'Now, the eyes. How would I describe their blueness?' She sipped her coffee. 'Like a stormy sea – the Atlantic. No . . . remember that exquisite silk you had a sample of, dyed from anil to give that amazing indigo?' Edie nodded. 'That's the colour I mean.'

'Fathomless,' Edie murmured, reminded of Tom's colouring. 'Well, that's three big ticks.'

'He's charming, yet, how you say, reticent?' Edie nodded. 'And dashing, yet speaks in a quiet voice. He's mysterious.'

Edie put up a fourth finger. 'No wonder she's wanted him since childhood!'

'*Absolument!* If the man wasn't a client's groom, I would have invited him home.'

'Shame on you!'

'Shame be damned. He's not married yet.'

Edie sighed. 'Well, he sounds like the dream.' She gave a small twist of her mouth. 'He sounds like Tom. I'm going to find him, Mads.'

'I know, darling. Is that tailor back who you wanted to ask about the man-who-would-be-Tom?'

'Don't mock me. I have every intention of talking to Percival Fitch on his return.' She reminded Madeleine of her plan to visit Fleet Street. Her friend gave her a nod of approval. 'And in the meantime, there's no harm in meeting Mr Wynter and seeing if he has any bachelor friends for us, is there?'

People passing by the Regency apartment building could hear women's laughter suddenly leaking out into the increasingly damp street as drizzle began to show in the pavement's gaslight.

Alex scampered into the club lobby, reaching for his fob watch, although he already knew he was running behind time.

'Mr Wynter?'

He closed his eyes and took a breath, turning and ensuring his expression was even. 'Yes, Henry?'

'A message for you, Sir,' he said. 'Miss Aubrey-Finch rang to say that she has "wangled" a car rather than a taxi for tonight and she plans to pick you up, at the new time of seven-thirty.'

Alex felt relieved. The rush was off. 'Oh, that's excellent, thank you, Henry. Traffic was crazy coming from North London.'

'It's the rain, Sir,' Henry said, as though it was an automatic response to every woe. 'Oh, and one more thing, Sir – a gentleman rang to speak with you just before you left. I couldn't get the message to you because you were in such a hurry earlier.'

'Yes?'

'Er . . . he's in the drawing room, Sir.'

'Here . . . at the club?'

'Yes, Sir. I said he could wait for you. It seemed rather important, I gather.'

Alex frowned. 'All right. Thank you, Henry.' Who the devil could be chasing him down at nearing six? He strode into the drawing room only barely noticing a suspension of tobacco fog that vaguely shifted around the chandelier with his arrival.

A tall, slim man with neat, wavy black hair wearing a dark three-piece suit and a bow tie stood. 'Mr Wynter?'

Alex frowned. 'Yes?' He watched the stranger approach.

'My name is Benjamin Levi,' he said.

Alex wondered why Levi was staring at him in a vague sense of wonder. 'Should I know you?'

Levi gave a smile. 'In one way, yes, but I realise why you don't.'

'Mr Levi, forgive me. I've had quite a long day and I am late to get ready to meet my fiancée, so if you'll —'

'Ah, yes, Miss Aubrey-Finch.'

Alex's gaze narrowed. 'What is this about?'

'Shall we move out of the lobby?'

He shrugged. 'You're not a member here, Levi, and you're also not a guest, I'm guessing. I hate to be churlish, but I am in rather a hurry, so —'

'In a hurry to marry?' he interjected.

'You're baiting me, Mr Levi.'

'I don't mean to.'

'But you don't deny it.'

Levi grinned, looking at the richly thick oriental rug splayed on the pale stone floor of the lobby. 'No. But then, I owe you.'

'Owe me?' Alex repeated. 'Owe me what?'

'Well, this, for starters,' Levi said, and threw a loose punch at the man facing him.

The blow, delivered from too close, missed Alex's chin and connected with the top of his cheek, by the eye. It was enough to unbalance him as he was moving away, and in that moment of amazement his shoe slipped on the fringe of the oriental rug, and he was falling. In less time than it took him to expel his breath in astonishment, he felt his head hit the flagstones.

When Alex opened his eyes he saw a cluster of familiar faces, all concerned, and Henry with a look of utter fury written across his. This felt horribly familiar.

'Preposterous! Keep that man still!' Henry ordered.

Alex blinked and shook his head to see club staff holding his attacker, who was breathing hard with a stare of hatred directed at him.

'Ben?' he said. It was out of his mouth before he understood how he knew the name. But then people were distracting him.

'Are you all right, Sir?' other staff were anxiously saying and he could hear murmurs and mumbles from his fellow club members. The drawing room had emptied into the lobby, men still clutching their first gins or whiskies of the evening. Several looked astounded, some appeared angry by the disturbance, and a few were just plain amused.

'Help him up, Charles,' Henry snapped at a younger porter.

'Don't fuss,' Alex pleaded. He was hauled to his feet and he gingerly touched the spot high on his cheek.

'You'll have a shiner there in the morning, old chap,' one wit laughed.

'Should I summon the police, Sir? Do you plan to press charges?' Henry was blustering.

Alex was shifting his jaw from side to side. 'No. Just leave us, please.' He made a gesture with his hand that they were to let the offender's arms go.

'Are you sure, Sir? Do you know this man, Mr Wynter?'

He regarded Benjamin Levi. 'Yes, I do recognise him,' he admitted, feeling the ghost of his past lay a chilled hand across his shoulder. 'I'll deal with this, Henry. I'm sorry for the disturbance, everyone. I'm sure Mr Levi is as well.'

The defiance didn't leave him, but Levi was able to offer a remorseful expression. 'My apologies to all.'

'Your apology should be to Mr Wynter, and when you have made it, Sir, I will personally escort you from White's,' Henry assured the interloper.

Alex caught the attention of a waiter. 'Get me a Scotch. Make it a double.' He looked at Ben with a query. 'Make it two doubles. We'll be in the billiards room.' Alex took a deep breath. 'Follow me, Ben.'

His visitor did so in silence until Alex pushed through the double doors and switched on one set of lights that glowed low over a single table, set up for the evening's play.

'They won't be in until later,' he said. Alex cleared his throat and leaned against the thick round corner of the table. They stared at each other in silence for a few seconds, Alex unsure where to begin.

'Did you volunteer to go to war, Ben?' Conversation had to begin somewhere, and he could see that his guest wouldn't start it. Unfortunately, it sounded like an accusation and Levi heard it that way.

'I'm no hero like you, Wynter, if that's what you mean. But I was conscripted in March 1916. Single men of a certain age were asked to join up and I did as duty called. Except —'

Alex never heard what happened to Ben Levi's war campaign because there was a knock at the door and his companion stopped talking. The waiter entered, carrying a tray.

'Your whiskies, Mr Wynter. Henry . . . I mean, Mr Johnson, asked me to bring the bottle too, Sir.'

'Thank him, please.' Alex took both glasses and the half empty bottle and waited for the man to leave before he handed a glass to Ben. He slammed the bottle down on the edge of the table and swallowed the slug of Scotch, wincing at the burn in his throat. Even opening his mouth hurt just now. His eye socket throbbed too.

Ben Levi drained his glass also and leaned against the wall. 'The repercussions of my actions could have me disbarred. It peeves me to say this, but thank you for not calling the police.'

Alex glared at him, wishing he could recall more, although memories were arriving regularly now and he sensed he'd never been closer than this moment to discovering the secrets of his past. 'Don't thank me. It was self-interest. I need a public scrap in my life about as badly as you do, Ben. You rang me after my father died. It struck me as strange then. What were you fishing for?'

'Let's just say I was testing the waters.'

'Of what? For pity's sake, man, speak plainly and spill what you've come here to say!' He poured himself another measure of whisky, larger than the last, but didn't drink it. 'Tell me,' he demanded, sounding disgusted, and watched his companion's pulse pound at his temples.

'I came here today not for you but for someone else. Someone I have hurt badly. Someone I have loved all my life and now lost – again.'

Alex sipped his drink, touching the back of his head where he remembered it slamming onto the stone. A distant headache beckoned. 'And what does it have to do with me, Ben Levi?' but even as he said the name, he felt a strange sensation of dawning moving through him. It felt as though he was walking down a dark corridor towards where candlelight illuminated a room he'd been searching for. But he had to find his way through a maze of corridors, pushing through cobwebs and parting curtains. Suddenly, with the curiously familiar shape of Ben Levi, head hung and mumbling what might be construed as an apology, he had the notion that he was about to start tearing through those cobwebs.

'Does the name Valentine mean anything to you?'

The whisky lost its sweetness and turned sour in his throat. 'Increasingly, yes,' he croaked. 'I discovered only today that the suit I was wearing when I was knocked down in Savile Row and regained my memory after years in a wilderness bore the label of Abraham Valentine. Also today, and quite by coincidence, I realised that my fiancée is having her bridal gown made by a salon in Chelsea called Valentine's, and I also learned a woman of that surname made deliveries to the hospital I was repatriated to.' Even as he said it, he felt the separate events beginning to mesh and it set off a reaction within that made him feel traumatised, yet elated. 'The same?' he asked, holding his breath as he met Levi's dark gaze.

Ben nodded. 'Abraham Valentine, the tailor from Golders Green, is the father of the designer of your fiancée's gown.'

'Then I need to speak with her,' he said, ramming down the glass. 'She may hold the key to —'

'Wait, Wynter! Hear it all. I'm sorry again for assaulting you. The fact that she's never stopped loving you and you don't even know her name got the better of me. I hate you with every ounce of loathing I can muster, but I'm ashamed of my actions towards someone I have loved for a lifetime, but I also can't let you marry Miss Aubrey-Finch when you already have a wife.'

The shock of these words hit Alex with a trembling sensation that seemed to arrive out of nowhere; up from his shoes, darting to all extremities and settling at the back of his throat until his lips felt numb and his mind scrambled with dizziness. Alex staggered slightly, had to hold on to the side of the billiard table to steady himself as more cobwebs were torn away and the candlelight became clearer. 'A wife?' he choked out. More events began to collide in his mind. Memories began to coalesce with speed and meaning. '*My wife*,' he repeated in a tone that was both anguished and filled with wonder.

'Do you remember her name, Wynter? Can you at least do that much and demonstrate that you deserve her?'

Alex was moving his aching head from side to side, slowly reaching, grasping towards the sound of clicking heels and the smell of violets. He could hear church bells and laughter, the splash of bathwater, the image of long dark hair against his chest. He groaned.

'Wynter? Are you . . .'

Alex couldn't hear his companion any longer. Levi's voice sounded as though it was coming from a long way away. He was hurtling on his thoughts, riding them like a wave of agony. Once on a childhood train journey to Scotland he had hung out of the window and felt the wind grab at his hair and whistle around his ears, taking away his breath, forcing him to close his eyes near enough but not so much that he couldn't squint at the scenery whizzing by. One moment he saw a farmhouse, the next it had moved behind him and his gaze was already locking on the next, only to flash past him. That's how this moment felt. Images, plentiful, fast-moving and like a waterfall rushing through his mind. And just like a waterfall, they all gathered at the bottom in a well. The well began to fill him, rising deliriously quickly, flooding his thoughts with familiarity and recognition. His head pounded with its speed and fury until he was sure the banks of his mind might break with the pressure as the sound of clicking heels suddenly delivered him a vision . . . and the vision had a voice. She also had a name.

He gasped.

'Edie,' he groaned and the well overflowed. Tears stung his eyes and slipped down his hurting cheek and Alex felt the choking emotion of memory returned in full as the last of the cobwebs were torn down. 'Eden Valentine,' he said, knocking his glass, which landed with a dull thud on the thick carpet of the games room, spilling whisky that splashed on his shoes in a hundred droplets like the scenes that were scattering in his mind, filling all of its corners with vignettes of life with Eden Valentine.

He heard the door softly close. Distantly and without really caring, Alex realised Benjamin Levi had left him to his memories.

30

Penelope Aubrey-Finch brazenly pulled in to the kerb outside White's Club in St James's and honked the horn of the new car she was driving. Not only did she relish the looks of disapproval from club members that she was receiving, but she loved the lack of inhibition this two-seater prompted.

'There you are, darling,' she said as Alex finally emerged from the club's glowing doorway into the night. 'I thought you were going to stand me up. Sorry I'm late, but perhaps you can understand why?'

He leaned over and pecked her cheek. 'Let's go, shall we?' he said.

She frowned but let his unreadable expression wait while she zipped the roadster into the traffic and gunned the engine. 'Did you see the looks of consternation your stuffy fellow club members were giving me?' She threw him an amused glance and waited a moment. 'Oh, come on, Alex. Tell me off or tell me I look wonderful, but don't just sit there like a sad sack.' She cut him a sideways look as she honked at a cyclist. 'Whatever is the matter with you, darling?'

'Pen, do you mind awfully if we don't go to Murray's?'

'Oh, Alex, why?' Her tone bled disappointment.

'I have a dreadful headache, actually, so jazz music is going to do me in, for sure . . . and . . . well, I want to talk to you.'

'Well, talk to me over dinner. We'll go to The Ritz. I'm sure César will fit us in.'

'Pen . . .' He let out a low sigh.

'Is something wrong?'

'Yes.'

'Oh.' She hadn't expected that. 'Well, where shall I head for?' she asked, looking perplexed.

'Just drive . . . drive out of London, somewhere quiet.'

They drove for twenty minutes in a taut silence and she was glad she hadn't thrown the hood of the car back as she'd intended. A night on the brink of winter was asking for trouble in an open-topped car.

'I don't think I want to hear what you have to say,' she said, puncturing the silence. 'I've never seen you so gloomy or pensive.'

He reached to turn on the heater, saying nothing.

'It has to be bad news,' she continued, 'or why else would you be behaving so strangely?'

He irritated her by keeping silent.

'Shall I take the Brighton Road?'

He nodded. 'Whatever you like. I don't care.'

Yes, she suspected she knew what was coming. Pen swerved onto the main road that led directly to Sussex and hit the accelerator. Maybe she could be happy if he didn't speak again tonight. She would drive them away from all of his problems.

'Whose is it?' he asked into the awkward moment, gesturing at the dashboard.

'Well, I think it's going to be mine.'

'You've bought it?'

'About to. It belongs to a friend of my father's. He's already moving on to his next purchase. Never thought he'd say yes to a sale, but he did.'

Alex said nothing.

'So, what do you think?'

'It suits you, Pen.'

'Yes, I think it does too. Fun but just a bit dangerous, eh?'

'Well, that's not how I'd describe you, but . . .' He didn't finish, staring out into the darkness roaring by them.

'I can't take this a moment longer,' she said suddenly into their gloom and swung off the main road as they were passing by Crawley. Alex barely registered her change of direction. She drove without a plan until she could see parklands and headed that way.

The night was frigidly cold out in the countryside and despite their scarves and warm overcoats, she knew the icy feeling in her body had nothing to do with the wintry night. She laughed into the awkward silence of the black moorland that reached beyond their vision.

'What's funny?' he finally said.

'Wynter by name, winter by nature.'

Alex surprised her by getting out of the car and slamming the door.

'What are you doing?' she demanded. 'Alex? Alex!' She followed him, struggling on her satin heels as they sank into the soft dirt. Pen pulled the fur coat closer, staring helplessly at the silhouette of the man she loved, standing alone and angry, it seemed. If not for the car headlights, she wouldn't have been able to see him at all. 'Darling, please. Let me help you with this. Whatever it is, we can face it and sort it out. You have to put off the wedding, right?'

He swung around and strode back to the car. 'Yes,' he said, sounding resigned, his voice uncharacteristically tight. She feared him now because whatever he had to say she sensed was going to cause pain.

And it was only now in the light with him facing her properly that Pen could see his cheek was damaged, his eye swollen. 'Heavens! Alex, what happened?'

He touched his cheek and nodded ruefully. 'I found my memory, Pen. This is part of it.'

She shook her head, frightened by what his admission meant.

'Listen,' she soothed, changing her tone to placatory. 'I can tell you're upset and something has happened, but I don't mind that we have to put off the wedding. These things happen. You're a man of business, leading a huge empire, and these are challenging times. I understand that and I'm not ever going to make life difficult for you, Alex. We can put off the wedding. Summer's fine with me – or, darling, let's just forget the whole bloody thing and elope.'

He cut her a dangerous look but she couldn't interpret the meaning and pushed on.

'I mean it. Let's elope, Alex. Forget all the society stuff, forget the pomp and noise and ceremony. I don't even care about wearing a fabulous gown. Let's just forget Eden Valentine exists and —'

'I can't,' he said, sounding choked.

She blinked. She was screaming to the heavens silently in her mind but to Alex she stood composed and found a calm voice.

'What can't you do?' she dared.

He shook his head hopelessly and his voice sounded broken. 'All of it, Pen. I can't elope. I'm ashamed to admit that I can't love you the way you want me to and the way you really should be loved because you are so adorable. You deserve so much better. I cannot marry you.'

She hated that even in this ugly moment of rejection her heart melted for whatever suffering was driving him to do this. She could hear it, see how much it anguished him, but still he was prepared to hurt her in the most spectacular fashion. Pen's body began to shiver with the shock. She couldn't feel anything except the cut of his words and how they were making her bleed.

'Why, Alex, why?'

'You said forget Eden Valentine.'

She shook her head, bamboozled. 'What's lovely Eden got to do with this?'

'Everything.'

'*Everything*?' she repeated and it forced him to explain.

'I remembered tonight something so important, so terrible, yet amazing at the same time that I can barely breathe.'

Still she waited, leaning dangerously close over an imaginary cliff where she could see herself staring into the beckoning abyss.

'You see, Pen,' he began, hesitating as the words caught in his throat.

'Just say it, Alex,' she said, dully.

'I'm already married.'

The words were like blunted clubs as they battered her.

'I found out an hour ago. A lawyer came to see me at the club and let's just say he found a shortcut for opening up the memories that have been shrouded.'

Pen couldn't give a fig about his memory returning, only the name of the person it had delivered to him.

'And this person you're married to is alive?'

'Yes,' he replied bleakly. 'I believe we may even have a child.'

'In England?'

'In London.'

Her sob exploded from her throat and it came out sounding like a retch.

'Do I know her?' she managed to ask.

He looked down.

Anger finally snapped. And it was all the anger and frustration that she'd shored up over the years, since her youth, when she'd watched Alex carouse and date women older than herself, and then through to university. And just when it looked like he would return home she lost him to the army and then to the war . . . yet not for a single beat of her heart had she accepted Alex was gone. It was her love, her optimism, her obsession, that had brought him home. Now all that fury infused her and she growled like a wounded animal. 'I said —'

'Her name,' he cut back, barely able to contain his own anger, an emotion she'd not seen before, 'is Eden Valentine.'

It took several horrible moments for the words to make sense.

'My Eden?' she finally whispered, her body rigid.

'*My* Eden,' he countered in a broken voice, all the rage gone. 'Forgive me,' he said in such an affectionate tone it hurt her even more to feel its gentleness, like a caress. 'This is not your fault. I am angry at the situation – losing her, finding you, hurting you both by loving you both. Pen, she married a man who had no memory, not even of his name. When asked to choose a name, he chose Tom, perhaps an echo of the father he couldn't remember. They became Mr and Mrs Valentine, who lived in a cottage on the edge of Epping Forest.'

Pen recalled now how Eden had spoken with such tenderness about the husband she called Tom. Pen covered her mouth to stop her cries but her eyes welled with tears, turning Alex into a watery silhouette.

He nodded. 'We didn't have a lot but we had our dreams and we were on our way. Eden was pregnant when I . . .' He shook his head, cleared his throat. 'I went to the salon today!' he groaned. 'I didn't see her.'

'She mentioned you this afternoon,' Pen said finally, just above a whisper. 'She said she was sorry she missed you.' She allowed the sickening feeling of deadness to give way as pins and needles of fresh dawning tingled through her body. Her fiancé was the father of Eden's child . . .

He gave a sound of a man being tortured, twisting away. 'My fault. This is all my fault! Oh, Pen . . .'

Penelope Aubrey-Finch felt her fleeting glimpse at the joyous chorus and the vision of Alex Wynter naked in her arms surrender to a vision of Eden Valentine wearing the bridal gown she'd made for her. A pulse of agony chased the numbness out and flashed through her body and she was sure she could hear fabric being torn.

This is what heartbreak feels like, she thought abstractly, as though it wasn't happening to her.

'Well, we can't have you committing bigamy.' It came out hard and toneless. 'Are you going to divorce her, Alex?'

His confused expression deepened into dismay. She knew him too well and she knew she had lost him fully now.

'I love her, Pen. I love her like you love me. It's not healthy, it's certainly not wise, but you can't help it and neither can I. I just didn't know it.'

'Neither does she, I can assure you. But she talks about Tom all the time, asked me to raise my glass to him when we were on the Orient Express because that's what she and Tom had always planned to do. Now I understand why you wanted to take me.' She gave a mirthless laugh that was harsh and uncharacteristically sneering. 'I could wish now that you had died in Ypres. I'm not sure how to live with the notion that you love someone else.'

He reached for her but she staggered back towards the car.

'I'm sorry, I can't love you, Pen.'

She sucked in a long, cold breath of despair and wrestled her heels out of the soggy ground, trying to climb back into the car. Finally slamming the door, she watched Alex's shoulders slump and he unhappily began to approach but she couldn't bear it. Couldn't bear the nearness of him; didn't want to see his broken expression again; couldn't live with his pity. She didn't want his gentle voice in her mind any more or to see his fingers touch the dial on the heater or adjust his scarf. She had dreamed of those fingers on her, in her . . . She didn't want this new world – loveless and bleak again without Alex in it. And the notion of Alex with Eden Valentine, the real Mrs Wynter, was like poison rushing through her blood. Viscous and toxic, it moved with dangerous intent through her veins, infecting every fibre with its pain.

As Alex reached for the doorhandle, she pressed the ignition, grateful that Freddy Bateman's promise that his car always started the first time was true. She swung the vehicle around and would have hit Alex if he hadn't leapt away. Pen wasn't sure what she was doing and she knew to leave Alex here, alone on the dark fringe of the moors, was cruel, but she had no room in her heart because her heart felt dead.

———————

Alex watched Pen spin the car dangerously away from him, sliding on the roadside gravel and screeching onto the main road. He could hear the roar of her engine as it growled, straining to reach a higher speed on the Brighton Road.

He let go of a long, painful breath. He'd hurt her terribly, but he knew now he would have caused her far more pain in years to come.

Stiff with cold, Alex walked to the local garage and paid someone to drive him to Ardingly. Within two hours he had come full circle and found himself sitting on the stump staring at Larksfell, trying to make some sense of his life. The house was quiet. It was only his mother at home, as he understood it, but suddenly lights began to go on in the house and he could see shadows moving around. Alex stood, only now realising how numb his backside had become, his bruised face stinging from the cold.

He moved gingerly, opting for one of the many side doors, but it seemed Bramson had already locked up for the night. He walked around to the back, tapping on the window of the parlour where old Mrs Dear was filling a kettle.

'What are you still doing up, Dearie?' he said affectionately, giving her a hug.

'Oh, Master Lex, thank goodness you're back, Sir. Something terrible's afoot upstairs.'

He frowned. 'What?'

'I don't know. Mr Bramson took a call from the police, I gather. They're on their way here now.'

'Police . . .' he murmured. Alex nodded at Mrs Dear, who was too disturbed to mention his swollen eye, and he hurried off through the bowels of Larksfell to take the steps two at a time, racing up to the ground floor.

He arrived via the servants' entrance to appear in the lobby where his mother and Bramson talked anxiously with pinched expressions.

'Lex! Oh, thank heavens!' His mother began to weep.

Alex moved to her. 'Mother. Whatever is it?'

'I thought you were part of it,' she warbled, quickly composing herself. 'Bramson . . .'

The butler cleared his throat, blinking. 'Master Lex, there's been a terrible accident. It's . . . well, it's Miss Aubrey-Finch.'

'Pen,' he uttered, his fears gathering. 'Is she all right?' His mouth was parched.

'We don't know,' Bramson said. 'The police couldn't tell us. They're on their way here now.'

Alex couldn't swallow for the tightness in his throat. His mind began to race ahead. 'What about her parents? Are they still in Rome?'

'Yes. Back at the end of the week,' Cecily bleated. 'The police called us because of you.'

Alex rubbed his face in fear of the truth and loathing for his part in it. It felt like a deepening nightmare. 'So we don't know anything?'

'A car accident is all we know, Sir,' Bramson said. 'Mrs Wynter, let's sit you down by the fire. Mrs Dear has put the kettle on. Should I fetch some ice, Master Alex?' Bramson nodded at Alex's bruising but Alex shook his head.

They drifted into the sitting room. 'I'll do it, Bramson,' Alex said, reaching for the poker and coaxing the embers in the fireplace back to life. It felt easier to be busy.

'We'd all gone to bed,' his mother stammered. 'Look at me, in my nightgown!'

Alex remembered what a state Pen had driven off in, the speed at which she had hit the Brighton Road, in a motor car she was unfamiliar with, and he felt his pulse quicken with dread that it was his fault. 'Mother, while we wait for word, I have something to tell you.'

She eyed him and there wasn't much tenderness in her look now that she knew he was safe. 'I've gathered as much, seeing as you're dressed for dinner and you were meant to be in London with Penny. Did you two have a fight? Is that why you have a black eye?'

He resisted touching where it was sore. 'That wasn't Pen.' He groaned and held his head, sickened by what he needed to say; what he'd already said to a beautiful young woman who was now potentially physically as much as emotionally hurt by his decisions. 'What a mess. Let me just talk and you can pass your judgement later.'

Tea came and then grew cold, untouched, as Cecily Wynter listened to the traumatic tale her son recounted, and when his words dried up and she turned to stare sightlessly at the flames, seeing only the blur of orange while her thoughts clattered with sorrow for everyone in his story, they heard a car arrive on the gravel.

Alex stood, helped his mother up and awaited the police. They heard voices and finally Bramson showed them in. Two men in plain clothes and one in uniform arrived wearing solemn expressions, hats in hand.

'Evening, gentlemen,' Alex greeted, his tone sombre.

'Mr Wynter, Mrs Wynter,' the eldest said. 'I'm Inspector Philips.'

They both nodded as he introduced the other pair, but Alex barely heard their names, and though it seemed churlish not to even offer a cup of tea at least on this cold night, he only wanted to hear that Pen was safe. He took the lead after the introductions were finished. 'Is Miss Aubrey-Finch hurt, Inspector Philips? She was driving a new car for the first time today,' Alex said.

The men shared an awkward glance. 'I'm terribly sorry, Sir, to have to tell you that Miss Aubrey-Finch had a car accident tonight and has died from her injuries.'

The room turned so still that Alex could no longer hear the crackle and spit of the fire. He was unable to take a breath as he repeated in his mind what the policeman had just said and was unaware that his mother had slipped away from his side to sit down.

'How . . . what . . . I . . .' He stared at the men, unable to find the words.

Philips saved him the search. 'It was instant, we're assured. She crashed the car at Hassocks, rounding a bend. She hit a tree. A nearby doctor attended the scene immediately but Miss Aubrey-Finch was . . .' He swallowed. 'I'm sorry, Sir, she was already gone.'

Bramson approached, clearly worried for his mistress. He stood near them both, no doubt in similar shock. Alex realised everyone was waiting for him to say something but his breath was now trapped in his chest and it was as if bumblebees were humming around in his mind in a great drone of noise that he realised was the sound of his heart pumping so hard he could hear the blood around his head as the policeman began to speak again.

'. . . her parents are overseas, we gather,' Philips said.

'Yes . . . yes, they're in Europe. Back at the end of the week,' Alex said, as if by rote, glad to finally find his voice. 'Do you wish us to contact them?' It seemed the polite thing to say next and helped him to focus. Action was always better than losing oneself in shock. He'd learned that in the trenches.

'Well, it might be best coming from a family friend.'

'Bramson, get both my brothers and Charlie home please,' he said to one side. 'Call them, wake them – whatever has to be done.' He was taking charge now as the immediate numbness gave way to sensation again and rational thought. This is what officers did on the frontline. They took control.

'At once, Sir,' he heard Bramson reply.

'I should tell you I was with Miss Aubrey-Finch this evening, Inspector Philips.'

The man's gaze cut sharply to meet his. 'Then we will need a statement, Sir.'

'Of course. Listen, can we get you anything? Bramson?'

The butler was just tiptoeing away. 'Leave it to me, Sir.'

'Come and warm yourselves,' Alex gestured, the tremble in his hand a sign of his shock despite his steady voice. 'I'll tell you everything I can.' He had experienced his share of trauma during the war, yet the pain of trying to absorb the reality that laughing, loving, generous Pen had died in the freezing dark, on a roadside and in bitterness at him, felt more agonising in this moment than all of his sufferings.

31

Edie put the phone down, pale and trembling; she wanted to believe she'd imagined the conversation just now and tried to picture herself waking up and feeling a flood of relief that it had only been a bad dream.

Madeleine walked back into the salon. 'Still alone? I thought Miss Aubrey-Finch would be here by now. I picked up cakes and . . .' Her words trailed off as she took in Edie's countenance. 'Eden, what's wrong?' She hurried to her friend's side. 'What's happened? Is Tommy all right?' She glanced around and saw Tommy playing in the corner.

'It's Pen.'

'Oh, thank heavens. She's late?'

'She's dead.'

'Dead?' Madeleine faltered.

Edie nodded, a hand trembling as it covered her mouth. She reached for one of the salon's seats and lowered herself, shaking, to the chair. 'Killed in a car accident last night. Mads . . . I had only spoken to her a few hours earlier. She sounded so jolly. We were having lunch today . . .'.

Madeleine sat carefully beside her friend, wearing an expression of deep shock. 'An accident?'

Again Edie nodded. 'Somewhere near Brighton. She sped into a tree. That was Charlotte Wynter. She's out of her mind with grief . . .' She shook her head and wiped a tear. Tommy had toddled over and she lifted him onto her lap and hugged him.

'Alone?'

Edie gasped. 'I didn't even ask about Mr Wynter's state. Oh, how dreadfully insensitive of me. Yes, she was alone.'

'He's presumably in terrible shock too.'

'He wants to see me.'

'Wynter does? Why on earth?'

She shrugged. 'Charlotte said it was important. It's very strange, Mads. He's not coming to the salon, which I can understand, so we're meeting at the Chelsea Physic Garden.'

'Maybe he wants Pen's money back?'

'I can't imagine that. No mention of money, although I'll gladly give back most of it. No, he's probably just trying to put together a picture of yesterday's events.'

'Perhaps the police need to talk with you?'

'Possibly, although Charlotte said there is nothing suspicious. Misadventure, according to the police report. Plain bad luck.'

'Oh, Eden, I'm so sorry. This was meant to be your big beginning.'

She shook her head. 'I don't want to think about that now but maybe it's a sign that I'm not meant to do this, Mads. Oh, that poor, lovely girl!'

'That's not the way to think. We have appointments in the book and for Pen's sake you have to try even harder now. She loved your style, Eden . . . so you mustn't let this sad and horrid tragedy throw you off the course she helped to put you on.'

'I know, I know. Mads, I'm just tired of having to pick myself up, only to get knocked down again . . . And every time I think there's a reason to feel more stable, to start looking at life with more optimism, something dark closes in on it.'

'What time are you meeting Mr Wynter?'

'Eleven. I can't believe he'd drive down to London, so soon after the event.'

Madeleine nodded. 'Shock can make you behave oddly.' She glanced at her watch. 'Shall I fetch your coat?'

'Thank you, and Tommy's too, please. I know I was going to leave him here over lunchtime but I think I'll take him with me on this meeting; might make it feel less awkward. But how will I recognise Mr Wynter?'

Madeleine gave her a searching look. 'I promise you, darling, you'll know him; even grieving, he'll be the most handsome man in the gardens.'

―――――――――

The cloudy skies gave a thin layer of warmth and though it was overcast, Edie didn't think it would rain but she had her umbrella with her just in case.

Expecting to lunch with Pen and her friends, Edie had dressed to impress today in a chestnut-coloured satin dress that was now covered by a daringly original scarlet coat. She'd fashioned it from a fabric imported from Italy and fastened it with polished horn tips that her supplier from Petticoat Lane had hunted down from Africa. The coat was belted low with a thin leather strap, its hem skimming her ankles above simple, pointed-toe chocolate heels that matched her leather gloves and small rouched bag. Her dramatic, oversized ecru-coloured fur collar swept up to cover her neck, while the sleeves hung low from wide openings ringed by the rabbit fur. A cream-and-scarlet cloche hat sat low and neat over her shiny dark-brown hair that tumbled in waves just above her chin. She knew the ensemble turned heads and had become accustomed to using herself as a walking canvas for her clothes, but today she wasn't enjoying the attention. She was thinking about her dead client and what she could possibly say to Penelope Aubrey-Finch's fiancé.

Tommy was walking beside her, his mittened hand holding hers tightly as they covered the short distance to the Gardens. Edie was reminded of how learning from Sol the tiny snippet that Tom had gone into central London to find a gift for her had felt so exciting to hear. Meaningless to most, but to her it was like a drop of pure gold . . . another little gift of memory to lock away in her heart. Likewise she would do her utmost to remember every nuance in Pen's voice, every moment of the conversation she'd shared yesterday, in the hope that it might bring Alex Wynter some solace . . . if that's what he was hoping for.

They moved at Tommy's pace as he kicked through fallen leaves past the newly named Chelsea Polytechnic on Manresa Road. The smell from the Imperial Gasworks at Chelsea Wharf caught her attention and encouraged her not to dawdle.

Edie approached the imposing, finely wrought iron of the double gates that led into the Physic Garden. Her gaze travelled to the oasis beyond and she inhaled the cold, fresh air, feeling that her spirits had indeed lifted. Realising they were fifteen minutes early, she looked up at the blue-and-gold crest on the gates – even faded, it looked dramatic with Apollo, the Greek god of healing, slaughtering the serpent of disease. These gardens belonged to the Worshipful Society of Apothecarists and were initially concerned with herbs for medicine but had since expanded to include all manner of plants. She picked up Tommy and walked on, preferring to use one of the smaller side gates to slip into the quiet gardens that she cut through on her way home via London's embankment.

Edie hoped Mr Wynter would not be late or her teeth would be chattering. She made for the Sir Hans Sloane statue, which could be seen from most angles in the garden and where she had suggested to Charlotte Wynter that she meet her brother. It had struck Edie as curious that Wynter himself hadn't made these arrangements. She'd been in too much shock to question it but it was an oddity that he'd used his sister to set it up. Then again, she thought, he would have been busy with police, no doubt barely able to think straight. Edie remembered that feeling of pure shock all too well.

The gardens were deserted. The temperature was dropping and a breeze was picking up. She shivered again and had her choice of all the benches, as each was unoccupied. She chose one and as she sat a slender, unshowy, stemmed shrub with long, leathery leaves and creamy-white flowers gave off a gentle, sweet fragrance around her that made her sigh.

Edie thought about her trip to Fleet Street tomorrow. It felt important – another defiance against surrender. She thought of Percy Fitch and visiting him after her trip to Fleet Street. It was a desperate, reed-thin chance that his client who was knocked over was Tom.

'Without hope, why bother?' she murmured to her child and only now caught sight of a tiny piece of his train set clutched in his hand. It provoked a quiver of pain, as she recalled who had given him the gift. *Damn you, Ben!* Birds called softly around her, new scents of spicy laurel and the pine fragrance of rosemary wafted over her, and Edie realised her mind was silently making a bargain.

If I forgive Ben, please, please, give me back Tom. That's all I ask. Just let him find me and I will never ask for anything more again.

She cast out her hope to every angel that had ever protected Tom through the trials of war, and as she did so, she did forgive Ben. Mads was right when she'd said that to hang on to her anger was to fill herself with the very poison that had led Ben to betray her. 'You're above that. You're kinder, more generous and capable of remembering all the good in Ben from childhood,' Mads had said.

Tommy had realised the chalky pebble he'd picked up could make markings on the pathway and was deeply engaged in drawing lines. Edie dipped into her pocket to find a handkerchief and smiled at the swatch of red fabric that was neatly folded in the middle. There it was. There was the sign. The angels had answered her. She glanced at Tommy.

'Daddy's coming,' she whispered, believing it in this moment to be the truth she would cling to.

Edie dabbed her eyes quickly and regarded the heart-shaped scrap. She carried it habitually and for no particular reason pushed it now beneath the soft fur of her glove so she could feel it against her palm and hold it there. She squeezed her hand into a small fist.

Come on, Tom. Find us, she urged.

———

At the salon, Madeleine answered the jangling telephone.

'Oh, hello, Mr Fitch. Yes, I do remember you. Do you remember me?'

'How could I forget a beautiful lady such as yourself, Mademoiselle Delacroix?'

She smiled. 'How can I help you, Mr Fitch?'

'I'm returning Edie's call. I've been away and have taken a few days to get back to her. Regretfully, I was swamped with appointments.'

'I'm afraid you've missed her, Mr Fitch. She has an engagement away from the salon and probably won't return today.'

'Oh, pity. Well, look, to save us all making another round of telephone calls, I wonder if you would be kind enough to pass on a message?'

'I'd be happy to.'

'Thank you. My assistant, Mr Elton, mentioned that Edie was enquiring after one of our valued clients.'

'Yes, Mr Fitch. Look, forgive Eden. She has been under a lot of strain lately and she's lost a lot of people she loves, including her husband and —'

'Good gracious, Miss Delacroix. When did she lose her husband?'

'He's not dead, Mr Fitch. But he's lost, gone missing.'

'But I caught sight of Benjamin Levi only days ago!'

'Mr Levi is not her husband. Tom is.'

The silence felt to Madeleine like a third person on the line it was so palpable.

Fitch finally cleared his throat. 'Well, well . . . I just presumed —'

'It's easier sometimes not to go through it again. Eden is family to me and I worry about her crusade to find her lost husband sometimes. He was a wounded returned soldier who was last seen not far from Savile Row.'

'Ah . . .' Fitch sighed down the line. 'I completely understand now. Oh, poor, dear Edie. I don't know what to say, and although I'm not in the habit of ever sharing names, in this instance I will break my own rule, if it might bring her some peace. The man in question is Alex Wynter. He —'

'Wait,' Madeleine interrupted. 'You aren't referring to Alex Wynter, the industrialist, are you?'

'Er . . .' Fitch sounded suddenly defensive. 'Do you know him?'

'We've met,' she said, her heart beginning to drum. 'He is marrying . . . well, was to marry one of this salon's bridal clients.'

'Good grief, small world, eh?' Fitch exclaimed. 'Well, there you are, Miss Delacroix.'

'Thank you, Mr Fitch, for your kindness. I'll let Eden know.'

Madeleine replaced the receiver and spent several moments staring at it in shock, her mind empty of everything but the echo of Fitch's words. *Alex Wynter couldn't possibly be our Edie's Tom.*

Edie looked up at the statue of Sir Hans Sloane, Irish philanthropist, physician and botanist, who was responsible for donating his

Chelsea home and grounds for the Apothecaries' Garden, the second-oldest botanical garden in Britain. Normally Sloane's backdrop was small woodland – yews and firs, elms and oaks. Now the winter trees were mainly bare and Sir Hans looked back at her somewhat gravely from a more naked scene, but she sensed a smile lurking beneath his outwardly sombre expression, convinced he approved of her bargain.

Edie let out a small sigh and checked the time on her wristwatch. It was eleven on the dot and the chimes of the nearby church confirmed the hour. Mr Wynter was due. She stood, put away her handkerchief, straightened her coat and hoped her eyes were not reddened. She pinched her cheeks in and bit her lips for colour.

She bent to retie the scarf around Tommy's neck and grinned as he sped off again – faster than ever – on tiny legs, heedless of the cold in his quest to chase after a dove. Edie was facing the main southern entrance but heard a footfall behind her on the gravel and swung around.

Everything in her life in that moment became still, including her heart, she was sure. She tried to swallow but her throat was so suddenly parched her mouth felt clamped but even so a strange, animal-like sob escaped.

'*Edie . . .*' the man said in an achingly familiar voice that released the spell of paralysis. Suddenly movement was permitted again and she was no longer shivering but shaking, her teeth rattling.

Edie bent forward her trembling body, clutching it as if in pain. In a couple of strides the long arms she had craved for so many tear-filled nights had wrapped themselves about her and picked her up. Perhaps he thought she might collapse. She couldn't believe she was being carried like a child, in a public place, but she also didn't care because Tom was here. Tom had found her, even though he didn't look like Tom but that voice was unmistakable – the hands were his, the broad chest was no one else's . . .

'*Edie*,' he whispered again, setting her down on the nearby bench.

She still couldn't speak. Couldn't utter his name, couldn't find a single word to convey even a smattering of the emotion ringing through her. She glanced at Tommy in the near distance scattering leaves and she turned to stare at his father, disbelieving through watering eyes, had to touch his cheek to be sure she wasn't dreaming. It was bruised.

'Does it hurt?' she whispered.

'I welcome it. Then I know this moment is real.'

'Is it truly you?' she croaked.

He nodded. 'I got lost, Edie,' he said softly, his voice sounding broken with grief.

'But you found your way back to me.'

Tom held her. They sat motionless and silent for several moments but it felt like a lifetime to Edie.

Suddenly her mind was crowded. She could hear Tommy talking to himself, realising he was hidden behind the statue.

'Wait . . .' she stammered, pulling back. 'How did you know where to find me? How could you —'

'Hush, Edie . . . I'll explain.'

She stared at him with eyes wide and alarmed, instantly soaking up details from his shaved face, which was every bit as handsome as Madeleine had attested to . . . but then Edie already knew that. In the same heartbeat she had noted the fine Savile Row cut of his suit, unmistakably an Anderson & Sheppard creation, and without any doubt it had the hallmark signature work of Percival Fitch. All of her random suspicions and hopes came together in one powerful realisation and her hand shook as she pointed, hardly daring to believe the words she uttered.

'*You're* Alex Wynter?' she accused in a small voice filled with both wonder and despair.

He nodded. 'I can explain.'

She twisted away from him and staggered up, holding on to the back of the bench because her knees couldn't support her.

'You were going to marry Pen?' Her normally husky voice sounded unnaturally high.

'Edie . . . I will tell all, but to jump to the end, I only remembered who I was last night when your friend, Ben Levi, paid me a visit.'

'Ben? You saw Ben?'

He nodded and gestured towards his blackening eye. 'Amongst other things he felt he owed me,' he began dryly. 'He filled in the gaps that had been missing since I was knocked over in Savile Row. You see, my darling, when that part of my memory returned it replaced what I had before, which was my life with you.'

She gulped back another sob.

'Hear it all and then judge, but first —' He stopped suddenly, his attention fully distracted as Tommy approached with two acorns proudly held out. He stared in shock, first at the small boy who plonked his prize into his lap, and then to Edie. 'Our son?' His voice shook.

She gave a watery-eyed nod. 'Say hello, Tommy,' she choked out, unable to help herself crying now. 'Here's Daddy.'

'Da,' Tommy said with a gummy smile.

Edie saw Alex Wynter gaze with teary wonder at the little boy who yawned and reached out his arms to his mother.

She lifted him up, glancing at her husband shyly, feeling her emotions colliding – from joy to disbelief and a sense of grateful unravelling . . . of letting go. *He was here*. She didn't have to be so strong any more. She wouldn't cry herself to sleep again or, as she woke to another empty day without him, rely on Tommy to always refill her well. And Edie wept to see the man she loved – who'd survived so much atrocity and despair – undone at the sight of his son.

She watched him dragging the back of his shaking hand across his damp eyes. 'Forgive me. I am grieving for Pen but Edie, this is also the happiest moment of my life. May I?' Edie nodded and the man she loved opened his arms to Tommy. She watched with a sense of overwhelming love as their son allowed himself to be held for the first time by his father.

'How about a hello, Tommy?' she half laughed, half wept. 'You know the way you kiss Mummy when I come home?' And in true Tommy style he planted a wet kiss on his father's nose and beamed him a smile bright enough to chase away all the gloom of winter.

'Tommy,' Alex whispered and hugged his boy close. 'This is what my dreams were telling me, Edie,' he said, his voice muffled as he held his child. 'To search for you both.' He drew Edie into his embrace and that's how they remained until their child wriggled to be free.

Edie laughed. 'He wants to get to the pond. We can talk there.'

They walked in a strangely comfortable silence following Tommy's half run, half walk to his favourite place.

And as Tommy babbled at the fish, Edie sat and listened to Alex Wynter, not noticing the cold or even whether anyone passed them by. In that hour she relived both their lives since 1920 and wept at the most painful part of hearing how Penelope Aubrey-Finch finally won the man she had loved since they were children. Edie had taken his hand as his voice had become small as he told her of the previous night.

'So she knew about me?'

He nodded, hanging his head in regret. 'I think somewhere deep in her soul Pen had always known there was someone else.'

Edie recalled how she'd noted Pen's curious wistfulness when she'd spoken about her fiancé only days earlier. 'She loved you so much,' was all she was able to say.

He let out a long, slow sigh. 'She did. I let her down. The truth is I felt like a ghost. I was moving through this life as Alex Wynter; I was there in body, but rarely in spirit. Do you know, Edie, the only time I felt really alive and connected was when I was trying to hunt down the owner of this?' He reached into his pocket and pulled out a red handkerchief.

Edie gasped softly.

'I've carried it with me always – I look at it every day, hoping for inspiration. I knew someone was out there. I've been searching for you blindly; *I could feel you.*' He edged closer on their seat. 'Edie, I can say that I have never loved another woman as I love you.' He hung his head again. 'I am ashamed for what's occurred. I will grieve for Pen but I would have made her miserable, Edie, because I loved you even when my memory stole you away. I loved you in my dreams – I could hear the click of your heels and smell your perfume and almost, but not quite, touch your skin, your hair. Your hair! I like it, by the way,' he said, smiling helplessly, and she laughed softly through her tears, remembering that bright smile; realising she too must look different to him.

'Be my wife again, Eden Valentine . . . you can even call me Tom, if that's easier. I've always liked it – it's my father's name.'

Edie gave a watery laugh, sniffing. 'No, there's Tommy now. Alex,' she said, testing it. 'I'm glad you found your name.'

'If you reject me now, I have to accept it, but I want you to understand that I will never marry again, for there will never be anyone else for me.' He stroked Tommy's dark head.

'I know that.'

'Do you?' he asked, his voice sounding desperate.

She nodded.

'Tell me – tell me how you truly understand that I have no future without you.'

Edie slipped off her glove and offered him her open palm, where a small scrap of red cotton unfurled. 'Because I believed if I always held your heart close, you would find me again,' she whispered and leaned in to kiss her husband long and deeply until their son's fingers, wet from reaching through iron railings to splash in the pond, grabbed theirs.

And as they set off to face the world beyond this momentary sanctuary, Eden Valentine felt the love she craved wrap itself around her heart again to send her spirits soaring alongside their son's giggling squeal of pleasure as his father swung him high onto his broad shoulders and pulled her close.

ACKNOWLEDGEMENTS

Where do ideas for stories come from? Writers are asked this constantly and more often than not it's hard for us to explain the inspiration that can originate from a series of ideas or coincidences. But for this novel I know precisely what triggered the tale. Our son, Jack, since taking on his casual sales role in the suiting department of a major store, has become passionate about bespoke tailoring. I think if he wasn't four years into his five-and-a-half year Law and Business degree, he might just disappear to Europe to learn more about this side of the fashion industry. While I was researching in the UK for *The Lavender Keeper*, Jack sent me on a garment-seeking mission to a particular gentleman's fitters in London and I found myself on Savile Row.

I must admit to becoming captivated by Gieves & Hawke at No.1 and my fascination intensified as I began to stroll the Row marvelling at the windows full of livery and hunting pinks, glorious tweeds and sumptuous tuxedos, plaques attesting to royal patronage, not to mention the general hush and whisper of the gentleman's domain that I'd dared to enter. It wasn't a leap for me to move from intrigued tourist to inspired storyteller.

I read a tower of books on life on the Western Front during the Great War to life in the early 1920s in Britain and yet it's the help from eager, generous others that always seems to unlock the greatest chest of information. Joanna Legg, thank you for all that vital information on the Great War. Thanks to Derek Killen in the US for his amazingly well-timed information on the financial pressures of that era, Tony Berry for walking me around London and sharing vignettes of life as a tailoress's son in the 1950s.

Special thanks to Ali Watts, my great champion and brilliant publisher of women's fiction at Penguin Books, who on reading the first draft gleefully rang to assure me I'd delivered 'exactly' what she'd hoped I might but then set me to work rewriting. Saskia Adams, thanks again for taking time from your snorkelling holiday to entertain me with your daily anxiety and despair for my characters as you read and copy edited in between dives. Heartfelt thanks to all the Penguins – my cheering squad, who work so hard behind the scenes – especially that fabulous and often unheralded sales and marketing team.

Thank you to Ian, for sourcing the mountain of research material required, and to my enthusiastic draft readers – Pip K, Judy B and Nigelle-Ann B. I never imagined writing such an outrageously romantic story but what an immensely satisfying journey this novel has been. I do believe it's my favourite. Thanks to all the booksellers for their ongoing support and to my wonderful, loyal readers.

Enjoy this one.

Fx

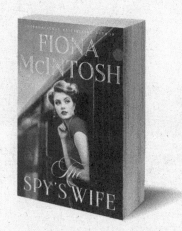

The highly anticipated new historical adventure from the bestselling author of *The Champagne War*.

Evie, a widow and stationmaster's daughter, can't help but look for the weekly visit of the handsome man she and her sister call the Southerner on their train platform in the wilds of northern England. When polite salutations shift to friendly conversations, they become captivated by each other. After so much sorrow, the childless Evie can't believe love and the chance for her own family have come into her life again.

With rumours coming out of Germany that Hitler may be stirring up war, local English authorities have warned against spies. Even Evie becomes suspicious of her new suitor, Roger. But all is not what it seems.

When Roger is arrested, Evie comes up with an audacious plan to prove his innocence that means moving to Germany and working as a British counter-spy. Wearing the disguise of dutiful, naïve wife, Evie must charm the Nazi Party's dangerous officials to bring home hard evidence of war mongering on the Führer's part.

But in this game of cat and mouse, it seems everyone has an ulterior motive, and Evie finds it impossible to know who to trust. With lives on the line, ultimate sacrifices will be made as she wrestles between her patriotism and saving the man she loves.

From the windswept moors of the Yorkshire dales to the noisy beer halls of Munich and grand country estates in the picture-book Bavarian mountains, this is a lively and high-stakes thriller that will keep you second-guessing until the very end.

*'Make these little vines count.
Love them as I love you.'*

In the summer of 1914, vigneron Jerome Méa heads off to war, certain he'll be home by Christmas. His new bride Sophie, a fifth generation and rebellious champenoise, is determined to ensure the forthcoming vintages will be testament to their love and the power of the people of Épernay, especially its strong women. But as the years drag on, authorities advise that Jerome is missing, considered dead.

When poison gas is first used in Belgium by the Germans, British chemist Charles Nash jumps to enlist. After he is injured, he is brought to Reims, where Sophie has helped to set up an underground hospital to care for the wounded. In the dark, ancient champagne cellars, their stirring emotions take them both by surprise.

While Sophie battles to keep her vineyard going through the bombings, a critical sugar shortage forces her to strike a dangerous bargain with an untrustworthy acquaintance – but nothing will test her courage more than the news that filters through to her about the fate of her heroic Jerome.

From the killing fields of Ypres to the sun-kissed vineyards of rural France, *The Champagne War* is a heart-stopping adventure about the true power of love and hope to light the way during war.

'It won't matter how many diamonds you find if you lose the love of your child.'

When six-year-old Clementine Knight loses her mother to malaria during the 1870s diamond rush in southern Africa, she is left to be raised by her destitute, alcoholic father, James. Much of Clementine's care falls to their trusty Zulu companion, Joseph One-Shoe, and the unlikely pair form an unbreakable bond.

When the two men uncover a large, flawless diamond, James believes he has finally secured their future, but the discovery of the priceless gem comes at a huge cost. A dark bargain is struck to do whatever it takes to return Clementine to a respectable life at the Grant family's sprawling estate in northern England – while the diamond disappears.

Years on, long-buried memories of Clementine's childhood in Africa and her beloved Joseph One-Shoe are triggered, as she questions who she can trust. To solve the mystery of what happened to her loved ones all those years ago, she must confront a painful history and finally bring justice to bear.

Her predator has now become
her prey . . .

Severine Kassel is asked by the Louvre in 1963 to aid the British Museum with curating its antique jewellery, her specialty. Her London colleagues find her distant and mysterious, her cool beauty the topic of conversations around its quiet halls. No one could imagine that she is a desperately damaged woman, hiding her trauma behind her chic, French image.

It is only when some dramatic Byzantine pearls are loaned to the Museum that Severine's poise is dashed and the tightly controlled life she's built around herself is shattered. Her shocking revelation of their provenance sets off a frenzied hunt for Nazi Ruda Mayek.

Mossad's interest is triggered and one of its most skilled agents comes out of retirement to join the hunt, while the one person who can help her – the solicitor handling the pearls – is bound by client confidentiality. As she follows Mayek's trail, there is still one lifelong secret for her to reveal – and one for her to discover.

From the snowy woodlands outside Prague to the Tuileries of Paris and the heather-covered moors of Yorkshire comes a confronting and heart-stopping novel that explores whether love and hope can ever overpower atrocity in a time of war and hate.

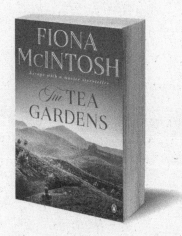

Spirited doctor Isla Fenwick is determined to work at the coalface of medicine in India before committing to life as a dutiful wife. With hopes of making a difference in the world, she sails to Calcutta to set up a midwifery clinic. There she will be forced to question her beliefs, her professionalism and her romantic loyalties.

On a desperate rescue mission to save the one person who needs her the most, she travels into the foothills of the Himalayas to a tea plantation outside Darjeeling. At the roof of the world, where heaven and earth collide, Isla will be asked to pay the ultimate price for her passions.

From England's seaside town of Brighton to India's slums of Calcutta and the breathtaking Himalayan mountains, this is a wildly exciting novel of heroism, heartache and healing, by the bestselling author of *The Chocolate Tin*.

Discover a
new favourite

Visit **penguin.com.au/readmore**